IMMORTAL AND THE ISLAND OF IMPOSSIBLE THINGS

GENE DOUCETTE

Immortal and the Island of Impossible Things
By Gene Doucette

GeneDoucette.me

Copyright © 2016 Gene Doucette
All rights reserved

Be not afeard; the isle is full of noises, sounds and sweet airs, that give delight and hurt not.

Sometimes a thousand twangling instruments will hum about mine ears, and sometime voices that, if I then had waked after long sleep, will make me sleep again: and then, in dreaming, the clouds methought would open and show riches Ready to drop upon me that, when I waked, I cried to dream again.

— CALIBAN, FROM THE TEMPEST, WILLIAM SHAKESPEARE

PART I

THINGS SLOW DOWN

CHAPTER 1

*S*unlight broke through the east-facing side of the house right on schedule, which woke us up more efficiently than any alarm clock or rooster might, and more permanently than I would have preferred.

By most metrics, I'm not a morning person. I probably used to be, back before we—as a species—had houses, but it's hard to know this for sure because my memory isn't absolutely 100% perfect when it comes to the first fifty thousand-odd years of my life.

This is potentially an act of self-preservation on the part of my brain, which is a normal human brain that was never (I'm guessing) meant to hold this much history in it. It's also possible that there just weren't a lot of memorable things going on in the nomadic life of the hunter-gatherer I used to be, so nothing made a real impression. I remember that we ate a lot and hunted a lot and slept only a little, and moved around all the time, so it was basically one long and terribly boring road trip story, and nobody enjoys boring road trip stories. Including, evidently, my long-term memory.

If I had any say in this arrangement, the sunlight would've had no way of reaching me in the bedroom, and I could have woken up on my own schedule. This sun-free bedroom would have also been located inside of a nice, safe interior space where predators couldn't find me. But this was one of the many arguments I lost preemptively, by never actually raising the issue when we first moved.

The house had an open floor plan, by which I mean there were almost no walls. This included walls *to the outside*. I'm not even kidding. There were gestures here and there suggesting the existence of a wall, but these were more like abstract representations. Prop walls, almost, like what stage designers do in the theater when they want to indicate a character is indoors, but they still want the audience to see the actors.

What we had was little sturdier than theater props, but that was about the best thing I could say about them, especially since I've never known a wild animal to be all that respectful of fourth-wall realism.

I was much more fond of the roof, which was stellar. I have always been a strong supporter of a solid roof, the kind that kept out sunlight and rain with equal efficiency, and also didn't fall when there was too much rain or snow.

Our roof did all of that just fine. Not that it mattered *too* much because if it was raining and windy at the same time all the rain from the outside skirted right past the hypothetical walls and coated the living room with a thin mist. This happened often enough that we had to waterproof all of the electronics. As for snow, we were in a place where that didn't happen. I assumed the roof would handle it okay, though.

It didn't rain very often, either, not really. And if I'm going to be completely fair about the whole setup, there *was* a way to close off the interior. It's just that doing so was sort of involved—there were partitions that swung down from the roof and interlocked with the partial walls—so it didn't happen often.

If a typhoon ever struck the island, though, we had hatches to batten down. According to all of the island's long-term residents, no typhoon had ever made landfall here, but in my mind that just meant it was overdue.

By the time I was awake enough to register the sunlight, Mirella had already been up for at least an hour. She was in the kitchen—or rather, the part of the very large room in which we lived, where we installed kitchen-like products and marble countertops—brewing cappuccino on the loud machine she had flown in from wherever expensive coffeemakers were hatched.

"Wake up, Adam, the day is half over," she said without turning.

She always knew when I was awake, even when I wasn't sure yet myself.

I could tell she'd been up for at least an hour because her hair was wet. She was wearing an oversized white t-shirt, and her long black hair was draining down the back of it, which made a portion transparent, which only proved she had nothing on underneath the shirt, in case there was any question about that. This meant she'd already had her morning swim.

"I prefer the days that start at sundown," I said, putting a pillow over my face. I couldn't remember if I drank the night before or not, but my head seemed to think that yes, I had. Many times in my life this would not have been a question that required asking, but I was trying to cut back.

"Stop thinking like a hunter," she said, sitting down on the bed to put a cup of coffee on the table next to my face.

I wasn't thinking like a hunter, but it wasn't worth saying so. I was thinking like a drunk who knew the best bars weren't much of anything before sundown. Plus the hunter-gatherer in me knew daytime was when to hunt. Night was when we hid.

Mirella wouldn't know that, though. She was used to being a top-of-the-food-chain predator, which meant hunting at night. Like most modern people, she had no real experience being prey.

"Drink, and wake up," she said, referencing the coffee. "We have nothing to do today."

"Then why do I have to wake up?"

"You have to be awake to appreciate that you have nothing to do. You *already* do nothing when you sleep."

"I can think of at least three philosophers who would be having a seizure right now."

"Come on."

A quick kiss, and then she left, confident I could handle the rising-from-bed part alone.

My wake-up process was considerably less involved than hers. I only needed a cup of coffee and a toilet, and both of those were indoors. I'd have considered going for a swim, maybe, but… well, we didn't have a pool. We had an ocean, and it wasn't all that easy to get to.

~

*T*here are times when I look at things and wonder how they might be interpreted by an archeologist in the future. You might do the same, except posit an alien attempting to examine us from afar. I tend to go with archeologist because that's in line with my own life experiences. Specifically, I am often at odds with archeologists who look at places I used to live or visit and have drawn conclusions that, while evidence-based, are fundamentally wrong. So when I perform this exercise of trying to guess what assumptions could be made about something through the lens of a couple thousand years, I'm drawing from life experience.

Anyway. If a scientist in the future or an alien hovering in lower orbit were to examine the floor plan of our house they might come to the conclusion that the bathroom was the most important part, only because it was at the center, and everything radiated from the center.

There were a couple of reasons why this was so. First, it was the only fully enclosed part of the building. No windows, just four walls that went straight up through the middle like a chimney, doing double-duty in supporting the roof at its highest point.

Ironically, this was the one part of the house I could have lived with having a window in. It wasn't like Mirella and I had any consistent company, and we were intimate enough to not worry all that much about clothing in any other part of the house, much less outside. But the bathroom was the one place she was extremely private about, to a degree that bordered on scary. It's possible goblins have a particular anatomical concern that requires full privacy, but I'd seen all of her parts so I'm thinking this was not the case. I'm thinking this was a woman thing.

Oh, Mirella's a goblin. I'll get to that in a little while, but just so nobody's operating under an incorrect assumption, goblins are human-looking enough to be mistaken as humans on a daily basis. This is a not the movie version of a goblin we're talking about, (it doesn't matter which movie, they all get it wrong) and thank goodness for that.

The second reason for the bathroom's location had to do with the plumbing. Our central plumbing was very much central. It was also extremely limited, and involved a septic tank that had to get cleaned out every six months by a man from the bottom of the island to whom we paid a tremendous amount of money on account of him being the only guy within two hundred miles willing to do something like that. He was maybe the second- or third-richest person on the island as a consequence. It was probably not worth it.

The building constructed around the bathroom was roundish, and consisted of multiple platform levels that corresponded to the uneven surface beneath the house, and the entire property was up on stilts to allow for rain from the higher points on the west side to make it over the cliff face on the east side without taking the building along.

A reasonable conclusion might be that a house already on stilts could also be a house with a flat floor, but whoever built the place didn't much care for this logic. Or something. I don't really know what the thinking was, but it worked because the various one-step platform levels allowed us to differentiate the rooms without resorting to having walls. Also, each platform was independently supported, making the entire structure the kind of sturdy one can appreciate when living at the top of a cliff.

After the necessary bathroom duties—I won't bother to describe them, but let's give another shout-out to my favorite invention, indoor plumbing—I refilled my coffee and met Mirella on the eastern side of the deck.

There was a deck around three quarters of the house: north, east, and south. The western side was the ostensible "front" of the building, which was where a gigantic boxy SUV and two ATVs lived. We had a front door there, which was probably the most entertaining part of the property: a door in a frame with a path leading up to it, with no walls on either side of the frame. Well, all right, there was a quarter-wall, and since the house was raised it would take a little effort to climb from the ground over the quarter-wall and inside, but still.

We were comically under-prepared for a frontal assault is what I'm saying. It was a wonder I was able to relax there at all.

Mirella was at one of the wood tables, looking out over the ocean, and eating sliced fruit from a bowl. For convenience, I'm defining *outside* as *absent a roof overhead*.

"It's going to be a nice day," she said, without turning.

"Are you sure? I think I see a cloud over there."

The sky was utterly, perfectly blue, so this was a joke. Mirella didn't laugh, but that wasn't something she was necessarily known for.

"No clouds," she said. "And, I never noticed before... on days like this it's nearly possible to see the sky curve with the Earth at the edge of the horizon."

I squinted.

"I can't see it."

"I have better eyes. Hard to believe your people thought the world was flat."

"*My people?*"

"You know."

"Humans."

"Yes, humans. Your tribe, old man." This was said with a smile, no less charming for the knife in her hand. She was using it to carry fruit pieces to her mouth, as one might with a fork or one's fingers. Goblins like knives; it's kind of their thing.

"Literally nobody thought the world was flat," I said. "Nobody who ever sailed a boat, anyway."

If you watch a sailboat disappear over the horizon the mast is the last thing to disappear. Thus, the Earth is curved. Everybody knew this, at least since there have been boats with masts.

"The Bible says the earth is flat," she said. "So does the Koran."

"Well, those authors didn't get out much."

"Tshhh," she said, which was really just a sound she made with her mouth more than it was a word. "You should take a swim."

"I'd rather a shower."

"The water's low. A swim is a better idea."

"We can get more water."

She raised an eyebrow at me, which is exactly as close as we ever get to a real argument. We were either doing something right or I was just too worried about pissing off possibly the deadliest person alive over a minor domestic inconvenience.

"It's not going to rain today, you should at least check the tank," she said, standing. "I feel like another swim. I wish you'd join me."

"I'll walk down later."

She took off the shirt, and as I said, she had no clothing on underneath.

I gawked. I wish I could say I had some sort of control over this, but I really didn't, even after seeing her naked just about every day since we'd moved in together.

She noticed, of course. I think maybe my jaw actually unhinged on these occasions. She treated me with a dazzling smile that was so excellent it managed to draw my eyes from the rest of her. She could give that smile to anybody, whether clothed or not, but so far as I could tell I was the only one who ever got it.

"You're sure? The water's perfect. It would take you forever to walk down."

"Positive. But that is a very compelling argument you're giving me."

"I know."

She threw me the shirt, then walked to the edge of the cliff and jumped off.

～

I think more than anything else, the cliff was what sold Mirella on the property. And, since it was technically her money that bought the place, the opinion of any cohabitants who may find a Jacuzzi more compelling than a cliff was largely ignored.

I say *technically* like there's an argument to be had there, but that's just me being petty, since I was the one who gave her the money and now I don't have any of my own. I gave away everything, actually—she only got a little of it—in an effort to disappear completely, so it wasn't like I misplaced it or gambled it away or had it stolen. I had no reason to be bitter about this because it was a conscious decision. And mostly I wasn't bitter, because when you're immortal, money is something you can always find time to get more of.

I wanted to disappear so people would finally just leave me the hell alone, and to that end it appeared to work. I do miss the money sometimes, though.

Having a lot of people trying to find you is the sort of thing that can happen when you're the only immortal man on a planet full of rich people who want to be immortal, and scientists who want to figure out how to make rich people immortal. Sure, some of those scientists were interested in curing diseases too, and I'm good for that since I never get sick. But mostly, it's the *get rich and live forever* people that are the problem.

I guess I can understand the appeal from the perspective of a mortal, but to be totally honest, immortality isn't all that fantastic. It's better than not being immortal, but not a whole *lot* better. I'm pretty sure the only reason I'm still around is I'm too stubborn to kill myself.

Okay, that's not really fair. There are other reasons to stay alive, like the days when the sky is a perfect shade of blue, the heat from the sun is offset by a nice ocean breeze, and my outrageously attractive girlfriend is taking off her clothes before it's even noon. Those are the kinds of days I go back to when times are bad, to remind myself what good times look like.

The house was on the easternmost tip of the island. From the edge of the property—the cliff—it was possible to see most of the eastern beachfront. Just look left, and down, and behold the nice sandy beaches. I would have been fine with a house that opened up on one of those beaches, but this was nice too I guess. Just a different kind of nice: private enough that we had no problem walking about without clothing in a home with purely hypothetical walls; close enough to civilization so we weren't going to die from some manner of privation. The only problem was that I preferred to walk down a steep, winding path that was only occasionally free of debris in order to get to the beach and the water, while Mirella liked to launch herself fifty feet off the cliff into what looked like rocky shoals. The water was about thirty feet deep at that point—the cliff jutted out—and it was probably perfectly safe to jump, but I've lived too long to die because I was wrong about something like that.

This, I suppose, was what happened when you took a professional killer like Mirella and relocated her to a place like this. She needed to put her life at risk every day, *somehow*, and diving off her own private cliff was as good a way as any. And if that wasn't enough, she usually scaled the cliff face to get back to the top instead of walking around the beach to the path. She said she did it because she was naked, and scaling the cliff meant not being seen from the beach, but she had a perfectly good bikini in the house.

Using the ocean for a morning bath was hygienically dubious, but eminently logical in this circumstance, which was: we were living on an island with a limited supply of fresh water.

This is one of the many, many things people who visit tropical locations like this don't take into account. It's also why I've spent so little time on tropical islands, to be honest. History is littered with accounts of shipwrecked sailors finding their way to remote islands and subsisting—barely—off of the land until rescued. Or *not* rescued, and found later looking much thinner and no longer alive. We as a species are now vacationing in places that used to kill us.

I've mostly stayed away from spots like this because it was hard to get my mind around the idea that isolation of this sort was a beautiful thing. Historically, I've taken vacations from mankind for hundreds of years by heading into the wilderness and fending for myself. This was whenever I felt it was time to disengage, or when I didn't trust myself around people, or when humankind was going through one of its really bad periods and I didn't want to deal with anyone involved.

So I know from isolation. But those vacations were in the

wilderness of the Eurasian continent, or Africa. There is a substantial difference between living alone on a continent and living alone on an island.

Fresh water is the biggest difference. This island had a natural spring replenished by runoff from the hills, but the spring was not bottomless and it wasn't near us. Every resident got a supply each month, and tourists used the rest. If we needed more we had to buy it, which was possible only if a water shipment made it from one of the not-at-all-nearby ports attached to proper continents. If there wasn't a shipment, well, too bad. No water for you.

A regular supply of rain helped. Most of the buildings on the island had Bermuda roofs, which were designed to catch and funnel rain water into a tank. From there it went through a ridiculously expensive filtration system and into another tank, which we then used for things like showers, the washing dishes, and making ice cubes to go with the cheaper bourbon. To supplement the water in the first tank, we also had an air conditioning system that doubled as a de-humidifier, and a device under the house that caught water off the mountain during the heavier storms.

Honestly, the tank—the second one—was almost always full, but sometime shortly after we moved, Mirella tapped into the collective water-rationing mania of the rest of the islanders. As a consequence, I couldn't take showers as often as I liked.

I'm sure it seemed like a minor inconvenience to her, but hot showers is near the top of my list of reasons I'm glad I'm still alive.

Food is another thing that can be scarce on an island. Large land animals on a continent aren't really a problem as long as you know where they run to and how to catch them. On an island, who knows? There are only so many waterfowl you can eat before you start wondering what the other sailors taste like.

I didn't know what animals were indigenous to this island because I never hunted on it. We hadn't had anything big wander into our living room yet, so maybe there weren't any, but it was also possible they were just too polite. Or, the devices mounted every ten feet around the deck to keep the bugs out—I think they emit an ultrasonic frequency or maybe a chemical or something, I don't know—also drove away game.

We ate a lot of fruits and vegetables, and ridiculous quantities of seafood. The vegetables were mostly from local gardens—the soil was volcanic, so plants grew insanely well—while the fruit was wild, and could be found more or less anywhere.

Once a year we bought a cow that someone was kind enough to slaughter and ship to us. We stored the parts in a freezer and pulled out the beef on special occasions or when the local fish looked off. Rumors of wild boar on the island had yet to yield us any opportunities for pork, so of course that was what I ended up craving almost daily.

The other problem with islands was the isolation from the outside world. That would have been a major issue if we were stranded, but we weren't.

I thought I'd miss the world. Except for the occasional trip into a forest here and there, I have been waist-deep in humanity for well over two thousand years. At first that was by choice, because those were a really interesting two thousand years— except for maybe parts of the twelfth and thirteenth centuries, which kind of sucked—and I had no interest in exiting. Then it became a thing where I couldn't figure out how to exit, because the world ran out of wilderness. Sure, there's still some here and there, but nothing on the scale I'm used to. I once lived for a hundred years in woods that were only a day's walk from down-town Athens, and you can't say that about a whole lot of places any longer. Maybe the Amazon.

That was before Mirella brought me to this island.

You're probably wondering why I haven't told you where it is or what the name of it is. That's because I'm not going to tell you. It's in the South Pacific, but that's all you're going to get.

Yes, it's a bona fide, honest-to-god secret island.

I know, I couldn't believe it either.

⌐

*M*irella climbed back up from the ocean, dried herself off and put on a proper set of clothes. We made a meal, and then went about doing not much of anything. I was reading a book and she was teaching herself how to paint, so we both did those things. Later, we would probably make a dinner, pick a movie, pick a wine, make love, sleep until sunrise, and start all over again.

Life had slowed down. Our only connection to the outside world was a satellite dish we used to rent movies, plus a very occasional foray onto the Internet to make sure nobody had blown up the planet while we were away, and that was all.

It was exactly the sort of break I needed, but failed at a decade earlier when it was a different island and a different girl. Back then, the girl wasn't really interested in quiet and isolation, so what was a planned vacation from the world became a thing where the world was being kept from her and it was my fault.

I hadn't heard a word of complaint from Mirella, but the circumstances were a little different. She picked the location and bought the house. I was just along for the ride.

"Hey," I said over my shoulder, putting down the book. "I was going to head into town."

Mirella was in front of her easel, staring at whatever it was she was painting. I wasn't allowed to look at it.

"Did you finish your book already?"

The books came from the island's remarkably extensive library. It was probably my favorite place other than our house and the pub. In another hundred years I'd probably be down-loading books from an online library instead. I wasn't ready.

"I did."

She snuck a glance at the bar on the other side of the room. We had a fully stocked bar, a modest wine cabinet, and a beer fridge. She would never say it, but she was trying to remember if she'd seen me having anything to drink yet. I hadn't.

I'd been good about the drinking. I learned I should only drink as much as Mirella does—which wasn't all that inconvenient, since she was hardly a light drinker when committed to it.

She had no interest in me when I was drunk and she was sober, though. Again, she hadn't said this; it was just something I figured out.

"Swap the spare while you're out. Don't kill any trees."

$\sim$

*a*s I said, the island is volcanic, but that only means it was formed by a volcanic eruption a long time ago and not—necessarily—that there's an active volcano on the premises.

This is an important distinction, because I do not have a great history with volcanoes. I lived on Minos when the volcano on nearby Thera destroyed the whole region, and I lived beneath Mount Vesuvius at exactly the worst time to live under Mount Vesuvius. Statistically, given how long I've lived, I'm bound to end up near a volcano at the wrong time, so it's not a huge surprise that I've had issues with them, but that doesn't mean I'm willing to just assume the next one I'm near isn't about to go off.

So we didn't have a volcano, but we did have a hill. Some called it a mountain, but it was a hill. The top of the island was only about a thousand feet above sea level, and there were homes to be found all the way up to—but not *at*—the top, which was something you don't see all that often on real mountains. All the properties above four hundred feet were called mountaintop estates, which was just good marketing, because *hillside houses* sounded less impressive. I couldn't be sure, but it was possible the decision to call the thing a mountain began with a marketing campaign.

There were access roads leading up to the estates: long, narrow, windy little paths I'm pretty sure used to be much wider, because I didn't see a lot of easy ways to get building supplies up to the top and there were some pretty awesome houses up there. Plant overgrowth had turned the roads into something slightly wider than a footpath since whenever the houses were built, though, and for that reason I'd have just as soon taken an ATV or just walked down to the lower island.

I had to take the mammoth SUV, though, because Mirella asked me to swap the spare generator.

There was a power grid on the island and we were connected to it, but the grid wasn't particularly reliable, so we worked off of generator power about half the time. It was rarely an issue because we didn't use a ton of electricity and were both capable of roughing it for long periods. It could still be a pain, though, like if the power failed in the middle of a movie or the food wasn't done cooking yet. As romantic as candlelight dinners on the deck overlooking the ocean could be, they were also a little annoying multiple days in a row. Plus the things we used to keep insects out ran on electrical power.

It had to be the SUV because the generator was too heavy to carry down and didn't fit on the all-terrain vehicle, and if it did it would just fall off at the first steep hill.

The problem was, I should not drive a motorized vehicle of any kind under any circumstances. On the ATV, at least, the *goal* was to throw oneself down a hill. Those were practically built for someone like me. But I'm terrible on roads. They could be flat, wide and well lit and I'd find a way to do something wrong with a car on them.

The island roads weren't wide or flat, and were only as well lit as the vegetation allowed the sun to make them. And the SUV was so wide it might have been square. It was a bad confluence of people and things.

Mirella trusted me to make this run alone because it was only about five miles to the bottom of the island, and about half of it was on a road that was literally impossible to drive off of. I could, however, damage trees on the way down, which I had done.

She may also have been operating under the errant assumption that I would be getting better at driving with time. I don't expect to.

Also, she probably didn't feel like going.

The trip down was pleasantly uneventful, but probably took a lot longer than it had to, because I was determined to make it down without taking any more paint off the side of the car.

Mankind should not ever build vehicles this big and then make them single-operator machines. Anything this large should require a team of competent people to operate and should only be used when storming battlements or breaking ice.

For about a year, I took to calling the SUV the "Hubris" because I think that's a good brand name for it. Mirella either thought I was just saying "Humvee" wrong or decided to ignore me. It was hard to tell.

Most of the lower island was dedicated to keeping tourists happy.

The island was very much a tourist destination, but only for a certain type of tourist, and only for the very select few of this type that could afford the cost of the vacation. Lower island was for them, because it was where one found the pretty white sands and the high-end hotel and the real bungalows: one-room shacks that were right up against the water when the tide is high. The hotel—there was really only one—was far more luxurious than anything in the bungalows, but somehow the bungalows were costlier. I didn't know why, but I was still adjusting to remote islands being a good place to go, so I wasn't the best person to ask.

The bottom of the island was also where the main public dock was, and the one proper town, if one could call anything this size a town. It had the public buildings—the local government was the approximate equivalent of a condo association—and all the stores and restaurants and so on.

There was also the library—which was much more useful to residents than tourists—the grocer, and the liquor store, and so on. A little further out, closer to the base of the mountain but still a part of the lower island properties, there were squat apartment complexes and other iterations of shared living space for the employees whose jobs were to keep tourists happy. And of course the airport was down-island, such as it was. We could only land planes at low tide because the runway was underwater the rest of the time.

I really didn't have any kind of ulterior motive for visiting the town, in case you're wondering. I had to pick up a couple of new things to read, swap the generator while I was there, maybe get some decent gossip from the two or three people I could rely upon for such a thing, and that was all. As I said, life had slowed down, and I was enjoying that fact very much. Two years in, I couldn't see any reason to do something different.

This probably sounds boring, and maybe it is. It's possible I have no compass to help determine boring, or maybe I have a different threshold than most people. From my perspective, though, the vast majority of human history has been boring, by which I mean *nothing happened*, and sure, that can be dull. On the other hand, nothing happening includes nobody trying to kill anybody, and specifically, nobody trying to kill me. That's the kind of boring a guy can get behind. I've learned to appreciate that version of boring, in other words, because the alternative is often far less pleasant.

≈

*J*parked the SUV in the lot behind the general store. It only took three tries to get the thing into an appropriately parked position, and I didn't hit anybody, but in fairness there wasn't anybody around. The roads didn't support a lot of traffic, and conveniently enough there wasn't a lot of traffic on a regular basis. Or so it always seemed to me. It was possible every time I took the car down the mountain, Mirella picked up the landline and warned everyone that I was on my way. That was something she would do.

The parking lot was flattened loose gravel without any proper lines drawn, which was nice because it meant I was never in the wrong space. I got out, jumped down, and headed for the back entrance. As I said, it was a beautiful, sunny day, with a light breeze. There was a constant whiff of ocean in every breath from just about every point on the island. It was impossible to forget the ocean was there even when it wasn't visible.

I was wearing flip-flops. I feel like this is an important thing to confess. Flip-flops, cargo shorts, a sleeveless t-shirt, and a pair of sunglasses. I was dressed the way a guy on permanent vacation should dress. I felt like a Roman senator inside the city gates, except there was no garrison of soldiers surrounding us, just a large body of water.

I had developed something like a permanent tan over the past two years and only wore shoes of any kind when the odds were decent I was going to be walking across gravel or seashells—a distressing number of surfaces here were made of crushed shells —or into an eating establishment of some sort. This was great because I don't actually like shoes. I see no point in them except under circumstances of extreme cold, but since the modern world likes to create surfaces that are unfriendly to bare feet I don't have much of a choice.

I'd carried the generator to the back of the car myself, but I wasn't about to do that when taking it into the store, both because it was a stupid thing to do in the first place—I did it because I didn't want to ask Mirella to help because for some reason I thought that was embarrassing—and because the store had a rack of two-wheelers at the rear door for this exact purpose. So instead I flip-flopped across the gravel and grabbed one.

And that was when the demon came up behind me.

CHAPTER 2

The demon was nearly seven feet tall, with an ugly flat face and a hairless head. His three-fingered hand gripped the doorframe as he shouldered his way through a space that wasn't really large enough to accommodate a being with his dimensions.

His name was Leonard. He was a pretty cool guy.

"Hi Adam, howzit going?"

"Hi Lenny!"

I said this a bit too loudly, because my first reaction on seeing any demon—even one who meant me no harm—was to panic. It's a pretty normal response, and the correct one about 99% of the time.

"Just switching out the portable," I added, in a more modulated tone.

"Yeah? No, no, put that cart away, lemme get it for you."

He got the rest of the way through the doorframe and headed for the SUV. I wasn't going to argue, because one doesn't argue with demons, especially ones who aren't trying to kill you. Or so I have to assume; Leonard was actually the first one I'd met who wasn't trying to kill either me or someone nearby.

Demons aren't some sort of hell-beast in any real supernatural heaven/hell sense, so everyone put away the bibles and calm down. They *are* large, thuggish monstrosities with skin thick enough to walk across gravel parking lots in bare feet—as he was doing—and take a knife cut without bleeding. They're nearly indestructible warriors of low intelligence with short tempers and an almost unparalleled bloodlust that makes them exceedingly difficult to control in large numbers.

Armies led by a vanguard of demons tended to win more often than not, so long as there weren't that many demons. More than a few—I think it may have been Genghis Khan who worked out the magic number of seven demons per battle, max—and they tended to just start killing everybody regardless of banner.

If you ever come across a demon, run. If there's a large body of water available, jump into it, because they can't swim. If you happen to have a vial of the flu in your pocket or something else pure enough to be reusable as a bioweapon, this is also useful because they have terrible immune systems. Other than that, you're probably out of luck because they will do *Terminator*-level damage to get at you if they have been tasked with doing so.

I wasn't running because Leonard wasn't chasing me. He wanted to carry my generator inside, and I was going to let him do that. If he wanted to pick up my car and move it to the other side of the lot I'd let him do that too. Another good thing to know about demons is that if they want to do something and that something doesn't involve disemboweling you with their fists, you should probably let them do it.

A thing that has been true of every demon I ever met was that they wore baggy clothing and large hats or hoods. This was to disguise the unmistakable non-humanness of their features, and it's why you've probably never seen one clearly enough to realize you should be running. But Leonard had on a pair of shorts and that was all. (There were a number of places on the island with a "no-shirt/no-shoes/no-service" rule. I'm pretty sure nobody was going to be telling him to abide by this rule. In fairness, he was probably not carrying any communicable diseases.) It was impossible to mistake him for anything other than a non-human creature from just about any distance. But that was all right, because there were hardly any humans on the island anyway. I was one of the few.

"Beautiful day, hunh?" Leonard said on his way to the car. "I love that breeze, yeah? Cuts right through the heat. Just great. And lookit that sky!"

"It's a nice day all right," I said. "It's always nice here."

"Yeah, ain't it? 'Cept the rain. Don't like the rain so much. No rain today tho."

This is really the deepest any conversation goes with Lenny, at least with me. We rehash the current and most recent weather-related events, he picks up something heavy, and we go on our way.

I met him my first month on the island. At the time I was dressed much the same, by which I mean I had no weapons onhand, I wasn't protected by heavy armor, and I had no way to radio in an airstrike. I had the SUV, and was debating whether to use it as a weapon or flee in it when he held out his hand and introduced himself. Then he talked about puffy clouds for ten minutes while I held my breath. Things have gone more smoothly since.

"Might rain later," I said.

"Nah." He sniffed the air. "Couple days, maybe."

I've learned that very nearly everything on Earth has a better sense of smell than humans. Even the ones with hardly any nose on their face.

Across the street, two tourists walked past the parking lot entrance, on their way from one of the local bed-and-breakfasts to the beach. They were incredibly pale-skinned men dressed in floral print shorts, carrying a beach umbrella, a couple of towels, and a cooler. If they noticed the demon in the parking lot at all, they didn't acknowledge him. But they weren't really men themselves. They were elves.

Hopefully, they packed sunblock. Their kind is not known to tan well.

Leonard waited as the car's back hatch opened. (I have a button that makes the back door open and close. Whenever I use it to do the latter I worry we have perhaps reached the point where technology has made everything *too* easy. Then I go on a nice long jog and I feel better.) Once the hatch was opened he reached inside and with one hand picked up the generator.

"Tapped out, huh?"

"It's a little low. Always keep a fully charged backup, you know how that goes."

"Sure, sure." He tossed it from hand to hand like a basketball. I closed the hatch. "Funny how they weigh the same."

"The generators?"

"The full ones and the empty ones. They weigh the same whether they're full or not. You figure when they're used up they'd weigh less."

I could have tried to explain to him that electricity doesn't weigh anything, or if it does it's not all that much, but to be honest I barely understand this concept myself. I will always be a caveman poking shiny things with a stick, but sometimes I'm good at pretending otherwise.

"Crazy, huh?" I said instead.

"That's what I'm sayin'. Let's get this swapped out for you."

～

*T*here are a lot of reasons for keeping the name and location of the island a secret, but the big one is that it's essentially a vacation paradise for people of means who don't happen to actually be people. These are goblins and elves mostly —they're actually the same species, but don't tell them that because they hate it—but also a healthy number of imps, satyrs, a werewolf or two, and lots of succubi and incubi. Even a vampire shows up now and then, which is just crazy, because sunshine and warm sand aren't typically attractive features to a vampire.

Those are just the ones who can safely pass as human beings. Supposedly, a troll lives in the hillside somewhere, and the island appears to have an indigenous tribe of pixies. Every bar has a resident iffrit, and I swear one time I saw a faery, although this might have been my imagination. Faeries are terrifying and don't play nicely with others, and almost certainly don't go on vacations.

I've also seen a few beings I thought were extinct. Within a couple of months on the island, I saw a djinn for the first time in a thousand years, and I've heard rumors of a real dragon in the woods on the other side of the mountain. I don't believe the rumors any more than the ones about a troll, but if ever there was a place capable of proving me wrong, this was it.

Perhaps the most amazing thing about the island is that there are natural enemies here that don't behave like enemies. It's a fully demilitarized zone. I don't even know how this is accomplished. It just is. It means a demon like Leonard—he's the only demon I've seen on the island—can hang around at the local general store and chat up customers, and not only does nobody run away screaming, nobody even thinks twice about engaging him in civil discourse. It's legitimately crazy.

I didn't know the island existed until Mirella brought me here, and I've been marveling at it ever since. She doesn't seem to understand how incredible this arrangement is, but she hasn't seen as much discord as I have, and is also perhaps a bit less cynical. That by itself is fairly amazing, because before retiring she was a bodyguard, and bodyguards are trained to anticipate the most likely violent outcomes in every situation. This place is one giant potentially violent outcome waiting for someone to show up with a tinderbox and a fuse.

That I am no longer anticipating such a possibility is surprising.

~

The generator swap took hardly any time thanks to Leonard, who after helping out went on his merry way, undoubtedly to find other heavy things that required lifting. As far as I knew, he mostly wandered around the bottom of the island looking for stuff to do. My theory was that moving stuff around all day was how he channeled his innate desire for violence, provided that was actually innate and not learned.

I always meant to ask him what he did for money and where he lived, but I never ended up in a conversation that lasted long enough to get to those questions. The answer might be the same as the punch line to the joke: where does an 800-pound gorilla sit? (Answer: wherever he wants. Cue laughter.) It was probably close to the general store, though, since that was usually where I ran into him.

Anyway, I didn't need to know that badly, obviously, or I would have figured out how to ask by now.

The only part of the island that deserved to be called a town was a five-block-by-five-block grid, all perfectly squared and equidistant, an imposition of artificial order on a landscape of natural variation. From overhead, the streets offended the eye. They were, thankfully, all gravel and seashell, but still struck a blow to the sartorial elegance of the nature around it.

Although perhaps that's just my personal reaction. For someone who grew up in a city, it might be comforting.

The order of the layout made it more difficult to get around than it should have. Since the whole grid had been built at the same time, most of the buildings on it were constructed from the same architectural plans, so the only way to tell if you were on one street and not two blocks distant was to look at the names on the buildings or the mailboxes. For instance, the town had a library in a building that was externally identical to the island's only hospital. I'm pretty sure these are two things that are bad to confuse with one another. I'd done it myself, about five or six times, but only when looking for the library and entering the hospital on error. I have no use for a hospital, but a great need for books.

I decided to walk to the library from the parking lot, because street parking was scarce, I cannot be trusted to parallel-park anyway, and it was only a few blocks. Plus, there was a nice bar between the lot and the library, and it had just opened for the day.

All right, so maybe I did have an ulterior motive for going into town.

~

I'm not an alcoholic.

Probably.

Sure, there's a mountain of evidence to suggest otherwise—like having blacked out on entire decades—but I just think the rules for an immortal man are different than for someone whose life expectancy is seventy-five years. I can waste a lifetime drink-ing. I can waste fifty lifetimes drinking. I'm not going to get cirrhosis, or catch pneumonia from exposure, or whatever. I might end up in a fight I shouldn't be in, but I'm generally not a mean drunk so that's unlikely, and I'm also good in a fight regardless of how much of me is composed of alcohol. I can function at a high level with a decent buzz for a long time.

What I cannot do is drive with that buzz on, but only because I'm an awful driver already.

Can I go without alcohol? Sure. Forever? Probably.

I'm not interested in proving that, though, to myself or anybody else.

Something I am *definitely* addicted to, though, is the cama-raderie that comes with drinking in public. This was a thing I wasn't getting out of my own personal bar in the house. The house came with an often semi-naked woman who liked me a lot, and finding someone like that is about a thousand times more difficult than finding a guy in a bar with an interesting story to tell. But I still missed talking to the guy in the bar now and again.

I was pretty sure Mirella knew this about me, and I was pretty sure she didn't mind. We'll see.

The name of the place was *The Fancy Mermaid*, and it claimed to be the oldest pub on the island. There were three other pubs that made the same claim, and I had no idea which one had the best argument. If you stacked up the creation stories against one another it was possible to conclude they were all built and opened the same afternoon and were arguing over what time of day they unlocked their doors.

I personally thought *The First Pub* had the best claim on the title, both because of the name and because it wasn't in the lower island proper. You had to drive away from the grid and onto a small side road and up the mountain a tiny ways to get to *The First Pub*, and that made it seem like the sort of place that might predate anything in the town itself.

Meanwhile, both *The Fancy Mermaid* and the other claimant, *Crabby's*, insisted the town was built around their establishments, in part because of their popularity.

It's a silly argument that people with short lifespans have all the time, as if surviving unchanged for a period of forty or fifty years is an achievement. But every establishment on the island was built in the late twentieth century, so to my ears they all sounded like three-year olds disputing a two-hour age difference. Last longer than Europe first, and then start bragging.

The Fancy Mermaid was not fancy, but wasn't a dive either. There were no proper dive bars on the island, which was nice from a tourism perspective, but it had the strange effect of making me miss them. This happens sometimes, where I discover nostalgia for something nobody should ever miss. Like hardtack, and plagues.

The interior of the bar was polished wood with the expected nautical themes, all tied to the iconic mermaid figurehead trussed to the ceiling and dangling over the bar.

I took a seat underneath her kelp-covered breasts and signaled Anh, the bartender, who soon had a pint of tap beer in front of me.

In terms of popularity, the *Mermaid* was somewhere in the middle of the pack. The most successful places on the island were the ones with a direct view of the beach, and the ones that were actually clubs playing ear-bleedingly loud music. We went to a club one time, and while Mirella seemed to enjoy herself okay, I was anxious the entire night. It wasn't until later I realized the rhythm and pace of the house music was the same as the drums we used to pound before going to war. I'm not a fan of the tribal war-drum sound as entertainment, it turns out. By the end of the night I was ready to brain someone with a femur bone.

There was a view at the *Mermaid*, but it was a view of the street. The windows were open to allow the trade winds through, and that ever-present sea smell was there, so the bar still felt connected to the island, but an ocean angle would have helped. I imagined the place was very popular with people who'd been at the beach all day and had had their fill of tides.

I mostly had the place to myself, but there were a few tables set up near the windows with tourists eating an early lunch. Goblin/goblin, goblin/elf, and human/succubus were the pairings I could see. I tried not to stare at the succubus, who was in a bikini top and short-shorts, with completely impractical four-inch heel sandals that I assume she removed when walking in sand. The human was every inch an American, and I mean that in the most unflattering way imaginable. He looked like the kind of guy who could afford to take a personal succubus to the most private island in the world while the bank he ran was busy wrecking someone's economy. I hoped she took him for a lot of money by the time she was finished.

I should mention that English was the main language on the island. This had nothing to do with location—if it did we'd be speaking Tagalog or Malay. It had to do with what language most of the people coming to the island were fluent in, and *that* had to do with what language the wealthiest people in the world were fluent in. I don't think anybody ever decided that English was to be the *lingua franca*; it just made the most sense.

Having said that, I spent ten minutes talking to Anh in Vietnamese, which I'm partially fluent in. I'm thoroughly fluent in every European language you can name, including ones nobody else alive is still fluent in, but the further East I go the less impressive my language skills become.

Vietnamese I'm okay with because at some point in I learned Khmer, which is similar. Most of the tongues native to the Philippines and Malaysia are new to me, though, as is a lot of Japanese. Chinese, I'm rusty with, but I can hold my own.

This is another way I keep from losing my mind entirely: finding practical things to learn. After this long a life you'd think I was mostly out of new stuff to pick up, but the world changes faster than I can absorb so there's always something else to get good at, even as old skills become useless. For instance, I know how to turn a live plant into papyrus, make a poultice from the blood of a wildebeest, perform a complicated rain dance, and track a wounded animal in a forest. I haven't needed to do any of those things for a very long time, although I did perform the rain dance for Mirella once, for kicks. It rained the next day, but I'm pretty sure that was a coincidence.

"Just the man I was looking for," said someone behind me. I turned to greet one of the few other human full-time residents of the island.

"Morning, doc," I said. "Here for a drink before you start your shift?"

"My shift just ended," he said, clapping me on the shoulder and sliding into the seat beside me.

Doctor Lew Cambridge was the chief resident at the hospital. He had the dubious distinction of being an expert in the field of cryptobiology, which doesn't officially exist. It's the study of beings that also don't officially exist.

I'm not sure how much the island pays him, but I imagine it's a tremendously large amount of money, because his research would probably be world-alteringly important if it ever got out and people believed it. Although maybe the second part of that sentence is the problem, because one thing I've learned about human beings is that we are really bad at accepting the idea of hidden species among us.

There are, as you may have already figured out, a great many sentient non-human species out there. Some are common enough and human-looking enough to have inserted themselves into society at large without being noticed. Others are rare and weird. A few are incredibly dangerous. I've come across most of them in my life, because it's been a really long life.

Doc Cambridge has come across a lot of them too, because many examples of impossible species live on this island. He loves talking to me for my evidently encyclopedic knowledge of these creatures, although he doesn't know where my knowledge came from. I'm a bit reticent to share the fact of my immortality with anybody, and especially not with someone in the medical profession.

I call him Doctor Moreau sometimes. I'm the only one who thinks it's funny, but that hasn't stopped me from doing it.

"How's the medicine biz, doc?" I asked.

He placed what looked like a stone on the bar.

"Take a look," he said.

I picked it up while he signaled to Anh for a drink. It was stone-*like*, but not a stone.

"Is this a bezoar?" I asked.

"It is!"

I handed it back to him.

"Ew," I said. "I feel an urge to wash my hands now, thank you."

"I pulled it from the intestine of a djinn."

"Not making it any better."

"But you understand the import of the bezoar, yes?"

His eyebrows wiggled with what I interpreted to mean he was excited.

He was an Englishman, but with hardly any trace of an accent. Pushing fifty, he was surprisingly fit. If one didn't know him, one might choose *tennis instructor* as his profession well before *medical doctor*. At least until the eyebrows started wiggling.

"Of course, but that's a somewhat non-scientific understanding, isn't it?" I said.

Bezoars are supposed to offset poisons. The word even means *antidote* in Persian. Generally speaking, the more disgusting something is, the more things it's supposed to cure. I don't understand it either.

"Long assumed to be the case, yes, but! What if the problem is not the bezoar, but the *source* of the bezoar?"

Doc had been working on a theory regarding a range of debunked medical remedies. His idea was that some of the old, since-disproven solutions to biological conditions *were* valid, just not for human beings. He got the idea after learning that a painkiller made from local tree bark was highly effective on succubi and incubi, but not on anybody else.

It was a neat idea. I'd rather he worked on answering the kinds of questions that have bothered me for a couple thousand years—like how do pixies reproduce—but he was trying to cure things, which I guess was more important.

"The source of this is a djinn, you say?"

"I was in surgery for three hours last night extracting that. Their biology makes them highly susceptible to intestinal blockage, as it happens. I washed it off since."

"Well thank goodness."

"But you understand my thinking."

It wasn't a question, more like a dare. He wanted to see if I could get to where he was. The doctor was incredibly curious as to where my expertise originated, and enjoyed challenging it.

"Djinn emit a toxin through their hands," I said. "It's like a poison, and it makes people highly suggestible for short periods."

"It's from their sweat glands. I believe biologically it's a defense mechanism, much like the psychoactive toad."

"It makes them incredibly dangerous too. You understand that."

"I wore gloves the whole time, don't worry. My patient is not that sort of fellow."

Djinn could make anyone think they're the most wonderful people in the world. That was the whole problem. I decided not to push that point, though.

"So to take your idea to the next step," I said, "if the being you took this from has a gland that secretes poison, a bezoar produced inside his body might be an actual remedy for poison."

"That's what I'm thinking, yes!"

"I don't know a lot about medicine, Moreau, but that doesn't sound anything like a logical progression to me."

"It's a possibility, though. I'm going to test it!"

"Let me know how it turns out."

~

I was nearly positive it wouldn't work, because there was a decent chance the idea that bezoars were a curative for poison was my fault.

I had this scam going. I want to say it was around 500 A.D., but nobody had the same calendars back then so I can't be sure.

It was a clever scam. First, I'd bring out a rat. (Rats, it should be said, were everywhere, all the time. If I didn't have one on-hand I would have been able to pick one up pretty fast.) I'd give the rat some poison—real poison, so this was just about the only overhead the business had—and we'd all watch it die. After the rat died, I'd make a big show of drinking the rest of the poison myself, and then pretending to suffer in the same way the rat had.

Then I'd swallow a bezoar and act like I'd been cured.

There were two elements to the trick. First, I actually did drink the poison, but since poison has no effect on me—for the same reason I can't get sick—it wasn't going to do any harm regardless of what I swallowed next. Second, I palmed the bezoar instead of swallowing it. This was because I was sort of afraid of choking on one, and also because bezoars are disgusting. Plus, why swallow it when I can sell it?

It was a lucrative gig. I ran out of bezoars several times and had to substitute clay instead, which worked exactly as well. Poison later became scarce enough that I started palming that too rather than actually drinking it. Rats I never ran out of.

I had to stop when someone decided my cure was actually a form of witchcraft. That wasn't so bad, except then people were asking me for things like love potions and what-not, and I just got tired of making stuff up.

Anyway, I wasn't going to tell the doctor any of that.

~

"Is this bezoar the only thing you're keeping from the djinn?" I asked.

"What do you mean?"

"I think you know."

"The toxin? Oh, well, now… that would be something if I

could figure out how to get it to work without a live djinn on the other end, wouldn't it?"

He was grinning, and I felt like I was missing something.

"You're not about to tell me you've already done it, are you?"

"No, nothing like that. I don't have the skill for such a thing anyway. I imagine what would be needed is a way to test active samples for long enough to ascertain why the chemical doesn't survive outside of the host, and then perhaps to work out a way to synthesize the components. But all of that would be a great waste of time. The uses are extremely limited."

I remembered nearly dying at the hands of a clan of djinn after my entire traveling party succumbed to the poison. *Limited* wasn't how I would have described what they could do. After that, you could have convinced me the djinn would run the world one day. That hadn't happened in the thousand-odd years since, so perhaps I was mistaken.

Unless they do run the world and I haven't figured that out. Never underestimate the appeal of a good conspiracy theory.

"Why is it limited?" I asked.

"The antidote to the poison is another kind of poison, albeit one that doesn't affect higher species: caffeine. A medium serving of dark roast and one is typically immune from the djinn for a day or two. I suspect one has to travel a long way to find someone with no trace of caffeine in their system nowadays."

I laughed. "That probably led to a lot of confused djinn."

"Well yes, I bet it did. It also led to a lot of dead djinn. Caffeine *is* toxic to them. That's why there are so few. I'm surprised you've even heard of them."

He side-eyed me, as he did whenever we drifted toward questions regarding my background that I wasn't going to answer.

I kept promising I would someday. That was probably true, but I needed to trust him a little more, or he needed to catch me a lot drunker than one beer deep.

That reminded me it was probably time I left the bar.

If I'm not careful I will spend an entire day in an establishment that serves alcohol, regardless of how unappetizing said establishment happens to be. After a certain number of beers I tended to forget things, like that I drove to town or that Mirella was waiting for me. After about double that certain number, I could forget where I lived or that I had a girlfriend at all. Double *that* and I could forget what century I was in and what language I was supposed to be speaking.

The safest recourse was to stop after one or two beers and proceed with my day. So far, over the past two years at least, I'd managed to accomplish this.

I threw some cash on the bar—American dollars to go with the language of choice.

"Time I headed on," I said to the doc.

"Oh, but I haven't even told you everything yet!" he said, his hand on my wrist.

"You showed me the bezoar."

"Yes, yes, but..." he pulled me closer so as to whisper. He was coming off a shift of at least twelve hours from the smell of him and the red in his eyes, so the ability to bring his voice down to a whisper was suspect, but there wasn't anyone else at the bar in earshot. "I have something I want to show you, in the lab."

"That's ominous."

"It was brought in yesterday. Washed ashore. Nobody knows what it is, but *I* think..."

He stopped talking and looked up at the ceiling. I followed his gaze to the figurehead directly above.

I sighed.

"There's no such thing, Doctor Moreau. Unless you're planning to build one. We've been through this."

The esteemed Doctor Cambridge authored research that stood on the line between fact and fantasy. If there were no such thing as goblins and demons and so on, his work would have been *pure* fantasy and he probably would have gotten locked up a little while ago. But they do exist, and because they do, most of the doc's research was perfectly valid, if utterly unpublishable.

The problem became in knowing when to stop.

I would have thought there was a minimum empirical bar. That's how I've approached things. If I haven't encountered a certain mythological being by now, I'm going with the assumption that it doesn't exist and/or never did exist.

A simple example: centaurs. Satyrs are a real thing, and satyrs are supposedly half man and half goat, so why wouldn't a creature that's half man and half horse also exist?

It only *sounds* like decent reasoning, though. Satyrs aren't really half goat, so arguing that their existence proves centaurs must also exist is silly. Also, I'm pretty sure the idea of centaurs began in tribes that didn't quite know what to make of the first men on horseback. And finally, I never saw a centaur, and I would have if they existed.

Admittedly, my argument has some holes in it. A decade or so ago I would have told you nymphs were purely mythological, and three thousand years ago I would have said the same thing about sea serpents, pixies, and faeries. I was wrong on all four.

It's still a better argument than *prove there is no such thing as mermaids*, because proving a negative statement is impossible.

"You should come to the lab," Doctor Cambridge said.

"Are you telling me you have a dead mermaid at the hospital?"

He shrugged. "Not an entire one, no."

"How much of one?"

"A tail."

"The tail of a large fish washed ashore."

"No, no, no. I believe what I have is the remains of a *shedding*. The creature came ashore and slipped out of its tail so as to walk among us on two legs."

I laughed. "Come on, doctor. By what biological process do you imagine that even taking place? You're talking about magic, not science."

Not incidentally, there's no such thing as magic. There are a lot of things that *look* like magic, but those things come with explanations not involving magical processes.

"More 'magical' than anything I've already seen on this island?" he asked.

"Yes, actually. I've never cut open a fish and found legs inside, have you? Even if that were a normal medical thing, you're telling me they just know how to *walk*? It takes humans months to learn how to do that for the first time. And how would one return to the ocean? Grow a new tail?"

Doctor Cambridge looked up again at the figurehead looming over our conversation, then at the bar as a whole.

"I've heard stories," he said quietly. "I know it sounds unscientific, but one of the things I've learned since I began working here is that stories having little merit on the mainland have a great deal of merit here. Come see what I have, before it deteriorates any further. It's withering away."

I clapped him on the shoulder.

"Another time. I've already been gone longer than I should have."

This wasn't entirely true, but *trouble with the missus* has been a good excuse to leave the bar since there have been bars.

"Be careful, then," he said.

"Why? Because the mermaids walk among us?" This was a joke. He wasn't laughing, though.

"Yes, exactly."

CHAPTER 3

here was a time when I thought mermaids were real.

As I said, I have a standard when it comes to the seemingly impossible things that actually happen to exist. Vampires and werewolves are two other really good examples, because for a long time I assumed they weren't real, but they are.

Meaning, they aren't actually impossible, just improbable and perhaps implausible, and the existence of such things as vampires and werewolves therefore made mermaids—in my mind— equally implausible and improbable, but no less impossible.

There's an important caveat: just because something turns out to have existed at one time or another doesn't mean it has the same properties as it's reputed to have. Dragons are my favorite for this, because they didn't fly or breathe fire. They were just big, dumb animals that died off eventually. Why? I don't know for sure, but they never adopted a proper pack mentality and were uncommonly bellicose, so maybe they just failed to develop into a creature that deserved to continue existing. The point is, they *did* exist once, only in a much more mundane iteration than any of the mythological descriptions spoke to.

In that same sense, perhaps it's not unreasonable to argue that mermaids are entirely real, provided we're sticking with the argument that men at sea for long periods, staring at vast bodies of water and thinking about things they wished they had, might justifiably mistake a manatee for a full-breasted woman. My only complaint about this reasoning is that a similar thing could be said about sea serpents, and I know for a fact that those are real.

Or were. I haven't seen one for a long time, but I don't go across oceans in boats when I can avoid doing so, because again: sea serpents! I'd rather not take any chances.

Anyway. My point is, I used to believe in mermaids, just as at one time I also believed in centaurs and devils. I put all of them in the same mental box as vampires and werewolves and pixies and all the other rare, improbable, but definitely real things.

All that changed between then and now is my standard of proof.

When I talk about things that happened in the distant past I like to pretend I'm a more evolved individual than the people of the time. To a certain degree that's true, because I have a much larger volume of personal history to inform everything I do. But I can't apply a perspective that hasn't been invented yet. I didn't have the benefit of Cartesian philosophy when arguing with Aristotle, or an awareness of astrophysics when determining whether an eclipse presaged a famine. If someone said a disease was caused by evil spirits I could doubt the existence of said spirits if I wanted—and I did—but I didn't have the germ theory of disease to counter with.

I was never more than a product of the time, basically. I was only as advanced in my thinking as it was possible to be for the period.

This doesn't mean I believed all the same things everyone around me did—belief in gods being an excellent example—only that if the people of a time lacked the tools to interrogate what was factually true and differentiate that truth from what was only *believed* to be true, then I too lacked those tools.

All of which is to say that when I thought there was a mermaid living in the Sea of Galilee, I had a lot of reasons to think it.

~

*W*hen I tell people I was a fisherman on the Sea of Galilee at around the right time to meet a certain famous person, I get weird looks. And I mean, from people who already know I'm immortal. (I would get entirely different weird looks if I ever shared that piece of information with someone who didn't already buy into my immortality, which I don't. I've found that immortality is a harder sell than *I was around for Jesus*.)

The thing is, you'd figure I would have run into the man, and I didn't.

The Sea of Galilee—we called it Lake Genneseret, but that doesn't exactly roll off the tongue—is huge. Not huge by the standards of certain oceans, or even some of the larger seas, but a whole lot bigger than your average freshwater lake. It was not only possible to make a living fishing in this sea without ever coming across the Nazarean, it was possible to fish there without ever hearing of him.

Also, his historical impact *in the moment* wasn't all that significant. Don't take that the wrong way, I don't mean he wasn't important, only that most of the significance associated with his words and life didn't get attached to him until after he was dead. At the time, the area had more than a couple of itinerant doomsday prophets, so it's unlikely that, had our paths crossed, I'd have even noticed.

So I mean, I guess it's possible I did meet him but I doubt I'd have remembered if I had.

Moving on.

Fishing on Genneseret wasn't a terrible way to make a living. It was big, and deep, and there was enough for everyone. I knew people who fished off small rowboats and caught enough to feed themselves and their family, and I knew larger vessels that caught fish in nets, cleaned and salted them on board, and brought them directly to market after only a few days on the water. That was the kind of fishing I did.

I was part of a team of twelve, on a boat owned by a man named Barukh. Seven of his sons were on the crew, as was Barukh himself. The other four were old men who had spent their lives on the sea, and me. I had *not* spent my life on this particular sea, but I'd spent six or seven full lifetimes on the Mediterranean, which meant I had more experience than anybody else there. However, my experience wasn't in net fishing, it was in things like *how to get a lot of slaves to row in unison* and *how to overpower pirates*. My expertise in square-rigged sailing was valuable, however, and I could gut a fish as efficiently as anyone. Plus I worked cheap. I had no family to support and lived in a shed on the small spit of land Barukh's family owned, fronting the shoreline.

I was going by the name Eleazar.

Barukh and his sons and the rest of us would spend two or three days at sea at a time, then one day at the market and one day of rest. Weather impacted when we left and how long we stayed out, and the Shabbat—honored by most everyone in the area—was almost always a second day of rest. I was Jewish in name but not practice, which added to my value as a crewmember. It meant on a couple of occasions I had to sail the boat alone, such as when weather prevented us from making it to shore before the Shabbat. It was a pain, but it only happened a couple of times.

There were eras in which it was a bad idea to not adhere to the same religious practices of those sharing the region, but this was not one of those times. Also, had I followed the dominant religion of the time, I would have worshipped the Roman gods, not the god of the Jews.

Barukh and his family likely realized that Eleazar wasn't the name I was born with, but people were really not that concerned with *real names* back then, so they never pried. The benefit of using a local name was that nobody much bothered me. I was a fisherman and a "Hebrew", just like a thousand other people, and if anyone got an idea that I should perhaps marry someone's daughter, they only had to pry deeply enough to discover I wasn't a practicing Jew and the conversation was over. It worked.

By the way, getting stuck in a situation where someone wants you to marry their daughter is a *huge* hassle, and it used to happen all the time. I think at least half of my approach to settling down in a particular area was finding a way to position myself as ineligible, because there was literally no easy solution to the daughter problem. When it happened the best recourse was to fake my own death and move on. I'm not joking.

When we were at sea I spent most of my free time talking to Nachum, who was one of the old men I mentioned. All of Nachum's children had either died or grown up and moved on, and none of the living ones embraced the sea in any real sense. Not compared to Nachum, whose life experiences with water lined up pretty well with my own. That is, he'd spent at least as much time on salt water as on fresh water.

He sailed the Mediterranean for many years, not fishing but shipping, on a trading vessel not unlike the kind I used to own back when I was a Carthaginian merchant. So we had some things in common. Plus he was the only guy I knew who was even close to being my age. That's a little like saying a rat is much closer to my height than a mouse, but when you live this long, you latch on to anything that looks like common ground.

Nachum was full of stories that wowed the younger members of the crew, and some of those stories might even have been true. A couple of those stories were about mermaids.

"Have you seen one yourself?" I asked one day. It was right

after he told a story in which he claimed to have done exactly that.

"You heard the tale," he said.

We were in the back of the boat stitching up the nets. The person the story had been for—Dor, who was Barukh's youngest —had already wandered off.

"I heard the tale, but now I'm asking you for the truth of it. Seems the only tales of mermaids I ever heard come from folk who know a man who saw one. I'm asking if you tell a tale told to you by one of those men and put yourself in that tale so as to improve upon it, or if you laid eyes on one yourself."

"It went just as I said."

"On the great salt sea."

"I tell you it was so."

If you were the kind of person who hung around people who spent a lot of time on boats, you heard at least one mermaid story, but most of those came from men who sailed the ocean, not the Mediterranean. It was atypical. As was sailing the ocean, actually. Not a lot of people did it. I hadn't, up to that point.

"Just to have this correct, you pulled a live mermaid up in a net on the great sea. This beast was half woman and half tail, and she could breathe the air and speak in the common tongue well enough to beg your captain to set her free."

Nachum eyeballed me unkindly.

"You have heard me tell this many times now, Eleazar. You call me liar only now? You, a man who claims to have survived a serpent on those same waters?"

"That was true," I said. And it was, but I changed some of the details. The incident in question happened ten generations earlier, but I wasn't going to tell him that. "We were chased by a Tanakh, but it did not, upon catching us, stick its head up from the water and converse in Greek."

"It's this portion of the tale you take umbrage with."

"It's one, yes. When we go to market we have one chance in

five of meeting with a buyer who knows no Latin, and two in five of meeting one who does not converse in Hebrew. And these are men who share the same shore as us. You would have me believe a creature can be wrested from the bosom of the sea and arrive on the deck of a ship with a full understanding of her captor's native tongue? I suspect a mermaid would have no under-standing of language at all, never mind the correct language for her circumstance."

"Well… perhaps it is an exaggeration on my part."

"The mermaid did not speak?"

"She pleaded, but did not speak. She expressed well her desire to return to the waters without words. The captain, on seeing her eyes fill with tears, had pity and set her free."

"Ah, but then you must explain the next portion, where she promises great fortune to him that release her. How might she have conveyed the availability of this spell without words?"

"Well that's common sense. Everyone knows a favor for a mermaid means great fortune. Otherwise we would have seen a dead one by now, would we not? The captain would have to consider the value of capturing and keeping a mermaid against the value of setting one free."

"Everyone knows, I see."

"Do not take that tone with me, Eleazar."

"My apologies."

We finished repairing the net in silence, and then it was time to do some fishing, and cleaning, and salting, none of which I'll describe because it's pretty gross and not terribly important to the story. I will say that we did not at any time catch a live mermaid in one of our nets, though.

By day's end, the deck was smelly from fish guts, which was unfortunate as the deck was where we all expected to sleep. Although we all smelled of fish guts too.

We slept in shifts, and it wasn't my shift to sleep yet, so I sat at the rear and enjoyed a typically fantastic view of the sky and the water in the light of the full moon. Except for the smell of the fish, it was one of those scenes that stick with an immortal man.

It wasn't long before Nachum hobbled up beside me. As was so with most old fishermen, he carried himself like a man whose joints were a grave disappointment.

"They've been spotted on this sea too," he said, slowly lowering himself to the deck to sit.

"Mermaids?"

"That's what I mean, yes."

"How would a mermaid get here?"

He shrugged. "Swim, I expect."

I laughed. "The waters of the Mediterranean are brackish and undrinkable. That's where you find mermaids."

"I don't imagine the quality of the water is a need for a being such as that."

"You misunderstand me, Nachum. There are great oceans, which I assume you know."

"Of course."

"These great oceans are filled with brine. If you say to me you saw a mermaid on the salt sea—as indeed you already have—I might believe this to be so because that sea is in communication with the waters of the oceans of the world. A creature could swim into and out of the great Mediterranean in the same way, and through the same means, as the waters. But *this* sea does not speak to the oceans. It is fed by rivers, and those rivers are also not speaking to oceans. If you imagine a mermaid to be a part of a tribe, or a herd, where would this tribe or herd live? Where do they come from and go?"

"Mermaids don't live in fresh water, is that what you're saying?"

"I am."

"You could have just said that."

"I thought there was a more thorough way to make the point."

"But such a waste of words! And to no account. Mermaids are

magic. Everyone knows this. If they wish to live in this lake, then they will live in this lake. Who are we to question?"

"I'm not satisfied with that explanation."

"Then find one which satisfies you."

"All right. What makes you say there are mermaids in these waters? Have you seen one?"

"Ah, no. Do you know old Menachem?"

"You will have to be more specific."

"Old Menachem, from the house beside mine."

Nachum lived on the seaside, a short distance from Barukh.

"You have no seamen beside you that I know of. Farmers, I took them for."

"Yes, yes, that's right. Old Menachem has the larger of the farms."

"And he saw a mermaid. From the shore."

"I'll tell you what we will do. It so happens old Menachem has sought me out for advice. When we next come to port he and I will be meeting to resolve his problem."

"His mermaid-related problem."

He smiled, which was a little unsettling, because he only had a couple of teeth left.

"I am going to bring you with me, and you can hear his tale from his mouth. Then you can decide on your own whether there are mermaids living in the waters beneath us."

❧

"It began before the harvest," Menachem said. He was a little man, brown and wrinkled and frail, but with sons large enough to bring into question the faithfulness of his wife. "With the ox."

Menachem had cows, a few goats, a bull and an ox. No pigs. I love pig. Used to eat pig regularly back when I spent most of my time in Greece, but this whole kosher thing had taken it off the menu in the entire region.

It wasn't a large farm by most standards, but large enough to sustain his family and produce some grains for market and an occasional calf for trade. As was the case for most of the farms in the area, Menachem used the obvious direct water supply for his farming needs. That included letting the animals wade into the shallows to drink.

We were standing at that water line as he told the story. The ground was muddy and the grass trampled to oblivion right at the edge. A soggy path led from the shore to the gated pen behind us.

"The fence is new," he said. "Before this, we only fenced the edge of the property and the field. The animals could walk from the yard to here as they wished."

"You didn't lock them up at night?" I asked.

"For what reason? There are no wolves in these parts, my neighbors are honest men, and none of the beasts have shown an interest in swimming to a different farm. We have a dog, but he is an old herder, and is thankful we've not asked him to corral any of the animals. He sleeps more often than not."

"All right, so you had to build a fence."

"We oversee them in the daytime and don't allow them down here at night any longer. Not since the problems began."

"I'm not clear on what the problems *are*."

Menachem shared a look with Nachum.

"You can tell him," Nachum said. "He will not believe you, but he won't laugh in your face either."

"That's a minor comfort. Very well, friend-of-my-friend. There is a mermaid trying to entice my animals to drowning."

"That is a bold assertion."

"As I was saying, it began with the ox. He *nearly* drowned. We found him one morning at the shore, on his side, breathing unsteadily. At first we thought him near death, but he recovered and was soon about again. But it happened a second time, and so we began to cage him up for fear that perhaps he'd been possessed in some way."

"Possessed?"

"Taken by a spirit with destructive intentions. Something that would compel an ox to take his own life. I don't know that such a spirit exists, but the rabbi considered it possible and so I do as well. To curb the ox's suicidal behaviors, one of my sons would walk him to the waters by day, and tie him up by night. Then it started happening to the others."

Menachem held his hand out to one of the two sons who had accompanied us to the water. The boy took his hand gently enough that it was easy to forget the younger man was a head taller than his father. "Haim was the one who figured it out. After we lost one of the cows."

I greeted Haim formally, as one did.

"In what way did you lose the cow?" I asked. "Did it drown?"

"It must have," Haim said, his head bowed. Young men addressing elders when in the company of their fathers often behaved with a degree of obsequiousness that would be difficult for a modern person to comprehend. I do miss that.

"You don't know?"

"We have many times over found two of our cows lying in the mud come morning, much as with the ox. We were discussing what sort of spirits to address on the subject when a cow went missing entirely. It happened overnight. We think she must have drowned and been taken further in. The water is very deep at about five paces, you understand."

"I do." There were several places on the sea that I knew of where the dropoff was drastic enough to allow for a deep-draft vessel right at the shore. "But what if—and forgive me, Menachem, I know you speak highly of your neighbors—what if she was simply stolen in the night?"

"We checked," Menachem said. "Discreetly, of course, but we checked. On the five nearest farms, no new cattle manifested."

"You are ignoring a more obvious possibility: Someone put your cow on a boat."

Menachem laughed, as did Nachum, and soon Haim, once he decided it was okay to.

"Have you ever tried to put a cow on a rowboat, my friend?" Menachem asked.

"I admit, I have not."

"If you had, you would understand why I laugh. Neither you nor the cow would be on that boat for long, I promise. Besides, this is not speculation. We saw the mermaid."

"You did?"

"Haim did. And so did Levi. I did not, but I am old and need sleep. I have sons to do things such as stay up all night." He turned to Haim again. "Go on and tell him."

"It was after the cow drowned. Father and the rabbi thought we faced evil ghosts, and asked us to hide nearby and wait for one of the spirits to take another cow, either in possession or in a song."

I thought of the sirens in the Odyssey, who are often depicted as mermaids, and wondered if young Haim was learned enough to make the reference a conscious one. I decided he probably was not, and that the phrasing likely came from the rabbi, who could have been sufficiently learned to know his Homer.

"We stacked a pile of rushes over here." He pointed to a spot beside a tree. "And hid beneath. This we did for four nights, with nothing happening. On the fifth night, we saw her."

"The mermaid."

"I promise you, it's true. She was only a head in the water at first, but even had we not seen that we would have heard the sound she was making. It was like a song, only not a song. I can't explain. But the cows knew the sound, and they went to it."

"How do you know it was a woman, if you could only see the head?"

Haim blushed. "She... emerged more thoroughly once near the first cow. We'd have missed any details had it not been a full moon on that night, but we both saw her from the waist up, and she had on no garments."

Levi, the younger of the two and therefore not expected to speak, did his part by nodding and looking deeply embarrassed.

"What did she... do, when she emerged from the waist up?" I asked.

"That was difficult to see. It looked like she was hugging the cow, speaking in her ear or... I will be honest, we didn't know what to do. We were expecting a spirit, not this. We were afraid."

"You didn't talk to her, then."

"We didn't move. We would have... father, you know we would not have let another cow drown, but..."

"It's all right," Menachem said. "If you had confronted her, I might be mourning the loss of two sons for all we understand about this creature."

"So what do you think now, Eleazar?" Nachum asked.

I was thinking Haim and Levi sold one of their father's cows and made up a ridiculous story to cover the crime, but I didn't want to say that and I didn't want it to be true.

"Has the fence worked?" I asked.

"It did at first," Menachem said. "But lately it has failed as well."

"It looks intact. Are the cows jumping over it?"

"No." He looked sheepish. "This will sound odd..."

"We're discussing mermaids, I believe we have passed *odd* already."

"The fence won't lock," Menachem said. "We latch it at night and on three occasions we have found it unlatched in the morning and the cows at the water. We have not lost one, but we can't figure out how they're opening the gate either, so I'm sure we will lose another in time."

"She might be opening the gate herself," Haim said.

"You're right, that does sound odd. If this is a mermaid, surely she would be unable to make it to this gate, as she would not be expected to have legs."

Menachem shrugged. "If she's not confined to the water, I'm not going to leave my sons out to fall victim to whatever other surprising monstrosities she might reveal."

Nachum clapped me on the shoulder. "No, that's what we're here to do."

"We are?"

"Yes, my uncertain friend. Let's catch ourselves a mermaid."

I sighed.

"All right. But we're going to need a net."

~

We also needed time ashore. Barukh was surprisingly understanding.

"Evil spirits are more important than fishing," he said. "We can manage a week short-handed."

Not unlike mermaids, it was assumed by most people that spirits—evil and otherwise—were real beings that required attention periodically. People still think this way, but most of the time we call it something else.

I was slightly less confident in the reality of the unseen. I won't say I had quite the same minimum empirical standards I employ for most things now, but I'd seen enough things taken as true, which turned out to be figments of somebody's imagination, to question conventional wisdom.

You'd be surprised how many things people believed that began as consciously employed tall tales or hoaxes. A whole lot of history can be understood the same way as an episode of *Scooby Doo*, to be honest.

We weren't going after a spirit. We had to catch a physical being, which was why we needed a proper fishing net. Barukh had no objection to us borrowing one of these—fishing nets aren't things you can find on a farm. It didn't seem at all strange to him that a net would be useful here.

Two nights later I was under a pile of rushes wrapped in a blanket next to Nachum, staring at a body of water that was barely visible in the moonlight.

It was not how I preferred to spend my evenings.

I've been on enough hunts in my life to appreciate the importance of staying awake and aware and still for extended periods, but that doesn't mean I enjoy the experience. It didn't help that Nachum had some sort of nasal condition that I never noticed at sea.

"Will you stop that?" I whispered, after hours of listening to it.

"It's how I breathe," he said.

"Then stop breathing. You'll probably alert the thing we're waiting for."

The thing in question didn't turn up that night, though, nor on the next two nights. That was enough time for me to figure out ten different ways to kill Nachum without anyone being the wiser, but that was all I figured out.

We took shifts to ensure one of us was awake when the mermaid showed. That was standard practice on hunts too, but on hunts I wasn't saddled with the second oldest person in tribe. Thus, when she did show up, on the third night, it was during Nachum's shift, and he slept through it.

"She used a spell!" he claimed. "It's the only explanation."

He said that shortly after we were both awakened by the sunrise, to find a cow standing in the shallows looking at us with bemusement.

"Yes of course, that's the only explanation. You falling asleep isn't at all feasible."

"Never!"

I walked over to the gate. It was clearly unlatched and not broken. If a cow had done it, I would have expected more damage. Also, the latch was on the outside only. A man could reach over the fence and unlock it, but a cow couldn't, unless the cow also had opposable thumbs and elbows.

I checked the ground from the open gate to the water. If it had been a mermaid somehow pulling herself fins and all from the water, I would have expected a drag trail. The distance was twenty paces, all matted grass and mud, but there wasn't a trail to be seen. Admittedly, the cow trampled the ground pretty well and could have disturbed the area enough to erase the evidence, but that seemed like an unreasonable possibility.

I walked the patch slowly until I found what I was looking for: a footprint.

"Come see," I said.

He leaned over to look.

"The footprint of a child," he said.

It was made by a bare foot, and we both had on sandals. It was also smaller than anything our feet could have done.

"Or a woman." I glanced at the water again. "It looks like your mermaid has sprouted legs."

"Well of course. They can do that."

"Can they?"

"When mermaids wish to cross onto dry land they shed their fins and come ashore on legs. Everyone knows this."

"By what means?"

"Magic."

"If the mermaid can use magic, why didn't she just magically open the gate from the water? Or fly to the gate?"

"That's a ridiculous suggestion."

"Right. Of course it is."

I looked at the cow, who continued to look like she had been caught doing something wrong.

"Maybe you can tell us what happened."

The cow mooed.

～

*T*he following afternoon I decided to put the net we borrowed to good use.

Up to that point we'd been keeping it with us, with the idea being to charge the mermaid and capture it by flinging the net into the water. It was a dumb plan, and in truth wasn't even a plan, so much as what we decided to do once we both realized we hadn't thought out the whole net thing beforehand.

It was a big net, though. Barukh only had one kind, the kind that required eight pairs of hands to extract from the waters when full. There was little point in employing it like a projectile. But as a trap, it had promise.

"I don't understand why you're putting it there," Nachum said, which wasn't helpful. Helpful would have been assisting me in hiding it.

I had spread it out on the ground between the water's edge and the fence and used ropes and a few conveniently located low-hanging tree branches to create a trap. Ideally, if whomever it was that came out of the water attempted to return to the water again, we could pull on the ropes and capture them before they made it.

"Where would you put it?" I asked. I was trying to bury the net in some of the mud from the shore. I didn't want the barefoot woman from the sea to feel the rope.

"*In* the water is where I would put it."

"I think a mermaid would have far less trouble detecting a net in the water than on the shore."

"In the dark?"

"This will also ensnare anyone else who might happen along the beach, regardless of whether or not they came from the water."

"You still doubt if she's real!"

"I only wish to plan for alternatives," I said. "My doubt is very healthy."

"The goal is to ensnare her before she can cast her spell to make us sleep, so it should be done while she's in the water. Once she's on land we will not be able to pull on the rope for being unawake."

"I see. By your reckoning, then, she can only cast the spell from the water, and not at all once ashore. Is this another aspect of mermaid lore I'm not familiar with?"

Nachum grumbled. "Very well, at least get some leaves down here. The mud alone won't disguise the netting."

~

Something that goes underappreciated nowadays is how very dark nighttime used to be.

The modern adult will describe someone as being *afraid of the dark* as if this were foolish and childish, but as far as I'm concerned it's perfectly sensible, because real darkness can be completely terrifying. In my lifetime, night predators were real, they were everywhere, and they were worthy of the active concern of adults and children alike. If you want to know why I spent so much of my life trying to latch onto various tribes and cultures—even ones where I was unwanted or whose beliefs I found barely tolerable—this was one reason. Having a bunch of people around meant both that there was somebody awake at night to sound a proper warning, and there was a large pool of other potential victims on hand.

The moon had been waning over the course of our nightly vigils, so we had less and less natural light to work with each evening. The only other real source of illumination was the stars, and that wasn't much. We could have lit a lantern, but that sort of defeated the purpose of the endeavor, as a lit flame generally signaled the presence of someone to maintain that flame.

It made for a tense evening. I didn't trust Nachum to either stay awake or to know when to trigger the net, so even when it was my turn to sleep I didn't. We had only one shot with the trap; I wanted to be as sure as possible.

That said, I nearly pulled the rope four or five times. Another thing that goes underappreciated in the modern world is how loud a quiet night is. It gets so quiet that very small sounds seem unreasonably large, and before long you're springing a mermaid trap and catching a bullfrog.

We didn't do that, but it was close.

I couldn't say what time it was when we finally heard something non-trivial. Based on the position of the moon it was probably well past midnight, but the moon was hardly there and I had let my talent for reading the night sky atrophy over the years.

What we heard was splashing. We'd been hearing something that we mistook for splashing all evening, but which turned out to be low waves cresting against the shore, and the occasional rambunctious fish. The sound a human-sized being exiting a body of water is much louder and largely unmistakable as something else, although we didn't entirely appreciate this until it happened.

Immediately, Nachum—who to his credit had remained awake—grabbed the rope, but I put my hand on his, a silent suggestion to wait.

The watery exit was followed by the *thuck-thuck* of feet in mud, and then we heard the latch thrown open on the gate. I counted to three, and then we pulled together on the net as hard as we could.

The net rose up and collapsed around… something.

She had been running straight for the water when the trap

was sprung, and in a moment we had her dangling in the air. I remembered thinking if she was a mermaid, this had to have been a deeply ironic thing, to have spent all that time in the water avoiding fishing nets, only to have been snared by one on dry land. This assumed mermaids had an appreciation of irony.

Our triumph lasted exactly long enough for me to ponder this, which was to say about three seconds. Then she let out a horrid shriek, the kind that wakes entire neighborhoods and causes adult men to throw themselves on swords, women to rend their garments and tear out their hair, and children to drop dead from shock.

A bad sound, basically. But that, too, only lasted for three or four seconds. Then the rope went slack.

We didn't hear her splash back into the water, but we couldn't hear much of anything, as well-rung as our ears had gotten from the horrible cry. But when we ran to the net and found it had been torn open it was clear the water was the only place she could possibly have gotten to.

~

"*T*his mermaid is much stronger than any I have encountered before," Nachum said.

It was morning, and we were at Menachem's table, having a small meal and reviewing our findings. Menachem's entire family —as well as probably half of Galilee—heard the cry that was still ringing in our ears hours later, so none of what we had to say was all that surprising.

"She tore apart the net?" our host asked, for a second time. I imagined he was wondering what she would have done to one of his sons.

"Without hesitation," Nachum said.

"The one you saw before was captured in a net," I said. "Clearly, this one is more powerful."

I didn't actually think this. What I thought was that Nachum never encountered a live mermaid before, and the reason he hadn't was that real mermaids were too strong to get caught in a fisherman's net. It was an excellent explanation for why there were no mermaids in captivity or dead ones on display.

"We will have to build a better fence," Menachem said. "Or move the animals further from the water. We have another field. We can just carry the water to them."

Haim nodded. "We would lose valuable farmland."

"Having our livestock drown would be a greater loss."

"I don't question your decision, father. And truly, the cows are looking much better now, I am sure it's safe to move them."

"Better?" I asked. "Because they're no longer drowning?"

"They were suffering from a condition," Menachem said. "We are fortunate not to have lost them all, between the disease and the mermaid."

"Tell me more about this disease," I said. "What were its symptoms?"

～

*I*t took most of the morning to convince Menachem and Nachum that the mermaid wasn't going to be coming back. I had to make up a reasonably large number of lies. That isn't all that difficult a thing for me, but usually I'm better prepared with a stock set of them I can repurpose to fit the circumstance.

This probably isn't surprising, but being an immortal man in a world where there is no such thing—or where such things are strong indicators of some manner of evil—means learning how to lie well and often.

The first lie I told was that the disease described by Haim and his father was a rare condition known to attract mermaids. I explained how similar skin conditions in sailors once resulted in an entire ship being overwhelmed and sunk, its sailors eaten. For proper effect I described the symptoms of scurvy. Then I turned to Nachum and said that of course, since he was the resident mermaid expert, he had heard of such a thing himself, and could surely back me up.

He wasn't going to contradict me, because he was far more interested in my continued belief in his expertise than in any truth. I'm pretty sure by the end of the conversation he'd convinced himself that not only had he also heard this thing about mermaids, he had witnessed such a happening first-hand. Within a week, I expected it would become regionally canonical mermaid fact.

I should have been all set after that one lie, because if the animals no longer had the disease they should have in theory no longer attracted the mermaid, but this didn't do the trick, so I had to make up a bunch more, such as that mermaids could only leave the water in certain phases of the moon, and then only three times a year, and then only thrice in a lifetime. Also, the cry she let out was proof that she was dying, somehow. I can't remember how I got there, but they believed it.

And of course there was the overarching lie, the one that every other lie was draped over: the mermaid was certainly coming back. It was only that I knew what to do, and I didn't want anybody else around when I did it.

~

Since I had camped out in their back yard for over a week, I was familiar enough with the hours Menachem and his family kept to know when it was safe to return without drawing attention. It was also easier by then to see where I was going because the moon was phasing in the right direction, so there was more moonlight to go by.

Rather than hide under the rushes again I just sat down next to the tree and waited.

It was probably a couple of hours of sitting. The lake was quiet, the cows remained locked up, and that was about all.

When it felt like the time was right—and I can't explain what *right* felt like—I walked to the water's edge. I had an old knife in my pocket, primarily used to gut fish. It was sharp, and too small to use as a weapon unless I got really close to somebody and cut in exactly the right place. I didn't need it for defense, though.

I made a thin slice across the top of one of my fingers. I would have cut the palm because it's easier to bleed a person from there, but I'd been cut unintentionally in the palm before and it takes forever to heal. Fingers are quick. They just don't bleed fast. But I didn't need much.

I dripped some blood into the water and then swished my hand in the shallows to get more in there, and then I walked back to the tree and sat down again.

Her head popped up about ten minutes later.

"Don't be afraid," I said quietly. I didn't need to speak all that loudly; she could hear my heartbeat from that distance.

When my words didn't produce a response, I repeated myself in Greek, and Latin, and Aramaic, and was about to move on to Urdu and maybe a Slavic tongue or two, when she responded in Greek.

"Who are you?" she asked.

"I am nobody of great import."

She took two steps forward, which raised her upper torso from the water. The shadows ruled over the moment, but I could tell she was unclothed.

"You know what I am," she said, "don't you?"

"Yes. It took longer than it should have. I wasn't thinking. It never occurred to me before that a vampire might live in a lake."

"There is no sunlight under the sea. Even near the surface, the light only tickles. It's difficult to catch fire surrounded by water. And I don't need to breathe. You are unafraid?"

"I have an appropriate dose of fear. Some of your kind have called me Apollo, do you know that name?"

"I do. If that's your name then you have lied. You are a person of greater import than most."

Vampires mostly think of me as a special version of them, because of the immortality thing. It's a lot more accurate to think of them as bizarre versions of me, but I'm the only one around willing to make that argument.

"Thank you for saying so."

"Are you here to kill me, Apollo?"

"I am not. What do you eat? In the water, what is there for you?"

"Fish have blood. It's awful. There are other things in the depths that taste better, but they are rare and difficult to capture, and they fight back. So, fish."

This would be why the oceans of the world aren't teeming with vampires, presumably.

"And the occasional cow and ox?"

"Sometimes. But they called for me. They still do, can't you hear them?"

"I can't. I'm sorry."

I've known vampires to have a deep connection with animals. Some have gone as far as to say vampires and animals talk to one another. I think that's an overstatement, but they share a certain bond.

"They were in pain. I helped them."

"You did, I know. They're better now."

"Yes. Their cries are different. Now they only long for my company."

"What happened with the one who drowned?"

"He was dying, and his pain was too great. I couldn't help him live, so I helped him die."

"That was very nice of you."

"It was more than the men would have done."

"That's true. But now I need to ask you to stop visiting."

She fell silent for a few seconds, perhaps to listen to her cow friends.

"They are calling. I miss their blood."

"Yes, I'm sorry about that. But the thing is, if you keep coming here the men are going to realize I was wrong when I told them their mermaid was never going to return. And someday it won't be two men with a net. It will be ten or twenty, or more. It will be more than you can protect yourself from."

She laughed. "I was a mermaid, was I? Why would a mermaid care about a cow?"

"I appreciate that. But will you agree not to come back?"

"As I said, I will miss their blood. But I can agree to this. How does *your* blood taste?"

"I've been told it tastes very good."

"Perhaps then you can let me taste you as a means to seal our agreement."

I sighed. "All right, but just a small taste."

~

I never saw that particular vampire again, and it was also the last time I encountered one living in a lake. That doesn't mean there aren't more out there, subsisting off fish blood and wandering land animals, only that I don't spend enough time in lake water to look for more. I also don't really fish in bulk any longer.

I did touch base with Menachem a few times after that night, both to see if his mermaid returned, and to assess the health of his livestock.

As I said, I can only understand the world as well as the historical period I'm in allows. Back then, we didn't comprehend disease at all. Most sicknesses were ascribed to evil spirits, and while I didn't really put much stock in this as an explanation, I also didn't have a better explanation.

As a consequence, I never knew what disease Menachem's animals were actually sick with. More importantly, I never learned what the vampire in the lake had to do with them getting better.

I still don't. I'm ruling out magic, but that leaves a lot of other options.

CHAPTER 4

I made it back to the parking lot about an hour after leaving *The Fancy Mermaid*, having swung by the library for a good long browse. In the interim, the lot filled up with the cars of locals, all parking in a neat row beside the SUV. This is a consistent source of amusement for me: there are no parking lines in the lot, but people pretend they're there anyway.

The other thing that filled up in the interim was the hood of the car. Mirella was sitting on it.

She was in shorts and a tank top, and had on her running shoes. Her cell phone was in her hand, but she wasn't looking at it. It looked like she was working on a tan.

"Isn't the hood a little hot?" I asked, unlocking the car with the remote.

"It's very hot. I anticipated your return would precede it becoming unbearable."

"Did it?"

"Yes, but only just barely. Another five minutes and I would have found some shade and left a note."

She slid off the hood, more or less literally, as there was a layer of sweat between her legs and the metal.

"Are you sober?" she asked.

"Of course. I took the car. Is something wrong?"

She looked at the spines of the books in my hand.

"More history?"

My reading habits consist of about 70% history books. People who know me think this is weird because I lived through all of it, but I could only be in one place at any given time, and I have a deep interest in learning what was going on in places I was not, because what happened in those places often had an impact on my life in some way. Ripples on the pond, and all that.

I also enjoy reading history books because a lot of them are utterly incorrect and thus inadvertently funny. I react the same way to every period drama I've ever seen, from the inexplicable regularity of white-skinned Egyptians, to Romans with English accents and everything in-between.

"Yeah."

I put the books in the car.

"Cousin called," Mirella said, waving her phone.

"So something *is* wrong."

"Enh. It's hard to tell with him sometimes, you know that. Wants us to *look into something* for him. I think he just wants an excuse to put dinner on his expense account. He's at the hotel. We can leave the car here."

～

*T*he island's police force, while small, was actually pretty impressive. I wasn't around for the founding of the local government structure, but I'm guessing at some point somebody realized if they were going to be inviting all of these exotic beings here, the local law had to be somewhat specialized.

Mirella's cousin Esteban happened to be an extremely specialized individual, which was why he was the perfect sheriff for this island. (They didn't call him sheriff, or chief. He was *capitan* to everyone, and I had no idea why. If I didn't know him I'd worry about a military coup.) He was a goblin. The whole force was, actually, and while this wasn't inherently impressive—half the island was goblin or elf—these particular goblins used to kill people for a living. More than that, they had a reputation for doing so. Basically, putting Esteban in charge of the police was an idea straight out of one of those westerns, where the gunslinger becomes the sheriff.

Not that they used guns. I mean they had them, but if it turned out the guns on their hips weren't loaded—were perhaps actually props—I wouldn't have been surprised. These were goblins, and goblins used swords. If you think that put them at a disadvantage, you've never seen a goblin use one.

"He didn't say why he called?" I asked Mirella, as we made the long walk from the lot to the hotel. She was keeping a pace that was hard to maintain in flip-flops. This meant she was a little annoyed with me, usually, although it could also have been that she'd jogged down the hill and was still working off the adrenaline.

"He wanted us to consult with him about something, is exactly what he said. I'm sure he meant you, since he has a team of experienced ex-mercenary goblins already, so I don't imagine he has significant use for me. I, however, know how to find you and bring you places, which I expect is all he needs me for. Also, I'm going to have the cell phone argument with you again later."

"Okay. So he called from the hotel."

"Whether he called from there or not, that's where he said to meet him."

Yeah, she was annoyed with me.

Here's the thing: I'm not really good at relationships. Real ones, I mean, the long-term kinds that last more than a weekend. I'd like to say this is mostly attributable to my simply not sharing a common upbringing—my cultural background is *settled caveman*, which runs contrary to just about every other background—but it's probably also because I'm just difficult.

In other words, while Mirella and I were doing pretty great, I was still getting on her nerves for stupid things. And I mean, that's probably totally normal.

Not having a cell phone was one of those things. From my perspective our life on the island was a vacation from the entire rest of the world, and on that vacation I'd rather not have a cell phone, because nowadays those things are a connection to the entire rest of the world, and I don't want to deal with the rest of the world. From her perspective, this isn't a vacation, it's a life decision, and that life includes being able to reach me on a phone now and then.

We're both sort of right, too, just for really sad and depressing reasons. Her entire lifetime is a short vacation from my perspective, but nobody wants to approach the argument from that angle because it's terrible.

Instead, we've gone back and forth. I've pointed out I'm with her all the time, and when I'm not, there are only about a dozen places I could be instead. On top of that, how many emergencies are there that would require immediate communication? I can think of hundreds of instances when having cell phone technology on-hand would have been tremendously useful, but this wasn't one of those instances, and I wasn't expecting there to be one later.

Her cousin asking for help was maybe an exception, but I kind of doubted it. He'd asked for help before. So far as I was aware, he was the only other person on the island who knew how old I was—not sure how he even found out—and liked to put my experience to use. I didn't mind, both because it was something to do and because I kind of liked the idea of playing civilian consultant to local crimes. All I needed was a private investigator license and it'd be some kind of film noir story.

Well, okay, we'd probably need a murder first for a proper

noir setting. Those happen all the time in the movies, not so much in real life, and so far as I knew there hadn't been one on the island yet. Admittedly, the government apparatus is the sort that could make something like a murder disappear (I feel the same way about Disney World, to be honest) but I imagine Esteban would have shared such a story if one existed.

Also, it's too sunny for noir.

～

The hotel was just "the hotel". It didn't even have a name over the front of the place, because it was the only hotel on the island and it was pretty obvious what it was, from every angle. It was also, needless to say, the largest building around.

Large, but not tall, partly because of the stability of the sea-level land it was resting on and partly because of the wind and the fact that a taller building would block the view from the rest of the lower island. The hotel was only two stories high, but those two stories were spread across acreage nearly as large as the town it was next to.

It was also only technically a single building. There were six distinct areas, with a seventh at the center for the front desk, the bar and restaurant, and the conference rooms. To the public, getting from one space to the next required walking outside, but the staff could go from area to area without doing that. This made perfect sense if you've ever tried to deliver room service in a rainstorm.

Each area was defined by grotto-like swimming pools. I don't entirely understand this, because the ocean was right there, but at the same time there's a lot of scary things in that ocean, so maybe it did make sense.

We walked past the front gates—there was a guard box at the

front, but I never saw anybody in there—and headed straight for the front desk.

Most hotels have large parking lots in front and the beach/swimming pools in back. This one was set up mostly the same way, except the parking was almost nonexistent because nobody vacationing on the island had a car. There were scooters to rent, but that was about all. Those weren't really used much either, because just about everything interesting could be walked to. Plus, there were a few cabs for hire.

So weren't a lot of cars, and there were also not a lot of people around, because we were at the landward side of the hotel and it was a nice day. Most everyone was at the beach or the pool, not loitering around near the front.

The hotel quite thoroughly blocked any view of the ocean from this side. We couldn't even see the pools. There were no inexpensive rooms with a view of the parking lot in this hotel, either. Everything faced some kind of water.

Mirella and her walking shoes reached the door before I did, waited for me to catch up, and then led the way inside. The air conditioning hit immediately. It was the kind of cold that was incredibly refreshing for five minutes, alarmingly chilly for the remainder.

There was nobody at the front desk, so she rang the little bell. This was not inherently unusual because nobody was checking in or out at this time of day or even this day. The flights were only twice a week, and the next boat wasn't due for another day.

"Hey," I said, "are you... mad at me about something?"

I've learned to ask these things when in relationships. It seems counter-intuitive, because a lot of the time it forces the other person to look for ways in which they might be mad about something, and maybe they wouldn't have stopped to interrogate their own feelings otherwise.

This is what happens when I think too much about these things.

"No," she said, but in a way that sounded almost like a yes. "I don't like having to hunt you down. It frustrates me. If there's an emergency."

"Is this an emergency?"

"This is a house call. You understand what I'm saying."

"Yes. But you and I haven't faced an actual emergency since we moved here. I've come to appreciate that."

"Have you? I wonder, sometimes, when you go off. Not with the drinking. Goodness knows, we're not going to be undoing four thousand years of training with you and alcohol."

"Hey, I've been pretty good."

"Yes, you have, which is why that isn't what I mean. I wonder if you're bored, and this is why you drift off and can't be found."

"No, nothing like that."

In my last actual relationship, I used to go on hikes by myself for two or three week stretches, just disappearing into the woods for a while. I told myself it was to stay in touch with nature, and that might have been true, but what was interesting—in hindsight—was that I was a lot closer to a lot more nature on this island, and I hadn't gone off on any extended hikes. So maybe it was the girl.

It struck me that this would be a nice sentiment to express to Mirella, but I couldn't figure out an easy way to say it. *You don't make me want to live off the land for weeks on end like my last girlfriend* wasn't a very greeting-card-worthy sentiment.

"You aren't bored?" she asked. "You don't miss all the excitement?"

"I don't miss constant peril. I like boring. Honest."

"Well then," she said, smiling, "maybe I'm the one who misses it."

I was glad she was the one who said it.

The door from the office area behind the front desk flew open.

"Hi, sorry, sorry. Can I... oh, hi, guys."

It wasn't true that every island resident knew every other island resident. There were important economic differences between a hotel employee and a resident of the upper island, for instance, which could easily result in one of us not knowing another of us. The island also had its share of hermits, or *very private vacationers*, depending on your perspective.

Mostly, though, we did know one another.

The woman at the desk was named Cathy, and she was an elf. She lived in one of the dozen or so off-the-beach apartment complexes a mile closer to the mountain. I drove past it on my way into town. It wasn't at all a terrible place to live, since the same rules about building heights were observed inland as they were closer to the shore, so the apartment buildings had the same open-air sprawl as the hotel. But the quarters were pretty small, there was no pool to speak of, and I was told the walls were unpleasantly thin. This would have been an unfortunate combination if all the residents were human. I couldn't imagine what it was like for the species mixture this place had going on.

"Is my cousin still here?" Mirella asked.

"I think so, is his car still out front?" She looked over my shoulder and out the panoramic windows of the lobby to answer her own question. "Yep, there it is. He always parks in the same place."

"Where can we find him?"

"Four twenty-two, Bali," Cathy said. *Bali* was the name of the hotel wing in this case, not the Indonesian island.

"Thank you," Mirella said.

"So, what's going on?" I asked. "Can you say?"

"Vandalism or something, I heard. Don't know why they called Stubby. Most times that's no big deal."

"Or why he called us," Mirella said.

"Yeah, don't know that either. You know the way, right?"

"We'll figure it out, thanks," I said.

Cathy waved and turned back to the office. On our way out

the door, I said, "I was kind of hoping for a murder or something."

I was kidding.

"So was I," Mirella said.

I don't think she was kidding in the slightest.

~

*W*e found Esteban outside of room four twenty-two chatting quietly with one of the hotel managers, a satyr named Paul. I knew Paul mostly for being one of only four satyrs in residence on the island. I have a certain affinity for the satyros, mostly because some of them think I'm a god and that can be pretty cool. If I wanted free drinks at the hotel I could probably tell Paul one of my more interesting names, but until I did that, to him I was just Adam, the human.

Esteban knew better.

"There you are," he said, shooting his cousin an unpleasant look. It was hard to tell what this meant, because about half of the average goblin's expressions appeared at least a little threatening. In Mirella, it was incredibly hot. In Esteban, it was mostly just alarming.

Esteban was shorter than his cousin, and a lot stockier than most goblins. He had a curious blend of Spaniard and East Asian that only really made sense if you already knew he wasn't human. He had a scar across his right cheek that turned purple when he was angry and when he was drunk. He never ever, under any circumstance explained where the scar came from, so I assumed it was an accident involving a kitchen knife or something along those lines. I've had scars like that. For about fifty years I had one across my nose that I claimed was given to me by highway brigands, when in fact I walked into a brick wall I mistook for a doorway while extremely not sober.

"It took some time to find him," Mirella said, "I told you this would be the case."

"Sorry," I said, "I didn't know there was going to be something urgent. I've been trying to avoid having to worry about urgent things. Afternoon, Paul."

"Mr. Adam," Paul greeted.

"Just Adam."

Paul gave that not-a-smile smile satyrs have been perfecting over centuries in an attempt to fit in with the rest of us. A real smile from a satyr tended to look like an animal baring fangs, so they went with a closed-lips sort of thing in public so as to not frighten people.

Paul always called me Mr. Adam, and I always corrected him and he hasn't stopped doing it yet. I have no last name, though, so he hasn't got a lot of choice, having already decided to address everyone as Mr., Ms. or Mrs., which I guess is a decision you come to when working in an expensive hotel.

I guess I could make up a last name. As it is, *Adam* isn't really my first name either, but my real first name was a sort of grunt so I can't go with that. (It's Urr, and the only person who still calls me that is older than I am.) I just never bothered to dream up a family name to tack onto the end of Adam, and Adam has really stuck with me of late.

"It isn't an emergency," Esteban said. "And I appreciate you taking time to offer your opinion."

"No, it's fine. Is there a body?"

"No, that would constitute an emergency. I also don't know what sort of situation involving a body would require your expertise, unless I considered you a suspect. You haven't been leaving bodies lying around of late, have you?"

"Not lately. I can't speak for Mirella."

"If I may, Mr. Adam," Paul said, "the problem is not that there is no body, it's that there is nobody."

This was an effort at a joke. It should be noted that satyrs are probably the most humorless people on the planet, aside perhaps from the Germans.

Paul opened the door to the room and stepped inside. I took a look at Esteban before going anywhere.

"Is this a crime scene?" I asked.

"We haven't decided yet."

"So I shouldn't touch anything."

"Touch what you like. Do you imagine we have a crime lab?"

What I imagined was that Doc Cambridge would fall over himself trying to use his laboratory to solve a crime if asked to do so. Of course, he'd also end up proving leprechauns did it or something.

Leprechauns aren't real, by the way.

Mirella and I stepped into the hotel room, and Esteban followed. Paul stayed in the hallway.

As I think I've made clear, the island hotel was pretty high-end. You had to be worth a lot of money to even consider a room, and worth even more to make it to the island in the first place.

The rooms were always a shock, then, because of how small most of them were.

Every room had wood paneling, a small terrace with a view, a big-screen TV and an above average bed (or two), springy carpeting, good air conditioning, a coffee maker, and... well, everything was all there like you'd expect it to be. They even had a live plant in the corner, which was a nice touch.

It was just small. I had a rough idea how much a room like this cost, and for the expense I'd have expected a hot tub, a sauna, and a bowling alley.

Room four twenty-two had two twin beds and precious little room for much else. I imagine it was an especially tight fit for some of the larger species. I mean, in fairness if you come to an exclusive beach resort and spend all of your time in the room you're vacationing wrong, but still.

The beds were unmade, but I couldn't see any personal items

to indicate the people who'd been staying in the room were still there.

Then I saw the writing on the wall, and I understood why Esteban asked for me.

"What is that smell?" Mirella asked. I couldn't smell anything.

"Sulfur, I think," her cousin answered. You can't imagine what it's like to cook in the same house as someone with that kind of nose sensitivity. She thinks I burn everything.

"I can't smell it," I said. "But sulfur is interesting."

"It's the writing that's interesting," Esteban said. "Sulfur could be a dietary curiosity."

I looked past him to the counter that doubled as a kitchenette. There was no proper stove, but the room came with a microwave.

"Any restaurants featuring brimstone on the menu?"

"Don't worry about the sulfur, what's the writing?"

The text was scrawled on the wall above the bed nearest the window: three neat rows of letters in a highly unlikely script.

"What's it written in?" I asked.

"That's blood, Adam," Mirella said.

"I was hoping it was blood-colored ink. Nice penmanship, though. They didn't use a finger. Fountain pen?"

"Blood in a fountain pen would be terribly inefficient," she said. "It would clog."

"I love you for having already thought that through, you know that right?"

"Yes."

"If you would please," Esteban said, rather loudly. Perhaps he wasn't enjoying the moment as much as we were. "What is the language? What does it say?"

"I think it might be Proto-Elamite. But I don't know what it says right now."

"What do you mean, right now?"

"It's not that simple. I need a little time with it. Mirella, do you have your phone?"

She nodded, and took a picture of the text, and didn't even give me a hard time about having found a circumstance in which I needed a cell phone.

"So you can't read it?"

"Stubby, there's a lot more questions in need of answering than just what this says. Finding Proto-Elamite graffiti on a hotel room wall is more or less completely impossible, for starters."

Mirella's eyes lit up, while Esteban growled. She loved the idea of a legitimate mystery, while he mostly just hated the fact that I called him Stubby. Everyone on the island called him that, but not to his face. It was a play on his name, obviously, but also a dig on his stature.

"Educate me, Adam, why is it impossible?" he asked.

"Because as far as I know this is the only written example of Proto-Elamite in the world. Nobody's spoken it for more than five thousand years."

"But you did."

"I did, yes."

"So why can't you read this?"

"I'm not sure if you understand how wildly different those skillsets are."

This is one of those things modern people don't even think about, but writing was once revolutionary. The process of creating a series of marks (on stone, in clay, on papyrus, whatever) which stood for words, or the syllables making up words, was something that had to be invented a hundred times over by different cultures, and the fact that so many of them did remains extraordinary.

"You spoke it but can't read it."

"It happens. The Elamites weren't super pleasant, and I wasn't in a position to pursue scholarship at the time."

"How do you know it's Proto-Elamite?" Mirella asked. "If you don't know the written language."

"I'm not one hundred percent sure it is, but it looks a lot like Linear Elamite."

"You're giving me a headache," Esteban said.

"That will happen with him," Mirella said.

"There *are* examples of Linear Elamite, which came after Proto-Elamite, and I know what Linear looks like because I'm curious about these things. But if you're about to ask if I can read Linear Elamite, no, nobody can. What examples exist haven't been translated, because nobody knows how. It's kind of a stand-alone language, so there's no descendant tongue to help out, and no one has uncovered an equivalent Rosetta stone."

I have a list of things I'd like to do at some point. The list helps keep me alive, in a way, because it's a periodic reminder that I haven't done everything there is to do just yet. On the list is, attempting to read Linear Elamite. As the only person on the planet who can still speak the language of the people of Elam (again, possibly except for a certain redheaded woman) I'm uniquely qualified to do this.

I expect I will someday, and I expect in doing so I will be disappointed. Every time I translate an old document it ends up being a recipe, a shopping list, or a rental agreement of some kind. Humans have always been sort of dull.

I didn't expect the writing on the wall to be dull, though, both because of the circumstance and the fact that it was in blood. People don't write recipes in blood. Vampires do, but vampires spend too much time listening to their own hype sometimes.

"I'm wondering, cousin," Mirella said, "when you are going to get to the part where you tell us why the occupants of this room can't translate it for you."

"They would be the first to ask," he agreed. "Unfortunately, nobody in the hotel appears to know who they were, or where they went."

"Where they went?" I said. "We're on an island. How far could they have gotten?"

"I agree, conditionally, but we have a jungle you're perhaps aware of. You've arrived at the core concern for my office. People were staying in this room and then they weren't, and nobody appears to know if they are missing, since to report someone missing one first has to know who was here."

~

A little while later, we were sitting in the hotel's manager office—I'd call it Paul's office, and for the moment it was, but there were five managers—and going over how it was possible for a hotel to not know who was in one of their rooms.

"This is incredibly embarrassing," he said, for the third time by my count. He was behind his desk running through the registration records on his computer.

The office was on the second floor, above the front desk, and had windows facing both the parking lot and the ocean, which gave it a sort of gateway-to-the-island feel. It had been a while since I'd watched one of the planes land, but I was pretty sure the windows also afforded a view of the inbound flight path.

Since the runway's existence depended on the tides, it was possible, in theory, to have a flight arrive and depart almost every day. That was never going to happen, though, because every full-time resident on the island despised everything about the plane, from the fact that it obscured the view of the sky to the part where it brought in people who couldn't afford to live on the island full time. (It also brought in cargo—food and so on—but not all that often. Most of the commodities on the island arrived by freighter.) The compromise was one flight a week.

This put a serious constraint on the hotel, because the plane wasn't big enough to carry a sufficient number of guests to fill up all the rooms. To solve this, the owners bought a cruise ship to ferry people from a nearby island that was large enough to land a jumbo jet. This was a great solution, except the ship was louder than the planes, and an even bigger eyesore. There was a proposal in the town council to limit the size of ships allowed to dock at the island. It was going to be an entertaining argument.

"The hotel's full?" Mirella asked.

"The hotel is always full," Esteban answered. "Or so I'm told."

"Yes, always full," Paul said. "Here we are. Seven days ago, the room was assigned to a Mr. and Mrs. Callaway. The Callaways requested a different assignment for unspecified reasons. They left on the last flight."

"Four days ago?" I asked, for clarification. Everyone on the island knew the schedule of the plane.

"Yes."

"So who else checked into the room?"

"According to our records, nobody."

"I'm sorry," I said, "but maybe you and I have a different definition of the word *full.*"

"Yes, I'm certain we do. Every hotel maintains a number of blocked out rooms that are considered filled while yet unoccupied. This is in the event of something unforeseen, such as a toilet backing up. *At capacity* is actually a variable number."

"All right. So you didn't have anyone in that room according to the computer. But someone *was* in the room, so how did nobody know who they were?"

"There was a breakdown in communication, which will have to be dealt with internally. After the Callaways declined the room, it went back into the available pool, and was assigned to another party… A Mr. Jenkins. But when he attempted to enter the room he reported someone was already there. This, mind, was at the height of the changeover, so when he went down and notified the desk that four twenty-two was already taken, we took care of him first, then blocked off the room. What should have happened next was that a note was logged so someone could follow up after the rush and determine where the error was, and who had that room. This didn't happen."

"Do these errors happen frequently?" Mirella asked.

"Oh yes. Any time you have twenty different people maintaining a constantly-changing set of records, there are going to be mistakes. That's why we have a protocol for resolving them, and why it wasn't impossible for there to have been a person assigned to four twenty-two that we had no record of."

"All right," I said. "How about the maids?"

"The maids were the ones who found the room in the state in which you saw it," Esteban said. "I've already spoken with them and went over their records. The room was marked as *do not disturb* for at least the past three days. I'm told the cutoff here is seven days before security is notified."

"What if the occupant is dead?"

"Nobody knocked until after the second day, and the maid who did that stated she received a reply from someone inside," Esteban said. "A woman's voice, but that's all she could say."

"What about keys?" Mirella asked. "They're electronic."

"Yes, there were no valid keycards for four twenty-two," Paul said. "But assuming someone was left behind to open the door from the inside, they would have needed no key."

"So they knew they weren't supposed to be there," I said.

"Yes that would follow," Paul said. "In these matter, usually, it gets resolved within 24 hours, which is how long it takes for an active key to become disabled programmatically. The occupant returns to the room, find the key doesn't open the door, and goes to the front desk. That didn't happen in this instance, so I'm assuming we're dealing with squatters."

I laughed. Squatting was something one didn't often see in an exclusive, private, super-secret five-star resort hotel. Probably.

"All right, so, they were here, and then they left, and the maids cracked open the room and found the note on the wall, and now you've got vandalism in a dead language."

"They left the room," Esteban said. "We don't know that they left the island, or necessarily the hotel. We're reviewing the manifests, but there's an excellent chance they are still here, and we have to treat them that way right now."

It wasn't until this moment that I understood why Stubby was involved, and why it was so important that the graffiti was translated.

What seemed at times like a miracle—that no violence ever broke out on the island despite the nature of some of its inhabitants—was at least partly carefully curated reality. Everyone, from residents to guests, had to be vetted thoroughly before being allowed to set foot on the shore. When Mirella and I moved in, we had to provide multiple references and survive several interviews with the residency board, which I promise you was a tremendous challenge for an immortal man who was supposed to be dead and had no references. Tourists had to survive a background review from the tourism board too. And everyone had to make it through a customs check regardless of their means of arrival.

This wasn't only a hotel record-keeping error; the island itself had a stowaway.

This was scary for a couple of reasons. First, it wasn't supposed to happen. Second, assuming it did, this was a secret island full of secret creatures who had their own closely-guarded secrets. An unauthorized guest could be anything from a conspiracist looking to prove a pet theory, to an assassin hired to eliminate one of the more important residents at the top of the hill.

"What about the blood on the wall?" Mirella asked.

Her cousin shrugged. "What about it? As I said, we don't have a crime lab."

"Doctor Cambridge at the hospital can probably type it for you," I said. "At least tell you what species donated it. Although... I can think of a short-cut."

"I'm in favor of all short cuts, Adam," Esteban said.

"Good, so am I. Any vampires in the hotel right now?"

~

*T*here did happen to be a vampire staying at the hotel, but it took an extra half an hour to get that information out of Paul. First, he claimed the hotel didn't track species and sub-species (vampires are considered a subspecies of humans) because it was illegal. This obviously wasn't going to fly, because there is no such law, and everyone knew it. Then he said it was rude to ask, and this was undoubtedly true, but since everyone there was pre-screened *someone* knew who was who and what was what, and surely this was shared with the hotel.

Finally, he said it would be irresponsible to share the information, at which point I asked him where the vampire rooms were.

"I don't understand," he said.

"Sure you do. Look, you don't have to tell us if there's a vampire in the hotel, or how many succubi are on the premises, or if you've got a rakshasa or a gremlin or an ogre. We all know a vampire would require different accommodations, and we've all seen them around the island at one time or another, so you must have a special setup. Just give us a room number and we can go knock ourselves. You won't even have to be there."

A few more minutes of hemming and hawing and he surrendered a room number.

The vampire room—there was only one—was beneath the front desk, in what could more accurately be described as a vault. It was also huge, which I guess made sense. It was the only part of the hotel where the room was the main attraction and not the beach.

The vampire was a Brit named Calvin. He wasn't happy to see

us, because we woke him. It being late in the afternoon, this was to be expected.

"You want me to what?" he asked, rubbing his eyes. He was in white cotton pajamas that had their heyday sometime around world war one.

"Examine some blood for us, sir," Esteban said, using his ultra-polite voice. He was being ultra-polite because that's what you do around rich people. It's also what you do around vampires.

"Is this something that can wait until later? Night-time would be really ideal."

"It's sort of an emergency," I said. "Sort of."

He focused on me for the first time, then sniffed. "Oh, hello. I think we've met. Apollo, isn't it?"

"Sometimes, yes." I had no memory of encountering him, but: alcohol.

"Sure, it was at that thing, wasn't it though? That Marie… Marie something. She was there."

"The… French Revolution?"

"No, no, no. In London. The late Eighteens sometime. Ahh, anyway. It's good to see you're still knocking around. Let me get my coat and my umbrella and I'll be along."

Soon enough, Calvin was dressed in a long overcoat with a high collar, a wide-brimmed hat, gloves, sunglasses and an umbrella. The poor man looked a little ridiculous, but the sun was definitely not going to reach him. There was a decent chance someone might conclude he was an incognito rock star—I could think of at least four famous musicians who weren't human—but that was only a little likely. Mostly, the get-up said *vampire*, especially the coat, which looked like it was last worn by Bela Lugosi.

"Is this Sanskrit?" he asked, when confronted with the message.

"Something like that. We were interested in whose blood it's written in."

"Right. Look, I'm not on board for any Satanic junk."

It's hard to contextualize how amusing it was to hear a vampire say something like that.

"No Satanists, so far as we know," I said.

"I mean, between the sulfur and the blood…"

"Do you know of any specific rituals this sort of combination might be tied to?" Mirella asked, beating her cousin to the question.

"Not really. I mean, kids play around with this stuff. Me, I seen it here and there, most times to try and drive *me* away, which is just… well, I bet the same's happened to you, at least once or twice."

"Once or twice," I said.

"Garlic would do it. Sulfur's bad, but it's no garlic. There's not many vampires in Italy, you get what I'm saying?"

"The blood, Calvin."

"Right."

He hopped up on the bed and sniffed the wall.

"It's a couple, three days old maybe. Came from the living. Or he was alive when he donated."

"You can smell the gender?" Mirella asked.

"No, 'course not, luv. It's not menstrual, though, I can tell you that."

"What a charming consideration."

"Not a bad idea, actually, if you're looking to write spells in ancient tongues in blood on the wall and you gotta do it regular."

"But it's arterial blood," I said, trying very hard to steer our blood expert back on-point.

"Yeah."

He licked his finger and rubbed the blood, then sucked on the finger.

"But I may be right, probably a man. Incubus, I believe."

"That's a surprise," I said.

"Well. *Could* be succubus, but I'm leaning toward my first answer. Why d'you find that interesting?"

"The people staying in the room went unnoticed, and I would never use that word to describe an incubus."

"An excellent point. Hang on…"

He moved to another part of the message.

"It isn't all the same blood. This first part is older. The passage was written at different times."

"How far apart?"

"Difficult to say. Few days, maybe."

He licked his finger and performed the same tasting ritual as before, which we all could have done without. He nodded slowly.

"Definitely different. This is some sort of animal blood. Preserved, I think. Very old."

"Animal blood?" Esteban repeated.

"Unquestionably."

"What manner of animal?" Mirella asked.

"Don't know. It's familiar."

Esteban looked at me. "A sacrifice?" he asked.

"You're hung up on satanic ritual, aren't you?" I said.

"It would track."

There is no such thing as a putative satanic ritual, not really. People have been playing around with the concept in recent years, but they're mostly just making stuff up that seems sort of legit, based on whichever Alistair Crowley artwork they happened to stumble across. Historically, though, "satanic" ritual ceremonies were actually pagan rites that had nothing whatsoever to do with the Satan of Christian theology.

What was sort of amazing was that the idea of a satanic ritual was so culturally ingrained that it was being floated to me as a serious theory by a goblin in a hotel run by a satyr, while standing in front of a vampire who was licking blood off a wall. I was surrounded by the nightmares of insecure Christians; Esteban worrying about a devil-worshipping cult was a little like the monster under the bed worrying that there might be other monsters under there with him.

"How old?" I asked.

"The blood? Possibly very old." He tasted some more. "There's a way to reconstitute dried blood. I think that may have been done with this. You know... this is gonna sound crazy. Hey, pull that shade, would you?"

I stepped around the edge of the bed Calvin was standing on and pulled the drapes closed. They weren't blackout shades and they weren't the sort to utterly seal off the sun even on the edges and the center, but they were good enough to keep a vampire alive.

"How's that?"

"That's wicked, thanks." He hopped off the bed and settled in the chair. It was one of those wicker things that must have cost a bundle. I couldn't help but think that the flammable chair combined with the curtain and the sunlight on the other side of the curtain was the exact right combination to murder a vampire if I was so inclined.

But that would be uncivilized, and rude.

Calvin pulled out a hand-rolled cigarette, which I was pretty positive he wasn't allowed to smoke in the room.

He lit it anyway. Nobody stopped him.

"Used to smoke when I was human. I get nothing from it, now, but I still love the feel of it in my lungs. I don't use 'em for nothing else, so... Apollo, you ever been to one of the gentlemen's clubs, used to be all over London?"

"Of course."

"Yeah, figured. Truth, you and I, we maybe met in just that kind of establishment. I can't recall. It was something with girls that didn't have much clothes on, so there you go. But I'm bringing it up not to embarrass you in front of your goblin lady friend, I have another cause. I'm remembering. I was at one of them places one time, except it catered more to my kind of folk.

Still had girls, mind. I think all the clubs did, even if it was the kind of club where nobody was interested in girls. Anyway, someone there, he had a special kind of blood. Very unusual, very rare. Kind of thing nobody had ever tasted before. We didn't believe him, of course, even when we were dropping shillings on the bar to have a touch of it. That's a good con, right? The kind where you know you're being conned and you still want to pay to get to the ending."

"You had a taste."

"I did. And I'm telling you, I think I just tasted that same kind of blood again off that wall there. I'm not fully sure, but I'm not gettin' there."

"You said animal."

"I did."

"So what kind of animal?"

"Well that was why nobody took the bloke seriously. What he said was, it was dragon blood. But everyone knows there ain't such a thing, right?"

CHAPTER 5

*W*hat we called the top of the island was actually a ring of flat land, which circled the real top of the island. The highest point was shaped like the tip of a thumb, had no trees and only a thin layer of wild grass, and was subject to uncomfortably high winds, and would be considered a cool place to be only in the event the mountain was much taller and there was some bragging to do after the fact.

Top of the island, then, was another real estate phrase, and like most such phrases it wasn't fully accurate.

One of the tourist expeditions involved a hike from the base to the top (the actual top) along a narrow, winding path that went past a lot of private property. Possibly the most dangerous thing anyone could do on the island was stray off that path, because most of the *top of the island* properties were violently private.

These houses benefited from the tree cover for privacy, and from the thick ground vegetation for the maintenance of their isolation. Also helpful, the ground was hilly and weirdly steep in places, so a lot of buildings were simply hidden by the earth, from multiple angles.

I was told it was possible to see most of the homes from the air, but from the ground they were virtually invisible. Even the roads leading up the mountain were all but impossible to find.

Fortunately, I wasn't the one driving. Mirella was. She didn't know where we were going either, but her cousin did, and we were following him.

"Where'd he go?" I asked, when it appeared Esteban's Jeep vanished into wilderness that looked indistinguishable from any other wilderness.

"I saw," she said, steering our SUV into a gap that wasn't there. To make it easier on both of us, I closed my eyes for a little while. The sound of tree limbs batting the side of the car was a sound I was familiar with, but I was used to hearing it when I was the one driving.

"Cars were a bad idea," I muttered.

"Today?"

"No, in general. As an invention."

She laughed. "You think shoes were a bad idea. You are not the greatest of authorities on this subject."

"Shoes *were* a bad idea."

The disturbingly narrow road did not lead to a ravine or a slope or a hidden crevasse of some kind—the sort of thing if I were on foot and traveling at a reasonable rate of speed I'd be able to adjust to in time—but to a gate.

A sentry stood on the other side of the gate. It was a goblin with a sub-machine gun, which was just a weird show of force in all respects. The amount of work involved to reach this entrance was so staggering—find the island, find a car, find the road—that anyone who made it this far would not have stumbled here on accident. Whereas a sub-machine gun (it looked like an Uzi, or a knockoff of one) basically existed to announce, "you have come the wrong way, you should turn around". This is especially so when the gun is in the hands of a goblin. The gun, then, was more than just alarming; it was alarmingly out of place.

I will grant, though, that an Uzi might be more effective

against a charging automobile than a sword, but the gate looked pretty sturdy from where I was sitting. It could probably repel a charging car.

There was a long exchange between Esteban and the guard, and then the gate was pulled open and we were all waved through.

The road continued around a corner defined by high trees, but only about fifty feet, and then the mansion was in view. It was a lot closer to the gate than it seemed it would be from the other side of the fence. From there, one got the impression there was an impressive amount of real estate to cover before reaching a vast building worthy of being called a *mansion*. But this was a small island, and the mansion in question only occupied a tiny part of it.

In other words, the building around the corner was surprisingly modest.

It took up roughly the same footprint as our house, but was much more traditionally designed, and with two levels. (Or possibly three. A sub-level was architecturally conceivable.) It was distressingly mundane, the sort of mini-mansion made to look larger by way of forced perspective, in the same style one might find in a suburb in Connecticut.

"Huh," was about all I had to say.

"You're disappointed."

"A little bit."

"I understand there's a pool in back."

"Unless it's the Playboy mansion grotto, I don't think it's going to change things."

"I thought your excitement related more to who lives here than in what the house looks like."

"Little bit of both."

I'd never seen this part of the island up close. Mirella and I had done the hike to the top a half-dozen times, but we took the path rather than stray into the forest, which was not an easy thing for me, I have to say. I look at thickly wooded areas the same way other people look at the street they grew up on. Also, if I wanted to invade someone's private property, I was skilled enough to do it without being seen, and no fence that stopped thirty feet beneath the top of the trees was going to prevent me from doing that.

Or I assumed. If I was wrong—if the owner of the property had a way of detecting me that I hadn't thought of—it could cause *an incident*, which was very much *verboten* on the island.

I didn't want to be the source of any local political turmoil just to scratch an itch, in other words. So instead, I saved my wanderings for the public land in the lower middle of the island. Nobody had snapped up that real estate yet for housing, and hopefully nobody would for as long as I was a resident.

I had some curiosity, then, about the estates that were taking up perfectly good forest. But Mirella was right; I also had my share of curiosity about the people living there. Especially in this case.

She parked the SUV next to Esteban's Jeep, and everyone got out. There was only space for four cars, total, in the driveway—six if you added in the space necessary to turn around—so we ended up blocking in the vehicles already there: two black SUV's that were smaller than what we were driving but looked bullet-proof. (Up close, you can usually tell.)

Another goblin, in a tux and tails, was waiting for us.

"Morning, Go-Go," Esteban greeted. He and the well-dressed goblin hugged, then parted as the sheriff made a show of checking out how his friend was dressed.

"You look stupid," he concluded.

"Shut up, I get extra to dress like this," Go-Go said in a poor approximation of an English accent.

"How much more for the accent?"

"It comes with the tux. Now get out of the way so I can greet that beautiful vision behind you. Mirella!"

"Hi, Go-Go." The two of them hugged, and I was beginning to feel left out in the hugging department, just a bit. I wondered if I should go over and hug Stubby, just to balance out everything.

"Adam, this is my uncle Gaugin. Go-Go, this is Adam."

Going by the hand he had on Mirella's ass, I was thinking they weren't legitimately related by blood, and *uncle* meant *family friend*. Although given the overall population size of the species, they were probably all a lot more closely related than they realized.

We shook hands as he sized me up.

"Pleasure," he said. His body language suggested otherwise, but that wasn't entirely unexpected. Goblin/human relationships were about as accepted as Jew/gentile; most people were okay with it, but there were some traditionalists with whom it bristled.

"Come on in," he said to all of us after three seconds of uncomfortable eye contact. "He's waiting."

Go-Go led us up the path to the front door, over the threshold, into a decidedly pedestrian entryway, and through two more doors (dining room, kitchen) to the back of the house. There we found… the Playboy mansion grotto.

More or less.

"Are you impressed now?" Mirella asked under her breath.

"A bit more, yes. Let's make friends with him so we can come back."

She grunted a modest disapproval. Or approval. Hard to tell.

We walked around the pool, which was an amoeba-shaped thing designed to look like a natural pond. It had genuine vegetation around it, and while I couldn't see it I could hear the rush of a waterfall. There was an enclosed space at the far end: a cave that was potentially artificial. That was probably where the water was coming down. If the architects wanted to they could have skipped the pool and made the house twice as large instead. I can't imagine why they would do that, but they could have.

At a corner of the poolside, more or less opposite the cave

opening, was a cabana. It looked permanent, with stay-cables bolted to the pavement keeping it from taking off in the periodic gusts of wind. (Mostly, the trees kept the upper island winds away, but some make it through.) It was a shame, because the cabana didn't fit in with the theme in the slightest.

There was a table under the cabana, and a cushioned bench with an assortment of throw pillows, a number of chairs, a stand-alone ashtray with traces of cigar use contained within, and an elf named Dmitri.

Dmitri was mafia, and everyone knew it.

~

I have what you might call a highly contingent moral code. This comes from spending most of my life in a world where *fair* and *unfair* were, on a good day, abstract ideas. Codes of conduct—moral, social, ethical, pick one—are new things.

Sure, okay, every group of people with a head-count larger than two had some sort of standard, but I wouldn't call them codes.

For instance, let's say the party we're talking about consists of five people, and all five of those people have to rely upon one another to continue in the world as five people, and not as three people, a dead person, and a dying one. It's reasonable to say that if in that scenario you anticipate being one of the three, rather than the dead or the dying, you're going to be okay with that, morally or otherwise. But the smarter ones eventually figured out there wasn't a lot any of us could do to control whether we were going to end up being one of the living, the dying or the dead. However, the other four people had a lot to say on that matter.

In fact, with a little *more* thought we figured out there didn't have to be a dead and a dying in this hypothetical party if all five of us were actively interested in keeping each other healthy and somewhat intact.

From that understanding came the realization that each person we added to the group improved our individual chances of not dying. This is more or less how tribes got built, and tribes led to civilizations once we figured out how to plant food and tame wildlife and so on.

This is the kind of morality I can get behind: you do what you can to keep me alive, and I'll do what I can to keep you alive. If you decide to believe in a god and that god tells you it's important to him or her, for some godly reason or another, to keep me alive, that's fantastic. I'm all in favor of you and your god and your god's moral code.

Anything beyond that, though, and I start to have questions.

Here's the thing: the bigger a group of relatively homogenous humans gets, the more rules they have to start stacking in. Now, a lot of these rules are *similar* to the 'you keep me alive and I'll keep you alive' code that I'm all in favor of, most obviously rules like: don't kill other people in this same group. However, some of the rules are frankly ridiculous and have nothing to do with keeping everyone alive and healthy, especially once those gods began distributing ethical codes that appeared to have a lot more to do with whatever sexual kink the priests or the royal family were into than with good, solid advice contributing to common survival goals.

Inevitably, rules start popping up whose obvious goal is *not* to keep all the members of the tribe alive, but to keep only certain members alive, and that's where I begin to get uncomfortable. I mean, I'm kind of okay with peasants having to grow food for royalty and then starving to death themselves as long as I don't happen to be a peasant, but that certainly makes me think twice about taking any of the king's other rules all that seriously. Likewise, if your tribe's rules about private property are more important than the rules that say *don't let people die from exposure*, I'm not going to pay that much attention to your laws about stealing. You're already showing bad judgment; I see no reason to take you all that seriously.

All of this is to say I don't really have a problem with the mafia or other iterations of the criminal element, in modern times or earlier. Sure, they can be dangerous and difficult to trust, but their naked self-interest and commitment to protecting their own is something I can get behind. I actually have more trouble trusting governments. At least with a criminal such as Dmitri, nobody is pretending to be following some weird set of rules. They are who they are.

One other thing I've noticed: the organized criminal elements of the world have always been overrepresented by members of species that are, technically, non-human. Elves and goblins in particular always thrived in these kinds of professions. I think it's because they're used to existing in secret, which just naturally lends itself to rule breaking. They're also gifted thieves, which I'm sure has something to do with it.

~

"Please, have a seat," Dmitri said, in a difficult-to-peg accent. It landed somewhere between Scandinavian and Slavic. He was skinnier than the average retired criminal, and his age only really showed in the laugh lines on his face when he smiled. My understanding was that he was at least sixty years old, but that was not at all obvious.

He was very pale, which was more a condition of his elven heritage than a reflection of his health.

We took seats around the table, and Go-Go left us, hopefully to fetch something alcoholic.

"Thank you for coming, Esteban, and for bringing your associates. This is your cousin, yes? I think I hired you once, dear girl."

"You did, sir, yes."

"I thought so. Was it to keep someone alive or the opposite?"

"As bodyguard, for one of your associates. It was some time ago. I'm surprised you remember."

"Of course I do. You're quite memorable."

Mirella always described her former job as one of a bodyguard, which was what she was doing when I met her. But she worked as an assassin for at least a little while. We never really talked about it. Anyway, the two jobs have a lot more in common than most people realize. I knew a guy who went back and forth between the roles all the time. His favorite story was how he got fired from guarding someone one week, and hired to kill him the next. Needless to say, I never did business with him, but it was a great story.

"I'm Adam," I said, extending my hand.

"Oh yes."

For my handshake, Dmitri rose from his seat, and shook my hand with both of his. It was a strange greeting from the most powerful man on the island, and possibly the hemisphere.

"It's my pleasure," he said. "I've been meaning to come down and introduce myself to you in *particular*, but... the truth is I hardly leave the house any more."

"Well, it's a pretty nice house. I bet this pool is popular enough."

"It is. And now that you've said so I must invite you for one of our events."

He sat back down again, which was the first time his age really showed. It was the knees. It's always the knees. I've seen more people get old than pretty much anyone, and those always go first.

"We have get-togethers up here," he said, to Mirella, sort of, "two or three times a month. You and... what shall I call you? Mr. Adam seems odd."

"Adam is fine."

"You should invent a furtherance of your name. A family identity with which to associate yourself. That's what I did."

Dmitri's chosen last name was Romanov.

"You picked the name of a Czar," I said.

"Yes, a symbol of strength and fear. My real name, much more pedestrian, not worth repeating here."

"*Romanov didn't work out all that well for Nikolai Alexandrovich,*" I said, in Russian. Because I'm a show-off.

Dmitri laughed.

"*An immortal man with the testicles to go by the name Adam shouldn't judge other people's choices in naming,*" he answered, in kind.

I decided I liked Dmitri. I also decided I needed to get him at least drunk enough so he could tell me who told him I was immortal, because that wasn't something he was supposed to know. Maybe Esteban told him, but I didn't think so.

"So, Capitan," Dmitri said, switching back to the common tongue. "I understand we have some unwelcome intruders in our paradise. Forgive my arrogance for asking you here to update me personally, but as I said I don't much leave the house any longer, and you can appreciate why such a thing would be a concern of mine. I of course speak for the council in this regard."

It had been five days since Mirella and I were shown the crime scene. I'd spent most of those five days staring at the Proto-Elamite graffiti and getting nowhere in particular with it. The Internet, which seemed to have an answer for almost everything, was proving astonishingly unhelpful, so I began reaching out to linguists. I probably sounded like a crank, but the first one who took me seriously was going to get the surprise of a lifetime in their in-box.

"I do understand, Dmitri, but I'm sure you have nothing to worry yourself about," Esteban said.

Dmitri smiled, but in a way that didn't convey amusement.

"I'm sure you're right, but still, I would like it if you were to humor me."

Esteban walked through the case for our host, omitting one or two key details, like the message and the fact that I hadn't been able to translate it, and also that I had a strong suspicion I never would be able to translate it. (I actually hadn't told Stubby this part myself.) Then he went through everything that had happened since.

A comparison of a month of ship's manifests, with the hotel guests, the bungalow renters, the B&B folks, and the people visiting local relatives for the same period, turned up a list of twenty-five people whose stay on the island couldn't be accounted for. (They did the same with the flight manifests, but those matched up perfectly. The plane is smaller, so there was less room for error.) Twelve of those people did end up being discovered after a little research, and had all been verified as leaving the island.

That left thirteen people potentially still ashore, who shouldn't be.

All anyone was really sure of was that room four twenty-two didn't have thirteen people in it, or if it did, not all at once.

I thought at least ten of the thirteen were the result of a clerical error, and maybe all of them, because I didn't think the people in that room came to the island by way of the chartered boat. There was too much vetting involved.

If I were planning a secret incursion to a secret island, I would find a way to get there that avoided the need for a passport: I would take my own boat.

You could charter a boat to the island, get within a mile and brave the sharks while swimming ashore from there. You could also get a boat right up to the shore and scuttle it. Both plans were risky, but neither was as difficult as getting past the vetting procedure necessary to get to the island via conventional means.

Whatever method they used to get ashore, what they did after that just made no sense. Squatting in a hotel room for a week meant risking detection, and then leaving it in the condition in which it was left meant notifying the authorities of your presence, which just seemed contrary to the whole spirit of being an illegal immigrant.

If it were my investigation, trying to figure that part would be where I'd spend most of my time, but it wasn't my investigation. Also, how they got here *did* still need answering. To that end we had learned that tourism and immigration control was a lot more vague than anyone realized.

"I appreciate that you are in a delicate circumstance, Dmitri," Esteban said, "but so far I've seen no reason for an elevated concern."

"Thank you, Esteban, I'm glad for your opinion. The number, though, it seems a large number."

"Thirteen uncounted persons is not thirteen missing persons. At this time our search is for the people who occupied that room, whether they are a part of the thirteen or not. All I believe we have proven to date is that the approach whereby we compare the ship register with the hotel ledger is inadequate."

"And you, Adam, what do you think?"

I didn't know I was there to have an opinion. We were tagging along because Esteban stopped by our home on his way up the hill, said where he was going, and asked if we could join him. I would probably have jumped at any excuse to get out of the house by then—trying to match a dead language phonetically to a written language is a good way to go insane—but this was a particularly good excuse.

"I think Esteban's probably right," I said. When this was met with silence and a long stare, I added, "I'm just consulting. We both are."

"Yes, I'm told. Why is that?"

"He has some expertise regarding certain details," Esteban said, without elaboration.

"You mean the message in blood on the wall, in a dead language," Dmitri said flatly.

Esteban sighed. "Di-Di, if you already *knew* all of this, why did you call me up here?"

"To hear it for myself?" Dmitri said. "No? All right, I have another reason for you to be here. For all three of you to be here, to be exact."

"Pool party?" I asked.

"I will invite you when the next one is scheduled. But for now…" he looked at his watch. "Well, it should happen in another moment."

I looked at my own watch. It was 11:25 A.M. locally. This wasn't a singularly interesting time of day so far as I was aware.

Then we heard a sound.

"What was that?" Mirella asked, looking at me.

"There will be two more," Dmitri said, still looking at his watch. "I wouldn't say they are clockwork as to when they begin, but they do happen, consistently, forty-seven seconds apart."

The second noise was slightly further away.

"They travel down the hill. I've spoken to a neighbor from around the mountain and downslope, he can confirm that after these three, the soundings continue, on his side." To me he asked, "What kind of animal makes this noise?"

It was almost a trill, like the sound a bird might make.

In the bush, centuries back, when we hunted, we signaled one another with a similar vocalization, but this was no human, and it didn't sound like a bird either. I could have come up with a list of land animals theoretically capable of issuing this sound, but all of them were very large, most were extinct, and none lived in the tropics. A mastodon could almost have made that sound, for instance, but you just don't run into them around these parts, or at all any more.

The problem was the bass note. It was just too low to be anything issued by a bird. At the same time the rapidity of the trilling could just about only have been done by a bird, or something with a quick tongue. It was such a deep, low note I could feel it in my groin. It was low enough that I was pretty sure I wasn't even hearing all of it, like there was more outside of my register.

I didn't think I'd heard it before.

"Some sort of instrument," Mirella suggested.

"A horn," her cousin agreed.

"Here it comes again," Dmitri said, and then we heard the third blast, but only just barely. As he predicted, this was the farthest of the three.

"It's not a horn," I said. "Or rather, it's not an instrument, or a tool, or a conch shell or anything that could be that loud."

"Why do you think this?" Mirella asked.

"It's hard to explain. There's a quality to all those things that's absent. You can almost hear the effort put into them, or... the air being forced through, I guess. This is a vocalization. When did they start?"

"Eight days ago. And I agree with you, which is why I again ask, what sort of animal can do this?"

"I don't know," I admitted. "Have you tried to track it?"

"We live in this jungle, but we aren't part of it. The burden of the modern man, wouldn't you say?"

"I wouldn't characterize it as a burden." To Esteban, I said, "you should consider putting a party together."

"Of whom? Bar patrons? Hotel maids? My own people have larger concerns."

"Are you certain, Esteban, that the strange noises are unrelated to your missing guests?"

"Dmitri, I'm here to reassure you that the island's stowaways are not hired assassin. I'm not prepared to address concerns that they may be changelings who have transformed into forest sprites."

"There's no such thing as forest sprites," I said.

"I was being sarcastic."

"Nymphs, those are real. That wasn't a nymph." If I knew there was a wood nymph in this forest, I'd be on the first plane out.

Esteban decided to ignore me. "My point is that I don't believe these people escaped the hotel and disappeared into the forest and are now associating with strange animals. It's probably a rare species of... something. I strongly doubt it's related, however."

Dmitri turned his attention to me. "And you?"

"I'm pretty curious. He's probably right. It'd be a stretch to say a new animal on the island had anything to do with the missing people. I mean, unless they were eaten by whatever that is."

"Adam..." Mirella said.

"Not that I'm saying that, of course."

"Of course," Dmitri said somberly. "The sounds began at roughly the same time the hotel room was evacuated, unless I have the timeline incorrect."

"We don't know when the room was abandoned," Esteban said. "It fits, but again..."

"I know, you can see no connection."

"Whatever it is, there are at least six of them," I said. "The only way to know any more than that is to get out there and track one down."

"I agree," Dmitri said. "I can give you two men. When can you start?"

"Two men?"

"Goblins."

"I'd be better off with satyrs, do you have any?"

Mirella coughed loudly.

"Adam, can I speak to you in private?" she asked.

She escorted me by the wrist to the other side of the pool and well out of earshot. I would like to say I went willingly, but whether she intended it or not, the grip she used would have broken the wrist if I resisted. I told myself that was just her instinct kicking in.

"What are you doing?" she asked.

"I don't understand the question."

"You're looking for danger again."

"Again?"

"It's what you do."

Looking for danger is the exact opposite of what I do. What I do is look for alcohol, and then I look for a place to sleep. If I'm unattached, I may also look for company, but that's about all.

"I don't do anything of the sort," I said.

"I've heard your stories. And I spent a year with you in which we both nearly died several times, when you were in a position to disappear at your own whim. I know you, Adam. You tell yourself you want nothing more than to do nothing, but you will jump into a dangerous situation with both feet and not a single contrary thought in your head. It's… it's heroic, and I love you for it, but we're here because we are done with all of that. I'm no longer a bodyguard and you're no longer a person in need of being guarded. So stop looking for trouble."

"I didn't think I was. A little hunting expedition is all."

"No, no, no, that's how it starts. You and two satyrs and soon they're both dead and there's a giant monster in the woods. We're retired. Let Dmitri slay the monster with those big guns."

"All right. But I was just curious. I don't see new things all that often, so you can imagine how I might find that appealing."

"I do. But the new things you find end up wanting to kill you at an unacceptably high rate."

I could swear she wasn't right about most of this. I mean, of course I have stories about barely surviving this threat or that, whether it's a sea serpent or a rakshasa, or just an act of piracy or gangsters with guns. But that's the point of a story: something happened, there was great peril, I barely escaped with my life, blah, blah, blah. Sure, a lot of stuff has happened to me, but look at the vast stretch of nothing that happened between the stories. If my life was nothing but jumping from one danger to the next I wouldn't have made it this far.

"I won't go," I said. Because that was a lot easier than arguing, when I was going to lose anyway.

"Thank you."

"It's probably just a bird or something, anyway."

"It's not a bird. But we'll let someone else figure out what it is."

"Yes, dear."

~

The happy medium between my not helping Dmitri in any way and my going on a week-long upper island hunting expedition was to offer him advice on how to locate the source of the mysterious sound on his own.

The advice was basic to anyone who's ever stalked prey over a one- or two-week period, which I guess nobody is really good at any more. Basically, they had to triangulate the feeding ground of the creature to within a few hundred yards, with the goal being to eventually be there before the prey is, preferably with some sort of net, gun or sharp thing, depending on their intent. I expected it would take two or three weeks if they did it right, longer if the thing they were stalking was smart enough to recognize it was being stalked. I also recommended a number of species on the island that might be good at this sort of thing. Goblins with sub-machine guns weren't at the top of the list.

An hour later we were back home and I was staring at the graffiti again.

"You're angry with me, for not letting you play in the woods," Mirella said after a time. The photograph of the untranslated text was on the big flat-screen television, which made it about the same size as it was on the wall of the hotel room.

She handed me a glass of whiskey, neat, as she spoke, sitting down on the couch by my side as if we were about to watch a show.

"Nah. I'm just really, really bad at domesticity."

"Me too," she said. She held up her own glass, which didn't contain whiskey. It was a veggie shake of some kind: a combination of sand and cilantro, so far as I had ever been able to tell.

We clinked glasses, as if we'd just completed a ceremony.

"But I do know danger," she added. "And that sound was the sound of danger."

"You think so?"

"Instinctively, yes. Even having never heard it before. My neck-hair stood on edge."

"Something visceral, then. Maybe species-specific, too. I didn't get that at all."

"Yes. But you run toward fires."

She put down her glass and lay across the couch so that her head was in my lap.

"I do believe you have too high an opinion of me," I said.

"When I was a child, I used to imagine what the man who would win me would be like, and what I imagined was a great hero. You're what I ended up with, so allow me my fantasy, please."

"All right. You want me on a horse, too?"

"Yes, a white horse would be excellent."

"Armor?"

"Goodness, no. A loincloth, or nothing at all."

"You have no idea how painful riding a horse in a loincloth is. Do I get a saddle, at least?"

She laughed. "No! Bareback."

"Well, between me and the horse, one of us is going to end up a gelding. Are there even any horses on the island?"

"No. Cousin said there was talk of establishing a ranch, for tourists to ride horses along the beach, but it was scrubbed. Ghouls."

"You're kidding."

"I'm only repeating."

Ghouls are essentially man-sized carrion birds, minus the *bird* part. They're skinny, bald, pale nocturnal things that I know almost nothing about, except that they tended to turn up on battlefields after major skirmishes to eat the dead. They greatly preferred horsemeat to human meat.

"I haven't seen a ghoul in more than a thousand years," I said. "But I don't recall them being much interested in living horses. Only dead ones."

"I've never met one, but I'm told having horses running about would have offended them in some way."

"I'll have to hang out at the hotel more often. I'd love to see a ghoul."

"Yes, that's my definition of a good time as well." This was sarcasm, but it was really hard to tell with her.

She pointed to the screen.

"What have you figured out about your words?"

"Almost nothing. I think this might rhyme, but that's nearly all I have."

"That's something."

"I guess. It's hard to tell, but I think the syllable count for each line is about the same, which makes me think the sounds represented at the end are homophonic."

"How are you counting syllables? The lines are different sizes."

"I know. A lot of languages have silent letters. Anyway, about the only thing I have going for me is I used to speak this language."

"Well." She picked up the remote and shut off the television. "I have an idea. Why don't we go to the bedroom so you can speak to me in your ancient language while performing terribly sinful acts."

"It's not a particularly romantic sounding tongue."

"Then switch to one that is."

"Well, all right."

~

*T*had an odd dream that night.

As you might imagine, someone who's been around as long as I have can end up with pretty interesting dreams. I thankfully don't dream all that often, but when I do I usually end up in a weird cross-cut of historical epochs, featuring people who could never meet doing things they would never do.

I'm sure other people have equivalent experiences, but I'm pulling from a much larger bank of memories. In a lot of ways, I think dreams are how my mind flexes old instincts. They probably also help keep me sane.

It was a decent bet the dream—or the start of it—was Mirella's fault, for asking me to speak to her in the Elamite tongue. Generally speaking, I'm entirely in favor of having a girlfriend whose kink (one of them) is dead languages, but it can lead to some strange mental associations, especially for the languages belonging to cultures I didn't particularly enjoy.

Elam was one of those places; I didn't really like it there.

The kingdom itself wasn't called Elam—this is a modern title. It was called Haltamti. There was a loose government apparatus that connected the city-states of the kingdom and—interestingly —it was a matriarchy. (This is only interesting in hindsight. At the time, it didn't strike anyone as particularly uncommon, because at the time it wasn't.)

Anyway, the dream. I was back in Haltamti, in the city of Susiana. I was a farmer when I lived there, which should give you an idea of how little this was like a modern city: farmers worked land within what would be considered city limits.

It wasn't really my property, because there wasn't a lot in the way of property rights. Everything was more or less collectively owned, and collectively eaten.

We served at the will of the high priestess, which wasn't a terrible way to live, to be honest, because she wasn't sending anyone off to war, and everyone was getting enough food to get by. I was a farmer because that's one of the things I happen to be really good at.

There was a guy named… well, I'm spelling this phonetically… Shif. Shif was the equivalent of a priest, which only meant he didn't work with his hands for a living. Shif was a pretty interesting guy, which was why I considered him a friend. (To be honest, about 95% of any population is just not worth striking up a conversation with, and this has been true since we invented conversations.)

Later, after I woke up from this dream, it was pretty obvious why Shif turned up. He was the first one to show me written language, and it just happened to be the language written in blood on that hotel room wall. Given this was well over six thousand years ago, it took an awfully long time for my inability to fully grasp the significance of the written word at that particular moment in history to come back and haunt me. I appreciated the written word *later*, after the Elamite kingdom was gone and it was too late to learn their alphabet.

In the dream, Shif was standing in front of a schoolhouse chalkboard in the middle of one of the mud temples. Through the window, in the distance, a volcano was erupting, but neither of us much cared about this. The hotel room text I was trying to translate was written on the board, and Shif was berating me, in Elamite, for not being able to read it.

"You always make the same mistake, Adam," he said.

"My name isn't Adam, it's..." but then I couldn't remember what name I was using.

"The same mistake," he repeated.

"What is that mistake?"

"Look out the window."

There was no word in Elamite for *window*, so what he said was, *look out the open*, but the open was a modern window, with a windowpane and glass and all that. A transparent sticker of a rainbow-colored bird was stuck to the window. It changed the sunlight's color from yellow to blood-red.

The bird looked like a large thing I used to hunt, tens of centuries before Shif's birth, in the African bushes. It was extinct by the time of Elam.

"Look out the window," Shif repeated, and the volcano was gone, and so was the room, and we were in a Roman bathhouse, covered in mud. We used to clean ourselves this way, by rubbing mud on our bodies and then rinsing it off in the baths.

"Why are we here?"

"You're making the same mistake again," Shif said, and that wasn't getting any less annoying. "Open your eyes."

"I know, and look out the window, I get it."

"He doesn't get it," a woman with red hair said, from the edge of the tub. It was historically feasible for this part to have been a memory, because it was theoretically possible for the red-haired woman—she's been going by Eve—to have actually been in that bathhouse. She was immortal too, and I know she spent time in the Roman Empire just like I did.

It wasn't a memory, though, because I would have definitely remembered it if it had happened.

"Priestess, how may I serve you?" Shif said, and we were back in Haltamti.

Eve was now dressed as the high priestess of the Susiana court, and my stomach lurched, because there was a real chance that actually *was* a memory.

"He doesn't pay attention," she said. "He won't see until it's time to kill again, and then he will."

"I understand," Shif said, and then the chair I was sitting in was an altar, and Shif had a sword.

The crowd beneath the altar muttered a sort of community approval for the sacrifice I was about to become—to the gods, for a good crop. Or maybe rain. Or to get the volcano to stop erupting. There was no volcano near Haltamti, but the sky was still full of ashes.

"The waters of the sea will meet the fires of the earth," Shif announced. The crowd began chanting, and then the chanting started to sound like a low trill.

"Pay attention," Shif said. "You're not paying attention."

"Can you sharpen that sword?" I asked. "It's too dull, you'll spend the day trying to get through my neck with that."

"This is how I rise," he said, and then he thrust the sword into my chest, and I woke up.

It took a minute or two to figure out where I was and convince myself I hadn't just been run through with a dull sword on a Mesopotamian religious altar, and another minute after that before I stopped speaking Elamite.

I didn't even try to go back to sleep. For one thing, that was the kind of dream that strongly argued against doing so, but for another, it wasn't exactly a meaningless kind of dream. I was missing something, according to a dead high priest from the Bronze Age. Something obvious enough for my unconscious to have already figured it all out. Unfortunately, my unconscious was being a jerk about it.

It took me the rest of the night to figure out what that was.

CHAPTER 6

"*Y*ou're saying it was a… fylgjur?" Mirella asked, the next morning. We were at the table on the back deck, eating a light breakfast consisting of fruit and strong coffee. "What tongue is that?"

"It's Norse. I've heard them called banshees too, but it was a Norseman who named it for me."

We'd already gone through the part where I explained why I was up before her and what happened in my dream. Listening to someone else describe a dream is one of the three most boring things that can happen in a conversation, so her capacity for patience and attentiveness was impressive.

"Ah, banshee is better. That word doesn't hurt my ears. So you say it was a banshee we heard yesterday."

"Or a fylgjur. I'm not exactly saying it was either of them though. What I'm saying is I now recall having heard that sound before, or something close to it, and when I heard it, the sound was attributed by people in my party as belonging to a fylgjur."

"Or banshee."

"Or banshee, sure."

"I don't see the difference between what I just said and what you just said. Either it was the thing, or, it was called the thing."

"The difference is that people make mistakes, and invent things that aren't real in order to explain things they don't understand. I'm not all that sure there's a real creature called a banshee, but the last time I heard that noise, a banshee was what I was told had made it."

"And you didn't investigate this? Whenever this was?"

"You would be surprised how rarely I find myself in situations where I can just wander off and explore. But no, I couldn't, because there was superstition involved."

"How so?"

"Fylgiurs are harbingers. Like comets, and blood moons, and a bunch of other things. The people I was with didn't know what really made that sound, but understood anyway that they needed to be going in the other direction as soon as they heard it. I wasn't in a position to persuade them otherwise."

It's not really fair to pick on the beliefs of ancient cultures, because we're all just trying to come up with a reasonable understanding of how the world works with the tools we're given. You and I might hear a weird noise and conclude it's the wind pushing through a tree knot, or an extremely distressed bullfrog, or whatever. Someone else might hear it and declare that the sound is coming from a spirit, and it's here to collect the dead, and since none of us are currently dead we had better run before it collects us.

Yes, the leap from bullfrog to a dead-collecting phantasm is pretty big, but still. We live in a world where someone might breathe a specific kind of air and die from it a decade later. Sometimes it isn't all that crazy.

"I see," Mirella said, sipping her coffee slowly. "Do you think we should notify Dmitri that you have indeed identified the source of the sound, and it is a mythical soul-eating monster?"

"No, but now I'm a lot more curious about what actually *is* out there."

"Mm. All right. I will consider letting you go play in the woods."

"Mythical soul-eating monster sold you on it?"

She stood, and took off her shirt, which would have been an extraordinary response under nearly all other circumstances, but was normal for us.

"Not really, but now I'm also curious as to what it might actually be. Maybe we'll go camping. Are you coming into the water?"

"Not planning to."

"Are you sure? Jumping in will undoubtedly help convince me to agree to your banshee hunt."

"How does that even make sense?"

"It will show the depths of your resolve."

"I'm a lot more concerned about the depths of the water under the cliff."

"I do it every day."

"Yes, but you're you. You killed a demon with a bunch of knives once. For all I know you can fly and just haven't found a way to tell me."

"Hah. Coward."

"Absolutely."

"Oh, come on, just run off the edge, you don't even need to dive properly. It's invigorating."

I was born in a jungle, and went five thousand years before I saw a large body of water that wasn't also frozen. I feel perfectly at home among trees, hunting banshees. I don't feel at home in the ocean, and never will. Not unless I'm on a ship.

But, I humored her, as I often did once we reached the name-calling stage, and walked the short path to the edge of our private cliff.

That was when I noticed the ocean was missing.

I heard Mirella's footfall and realized she was about to perform the very same kind of leap into the ocean she insisted I attempt. Usually, her dives were relatively sedate, requiring not much more than a little jump, but since we'd entered into a sort of unspoken pissing contest—which can happen when you're in a relationship with a goblin, just so you know—she was aiming for a more impressive performance. I'd seen her do this a couple of times before. She went from a run to a leap that was about twice the length of what one might expect from an Olympic-caliber athlete.

It would have been very impressive, but not impressive enough to reach the water.

"Wait!" I said, but words weren't half as effective as the arm-tackle I had to commit to in order to get Mirella to the ground.

"Ow!" she exclaimed, as I landed atop her. The surface at this spot was a combination of loose dirt, scrub grass, and rocks, which was not a great landing when one is naked, as she happened to be.

"What are you *doing?*" she asked.

"The ocean's gone."

"What are you talking about? Oceans don't disappear."

I helped her to her feet.

"This one did. Look."

All the way down the beach to the hotel, the ocean water appeared to be missing, like low tide had come and then come again three or four more times without scheduling a high tide along the way. Either the water decided to pull away from the land further than it ever had before, or the island was rising.

Or, option number three.

"Oh my god," Mirella said. "We have to call Esteban."

A siren sounded in the distance.

"I think he already knows."

It was an air raid siren, so as soon as I heard it I instinctively look to the sky for bombers. But that was the wrong place to be looking. The place to look was the horizon, because the ocean hadn't disappeared. It had backed up, regrouped, and decided to charge.

In other words, there was an impressively large wall of water approaching the island.

"Well, that's a sight," I said.

"You've never seen this before?"

"Nope, first time."

"Then we can say the day has been an accomplishment, for giving you a new experience. How tall do you suppose that is? More than ten meters?"

My eyes ran across the vast wave until I was looking straight ahead from our cliff vantage point.

"I think so, yes. How fast do you think that's moving?"

She followed my gaze.

"Oh."

"Pretty fast?"

"We have to go. We have to go right away."

She spun and ran straight into the house. I was mesmerized, and not otherwise moving, because frankly it isn't all that often you get to see an entire ocean of water racing to slap you in the face. It reminded me of the Hollywood version of the Moses story, with the Red Sea parted on both sides as the chosen people ran across a dry seabed.

Needless to say, that never actually happened, for a lot of obvious reasons. For one, speaking as someone who personally fled Egypt, that wasn't even close to the best route. Plus, there's a chasm at the bottom of that sea that would have been a little tough to cross, and I don't recall reading about God throwing in a suspension bridge.

Anyway. At the edge of the cliff I was having one of those moments of disconnect one has when witnessing something one had only ever seen previously as a special effect: that quality of unreality in the midst of everything nearby and provably real.

The last time I recalled experiencing this sensation was at the base of a live volcano during an eruption—when I had no cinema to compare it to. Then I remembered the volcano from my dream and wondered if I'd experienced a prophetic event.

"ADAM!"

I turned at the sound of my name, which broke the spell. Mirella had put on clothing, and was slipping on a pair of track shoes.

"Get what you can, quickly!" she said.

"Right. Impending death, right."

I ran back into the house. I was wearing shorts and a basic T-shirt and nothing else, and so I went to the dresser where I kept a more comprehensive set of clothing, at which point I froze because I had no idea what I was going to need.

I'm not enormously attached to a lot of material goods. I've been known to hang onto one or two uniquely irreplaceable objects—I once carried a sword made of Damascus steel around for four centuries—but I had nothing like that with me on the island. Off-island, I had caches of things I expected to want again someday, in places where they would last for a while without being disturbed, but again, none of that was on the island or in the bedroom.

So since I had no laptop containing a vital manuscript, or a locker holding a rare illuminated Bible, or a one-of-a-kind codex, or any of the other things someone in this circumstance might retrieve, I got hung up on what I might want to have in the near future.

Unfortunately, I didn't own any scuba gear, or a surfboard.

"Too late, must go," Mirella said, as she ran straight past the elevated bedroom platform and toward the front of the house.

I looked back. It appeared the ocean was now coming over the back deck and through our open floor plan. Any questions I might have had about the force of the wave were answered by witnessing it demolish the table on the deck, and rock the kitchen island. Crashing waves combined with groaning wood and stone and glass, and a new reminder that everything in this world is temporary.

I was right behind Mirella after that. I was also empty-handed, as I never bothered to retrieve anything from the bedroom or any other part of the house.

We didn't stop to open the front door, which seemed like an even sillier contrivance in this context. Instead, we jumped out of the building over the short wall that stood on the side of the door, just as the water was going to be doing in a moment or two, since it sounded like it was directly behind us. It would have been nice if the ocean respected the door and the fake walls a tiny bit more, but that was nature for you.

I landed beside Mirella, who'd hesitated long enough to ensure I was with her. This was possibly a fatal error on her part, as I think she would have escaped what happened next otherwise.

Just as I turned to discuss a plan involving reaching the nearest tree and climbing above the oncoming water, our legs were cut out from beneath us and down we went.

What happened, I realized later, was that while the water going through the house was slowed by the furniture and various platforms and half-walls, there were no such obstacles beneath the house other than the occasional support beam.

It was knee-high and moving fast. We were both submerged almost before recognizing what was happening. I had enough time to get a gulp of air and grab Mirella by the hand, but that was all.

The current carried us from the house and straight for the hillside. I held onto the air, but not to Mirella. The force of the water tore us apart, and I didn't have time to evaluate the consequences because I was too busy worrying about the fact that I was being propelled toward rocks at an unreasonable rate of speed.

There were trees, too, though. A tree trunk was just about as forgiving as a rock when it came to hitting one at ramming speed, but they were easier to grab, and offered some vertical promise. I was able to maneuver myself—or perhaps I was just lucky enough to already be heading that way—toward a particularly sturdy tree with an equally sturdy low bough.

I caught it with my left elbow, grabbed my left wrist with my right hand, and held tight against the sensation that I was dislocating my shoulder while riding out the force of the wave.

I'm not an exceptional swimmer, but I can hold my breath for a very long time. This comes from having been born into a world where long-distance running was how we obtained meat. They're good lungs, I'm saying. I can't explain why they're still as good as they were sixty-thousand-odd years ago, but I can't explain why I'm still alive either. I imagine the explanation for both is the same, whatever it might be.

Still, I was underwater for just long enough to worry that I might actually drown. But gradually, the pressure subsided enough to enable me to move from the tree limb to the trunk. From there I shimmied in what I hoped was the right way, until the combination of my moving upward and the water level moving downward worked together to get my head to some air. I took a deep breath, and kept climbing. Soon, I was completely out of the ocean, and the water was falling away from the hillside.

I'd been carried downhill a lot further than I realized. It took a minute to even locate the roof of the house. I had to climb more than halfway to the top to see it, which wasn't at all fun because my left shoulder, while not dislocated, was extremely displeased with me, and no longer felt all that interested in behaving like a weight-bearing joint.

It was a miracle I hadn't been crushed en route to the tree. It looked like I was swept along the road quite a distance, before the road turned and the water didn't.

Only then did I start worrying about Mirella. I couldn't see her anywhere. I kind of thought of her as bulletproof, but she needed to breathe just as much as I did, and was no less capable of being crushed against a rock face, rammed into a tree, or dropped over the side of the hill. No amount of skill would have helped her if she couldn't control her direction or if she wasn't conscious when the time came to act defensively.

A tsunami wasn't going to care how good she was with a sword.

I shouted her name five or six times, but got only silence in return. I told myself that didn't mean anything except that she wasn't in earshot.

The silence was, in itself, unnerving, because not only was Mirella not responding, nothing else was making noise either. Ordinarily, the jungle was alive with some kind of sound.

I climbed a little higher.

From the top of the tree, I was able to see the whole lower island, or rather where it used to be located.

I could see the roof of the hotel, because it was the tallest and widest thing down there, but that was about all. The rest was ocean water in every direction. The roadway grid, the municipal buildings, the bungalows along the beach… all of it was just gone.

Then I heard a noise. Up the hill some ways—no telling how far—was a low trill. It was met by a second, from closer, and a third from further away.

It was the call of the banshees. They'd come to collect the dead.

PART II

THERE AND BACK AGAIN

CHAPTER 7

$\mathcal{T}$he events surrounding the first time I heard a banshee cry were frankly a good deal more interesting than the sound itself, because when I heard it I was on my way to an entirely different monster.

This was something I ended up doing from time-to-time, especially in situations where people around me had some idea of who I was and what I knew. For a lot of early human history, reality and mythology were pretty fluid concepts, so my being an immortal man was something a lot of people were cool with, and didn't consider it all that big a deal.

A bigger deal was my vast experience, specifically when it came to important knowledge such as how to kill various large things.

At the time, I was eking out a living on a small spit of land near the rocky shore of the North Sea. I'd put this somewhere around 500 years after my time as a fisherman on Lake Genneseret. Not that I was counting the years; I'm piecing it together after the fact.

This was pretty far north for me. I had a personal preference for more temperate climes, which is what happens when you experience an ice age first-hand: you learn to really appreciate equatorial weather. But it wasn't *too* far north, just around what's now Sweden and Denmark. (I don't know which one of them I was in. They're next to each other and we didn't have maps.) If I wanted to wear dead animal fur year-round and spend a lifetime rowing small boats or sailing larger ones I could have gone further north still, but I have only so much patience for snow, less for cold-weather-appropriate apparel, and almost none for ocean-going vessels.

But, gadding about the fertile crescent for thousands of years can get astoundingly dull over time. Heading to what would later be the top end of Europe was an attempt to find a little adventure, or at minimum something new.

Adventures I had, but most of those adventures involved mead and taverns, and having my well-being threatened by men who smelled terrible. Once I grew tired of it, I went back to one of the things I did well.

~

I belonged to a small community of farmers and fishers. By small, I mean there were only maybe ten families all told, and we only considered ourselves a community because we traded food. We had no governing structure, but we also owed fealty to nobody.

If anyone came along who wanted to take the land, I suspect I was the closest thing we had to muscle, which was too bad because I had no weapons worth mentioning. I did have a goat, but he wasn't a large goat, and neither particularly fierce nor belligerent.

It wasn't prized land, though, so nobody came along to take it from us.

Then one day, a warrior appeared on my land.

"That is quite a goat you have," he said. I was prepared to

lunge for a large stick nearby as a means of defense, until he spoke, and then I recognized him.

"He will tear off your leg if you glance sideways at him," I said.

"I believe it. Fearsome, indeed."

"How are you, Unfer?" I asked. "And how did you find me?"

"Why, I asked for directions to the richest man on the hill, Beuvulth," he said, calling me by the name I'd used in his company. I was the richest man on the hill, because I was the only one with a goat. The bar was low.

"I don't go by that name here."

"Well if you don't mind, I'd rather you did go by that name where we're going, or we will only confuse everyone who has heard of you."

"Where is it you're expecting me to go?"

"Sköld. I'm here to relieve you of your debt."

I sighed grandly. As it happened, on an evening not so long before this meeting, somewhat more north and in a considerably more violent environment, Unfer saved me from having to kill several men. In his estimation, he talked them out of killing *me*, and thus was I supposedly indebted to him. I didn't see it that way.

"Will I need a sword? I don't have one. And the goat doesn't travel well."

"Leave the goat. I'll get you a sword."

"Come inside. I have a fermented brew I keep for guests. We will have some, and then you can tell me what I am agreeing to and I will decide for myself if it satisfies the debt you feel certain I owe you."

~

*M*y home was a square stone hut. It was sturdy, and passably comfortable, only because I stuffed a few sacks with dried grass to sleep on. I had two chairs, a table, and a pile of animal furs for when it got cold, which was essentially every night. I also had jars of preserved food, and this fermented milk thing that was the best I could do.

"This is extremely awful," Unfer said. "I mean that."

"Thank you, I know. But it's the only spirited drink fifty leagues in all directions, and I have certain needs."

"I recall."

Unfer was a large man with blond locks he kept in a braid. He wore light armor made of iron, and brown leather. Since I last saw him he'd gained a scar on his left cheek and lost a finger on his right hand. In those days, that just meant he was aging nicely.

He looked like a formidable opponent, whereas I was exactly as I am now, only with different clothing and smelling somewhat more like goat shit. (Unfer smelled like a horse, which was interesting given he arrived on foot.)

To just about anyone, the idea of him coming to me for assistance, warrior to warrior, hardly made sense. He looked like a warrior. I looked like the guy who needed to hire a warrior.

"What is the issue?" I asked. "Does it involve whoever gave you that scar?"

"No, no. A woman gave this to me, and I earned every part of it. No, I come on behalf of the great king Hroar. You have heard this name."

"I have not, no." I was being honest, actually hadn't.

"But… the tales of his… never mind. You have been on this farm for too long."

Unfer's people and their constantly burnished sagas made for a community that was convinced they were a good deal more famous and legendary than they actually were.

"What does this king need of me and how does he even know who I am?"

"For his knowledge of you, I am to blame. For what he needs, I am also to blame. We need a man with a great understanding of the beasts of the world."

"Is he starting his own farm?"

"Not that kind of beast. The kind that requires slaying."

"This far exceeds the debt you're owed."

"Perhaps. But I would also appeal now to your sense of rightness."

"I have no such sense."

"I am prepared to convey you by force."

"That is a more compelling argument. What kind of creature, and why does it need to be slain?"

"We've never seen the likes, but I can swear to you it is a challenge to the greatest swords in the king's land, and now only brings shame to Hroar's house."

"Maybe you should explain."

Unfer explained.

It seemed the great king had built a great hall for his great feasts, but the first time he held a feast there, he and his guests were attacked by an ill-described 'monster'. That same monster had since taken up residence in the hall, and none had proven capable of dislodging him.

Two things were clear from the narrative. One, Unfer didn't know what kind of beast this was and neither did anyone else, and two, Unfer hadn't faced it, so he didn't really know what it looked like. His description was therefore filtered down through the memories of the feast attendees who survived. This made for a description that didn't at all correspond with anything I'd ever heard of before.

I decided to make the second observation aloud.

"I must conclude that since no man has faced the creature since and lived, you yourself have not done battle with this gigantic five-armed fire-breathing beast yourself," I said. "As you sit at my table and do still clearly live."

"I prefer to employ wisdom before strength, Beuvulth. Of all who stride the Earth, you are most like to appreciate this. Will you come?"

"I will, but not for our debt and not to slay any great beast. I go to find out what manner of thing it actually is. If my generosity intercedes, I may tell *you* how to slay it, and simply go home."

$\sim$

The reason Unfer had no horse was that he and his men took a boat from across the sea to reach me, which indicated he knew more or less exactly where I was to be found.

The obvious conclusion was that he'd been keeping track of my movements in some way, perhaps for an occasion such as this. Or maybe he was just shrewd enough to appreciate that one did what one could to keep an eye on the only immortal one knew.

It was eight men in addition to Unfer; so, four oars a side for when the winds were unfavorable, or seven to man the riggings of the sails when the wind blew true, with one to steer.

I'd like to say the kind of people I'm talking about were Vikings, but I'm going to be honest with you: nobody called them that. I sincerely don't even know where the name came from. Seriously, I think someone just made up the word one day. Wagner, probably. He's at least partly to blame for those ridiculous bull-horned helmets nobody wore. Also, if the word Viking were even in use at this time, it still wouldn't apply, because these were land-bound men, not high seas piratical invaders.

Anyway, they were either Danes or Skjöldungs.

We had just reached the boat when I heard the noise.

"Hurry!" one of the men hissed as we approached.

"We would have reached you sooner had you not doused the torches," Unfer groused. We had to walk the coastline for a little while.

"And we'd have left without you had you not arrived before now," the man said. "Did you not hear?"

"That peculiar keening?" Unfer looked at me. "Some animal, no doubt."

"No doubt," I said, although in truth I'd never heard an animal make this noise.

"It's the fylgjur, come to collect the dead," another of the oarsmen declared. "It's why we put out the fire, and why we should be gone from this land."

"Well get us on the water, then," Unfer said. "Even though we've no dead for collecting."

"She would sooner make her own dead than leave unsatisfied," the first man said, as the others lifted the boat to the water. "I know where your thoughts are on this, Unfer. You're not a one to give in to superstition. Well neither am I, but I know enough to respect them, when being wrong can mean my death. We can be doubters in the daytime."

The boat was at sea shortly after. I heard the odd howl twice more as the men rowed furiously. The last howl, strangely, sounded closer than the first, even as the shore was getting further away. We never did see what was causing the noise.

If it seems as if this is really something I ought to have remembered the minute I heard the sound again, you aren't wrong, although let's keep in mind how many years passed between encounters. Also, what happened after that was so much more memorable, I think I can be forgiven.

❦

There were horses waiting on the other side, along with provisions. I was happy to see both because I was hungry, and unwilling to walk an untold number of leagues just to satisfy my curiosity.

There was a time when Unfer and his tribe were considered the greatest warrior horsemen around. They rode into battle with boar's-head helmets, swinging heavy iron swords atop armored mounts, and it was terrifying. (I saw this from the edge of a battle I wasn't directly engaged in personally, and I went the other way immediately.) Even though the crested helms didn't really look much like boars, the overall effect was to be witnessing something not human. Fear is an impressive weapon in a battle.

In recent years, though, their battles had taken place without a horse beneath them. This was one of the things Unfer and I discussed as we rode north.

"Too many wars and not enough horses," he said. "It takes a lot to keep a horse healthy and strong in these climes, and a mount in heavy snow is not near as much an advantage as you might think. You end up on a slow-reacting beast with perpetually exposed flanks, ready to die with his rider's leg pinned beneath. In a springtime battle on a southern field I would gladly ride. Otherwise, to keep my blood in my body where I like it, I'll stand."

I checked my horse, who was stubborn, and perpetually looking to graze. This didn't escape my friend's notice.

"I'd have thought a man who saw the first sunrise would hold better command of his mount," he said.

"Some things take more than one lifetime to master. And horses this size haven't been around as long as you would imagine."

"This size?"

"They used to be smaller."

He laughed.

"Is that so? Was this true of many things?"

"Some. Most were much larger."

"And man?"

"Man has gotten smellier and smarter in equal measure."

We camped on the side of the road—a path, really, not a proper road in the Roman sense—overnight and dined on salted meats. I was supplied with additional furs when it was clear the cold was only growing more intense, and we were heading in the wrong direction to escape it. I was also supplied with the sword I had been promised.

Swords in those days required tremendous upper body strength, because they weren't terrible sharp or well-balanced. I didn't have tremendous upper body strength, and in battle tended to rely upon my opponent's clumsiness. You'd be surprised how effective this was. Also effective: not going to war in the first place. I was exceptionally good at that.

The sword was so I would be a better night watchman, as it was understood that I would be taking a turn so others could sleep without waking up eaten. This is probably the second-oldest task I have ever performed, after hunting. It's the sort of thing people don't have to do any more, although we also mostly gave up sleeping outdoors on the side of the road.

My shift was shared with the man who warned of the fylgjur. His name was Aescher.

"I would say," he began, after an hour of silence, "you do not look to me like a great warrior."

"Don't I?"

"No, you look to me like a goat-farmer."

"I am indeed a goat-farmer, and a farmer of other things as well. Do you imagine a world in which a man can be only one of these things?"

"I can imagine many things. Whether they match the world I see is another matter. Great warriors who retire to farm do not look as you look. Nor are they so young as you. And none are without scars."

"Scars fade. What led you to call me a great warrior?"

"Such was the premise which informed our quest to retrieve you."

"I understand. It is true, Aescher, that I can best most in combat, but that is not why I was sought. I am here for my wisdom."

He huffed. "The land is full of wisdom. What we are short on are men who can win the day against a monster. You do not appear to be such a man."

Aescher really wanted to challenge me on my first point, but that wasn't how one was supposed to spend guard duty, so he didn't. Also, *oops, I killed the guy we went all that way for,* was going to look bad, pretty much from every angle. He spent the remainder of our time together muttering unpleasantries under his breath.

We reached the hall the following evening.

I don't know when the Scandinavians started building mead halls, but the halls never really made a lot of sense to me and they weren't super good at building them.

The Greeks built similar structures, mostly for religious reasons, but the Greek versions were mostly open-air platforms with a roof and lots of Ionic columns. And they used stone. Those things lasted forever, but also had no walls, tables or chairs, so they were *similar,* but not precisely the same.

The Romans copied a lot of the Greek structural ideas, but aside from the bathhouses, didn't have much use for a building with only one room in it. No Nords were going to be copying the Romans any time soon either.

A mead hall was literally just a standalone dining room. That was it. They were built out in fields and attributed the same sort of value a modern person might ascribe to a vacation house in a nice area. Kings had them, and they were about the only ones. In fairness, local kings had very little else. Everything in this territory was made of mud and wood.

Hroar's hall looked like as stiff wind could collapse the entire thing. It was built out of wood slats in approximately the same oblong shape as their burial mounds, only with periodic angles, since the layered wood slats that constituted the walls were flat and not curved. The roof had semi-hidden vents to let smoke out, which was important in a building with no windows in a time when fire was the only source of illumination.

Speaking of fire, nobody with a healthy respect for it would ever go inside a building like this.

"So now we are here," I said, "what's the next part?"

"We go inside, find the monster and with your help, slay him," Unfer said. "And then people will write poems about our bravery and we will live forever."

"I already live forever. Is that really the entirety of your plan?"

"You have other suggestions?"

"Not without seeing your monster first, no. Why do we not just burn down the place?"

"The beast resists fire," Aescher said. "And destroying that which we are here to save is a poor solution."

"Kill the monster, and build a new hall on the same spot," I said. "If you do it fast enough…"

"You are delaying intentionally. Are you coward?"

"You will show respect, Aescher," Unfer said.

"How do you know about the tolerance for fire?" I asked.

"He is the only man to walk away from the last party to attempt to slay the monster," Unfer said.

"I thought you said none survived an encounter?"

"It made for a better story."

"I dined with the king the night it attacked, and many from that night lived," Aescher said. "And on that night we tried to set it afire, but it shook off the flame like water."

"Interesting."

Unfer raised an eyebrow in my direction. "Do you now know what it is?"

"No. It's interesting only for being information I didn't have before. I still need to see it to know."

I was thinking it was a demon. They had skin so thick they could hold their hand in an open flame for a good minute before complaining about the heat. A demon didn't really match the description I'd been provided, but nothing else did either. Plus, demons weren't all that uncommon in this part of the world at this time in history. It was likely, though, that at least one of the men of Hroar's kingdom had seen a demon in their lifetime and could recognize one, because it's not something you forget.

Dragon was another possibility, but the odds were much worse in that regard. Dragons were really just big dumb animals that mostly stuck to wooded areas. A dragon wouldn't attack a large party of men armed with swords any more than a wolf or large cat would, which was to say they wouldn't as long as the numbers weren't in their favor. They also wouldn't camp out inside the hall unless they were wounded and couldn't move.

Dragons might have had tough enough skin to be considered fireproof. I'd never tried to set one afire, so I couldn't know for sure. If they actually breathed fire, that'd give me the answer to the question, but they didn't.

"If you need to see it to tell us how to slay it, we shall have to make sure you see it," Unfer said. "Take a torch, everyone. Search the floor after we've got the braziers lit, or we'll be grappling it in the darkness. For all we know the damn thing can see in the dark."

Unfer and Aescher led the way, both with a lit torch in one hand and a sword in the other. A third man pulled open the main double-doors to the hall to allow them entry, given they only had two hands apiece.

In they went. I followed, with four men at my back.

⁓

I don't know of any other species that is quite as good at finding stupid ways to die as humans. I say that despite being an actual human. If you look at my history you'll find I may be more directly responsible for the current nature of humankind than anyone else around, but all the same I don't recall promoting this kind of stupidity.

Not that I'm really complaining. Taking advantage of stupidity is one of the things keeping me alive.

But okay, to use my favorite example, have a look at the Crusades. Basically, a large number of wealthy people with their own castles and land decided one day that despite living better than all but an extremely small handful of people on the planet, what they really wanted was the land in a different country a thousand miles away. This was weird enough, but it got worse because that land already had other people living on it, and those people had done the sorts of things one does on one's own land, such as assembling large defensive apparatuses.

If you're ever hanging out with a bunch of people, and one day that bunch decides it would be fun to travel a vast distance in order to attack a settled army behind fixed battlements because they think the land that army is standing on is super important, what you're going to do—if you're smart—is go find a different bunch of people to hang out with.

Wars are started for reasons that seem stupid in hindsight but make sense at the time. I get that, but there are also occasions when it seems like human tribes put a little bit extra effort in finding ways to die in large numbers for small reasons.

The assault on the mead hall was a smaller version of the same lack of thought, which was particularly galling considering I was in the middle of this one.

We were heading into a dark building fully aware there was something inside that could kill us with its bare hands and had an apparent active interest in doing exactly that. We were holding the only light sources—I really cannot stress enough how important this was in the days before electricity—which meant we could be seen but weren't going to be able to see much of anything until our eyes adjusted. On top of all of that, our source of light was fire, and we were walking into a wood building.

The second most rational thing to do—after just burning the place to the ground—would have been to tear down the walls to expose the creature, and fight in an open space where there was plenty of room for other assault options, like a hundred archers.

Instead, since the pride of the king and the integrity of the building were more important than the lives of the people sent in to deal with the problem, we willingly charged into a potential ambush.

Sometimes I wonder how mankind made it this far.

~

*W*e weren't attacked and eaten as soon as we entered the hall, which was a little unfortunate, as an early demise would have saved us from the smell.

If you took someone from today and dropped them to just about any point in the past, I'm pretty sure the first thing they would say is *dear god, what is that smell?* It wouldn't be any one thing, either; the whole world was a stew of body odor and dung and rot.

A lot of the reason mankind spread out and settled down across vast territories was just to get away from the smell of each other, something that was forgotten by the time we got around to building real cities. Then, the solution was to put flowers in our breast pockets to give us something to smell other than the world. When that didn't work, people—the rich ones—started manufacturing their own soaps. This wasn't to keep themselves clean; it was so their whole body smelled the way the flowers in their pockets were supposed to. Perfumes were the same deal. We didn't create these things so other people thought we smelled nice, we did it so we couldn't smell the other people.

Somehow, this never comes up in period dramas, which is another reason I can't take any of them seriously.

The smell that hit us when we walked in was worse than any

I'd encountered before. I anticipated a stench from rotting bodies, as I was told there were multiple dead in the hall, on top of which there was all the food from the banquet the monster interrupted. But that wasn't what hit us at all. This was pure body odor.

Unfer gagged, while Aescher spat and cursed and nearly lost his torch flame for all the waving he was doing to try and eradicate the smell in the air.

"Spread out," Unfer ordered in a harsh whisper, over his shoulder. "Light the braziers and try not to vomit."

We spread out. I was at a tiny disadvantage because I'd never been in the hall before, but as I said, architecturally this was not a terribly complex building. Big long table in the middle, chairs around the table, an entrance on either end of the room, and that was about all. If Hroar was extra-fancy about it, the far end had a raised platform for him to stand atop so he looked more important, and there was the possibility of a side table or two for food and libations, but that was about it. The food would have been cooked elsewhere and brought over by wagon, carried in through the back of the hall.

Oh, and there were the braziers, which were torches on tall, free-standing staffs embedded in a wide base that one hoped was difficult to topple. Quality varied region-to-region. The best could withstand an unintentional assault from a drunken swordsman. The worst fell over with a sneeze.

As I stumbled across my first upright brazier, I was happy to discover the thing looked decently sturdy, and my hope to not die in a fire while fighting for my life against an outrageously smelly monster increased somewhat. I lit it.

The others performed the same task, slowly bringing illumination to the modest interior.

In the improving lighting, the tabletop was the first thing I took note of. The remains of the interrupted banquet sat where it was, looking a little like how one might imagine a frat house kitchen after a party, if everyone in the house died overnight and nobody found the place for a month.

All right, the analogy is a stretch. The point is, there was a lot of half-eaten food, dirty plates and goblets, upturned mead pitchers, and so on, and the entire mess was alive with the irritated motion of flies. It was a testament to the severity of the extant body odor that we couldn't smell the rotting food over it.

Because of the size of the room, I'm not entirely sure what happened next. One of the men on the hall's far side—more or less as far from me as they could be—either stumbled on and awoke the creature, or was surprised by him. Either way, there was suddenly lots of shouting and sword-clanging, a torch bounced along the ground, and other men began running toward the scene.

And, there was a deep, eardrum-rending roar. It was the kind of enraged bellow that hundreds of thousands of years' worth of evolution trained humans to run away from. It might be the cry of a herd of mastodons, or the low thrum of a large cat standing right behind you. It was a warning that the creature coming your way was bigger, and you'd best turn around and head the other way as fast as you can.

But, since bravery often means acting contrary to instinct and basic common sense, we all got our swords out and headed toward the noise. This was particularly stupid of *me*, because once I heard that howl I was pretty sure I knew what was on the other side of the room. If I was right the sword wasn't going to do all that much good.

The ensuing melee lasted no more than forty seconds, but amounted to a master-class in how not to fight in close quarters. The hall's dimensions were decently large and the actual fight took place away from the table and the chairs and near the back corner of the room, but there were eight of us, all wearing some sort of battle armor and wielding swords that required vast backswings in order to be truly effective, and seven of us were unusually large examples of our species. (In terms of height, these Norsemen and I were about the same, but where I was skinny and built for running and hunting, they were wide-shouldered and thick, built for rowing and fighting.) And the thing we faced was nearly twice our size.

I could understand why it had been described has having five arms. It didn't stay still long enough for anyone to count them, and the darkness made it seem as if it were moving much faster than it probably was; it seemed like there were arms everywhere.

Anyhow, I'm doing a terrible job describing the melee because I couldn't follow it. I saw Unfer get in a powerful attack, which involved leaping in the air and swinging his sword down with a two-handed overhand blow, as if with an axe, and I heard the attack land true on what (I'm assuming) was the creature's shoulder or head. I heard the monster roar in pain, and then there was a thud, and Unfer flew past me and onto the table. I saw another man have his head caved in with a heavy fist, and I saw Aescher crumble from what looked like a lethal blow to the ribcage. And I would love to say I got in a few good swings of my own, parried the creature's attacks, and retreated to safety to regroup and reconsider, but that's only half-true. I only offered token engagement, just enough to get a closer look, and maybe so nobody would give me a hard time about not trying. I did, however, retreat exceptionally well.

I found Unfer on the floor on the other side of the table. He was looking for his sword.

"I struck a killing blow, Beuvulth. Did you see?"

"I saw. Yet it didn't kill him. Most killing blows meet that standard. Do you want some help?"

"I drew blood, though, I saw it. The beast is not invincible. I need my sword."

"Not invincible but very, very large. You've lost four men already, and I believe your killing blow shattered your sword.

Here is the end of it." I kicked the haft of his sword in his direction.

"Then tell me what it is, and give me yours, so I can go end this!"

"It's a troll, my friend. And you should stay down."

~

Trolls are basically gigantic people. That's an over-simplification, but it's about right. They're the things legends are usually talking about when they're describing giants.

Your average troll is about 60% chest and arms. They have short, thick legs, which makes them terrible runners but excellent close-combat fighters, and they're great if you want a bunch of heavy somethings lifted. I'm told two of them helped move Stonehenge to its current location, and while I didn't see any trolls in Egypt I had to leave town before they began work on the great pyramids. I wouldn't put it past Khufu to have employed at least one.

My first-hand experience with them came way back before the pyramids and before Stonehenge, and... well, before everything else, too. For a short time, we had one in our tribe. He helped us hunt mammoths.

Before science proved me wrong about this, I would have said trolls were humans, only they were the megafauna versions. Back when most of the game we hunted—and most of the animals hunting us—were enormous, trolls made perfect sense. I *think* we found one as a baby and raised him as one of us, and that was how we ended up with a troll in our tribe, but my memory is a little shaky here, and it's hard to be positive how much is recollection and how much is just something that sounds like it probably makes sense. In this case, I also just described *The Jungle Book*, and the beginning of the movie *Elf*, so it's hard to be sure how accurate it really is.

What I do remember is how we employed our troll, once he came of age. He couldn't run with us, so he couldn't chase down game like we did. But we could drive our prey in a particular direction, with said direction being advantageous to us in some way. A lot of times, this was toward a wall (so they would be cornered) or toward a cliff face (so they would fall to their death.) With a troll, we could drive them toward him, and he could punch them very hard until they fell over.

Honestly, there are maybe only one or two things in the world that are cooler than watching a troll drop a wooly mammoth with a roundhouse punch.

If you asked me, back in the seventh century, if trolls were still around, I'd have said no, which was why when embarking on this little adventure to de-monster king Hroar's mead hall, *troll* wasn't on my mental list of possible creatures.

~

I jumped up on the table, which put me approximately eye-level with the troll.

"Ho, monster," I said. "We speak, now."

"What are you doing?" Unfer asked, from behind the table.

"What does it sound like?" I asked him. "I'm starting a conversation."

"Monster?" It was the troll who spoke. His voice was a thunderstorm. "*You* are monster."

"It speaks!" Unfer muttered.

"I am Beuvulth, the thane."

I wasn't a thane, but that was how Unfer knew me, for the most part. I've always found it easier to claim lineage with a local tribe when I could, especially when the claim couldn't be validated independently. I still do this sometimes, only instead of identifying as a thane I call myself a Canadian. Nobody bothers Canadians.

"What shall I call you, besides monster?" I asked.

"Beuvulth the thane... I am Gren the... I am Gren."

"Gren, it is my honor to speak with you. Do you not know what you are?"

"I am Gren."

"Yes, so you said."

He grunted.

"Come closer with that pointed metal, and I will show you what I am," he said.

"I think we've had enough of that for now, do you agree?"

"It is never enough for you small monsters. Gren is ready."

One of the warriors in the room was agitating for a renewed assault. I could see him creeping forward, to the right of Gren.

The man seemed to think he was catching Gren unawares. The troll took a step forward and into better lighting, ostensibly to look me in the eye. The truth was, the forward position improved his range of movement for the attack about to commence. And he saw that I knew this as well.

"Gren is ready," he repeated.

I looked at the warrior to Gren's right, and shook him off wordlessly. I would have called him by name, but I wasn't paying attention when we did the introductions. It's all I can do to recall the ones I already know, including whichever name I'm using at the moment.

The man lowered his sword and stepped back.

"I mean no treachery," I said to the troll.

He remained at the ready—knees bent, hands curled into fists, head forward—until I realized he was not ignorant of the fact that I still had a sword in *my* hand. To that end, if I were to launch myself from the table and bring the tip of the sword forward, I might have had an opportunity to spear him in the eyeball. I'd say the odds of success were approximately equal the odds of failure. Risky, certainly, but it was still the best attack at our disposal.

I knelt down and put the sword on the table instead, then stood again. Gren relaxed a little.

"I am not a thane," Gren said, after a lengthy silence.

"I can see that."

"You ask if I know what I am. I am not a thane."

"But what are you?"

"I am Gren. What does the thane care what Gren calls himself?"

"I ask because I have traveled great distances to arrive on this table. I came because I know what Gren is, and I know how to kill Gren."

Gren roared, which was terrifying, but he didn't do a lot else.

I wasn't attacking, which put him at a disadvantage. Trolls are really good at defending themselves—and castles, and bridges, and so on—but less dangerous on offense. Gren might not have known what he was, but he had good instincts about his combat strength.

"Well then! Come at me!"

"I tell you this only as a warning. I know what Gren is, and so I know Gren's weakness."

"Show me! We will see how well you know what it is you think you know."

"But I do not wish to kill Gren."

From beneath the table, whispering, Unfer said, "Tell me his weakness and I will do the killing, Beuvulth."

I ignored him.

"Then you lie, Beuvulth the thane," the troll said.

"It could be so, Gren the Gren. If I prove wrong, it will surely mean my death. But I am not wrong, and in not being wrong, my proof would be *your* death. Do you truly wish to see my proof?"

He looked uncertain.

Most trolls I've seen have large wide foreheads and door-knob-sized noses, which combine to make their smallish eyes nearly invisible. They're so sunken, it's easy to mistake them for a single eye, as was the case with the Cyclops in the Odyssey. (I knew Homer—or, more precisely, I knew one of the Homers, as there were several—and this was my biggest complaint.) It made their expressions hard to read, although the long cheeks and wide mouths betrayed a great deal. As much as it could be said that trolls can think and reason, this one was doing that.

"How is it you came about this knowledge you claim to have?" he asked.

"I know of all the beasts, for I have slain all the beasts: the great hunting cats and the mammoth horned monsters, dragons, demons and men, and more. All great strengths hide great weaknesses, in all things, even in Gren. You would know my name, and fear it, but that none who have faced me have lived to speak it."

This was mostly all true. Eighty percent, let's say.

"Yet you would not kill me."

"I would not. I would ask you to leave this place and not return."

"Why would you do this?"

"For the very reasons we have already discussed. If none live to hear my name, I must undergo this speech on each occasion, and it is tiresome. I no longer wish to rid the world of the great and fearsome beasts, for there are so few of you remaining. You must recognize this yourself. Do you know of another Gren?"

"My mother, but she is not Gren."

"She is the same as Gren, though, as I am both a thane and a man."

"Yes."

"Do you know of any other?"

"No."

"That is because so many have been slain."

"By you?"

"Or men acting for me."

"Then tell me my weakness."

"But why would I do that, Gren the Gren?"

"So I can tell you if you are correct or not."

"This is a mistake on your part, Gren, for you do not believe you have any weakness, and so no matter what I say next, you would laugh and insist I am incorrect, and then we would fight and you would die."

"I should know my own weakness!" he shouted. It sent a wave of bad breath in my direction to accompany the body odor that was still making my eyes tear.

"But knowing will not make it any different," I said.

He looked lost.

"You say you can kill me but offer no proof," he said. "You ask that I leave here and never return on your word that you know how to slay me elsewise. How do you expect me to accept this?"

"You are much shrewder than any I have met, Gren," I lied. "None have taken my word before, and so none have lived."

Gren roared in frustration. Aescher, halfway across the room and standing only thanks to a stubborn refusal to accept that he had broken ribs, appeared ready to attack. I knew of two other men in my sightlines with the same idea, and no doubt Unfer was eyeing my sword and thinking the same thing.

"If I leave, and never return, how am I to know these men will not come find me?"

"They want only for you to leave. If you never return we will swear to all that you have *been* slain and none who are not in this hall will look for you."

"I am safe here, why would I leave?"

"But why did you come at all?"

"I heard..." he began, before the words got caught in his throat, and I realized Gren was on the verge of tears.

It was only at this point I realized something that should have occurred sooner: Gren was not an adult troll.

It was difficult to get the full measure of his physical dimensions inside the mead hall, but it was clear he could stand upright near the corner, which would have been difficult for an adult troll insofar as the roof was sloped. He mentioned his mother, too, which should perhaps have been a hint.

"You heard carousing," I said. "And you came to see."

"Gren was attacked by the small monsters. They still attack me, Beuvulth the thane. I am safer here."

"And I tell you, Gren, you cannot stay. Were I not now to kill you, there would still be more men coming, and one day you would fall. If you wish to live, you will have to do so in whatever cavern or forest you call home, or not at all."

He thought about it, while I held my breath and hoped nobody screwed this up by launching a knife at him or something.

"In truth, Beuvulth the thane, I tire of eating your dead each night. I much prefer goat and night-bird. If you secure my passage to the trees, I will permit you to not kill me."

"I will lead you out myself, Gren of Gren." I bent down and retrieved my sword. "And any who would interfere with your exit will have to do battle with me first."

~

*N*obody got in the way as I walked him out, nor did anyone attempt a rear assault, which was frankly a surprise.

As soon as he reached the outside, I wished him well and turned around to bar the exit. This turned out to be a wise decision.

"Stand aside, Beuvulth!" Unfer declared from halfway across the room. He was waving the end of his shattered sword around as if it was useful. "You've lured him out of the building; now we can finish him off!"

"I will not."

"You are a madman and a coward," Aescher declared. He was

close enough to try pushing me aside. I popped him in the broken ribs with the flat of my hand, which brought him to his knees. Another man tried to rush past us as I was felling Aescher, so I had to spin quickly and sweep his legs out. Then I had my back to the doors again, and everyone held off.

"Be reasonable, Beuvulth," Unfer said. "That creature killed a dozen men."

"I know, and he ate a good portion of them while he was here."

"He will continue to terrorize this countryside unless we stop him, and now is the time to do that!"

"If he terrorizes the land, it is your own fault for having nurtured his malice."

"How dare you…" gasped Aescher.

"Unfer, you called me here for my experience, and I can now tell you that your monster is a troll. Trolls are not malicious by their nature. It is only because men attack without thinking that you face this mess at all. If one man had thought to speak to Gren when he came for this banquet, you would have made a valuable ally, rather than a terrible foe."

"But, now that he has been made enemy, we would be foolish not to strike at him with numbers on our side, in the open."

"Then you were not listening, for that was a young troll. The adults are much larger. All the trouble this one gave, do you believe his mother would be less difficult an opponent? I can only imagine what she might do to this land once you've murdered her son."

"But you know their weakness," Unfer said, "and you can tell it to us. With that, we would have no fear of any in his family, should they even be real."

"The weakness I spoke of is that trolls are very stupid, and so, they fall prey to trickery. It was how I convinced him to leave without doing us any more harm. It will do you no good if you mean to speak to him with your sword instead of your voice.

Now, you asked my help to rid your mead hall of a monster, and this I have done."

Aescher stood, extremely slowly, because he really wasn't breathing well.

"What would you have us tell our king, when he asks how we freed his hall?"

"I don't care. You're Danes. Think up a good story and put it in one of your sagas."

CHAPTER 8

I stayed in the tree for another hour while the water drained off the hillside, and because I'm sort of comfortable in trees anyway. It's a good place to hang out if you're feeling overwhelmed, or at least it used to be back when the most common cause of workplace stress was large, ground-based predators. That was actually a brief window of time once large cats started to figure out how to climb trees, which is why I don't like cats but I do like trees.

Anyway. I associate the tops of trees with a certain amount of safety and peace, so I remained there and watched the world below reformulate itself.

The town that took up most of the lower island didn't return in that time. The water abated considerably, and buildings that had a second floor were showing up again, provided the buildings hadn't been ripped down from the force of the tsunami.

It seemed as if a lot of them were still there, but it was difficult to tell. I couldn't seem to successfully contrast the way it looked after the wave with the way it looked earlier in the day. I have the same problem whenever I stand in a spot I'm told *used to be* the location of such-and-such an important thing, mainly because I'm the only one who remembers what that important thing looked like, and it's nearly impossible to reconcile that with the modern world. This is basically how I experience all of Europe.

The difference here was that I had been looking at this landscape as recently as the day before, and yet when I saw roofs missing in the neat crisscross street grid, I couldn't remember what kind of roofs were missing or what they sat on top of.

The water was still at least six feet deep, which was perhaps ten or fifteen feet higher than it should have been, given the lower island was effectively at sea level. I wondered how much more it would come down, or if it would at all. Maybe this was the new normal for the place. That would be a problem when it came time to land a plane, since there wasn't any flat land anywhere else.

It also remained alarmingly quiet, which was really disturbing. I've been through quite a few earthquakes, and there's always a moment of stunned silence when the ground stops shaking that's nearly as memorable as the quake itself, but that moment doesn't last all that long, and certainly not as long as this one was lasting. Even if I was too far from the town to hear people moving around and calling out for help, the forest should have been awake by now, and it wasn't. It was silent, and perhaps as shocked by recent events as I felt.

All except for the banshees. They wouldn't shut up.

I didn't see anyone moving around down-island either. Yet there clearly had to be someone. The top floor of the hotel was still standing, and even if the water hit that floor—and the wave would have impacted the building at an angle and not head-on—the structure was solid enough to deflect the force. On top of that, there were a lot of beings living down there that were more durable than humans. Granted some of them—Paul the satyr, for instance, or Lenny the demon—bore a genetic hatred of water that likely resulted in them drowning, but the rest...

They couldn't *all* be dead. I mean, that would be awful.

I lowered my still-bare feet onto the damp, squishy ground, and tried to imagine how much the briny ocean water was going to harm the plant life. This was perhaps an ecological question that could wait, but the mind goes in interesting places in times like this. When France fell to revolution, my first concern was whether I could still get my hands on a good brioche.

The walk to the house was a lot longer than I expected. It felt like at least a mile, but that might have been the shock, and the general difficulty the terrain offered. It wasn't that I was bare-foot; it was the detritus. I know better than most that the ocean has a whole bunch of weird things living in it, and it looked like a lot of those weird things decided to take a ride with the wave. Now they'd found themselves in entirely the wrong place. Many were flapping about madly, gasping and dying and not at all clear exactly how far they were from the nearest collection of water. I couldn't really help them, but I did my best not to step on them.

I was beginning to wonder what it meant that I could hear the banshee cries now, where before I had to climb up to the top of the island. I wondered if they were connected to the wave, and if so, how. And, I wondered if they represented a real danger, and not just a curiosity.

~

I didn't want to admit it, but I was in kind of a lot of trouble.

There are certain things I learned how to do over the various millennia of my existence in order to ensure continued survival. One of those things was to always have a back door, and by that I mean I did what I could to make sure full retreat was an option. Basically, if for any reason a situation gets dangerous, I want to know I can drop everything, abandon whatever I was calling myself in whichever civilization I had ingratiated myself to, and disappear.

This meant avoiding situations where I was cornered. No deserts, no cities on mesas, no mountaintops… and no islands.

I broke the island rule many times in the past hundred or so years, for a couple of reasons. One, they didn't represent the kind of isolation they used to, in the modern world. I *owned* an island for a short time, and I was okay with that because I was alone on it—except for a pixie, a girlfriend, and the occasional guest—so there was no civilization to worry about, and because I was in regular electronic communication with the mainland, which was only a short helicopter ride away. Likewise, I'd vacationed on an island a couple of times.

But this was my mistake: if Hawaii's volcano wakes up or a huge wave takes out part of Indonesia, people know about it. That's the joy of modern communication.

I couldn't rely on that here, because I was living on a secret island.

I didn't know who knew we were here, or if word got out that we were in trouble. Provided an alarm was raised onshore some-where, I didn't know who would come, or when. So far as I could tell, all the people who did know these things were dead or missing.

Basically, I was stranded on an island with no way of telling anybody I was stranded on an island. I didn't know the island well enough to identify a source of food aside from the fish dying in the sun, and I couldn't locate the nearest available fresh water other than the tank under my house. Unlike just about any conti-nent, then, if left to my own devices indefinitely, I couldn't survive here alone.

Oh, and I was doing my best to not think about it, but my girlfriend was missing, and I was worried she might be dead.

J was a tiny bit surprised the house still standing. The force of impact from the wave had to be considerable —albeit less than what hit the lower island, surely—but the building still looked structurally sound. I remember reading one time that the thing to do when a tornado was heading your way was to break the windows in the house to keep the wind from taking the house away. I was always dubious of this advice, but maybe there was something to it. Maybe the wave spared our house because we had no walls.

Unfortunately, as might also be the case in some hypothetical tornado scenario, the contents of the home didn't do so well.

Portions of the place were semi-waterproofed, especially along the edge. We obviously got rain, and living on a cliff meant getting wind with that rain, so a combination of fine mist and actual raindrops generally made it five to ten feet inside. Everything kept in that area had to cope well with water.

We planned for that. We didn't plan for the ocean jumping up and attacking. Not that there was a real way to plan for that sort of thing.

The televisions were destroyed. That was the first thing I noticed, which can be put in the pile of *the weird things that come to mind* along with brioche and soil quality.

A quick look at our upright closet—which was now neither upright nor, strictly speaking, a closet—confirmed that the clothes I'd fled in were pretty much the ones I was stuck with. That included footwear, which—again—I didn't mind much, except I'd rather have shoes on when accidentally stepping on a jellyfish, or whatever other oceanic goo might be waiting in the hillside.

I found an unshattered drinking glass sitting in a cupboard that used to be in the kitchen, and was now lying on our mattress. The mattress wasn't on the bed, but it was still in the approximate correct place for our bedroom. The bed itself was missing entirely. I sort of wished I had video footage of the wave strike, just to see what sequence of events could have resulted in the heavy bed being carried off while the foam mattress stayed in place.

I took the drinking glass to the kitchen and turned on the tap. What came out was fresh water, so I drank some of it, and then considered whether it made more sense to stay here and wait, or find a canteen or a loose bottle, and leave. That would mean knowing where I was going next, and I didn't, but it was good to know I could. Then the water in the pipe ran out and got replaced by what was in the tank.

The ocean had compromised the supply. I would have to find fresh water elsewhere. That probably meant leaving the house.

There was also a question of food. The refrigerator was nowhere to be seen, but our freezer was still there. It had frozen meat in it. I was in the middle of considering what, exactly, I could do with a twenty-pound side of frozen beef, and whether it made more sense to leave it where it was and come back later, when I heard movement.

"Mirella?" I asked.

Someone was around the corner, behind the opaque center column that supported the roof and hid the bathroom, near the now entirely hypothetical front door. Whoever it was, they breathed, walked on two legs, and didn't answer to Mirella's name. I started to consider whether or not to look for a weapon —perhaps this was where a slab of frozen meat would be useful— when I got a response.

"No, not Mirella. I'm sorry."

It was a woman's voice. I didn't recognize it.

"Why are you sorry?"

She stepped out from the corner: brunette, tall, incredibly fit, in shorts and a halter top and hiking boots. She was dirty, and her hair was a tousled mess, and she looked utterly fantastic.

She was a succubus. They fall out of bed in the morning looking ready for a photo shoot.

"I'm sorry, because I'm not her. I imagine she's… with the wave, I mean, she may be…"

"Oh, no, I'm sure she's fine."

I was not at all sure Mirella was fine. I was on the cusp of panicking that she might be entirely the opposite of that. It was sort of annoying, because one of the great things about Mirella was that she was one of the most capable people I'd ever met. If there was rescuing to be done, it was typically her rescuing me and not the other way around. This was perhaps part of what I found so appealing.

She would turn up eventually. I was sure of it. All I had to do was convince the knot in my stomach it was true, and it would be.

"All right," my guest said. She had an accent. It was gentle, but enough to give her a kind of *sexy Russian spy* flavor that she undoubtedly worked to an advantage.

"*Are you Croat?*" I asked, in Croatian. I hadn't spoken it in many years, but I was fluent enough.

She looked surprised.

"I am," she said, in English, "But I prefer this language. My name is Gordana."

"What can I do for you, Gordana?"

"I thought… we're here to collect you. I thought you would… no, never mind."

"He doesn't know anything, you cow," said someone from behind me.

I didn't know he was there. I should have, because I'm not supposed to be all that easy to surprise, but I was staring at Gordana and became distracted. This is what happens when you're around a succubus, and it will happen regardless of whether you're in a committed relationship or not. Mirella could be standing right next to me, and it would still happen.

In the same vein, the man who had come up behind me would have—had Mirella been there—commanded *her* full attention, because that's how thing work with an incubus. This one was blond, muscular but not obnoxiously so, tan, with blue eyes and perfect cheekbones. If someone were doing a photo spread for a line of clothing targeting sallow urban Europeans who wanted to dress like they were rugged outdoorsmen, he'd be the man for the job.

He was standing on the other side of where our kitchen would be, next to the cooking range. The range—thankfully electric and not gas, as otherwise we'd be looking at a real risk of an explosion—had been relocated to the outside of the building, some five feet beyond the edge of the ground-floor platform.

"An incubus and a succubus in the same place and nobody's trying to kill anybody," I said. "This must be the end of the world."

Nobody laughed, and Gordana's expression was such that I became concerned that it actually *was* the end of the world.

"Listen," the incubus said, "all you have to know is that we have food and water, and a place up in the hills that didn't get hit by the wave. We are here to bring you there."

"This is my brother, Bruno," Gordana said with a little acid in her voice.

"Well, Bruno," I said, "I appreciate the offer, but no thanks, I have a girlfriend to locate and I'm afraid that will be taking up all of my time."

"You will need food," he said, "and you will need water."

"I heard you the first time. I'll pass anyway."

When it comes to matters not explicitly sexual, incubi can come off as real assholes. Actually, I think they come off as assholes all the time, but that's me.

"You see, this is why you shouldn't handle these things," he said to his 'sister'. They weren't related, aside from being of the same species. This was obvious from looking at them. Not that actual siblings would have hated one another any more or less. "Now he's suspicious."

"You realize I can still hear you?" I said. "To be honest, I would have been 50/50 on it if she asked, but you're not filling me with a lot of confidence."

"Of course you would have. You're a man. It's how they get what they want. That's why she sent her."

"Yet she also sent you, and you are intolerable," Gordana said.

"I'm here because we are both meant to be here. Don't question these things, cow."

"All right, number one, stop calling her that," I said. "Number two, who is this person that sent you? Do I know her?"

Bruno just shook his head.

"This is complicated, Adam," he said. "It would be better if we left here first and worked out the why, and who, and how, some other time."

Bruno was dressed in khakis and hiking boots, with a loose sleeveless T-shirt, and a knapsack on his back. He had a handgun tucked into his belt. It was hidden by his shirt, until he lifted it to reveal the butt. This was how he planned on convincing me to go with them.

Oddly, knowing incubi tended to be assholes meant I was more tolerant of this particular approach.

"Oh, for goodness sake," I said. "Put that in the bag, that's about the dumbest place to carry it, and if you actually tried to use it on me I would just take it from you. Seduction isn't going to work and neither are threats. Right now, I need to head downhill and see if I can figure out whether Mirella survived the morning, and maybe see who else made it. I'm not going to go uphill and away from her based on the say-so of two people I just met. Not without a little more. Why don't you guys start at the beginning?"

"The beginning?" Gordana asked.

"From when you trashed the hotel room."

They shared a look, but that was all. The silence was answer enough.

"That *was* you guys, right? Some of the message was written in incubus blood, I assume that was yours."

"We ran out of the other kind," Bruno said. "Had to improvise."

"Adam," Gordana said, "that is your name, yes? We have this correct?"

"You can call me Adam, sure."

"Adam, Bruno is right. There's a tremendous amount of information you do not have, but we aren't the people who should be providing it. We can bring you to the one who you should speak to, but you need to trust us to go at least that far in our company. We have a long way to travel, and the hillside is going to be much more dangerous when the sun goes down."

"Why is that? I've lived here a little while, the woods seem pretty safe."

"That was before," Bruno said. "This is after."

"Please," Gordana said.

"Tell me why the hillside is going to be more dangerous when the sun goes down."

Bruno looked at me like this was the dumbest question ever.

"You've heard them," he said. "You can hear them now."

"The banshees."

"If that is what you would call them, then yes."

"What do *you* call them?"

"We have no name for them, but we know to fear them."

"How do you know?"

"We were told," Gordana said.

"It's like you guys are trying extra hard to be as vague as possible, and it's starting to piss me off."

"Everyone downhill is dead," Bruno said. "If your woman was down there, she's dead as well. And so will you be, if you go that way."

"If you want to live, you need to climb," Gordana said, in case Bruno wasn't being clear enough.

"Were you told this as well?" I asked.

"Yes," she said. "And we really can't tell you by whom, but you must appreciate the truth behind what we say, literally or not. Even if people endure downhill there is no food and no water, and the sun is hot and unkind. You are a survivor, Adam. If what we understand of you is true, this is your singular quality."

She was right, which was a tiny bit aggravating. My own instinct was to head for the shelter of the trees. It's what Mirella would do too, and if she was alive that was where I'd probably find her. Going down meant I was looking for a body, and I didn't want to do that.

It was also a tiny bit aggravating that my erstwhile saviors were behaving as if they'd booked this meeting, months in advance, like it was on my calendar. If I had a calendar. That was a little weird.

"Yeah, all right," I said. "I can't stay here and I shouldn't go down, so I guess up makes sense right now. Doesn't mean I won't ditch both of you if the need arises."

I walked over to Bruno, who was closer, and extended my hand.

"Partners," I said.

"Yes."

He reached for my hand.

There's a pressure point on the wrist. Grab it right, it feels like the wrist is getting snapped in half. I grabbed it right.

"Owwww!" Bruno exclaimed, as I took the gun away from him. I let go of the wrist, and he fell to one knee. Gordana, who was only a few paces behind us, froze where she was, which was wise as I had just armed myself.

"Some advice," I said. "Threatening to kill me if I don't come with you is stupid when it's obvious killing me isn't an actual option. Also, don't show off a gun if you don't know how to handle yourself."

"I know how to handle myself," Bruno spat. He stayed down though, his eyes to the ground, possibly anticipating a bullet to the brain. People who are expecting to get shot tend to duck their heads and tighten their shoulders. It's some strange kind of instinct.

"I would rather you not do that," Gordana said.

I laughed. "That was impassioned."

She shrugged.

"He knows the way back better than I do," she said. "We might get lost."

I flipped the gun around and handed it back to Bruno. He took it, slowly, and got to his feet even more slowly.

"I would appreciate it if you stowed this somewhere," I said. "If you're right that nightfall brings danger, it might be useful. For me, not you. I know how to use it."

"I know how to use it!"

He was of a fairer complexion than Gordana, so when he got angry, he reddened a lot more than he probably realized. He was beet-red.

"I'm not going to test you. Just put it away. If you're worried it's going to go off in your bag, I wouldn't. The safety's on."

He glanced at the side of the gun to verify this, which said plenty: he looked in the wrong place for it.

~

*T*he first step to really understanding just about any species is figuring out how the perpetuation of that species is carried out. For instance, imps are gifted storytellers, they're all male, and they reproduce with human women. Satyrs, who also only reproduce with human women, are incredibly charmless. So, imps tend to strike off on their own, convince a woman to mate with them, and start a family that is largely isolated from the lives of other imps. Satyrs are socially close-knit, in closed communities where daughters are raised with certain cultural expectations.

This tells me a whole lot about imps and satyrs, their children and half-children (a half-satyr is sometimes—not every time—a werewolf) and so on, and that makes it easier to deal with them. In contrast, I know very little about demon families, and I know nothing about how pixies reproduce. I can tame a pixie, and I know how to kill a demon, but I don't *understand* them.

When it comes to why incubi and succubi don't get along, reproduction is the answer to everything.

They have a lot more in common than not. I mean, aside from being different genders in the same species. They both treat sexual intercourse like commerce, and treat being adored like a flower treats sunlight. (Adoration is more important. They derive much more pleasure from being wanted than from being bedded.) Their conquests—the heterosexual ones—are human rather than other members of their kind. They have the same approximate lifespan of somewhere close to eighty or a hundred years, and they look twenty-five for most of that life. And, they despise each other equally.

The key difference is fascinating: succubi are infertile. Incubi are not. The only reason the species still exists is because there are incubi out there knocking up human women.

This would seem to be an unreasonable sort of burden on the average incubus, but fortunately they handle it about as poorly as possible, so we're all spared from having to feel badly for them.

An incubus won't do what, say, an imp or a satyr would be expected to do, which is to go out, meet a girl, marry her, and father her children. The incubus was not put on this world to perpetuate monogamy and the nuclear family. What they'll do instead is woo a girl, get her pregnant, and disappear.

What responsibility the incubus does feel for his children is best reflected in his choice of mates. They tend to gravitate toward financially well-to-do women with either rich families or rich husbands. It increases the likelihood their bastards will be taken care of, even if it's by a cuckolded and resentful human man.

Of course—and this is the really interesting part—the abandoned bastard child usually grows up resenting and/or actively hating the incubus father for having abandoned them in the first place. It means an adult succubus despises all incubi and, interestingly, nearly all adult incubi loathe both other incubi and themselves.

When functioning properly, this is a reproductive dynamic in which daddy issues is an expected outcome. If people knew incubi and succubi were real, there would probably be an entire branch of psychotherapy devoted to them.

~

There was a walking path that terminated on the uphill side of our house. I was very familiar with it, as Mirella and I went on the occasional short-distance hike around the area, and the path was where we began. I say *short-distance* because we were never more than two hours from the home. I don't know if that is everyone's definition of short or not, but to me a long-distance hike would be one that required overnight plans and a way to catch dinner.

We started there. Bruno led the way, I followed and Gordana took the rear. This was not an ideal arrangement as I spent most of my time staring at Bruno's backside, which really did nothing for me. (It was an impressive backside nonetheless.) It did mean if I wanted a conversation with the considerably less detestable Gordana, I could just slow down and talk over my shoulder, so it wasn't too terrible.

"How far did you say we had to go?" I asked her, in a moment when Bruno was out of view around a corner I knew was coming. The path went in a winding uphill direction for a time before leveling off and circling around a large tree and meeting up with itself again. It was at that point I'd have to pay attention to where he was going, because continuing on the path would just loop us back to the house.

"It's a long way," she said. "I couldn't say exactly how long."

"But more than a day?"

"Possibly. We've planned for it."

"Okay. So how'd you guys know the wave was coming?"

"We didn't."

"Aw, come on. The tsunami hit a few hours ago and you came from more than a day away. How'd you know?"

Bruno was in view again, having slowed on the other side of the turn. He caught some of what we were talking about.

"You'll have your explanation when we get there, Adam," he said. "Just keep moving."

"I can walk and talk at the same time," I said. "And how do you guys even know my name?"

"Enough with the questions. The talking will attract attention. We don't want attention."

The banshee cries remained consistent yet far away, but I couldn't argue with the suggestion that whatever was making the noise was something I didn't feel like meeting, or not yet. I would prefer to be better armed first, and in the company of more dangerous individuals.

I wasn't feeling great about getting too far from the house. I couldn't tell exactly where a day's travel through the island's jungle would even get me, geographically, because I wasn't sure how easy the trip was or what kind of hiking skills to expect from my escorts. It was still a day of travel that could be taking me further from wherever Mirella was. That is unless the person who sent these two also sent someone for her. I felt like that was something someone would have told me already, though.

It was a little over an hour to the flat area and the circumnavigated tree. On the far end of the loop, Bruno hesitated, studied a couple of the trees in some detail, and then pushed aside a handful of low branches and motioned us to join him. He was sticking to a route that was what I would call unmarked, and to most people nonexistent. I could see the signs that at least two sets of bipeds had traveled this way recently, though. Those bipeds, I assumed, were the same ones now escorting me.

Tracking people and animals in the woods was something I was reasonably good at, having spent a whole lot of my life as a hunter. I could see paths that weren't really paths—as distinct from the heavily traveled one we'd just gotten off of. What I was seeing, though, was not the same thing Bruno was seeing. His approach involved markings on the lower part of some of the trees. They were subtle enough to be missed if you weren't looking for them.

Assuming the rest of the trail was marked the same approximate way, I could probably go it alone if I had to. I didn't have to, but if we lost Bruno to some catastrophe, it wouldn't be the worst thing ever.

On that point, he would probably not agree.

We were off the path for about twenty minutes when we heard the trill of one of the banshees that was close enough to cause Bruno to drop to a crouch and freeze. He shot a look back at us, the clear implication being we had better do the same. So we did.

"Have you seen one?" I whispered, to Gordana.

She shook her head no. She looked frightened. My first instinct was to hug her and protect her. Because: succubus.

"How do you know to be afraid?"

I asked this even though the sound was a little terrifying, and that fear didn't necessarily require detailed explanation.

"We were warned," she whispered.

"By the same person who told you about the wave?"

"Shh!" Bruno hissed.

Something approximately man-sized was moving through the forest to our left and uphill. It was wreaking havoc with all my natural impulses, because it sounded like it was about the same height as a human, but it *felt* like something heavier.

It passed soon enough. We stayed where we were for a few minutes anyway. Then Bruno stood up, looked around, and waved for us to continue. I picked up the pace until I was close enough to him to whisper properly.

"You don't know what it is," I said.

"No."

"But you know enough to be afraid of it."

"I saw your face, Adam. You knew enough to fear it knowing even less than we do."

"Fair point. But you have nothing else?"

"What do you mean?"

"I mean you seem to know more than you should about things that only just happened. I'm asking if that knowledge extends to a detail or two about whatever we just encountered. Anything, even if it doesn't seem important."

"Only to avoid them."

I wasn't a hundred percent sure I believed him.

~

*S*undown arrived before we reached wherever we were going. Exactly where that was would have necessitated —at minimum—an understanding of where we currently were, and I had no idea at all. We'd crossed two of the roads which ran up the hill, but the roads on the island were an illogical series of loops and whorls, so there was no way to use them to figure out where we were heading, other than *up*.

The roads were as they were because they had to reach the various private estates dotting the hillside, and given we'd been hiking a relatively straight path, I was certain that if we hadn't crossed into private property already, we were going to be soon. Some of that property was guarded by people with guns. I wondered if my new friends were aware of this.

Nightfall also brought cooler temperatures, and I was still dressed in shorts, a t-shirt and no shoes, and everything had a lingering dampness from when the ocean knocked on my back door. I can't get sick, but I'm pretty sure I can freeze to death.

All right, it wasn't *that* cold. We were still in the tropics and everything, and I wasn't about to lose a limb to frostbite. It was enough, though, to make for an uncomfortable evening, so I was grateful when a sweatshirt my size came out of Gordana's bag.

"Nothing for you?" I asked, as she was still scantily clad. Her skin was shiny from sweat, and she looked like she was ready for a photographer.

"We don't suffer from temperature changes as much as… as humans."

"Oh. Yes, I guess you don't."

I'd really never thought about it, but succubi and incubi did spend a lot of time wearing very little clothing, so it made sense.

"Not that you are human," Bruno said. "I mean, you aren't really."

"Sure I am."

He smiled like we were both in on a joke of some kind, except he was the only one, so his expression turned to bewilderment.

"With your… lifespan, I mean to say."

As he spoke, he started pulling things out of his knapsack: a blanket for the ground, a single waterproof sleeping bag, a handful of protein bars, and a tin box big enough to hold a pack of cigarettes. Bottled water had been emerging from Gordana's bag for most of the day already, and now three more bottles came out. They were prepared for exactly one night in the woods. And possibly a smoke or two.

"I know what you mean," I said. "You're wrong, but I know what you mean. I'm as human as the next person."

"Of course," he said. "And so am I."

I didn't feel like debating him on the finer points of my humanity, because I didn't actively care about what he thought either way. As long as he never decided I was bulletproof or bite resistant or something, it wouldn't matter.

Our campsite was in a small cavity on the hillside. It was created by a combination of soil erosion and a dense root system, and was more or less the ideal place to set a certain kind of trap if I had a good knife, a few vines, a small collection of leaves, and an inclination to trap something. It wasn't the sort of place one stumbled upon by accident, either. I was pretty sure they scouted it ahead of time.

"I'll be honest, when I was promised food, water and shelter, this wasn't really what I pictured."

"It's just for tonight," Gordana said. "We can only carry so much between us."

"We'll be safe here, though?" I asked.

"Yes."

"I'll keep watch," Bruno said. "While she keeps you warm."

"I see. I did mention the girlfriend, didn't I?"

"We can literally keep one another warm," Gordana said. "Without euphemism."

"All right, I guess that's okay. But when we meet up with Mirella, you can be the one to explain this arrangement. If she kills you first, I may have enough time to get away."

Sleep was a long way off, though, so in the dwindling light we sat in a huddle on the ground covering, chewing our protein bars and drinking our water.

I'm not in favor of whatever current food trend resulted in the creation and dissemination of protein bars. I appreciate their convenience, but that's about all. I mean, up until very recently, new gastronomic inventions resulted in things that tasted better, not worse. Raw meat to cooked meat? Fantastic. Rotten meat to salted meat? I'm all aboard for the invention of bacon. New spices and ways to cook things, preservative concepts like pickling, these are all great ideas. And of course there's the best idea ever: fermented drink for when there isn't enough potable water.

But then came protein bars, part of a larger movement toward blander food, and I think we're just going in the wrong direction here.

I admit I'm spoiled. People just want to be healthier, and that's great, but I'm an immortal man who doesn't get any fatter; I could eat sticks of butter all day if I wanted and be totally fine. (Okay, I'd be on the toilet for the second half of that day, but you get my point.) Besides, we used to have protein bars, and they were delicious. We called it beef jerky.

Anyway.

We ate in silence. I wondered, again, where Mirella ended up and if everyone we knew from the lower island was dead. I also wondered if a warning went out. Nearby islands got tsunami warnings after regional earthquakes, and while I never actually considered the question before the wave came, I just sort of assumed we would get the same warning. But maybe not. Maybe this was another one of the drawbacks of living on a secret island.

There was also the question of whether a warning would have mattered. The lower island wasn't really built to anticipate a disaster of this magnitude, but saying that implies there is a way *to* prepare for such a thing.

On a smaller scale, sure. Gordana and Bruno appeared to have been the recipients of advance notice, and to have benefited from it in the form of being alive and unmolested by salt water. I hadn't devoted a lot of time to understanding how that could be.

Generally speaking, catastrophically large tidal waves weren't deliberate creations, so they probably weren't in on it. (I know: obviously. But if someone says *a bank is going to be robbed next week* and then it happens, the first question is always going to be, was the person who predicted it in on the robbery in the first place?)

I began to wonder if they knew all the way back before they trashed the hotel room with cryptic messages in dead languages, and if the oncoming wave was the reason they fled for the hillside. The timeline made sense.

It didn't explain why they came to the island in the first place, though. Assuming they stowed away or employed some other secretive means to get to the island, the question had to be, why did they go through all that trouble to put themselves *into* danger?

That led back to the question of whose advice they were really following, and why, and what the deal was with the indecipherable stanza in dragon's blood. What would be the point of a message they knew perfectly well nobody could read?

It hit me then, and I laughed out loud before I could help myself.

"What are you finding funny?" Bruno asked. His expression was one of somebody who felt more or less the same about protein bars as I did.

"You guys," I said. "You don't know what the message you wrote on the wall meant, do you?"

They looked at each other.

"Do *you*?" Gordana asked.

"No! But that wasn't the point, was it? You didn't put it there to be read. It was there because you knew who would show up to try and read it."

"We didn't compose the message," Bruno said.

"You were there when it was written."

"Yes. As you know, some of the blood was mine."

"It was put there by the person you're bringing me to see. That person didn't tell you what the message meant either, did they?"

"No."

"We asked," Gordana said. "But she only rarely answers."

"She didn't know what it meant either," I said. "That's why she didn't answer."

"All right," Bruno said. "And how do you know that, immortal man?"

"I know that because I just realized who you're bringing me to see. You're working with a prophet. And we're all in a lot of trouble."

CHAPTER 9

*P*rophets can see the future.

Look, I know I've said a bunch of times that there's no such thing as magic, and I stand by that statement completely, because in all my time on Earth I have yet to see something that didn't end up getting explained eventually. Certainly, a lot of those explanations came many generations after the original observation, which is why people stick with the *magic* explanation, but that doesn't make it accurate.

Also, some people's minds just work differently. I've seen this often enough to appreciate it as an actual thing that seems fundamentally true, on a... well on a wiring level, if I can use a modern corollary. Some of us are just predisposed to seeing mundane things in a way that confirms the existence of the supernatural from their specific perspective.

I'm very much tied to logic and observation, and have been since before those were concepts. As much as I respect the magic-as-reality viewpoint, I think it's fair to say one of the reasons I'm still alive is because my brain doesn't work that way.

Despite everything I just said, it's also the case that there are some people in the world who get glimpses of the future. Please know that this is hard-fought knowledge I resisted for an extremely long time, as I have incredibly high standards of proof for a modern caveman.

The most common kind of future-seer is the oracle. These are women—they're always women, don't ask me why because I don't know—who under certain altered states can glimpse, quite briefly, the future of a person. There are all sorts of rules about this: the oracle has to be stoned enough to enter the correct mindset; the person has to be ready with a specific question; the prophecy, once delivered, can't be clarified and is wide open to interpretation.

Oracular declarations are always incredibly vague, and suffer from a deserved reputation of being badly misunderstood until too late. The famous Delphic oracle story is of the king who was told that taking his army across a river to engage another army would result in "a great kingdom falling". He mistakenly assumed the kingdom in question was his opponent's. It wasn't; crossing the river was a huge tactical error, and the outcome was his own kingdom's fall.

Anyway, oracles are rare, but there are still a few around. The ability appears to pass down through generations, but a lot of the ones out there don't even know what they are.

Prophets are a little different, and a lot more dangerous. They don't have to alter their mental state to get a glimpse of the future, because for whatever reason they see it *all the time*. That future isn't specific to an individual, either; it's the whole, big picture. As with the oracle's pronouncements, a prophet doesn't always understand what he or she is seeing and can't make it any clearer to themselves or anyone else. But some of them do understand, or claim to. They're the really dangerous ones.

Prophets deliver an almost-constant stream of scattershot declarations about oncoming events. It makes them really difficult to be around. They are also, almost without exception, batshit crazy. Mercifully—for them—prophets also tend to die young.

There's a third kind of future-seer, but they're the rarest of the them all. Some select few people can see about five seconds into the future. Like the prophet's future-sight, it's something they can't turn off, but since it's only a rolling five seconds—and it's only the events happening in their own future—they can learn to cope well enough to appear outwardly normal under most circumstances.

This ability makes them perhaps the best warriors on the planet. I've only encountered one such person face-to-face, but I've kept tabs on his descendants, and at least one or two have the same skill.

Outside of this family, I've never seen it. It's so rare, in fact, nobody has even come up with a name for this type of person. I just call them Corrigans, after the surname of the one I met.

~

"We don't know what she is," Gordana said quietly, ignoring Bruno's disapproving stare. "We only know she's kept us safe this far."

"It's not something we talk about," he said.

"She brought you to an island that was hit by a tsunami fifteen hours ago and you've been living in the wilderness for two weeks, hiding from the local police and whatever the hell is making that noise. Seems like she's put you into a lot more harm than not."

"That's only because you don't know anything about us," Bruno said. "I can't speak for this one, but my life was worse before."

"Why do you say we're all in trouble?" Gordana asked. "Trouble *because* of her, you meant."

"That's exactly what I meant."

There are two things that happen a lot around prophets. First, they tend to either attach themselves to religions or create new ones from scratch. (This happens a lot, although generally the person identified by history as the prophet is usually actually the scribe. The Bible is full of mistakes like this.) Modern iterations end up being called cults, but they're basically the same thing.

Second, prophets leave a trail of bodies.

This isn't done with any real intent. The problem with prophecy is that the future is inherently amoral, and will happen a certain way without regard for the preservation of life. People following the word of a prophet expecting to find themselves in a better world may not know their death is part of the trade-off for that hypothetical better world. And generally, the prophet doesn't know it either. All they know is, if they tell scion number one to go somewhere and do something, this other thing—presumably a desirable thing—will happen. Scion number one may have to die for it to pan out, though.

I do everything I can to stay away from prophets. I mean, I know the future is what it is and all that, but the *free will vs. fate* thing is an argument I've been having for probably thirty thousand years and I find it unbelievably tiresome.

"I don't trust them," I said. I could have told her all of the rest, but it wouldn't have done any good. People don't like being told they're in a cult, for starters. "You shouldn't either."

"She told us to find you," Bruno said. "If we hadn't come along, what would you have done?"

"I would have gotten by," I said. "I've lived alone for centuries before now."

"I don't think you understand, Adam," Gordana said. "We didn't come to the house to save you. We came to the *island* to save you."

This was a surprise.

"A warning about the giant wave would have been awesome,"

I said. "I think a lot of other people could have benefitted from that too."

"Specifics were unknown until today," Bruno said. "If you are familiar with… with prophets, you would know this."

He said the word *prophet* like it was the first time he'd considered applying this word to the woman on the other side of the predictions. Maybe it was.

"I do," I said. "I imagine whatever she was saying about today didn't make sense until this morning."

"She called it the decimation," Gordana said. "We didn't know what it meant."

"How many of you are there?"

"More than the two of us and her," Gordana said. "Beyond that I shouldn't say."

"She couldn't send more people to deal with those things in the woods? I mean, a decent-sized escort would have been good."

If these were the most combat-ready people in this little cult, I didn't have any confidence we were heading someplace safer than where we were at that moment. If Mirella were with me I wouldn't have to worry about these things.

Gordana looked like she was ready to answer, but she was stopped.

"No, enough questions," Bruno said. "We will all be there tomorrow, and you can see for yourself, and ask what you please, and perform your own head-count if that is something which interests you."

❧

I didn't get a lot of sleep. Under very nearly any other circumstance, my saying I shared a sleeping bag with a succubus would naturally lead to the statement *I didn't get a lot of sleep that night,* and no further explanation would be necessary. But that wasn't the reason.

It certainly *could* have been. Gordana wasn't like a lot of the succubi I'd met, in that she didn't seem to carry herself with the same sort of quiet confidence—equal parts intimidating and exciting—most had. It was like she'd turned off that part.

This had less of an effect on her appeal than one might have imagined. The biggest difference was that most of the time, when you're around a succubus, they make it so clear they're game, the only lingering questions are *when* and *where* and *for how long?* With Gordana, I felt welcome, but I also felt like I had to ask first.

I didn't ask. We huddled together under the light sleeping bag, for warmth and only that.

She wasn't what kept me up. What kept me up was the idea that there was a prophet, somewhere on the island, who saw far enough into the future to come all the way here specifically to save my life.

There was a lot to mull over. For starters, I'm not nearly that important. Sure, I've been around for a long time, but if I died overnight, the world would go on just fine, with maybe only a couple of people available for mourning. This is not to say I don't have a lot of friends, only that the vast, vast majority of them have died of old age. On top of that, a few years ago I severed my current real-world connections by staging my own death. The necessary people know I didn't actually die, but they also know I may as well have, because the whole point in staging your own death is not reconnecting with the people who knew you when you were alive. The point is, if I died on this island, there would be no way for any of them to know it.

Mirella would know, and would mourn my passing, but that only counted if she was still alive herself, something I was becoming more anxious about the longer I thought about it.

In my admittedly limited direct experience with prophecy, I've found predictions tend to revolve around large events, not small ones. Prophets don't bother to announce things like who is going to have a ham sandwich next week and which celebrity is getting pregnant soon. They deal in sinking continents, extinction-level events, and wars. Acts of God, if that's what you're into.

Coordinating a trip to this secret island for however many people were in this little cult, in order to set up a hidden camp in the hillside specifically to support *my* rescue could only have meant one thing: I was supposed to do something important in the future.

This was why I hated prophecy so very much. This important thing could be literally anything, including doing something *bad* which caused a great deal of terrible death and destruction. It could mean I was still going to die but in a different way, elsewhere, for different reasons.

The idea that I was meant to live in order to do a thing wasn't at all comforting, basically, especially given that this thing was significant enough to endanger the life of the prophet, Gordana and Bruno, and however many other people who were living in that camp in the hills. For all I knew it even had something to do with the tsunami itself, although I couldn't imagine that as a deliberate act. That seemed only possible if one subscribed to a certain degree of paranoia, along the lines of "the government can control the weather."

And look, sometimes—rarely, but sometimes—I do something legitimately important. Like save a lot of lives in a fire, or prevent an assassination. But this is almost always an accident of my happening to be someplace at some time. Half the time I don't even know what I've done for a generation or two. If that seems weird, consider how long my life has been and how many "oops, I just saved a baby who turned out to be Hitler" situations it's possible to end up in over that span of time. (I did not save baby Hitler, he's just the best current version of this point. A hundred years ago it would have been baby Napoleon, probably. Although you really can't go wrong with baby Genghis Khan in just about any year from 1200 onward.)

Most of the time, though, I keep my head down and go about my life without worrying about the certifiable Big Things going on in the world. I don't want the attention, and "big things" are never that big in the larger context of history.

Also bugging me was my apparent rescue from death. I couldn't tell if that was happening now—perhaps I would have starved to death or been mauled by one of those banshees if left alone—had already happened, or was going to happen later. Worth considering was that by the time the wave hit my life had already been altered by the prophet when the message was written on the wall. Possibly, without that message I'd have been on the lower island in the morning, rather than at home. It seemed like a stretch given the time of day the tsunami made landfall, but it couldn't be ignored out of hand.

Prophets screw up everything. They don't just make you re-examine the future, they make you re-examine the past. I have enough trouble with the present.

Anyway, I couldn't sleep. As a consequence, I was awake when the attack came.

Since we were lying in a depression on the side of the hill, all the sound coming from the uphill side was gone. This is a peculiar sensation, a little like losing the hearing in one ear temporarily. We could still pick up the noises of the forest on the downhill side, but that was about all. I couldn't hear or smell the ocean any more, which just added to the unfamiliarity of the situation, as if the sleeping bag and the strange companion weren't enough.

The keening of the banshees came through just fine though. They sounded every half hour, roughly, from different parts of the hillside. None close by, or so it seemed.

Bruno was on the top of the hill, at the lip of the depression, holding the gun he didn't know how to use.

I couldn't tell you what time it happened. After Midnight, based on the position of the moon, but beyond that I wasn't sure, because I stopped wearing watches when I moved to paradise. (I appreciate the importance of timekeeping to the world economy, but that doesn't mean I think the invention of hours, minutes and seconds was a good idea. I'm not fully sold on calendars either.)

There was a cry of surprise, and then a gunshot, and a scream, all from Bruno.

I rolled over and started to climb out of the sleeping bag. Gordana latched onto my arm.

"No," she whispered. "You must stay."

"He's in trouble."

"This was foretold."

I shook free of her grip.

"No kidding. Did anyone tell Bruno?"

Again: this is why I hate prophets.

I scrambled out of the concavity with the help of several conveniently-placed tree roots in time to hear a second gunshot and see… something.

Bruno was grappling with a squat, pale creature. It seemed as if it glowed, but that was only because its skin was so white. I was reminded immediately of the fae, because faeries were just about that pale. But faeries were also seven or eight feet tall, and this creature looked shorter than Bruno, who was in turn shorter than me.

I couldn't see a lot more than that, both because the canopy of trees blocked out a lot of the moonlight, and because I was at the top of the ridge and on my feet for only a couple of seconds before Gordana grabbed both of my ankles and pulled.

As you might imagine, I was upended rather effectively. I braced for the part where my upper body slammed against the edge of the hillside—my elbows took the brunt—and then down I went.

She was on top of me then, and not in a really cool sexy way. Well, okay, it sort of was, but this wasn't the time for any of that.

"You *must* stay here!" she said. Her legs were on both sides of my torso, and my arms were pinned up against them. She was squeezing her thighs to hold me still, which was actually pretty impressive.

"Ow," I said. There was something hard and lumpy on the forest floor located directly beneath my lower back, just slightly to the left of my tailbone. In hindsight, I was probably lucky I didn't have a broken back from that maneuver. "It's going to kill him. You know this."

"I know this, yes," she agreed. "It's preordained."

"Lots of things are preordained. That doesn't mean you're supposed to just let them happen. We have to help him."

"Shhh!"

She sat down on my crotch, her knees still forward and her thighs still pinning my arms. Then she folded her own arms over my chest, covered my mouth, and lowered her chest against mine. I couldn't move at all, not even to tell her how painful the root sticking into my back was—doubly so with her weight added—or to apologize for the part of my anatomy that thought we were doing something wholly different than what we were actually doing.

She was trying to hide us, and also shield me from whatever was up there.

I could hear it, shuffling along the edge of the concavity, right about where Bruno had been standing watch. Gordana heard it too. Her heaving chest against mine stopped heaving—she was holding her breath, not dying.

I held my breath as well, although in my case it was sort of mandatory, because I couldn't really breathe anyway.

After about thirty seconds, she sat up and we both took in all the air we could find.

"All right," she said. "It's done."

She released me, and I rolled over to make sure my legs were where I left them and still took orders.

"You were told to let him die," I said.

"I was told to keep you safe, here, regardless of what was happening above. And that you would resist. I didn't expect you to be so good at resisting."

In this, I was pretty sure we were talking about sex, not my interest in rescuing her annoying sort-of sibling.

"I told you I'm spoken for right now."

She smiled. "That has never been an issue before."

I got to my feet, slowly.

"An issue with you, or with me?" I asked.

"I don't know enough about you to know, Adam. I was speaking from my own experience."

"Well, don't take it personally," I said.

I scrambled back up to the top of the ridge. My back was sore, and so was my right knee, which appeared to have gotten twisted when I went down. Other than that, everything was in working order.

This was more than I could say for large portions of Bruno.

Both of his legs were broken, as was his collarbone. It looked like his chest had absorbed a great blow, and his arm—the right arm, which used to have a gun on the end of it—was horribly mangled. The gun was nowhere in sight.

I knelt down next to him, and heard Gordana come up behind us.

"What did this?" I asked her. "Did you see?"

"No. The important question is, did it see us, and I think that answer is also no."

Bruno gasped, which was a shock, since we were pretty sure he was extremely dead.

"Hey," I said, because what else was there to say? "Are you still with us?"

He was breathing, but it wasn't great breathing, not like what you'd anticipate from a healthy person. It sounded like he was only using one of his lungs, for starters.

"Is it gone?" he asked.

"Think so," I said. "Did you see what it was?"

"No. An eel. No. Foot loose. I can't feel mine. No."

"He's delirious," Gordana said.

"A little scrambled, yes," I agreed. "He must have taken a shot to the head."

"We have to leave him here."

I took a long look at her. I appreciated that succubi hated incubi, and I knew exactly why that was so, but this particular one had saved our lives.

"No, we certainly don't."

"Adam, look at him. He can't walk. He may be dead by sunrise."

I stood, and walked us out of Bruno's earshot.

"Look, I appreciate that you guys have been living off the grid for a couple of weeks. It's all very life-or-death commando stuff, and sure, okay, but this morning I woke up in an actual bed a couple of miles from a real twenty-first century town with a hospital and modern medicine, and I'm not ready to jump back into kill-or-be-killed right now. I can live off the land if I have to, but let's keep in mind that we don't *have* to. There are probably three estates within a mile of where we're standing, and I bet at least one of them has electricity and a damn first aid kit."

"This is not how it's supposed to happen."

"According to the prophet."

"Yes. He was to die in combat, and you and I are to continue to the camp alone."

"Look, you can't have it both ways. If his death was predicted and it didn't happen, that should tell you the future isn't nearly as preordained as you thought it was. Besides, I thought he was the only one who knew the way."

"I had to say that to make sure we got to this point. I know the way just fine. And the only reason it didn't happen as it was supposed to is because you tried to intervene."

"Because that wasn't supposed to happen either."

"Now you understand."

"So rather than recognize maybe your prophet isn't a hundred percent correct, you're going to do everything you can to reset things to match what she said was going to happen. By letting him die."

"By allowing him to die as he was supposed to."

"Right. Fine, then you're going to have to go over there and kill him, because if you don't do that I'm going to put something together to carry him on, and tomorrow we'll be looking for help, whether you're with us or not."

She looked past me at the still-breathing Bruno, and it looked like she was considering it.

"All right," she said. "I'll help. But only if we carry him back to the camp. We have a doctor."

CHAPTER 10

A stretcher is one of those things I know how to make from scratch. It's possible I made my first one more than fifty thousand years ago, at a time when we certainly didn't call it a stretcher, or any other word, because we barely had words.

What we did have was a regular need to transport large, heavy, awkwardly weighted collections of meat great distances using the combined strength of more than one ambulatory person. Typically, we were carrying dead animals, so there was no need to worry about things like whether we tied them to the log too tightly.

Every now and then, it turned out the animal in question wasn't *entirely* dead, which led to the kind of fun you just can't have nowadays. (I'm being sarcastic. It was terrifying. Kind of funny in hindsight, but not at all pleasant in the moment.)

Very occasionally, we would apply the same technology to get a member of our own hunting party back to the rest of the tribe. When doing this we *did* have to care about the wellbeing of the person we were carrying, so the technique was a little different. Instead of being lashed to the bottom of a log, they had to be tied to the top of two or three logs, and for the most part we had to be a lot more careful about keeping them stable and as levelly horizontal as was reasonable. And in the event of a larger predator turning up at the sight of an easy meal, we couldn't just drop the tied-down meat and run, and then circle back and kill the predator.

(This happened a lot. We had a word for it, the rough translation of which would be *trading up*.)

We didn't do this all that often for people in our hunting party, because of the whole large predator problem. Traveling with someone immobilized put the whole party at risk. A wounded man on a six man team could mean we were guaranteed to return with only five men, or we could take a real chance that none of us made it back. Usually, then, if someone was carried it was because they were considered important.

When it was my turn on the stretcher, thankfully I was considered important enough.

My point is not that Bruno was especially important, though, it's that I knew how to make a good stretcher. Unfortunately, that knowledge was based on my standing in an African equatorial jungle. These were different trees.

What kind of trees? I don't even know, just like I didn't know what the names of the African trees were. But I knew how to spot limbs that were sturdy enough for use but weak enough to snap off the trunk without anything sharper than a slightly pointy rock, and I knew how to turn thin twigs and vines into rope.

In Africa. We weren't in Africa.

After about an hour of looking, I was able to come up with two passably utile long sticks, but nothing I could use to make rope from, which made the sticks not at all useful. Then I remembered we also had a sleeping bag and a blanket.

By morning, Bruno was wrapped up in a cocoon with sticks on either side. Given there was no support underneath, the setup was especially sensitive to movement, so the trip was going to result in him being in a lot of pain.

In my opinion this was better than dying from a combination of exposure and whatever wild animals were out there that liked the taste of incubus flesh. I can't say for sure Bruno saw it the same way. By morning his head had cleared up enough for the words from his mouth to start to make a little bit of sense, which was both good and bad.

"You bitch, you bitch, you bitch," he muttered over and over.

"Hey," I said, after a good hour of this. "Enough with that."

I was holding him at the head end of the stretcher. Gordana had the feet. She was leading the way, which meant she held the stretcher behind her as she walked. This was awkward, so we switched positions regularly, with her directing me from behind. It was slow-going no matter what, because while it was a gorgeous day, it was also hot, the kind of day Mirella would have spent just diving into the ocean over and over, to wet her skin and let it cool in the cliff-side breeze.

The heat made everything feel heavier. We had the two back-packs tied to the poles underneath Bruno, who was already a dead weight, and we were all sweating, and quickly running out of bottled water.

"She knew," Bruno said. Then he gasped in pain from a light jostling caused by uneven ground.

"Who knew? Your prophet, or your sister?"

"She's no sister. I have a real sister. She's a bitch too."

"I told you to stop saying that."

"Cunt, then."

"Not any better."

"She was told to expect my death."

"So she was. And she didn't tell you."

"Why shouldn't I curse her then? I already knew her as a bitch, this only secures it. Tell me I'm wrong."

"You both follow the same lunatic, don't you?"

"Don't call her that. But yes."

"If this prophet told you Gordana wouldn't live to see the

camp again, but that you had to keep that to yourself, wouldn't you have?"

"Yes, of course. But that's different. Her kind is useless. A biological accident. Her death would be a correction."

"I'm beginning to think she had a point about leaving you to die."

"She was right."

"Was she? Because we could still do that."

"No." He hesitated. Or, he was in too much pain to continue right away. "Thank you for trying to help. If I don't sweat to death in this oven you've constructed for me or suffocate from my internal wounds I doubt it will be worth much, but I appreciate you trying."

"Well you're welcome. Don't take it too personally, though, I really don't like you."

He laughed, coughed, cried out in pain, and then didn't say anything for a while.

~

"I have to stop," Gordana called out, after another hour. "He's too heavy."

We'd been going uphill, and the path—which was hardly a path at all—didn't have much in the way of clearings or flat space. So, we just stopped where we were, slid the stretcher to the ground between two trees, and sat on the uneven mossy earth.

I unzipped the side of the sleeping bag. Bruno gasped.

"It is a thousand degrees in this, thank you."

His body was still a twisted mess. Before sealing him up in the bag I'd done what I could to splint the broken limbs with branches and torn bits of clothing, but he still looked as if a giant had picked him up and crumpled him into a ball like a piece of paper. He was also covered in sweat, and steam was rising off.

I put a bottle of water into his good hand and propped up his head so he could have a little.

"We are going to run out of water soon," Gordana said.

"Then we'll find some more." I said.

"Where?"

"One thing at a time."

"We're not going to make it to the camp before sundown," she said.

"As I said, one thing at a time."

"Our leader said…"

"Don't. I don't care. For all we know, she told you what she told you so that what's happening now ended up happening. Trying to align yourself with fate is a waste of time."

Bruno was getting greedy about the water, so I had to take it away before he made himself sick. If he had any crude words to say about this, they didn't come out.

"Last night," I said, to Bruno, "you tried to describe what attacked you. Do you remember?"

"Do I remember describing it, or do I remember what attacked me?"

"Pick one. What was it?"

"I never saw anything like it before. Short, slimy. Very strong. He had no feet."

"What was he standing on?" I saw enough to recognize that the thing in the forest the night before was a biped.

"Legs? I don't know. Tubes. Macaroni. I didn't ask."

Bruno rubbed sweat from his forehead, and then something weird happened. His fingers came off gummy. Like mucus was coming out of his pores.

"Would you look at that. On top of all else, I think I may be melting."

~

I had almost no understanding of the medical intricacies of his species, but it was pretty clear that what was happening to Bruno was decidedly atypical. Gordana clearly never saw this before, based on her expression—something between surprise and disgust, but not familiarity—so if this was how they died normally, she'd never seen a member of her own species perish. Given their lack of proper family dynamic, this was entirely feasible.

Possibly, incubi melted as they died. That sounds a bit loopy, and I get that, but I also know some of these impossible beings actually do melt, albeit *after* death. That's what happens to demons. When one of them dies the body breaks down almost immediately. I don't know why or how, it just happens. Bruno wasn't a demon and he wasn't dead, so his gradual dissolution still didn't make a lot of sense, but notionally it wasn't entirely out of bounds.

Thinking maybe the heat was causing it, we didn't bundle him back up in the sleeping bag, even though it made him much harder to carry. Instead, we zipped the bag up and put him on top of it. Short of stripping him down naked and using his clothes, though, we had nothing to tie him down with, so we did our best to keep the stretcher flat and went a little more slowly.

But then the climb got a lot steeper, and it became pretty clear pretty fast that we were going to require another solution.

"We *have* to leave him," Gordana said for probably the eighth or ninth time. She wasn't bothering to say this quietly any more, perhaps hoping Bruno would volunteer to die sooner. He was lying at an angle on the forest floor a few feet away, muttering curses under his breath and humming show tunes in an odd, atonal way. It wasn't clear he was fully in attendance. "We're only a half-day's walk from here. If we hurry, we'll make it before dark. We can return for him in the morning, with more people to help with the transport. If he's well-hid... don't look me that way, it's the best we can do."

"I'll stay with him. You go; I'll be waiting for you."

"That's not how it's supposed to happen."

"It's either that or you give me some very good directions and *I'll* go ahead while you wait with him."

"Directions."

"Like, make a left at the big tree, go straight when you see the leaf."

"I don't think that would work."

"I don't either. I thought the sarcasm made that obvious."

"You would have to keep the rest of the water and the food, and ration both. You will still run out before morning."

"Then I hope you're right about it being only a half-day from here."

She sighed, and was perfectly lovely when doing so.

I have maybe not underlined this enough, but being in the middle of the tropics with a succubus—where there is little clothing being worn and what is worn is soaked through with sweat—is under almost every other circumstance the definition of paradise. My luck to end up in one of the only times this was a bad thing.

"She will be angry with me for leaving you."

"You can tell her I was too stubborn to go and you weren't strong enough to overpower me. It's the truth."

"I haven't tried to overpower you via every available means, Adam," she said, smiling.

"Well, I appreciate that. But I prefer my sex recreational, not coercive. You understand."

"Better than you think. All right. I will go. If you must move... if there is danger, I mean, try and move uphill. I expect to see you here in the morning, alive."

"I'm all in favor of that too."

"And if you aren't here, we'll look for you. Oh, gods, I'm going to be in so much trouble for leaving you here."

"I can take care of myself."

"Just stay safe. Hide."

She hugged me, I hugged her back, and with nothing more than a side-eyed look of disgust directed to Bruno, she headed up the hill.

I watched until she was no longer visible, which happened pretty fast. The jungle was thick.

Then we were alone. I sat down and pondered the fact that I didn't know where I was.

It was pretty alarming to think that I could travel on foot for only a day, on an island I'd called home for over two years, and end up completely lost. I mean, you can go a long distance in a day—longer if you run most of it, which I certainly had in me—but we were talking about an island. There was only so far to go, and only so many ways to get lost. I grant that a largely undifferentiated jungle setting differed significantly from an island like Manhattan, with its numbered streets and right-angles, but this island was also smaller than Manhattan.

I checked on Bruno. He was still oozing, or melting or whatever, but seemed to be sleeping somewhat comfortably for the moment. Well, or he'd passed out from the pain or lapsed into a coma, but sleeping seemed like a nicer option. Plus he was still muttering things, and people in comas didn't tend to do that.

With him looking about as okay as he got, I climbed the tree under which he was resting. It was the best way to figure out where the hell I was.

All I could see from the top of the tree was water on one side and the high point of the island's miniature mountain on the other. No lower island, no village. And I was really upset about this for about five minutes until I realized I was looking at water because we'd walked around to the back of the island at some point. Tsunami or not, I would have had the same view.

That made plenty of sense. If you can see enough of the future to anticipate a tidal wave, it's a good idea to camp out above the water line, but an even better idea to pick a spot on the blind side of the island. This side didn't get much tourist traffic either—it had beaches, but they were rocky, and the way down to them was steep and unpleasant—so there was less chance of being discovered. Plus I'm told the sharks preferred that side.

I imagined that the point in which our trip went from a slight incline to a steep one coincided with the point at which the path we followed turned for the direct climb up the mountain.

A half-day's travel from that point was probably just short of the top, where all the best estates were. I wondered how a group of squatters managed to go unnoticed on that land.

I was about ready to climb back down when some movement caught my eye. To the right and downhill, treetops were moving in a pattern contrary to the push of the wind. It was slight, but not incidental: something large was traveling below the canopy over there. In a leisurely sort of way, it was heading towards us.

I slid down the tree. It was time to hide.

～

*T*here was no natural depression in the ground to work with this time. We were basically where Gordana and I jointly decided we could no longer continue to carry Bruno, and it was an exposed area. Rather than try and figure out a way to move him, I spent the afternoon collecting what loose plant life I could from the forest floor, and then I essentially buried him under it. I could have, at that point, tried burying myself, or at minimum disguised my scent with some dirt and moss, but decided it made just as much sense to climb back up the tree and hide out there for the evening. It would hardly be the first time.

"There is a box," Bruno muttered.

"What's that?"

His voice was barely audible.

"A box, I said. Metal. A tincture. In my pocket."

"Hang on."

I had to unbury him a little to get to his pants. It was in the back pocket.

"Ah yes, thank you. Could you open it? Carefully."

I sat beside him and slid the top of the container off. There was a yellowish substance inside.

"Sulfur?" I asked. It smelled like it.

"And some other things. I don't want to be a bother, but could you put some of that on your finger and hold it under my nose?"

I did, somewhat reluctantly. He whiffed it up, held it for several seconds, and then started breathing normally again.

"Yes, that's good, thank you," he said.

"Is this like snuff?" I asked. People used to inhale finely ground tobacco, and they called it snuff. I know, it sounds dumb.

"It's a palliative. It wouldn't work on you. Particular to my kind."

"You made this in the hotel room."

"I did, yes."

"And it's a drug?"

"Closer to aspirin than to heroin."

"Medicinal, not recreational."

"Yes, that's it," he said. "I've been fighting a cold."

He drifted off into something that should have been a laugh, but laughing hurt too much, so it was mostly a wheeze and a gasp.

"Funny, now that my body has been destroyed and the skin is dribbling off my bones, to think my largest concern two weeks ago was a sneeze. Tell me something."

"Sure," I said.

"Why?"

"Why am I doing this?"

"We both know altogether well I am dying, and I will probably be dead by morning. You owe me no allegiance and as you've said, you don't even like me. So yes. Why."

I leaned back against the tree I was planning to re-climb shortly, and thought about the question.

"Not sure," I admitted.

"Are you as old as she said?"

"How old did she say?"

"She said you were as old as the world."

"That's very poetic, but... guess it depends on your definition of *the world*. But I'm older than any civilization, and older than most races, and older than every language. I don't know how old, but, pretty old."

"Then you are a survivor."

"That's part of the package, sure."

"A survivor would have left me yesterday. It was the smart thing to do. Do you no longer wish to be one?"

"It's not like that. You know some people think I'm a god?"

"That follows, yes."

"Sure, but I'm not."

"Who would be qualified to judge?"

"Right, but... gods. Gods exist so all of this makes sense. Either they reward people for their suffering and senseless death, or they're to blame for it. We create gods to understand the random and inexplicable, because even if people don't get what's happening and why, the god they believe in... well, he's got a plan. It could be a terrible plan, but he surely has one. If I'm a god, everyone's in trouble, because I don't know why people suffer and die. I just don't want it to be for my sake."

"You're upset because of my sacrifice."

"The list of people who have died so that I could live is so long I can't begin to name them all."

"But I didn't do it for you. I did it for the prophecy."

I laughed.

"That's not any better. If it isn't a god out there with a plan, it's a prophet with a peek at things to come. It's all just another way to give meaning to something meaningless. Maybe I'm here because I'm tired of letting people kill themselves for my sake. Maybe it's just that prophets piss me off. It's probably nothing personal. I mean, you *are* a prick."

Bruno smiled.

"I am. But thank you for being kind. If there is a place to go after this, and that place has gods in it, I will be sure to tell them you acquitted yourself well."

He held up his left hand, which I gripped tightly. It was moist and sticky, and… well, pretty gross, and if I worried about things like disease I'd probably be really concerned. As it was, I probably could have used hand soap and a sink.

"I hope there is such a place," I said, "even if it's half-full of people I sent there."

~

I didn't climb the tree. Some combination of the hiking/carrying of Bruno and the lack of sleep from the previous night conspired to enable an outcome in which I dozed off against the trunk next to him, his clammy hand still in mine, and the open tin of sulfur powder still in my lap.

I woke up to the sound of something large moving through the woods. It was easy enough to pick out because the entire forest floor had gone silent.

Like I said before, jungles make a ton of sound; bugs crying; small animals running, climbing and slithering; trees creaking in the wind; moisture rapping against leaves; birds flying; bats flapping; and on and on. It's always something, and it creates a sort of low, undifferentiated hum that after a while you don't hear any more, right up until it stops.

What makes everything in a jungle stop what it's doing and stay still can either be a large predator or an impending storm. If you ask me how a meerkat or a buzzard or a deer knows when a storm is coming (or an earthquake, they're really good at that too) I couldn't say, but that everyone knows when there's a predator... that's pretty obvious. The ones who can sense a predator are the ones who are still alive. The loud ones. who can't tell, were eaten by the last predator to come through.

I knew enough not to move, but at the same time I had to move. I needed to know what had done this to Bruno. I mean, I was pretty clear that a banshee had done it. My question was, what the hell was a banshee?

I listened to them all day, in the distance, making that weird noise, and as much as I didn't want to run into one after the beating Bruno got, I very desperately wanted to see what they looked like. Large, scary, monstrous things that can pulp a human-sized person do not just pop into existence, and the one story I had—where I heard them from afar on the Danish shores some fourteen hundred years ago—just wasn't enough for me. If these things were real, they weren't something new. They had another name.

But to know what that name was, I had to see one. Once I saw, I would know how to deal with it.

All right, probably not, but one thing at a time.

I let go of Bruno's hand, set aside the tin of sulfur, and got to my feet as quietly as I knew how, which for the record is pretty quiet. It helped a lot that I was still barefoot, as I always traveled better off-road that way. You'd think after years of mostly having on footwear, the thick skin and calluses would have softened, but they never seem to.

I took a cautious step around the tree, had a look around, and another step. The forest floor was still dead quiet, but that could mean either that the predator was coming, or that it was right behind me. There's always that risk.

Then I heard it, heading down the hill to my right. Big, moving on four legs, with another consistent with a tail. I took a couple of steps toward the sound to see about getting a good view of it before scampering up a tree when I realized my error.

Something big was on the way, all right, but something else was already there, behind me.

It was big too. It stood maybe ten feet away. Pale skin, almost translucent. What I thought the night before was that it was practically glowing in the moonlight, which I interpreted as paleness, but this was something more. The thing's skin picked up what light there was and reflected it back in a white glow. I might have thought it was a ghost if I lived in a world where ghosts existed and also glowed.

I put it at no more than five feet in height, and with a body shape that only barely corresponded to a human one: there was a head and a torso, and arms and legs, but those component parts formed something closer to a pyramid than a person. There was a great deal of fat on its frame, most of it settling in the lower region. The shoulders and arms displayed an astonishing musculature, but the stomach and waist suggested a grossly overweight man. The parts didn't match up.

The head looked like the top of a rocket. There was no nose, and no visible ears. The eyes were huge and black, the mouth closed and bearing an expression I couldn't interpret.

I had no idea what I was looking at.

It seemed to have some dim idea of what I was, though. It stepped closer. As it moved from the tall grasses on those enormous, thick legs I saw what Bruno meant when he said it had no feet. It didn't step, precisely; it glided. There were two legs involved, but they didn't bend at the knee. Instead, some kind of cilium action going on down at the bottom, like there were hundreds of tiny toes helping it scamper along.

I say *it* although it had no clothing on and a breast-free chest, so I could have said *he* just as easily, and maybe I would have been correct about that, but this thing looked so alien—I wasn't ruling out an extra-planetary explanation at this point, either—

that there was no telling if the external indicators of species gender even made sense.

I didn't know what to do, but it was coming my way, so I figured I had a few seconds to sort it out before trying to escape up a tree.

"Hello," I said. "I mean you no harm. Um, greetings."

I waved.

It stopped, looked at my hand for a second, and then opened its mouth to reply. By screaming.

I don't know if the scream was all it had. By that I mean, maybe it didn't have an indoor voice, and it was either scream or say nothing. I did know that in screaming, it revealed two rows of sharp teeth that were the sort of thing people have nightmares about for the rest of their lives, and that getting a good distance away from those teeth was a really great idea.

I turned to grab onto the nearest tree at around the same time the creature decided I was someone he wished to attack.

Fortunately—and I may never consider this a matter of good fortune again—I'd forgotten about the other large predator traveling through the forest.

It reached the scary pale thing before the scary pale thing reached me, and well before I made it to a tree. I decided then it was better to dive to the ground behind a trunk and next to Bruno and bear witness as two large beasts grappled with one another, especially since neither was focusing on me.

I was very lucky the second thing in the woods wasn't another banshee. It was taller, and it didn't glow in the light. It roared a lot, and growled, and acted as we all expect most large land animals to act in general. About half of that was for show, which is typical: animals don't often combat for sport, and would rather scare off an opponent than engage with one.

There wasn't a fight, in other words. The banshee quickly retreated, leaving my savior alone to do what it wanted with me.

I wasn't going to escape up a tree to get away from this predator. I knew what it was and I was pretty sure it could get at least ten or twelve feet up a tree before I could climb past the ten or twelve foot point, and it was possible it could even *climb* a tree if it really wanted to.

It growled a low, lizard growl and walked on four legs toward me, claws uprooting clumps of grass. An oblong head showed off rows of teeth nearly as impressive as the last guy's.

It headed my way. I knew what it was, and I knew how to kill it, but I needed a sword and a lot of help and I had neither of those.

It was a dragon. And it wasn't supposed to exist.

CHAPTER 11

*D*ragons never got as big as houses, they couldn't fly, and they didn't breathe fire. They also weren't self-aware, in the way that people (and goblins, and elves, and even pixies) were. They were large land animals, megafauna lizards that went extinct a while ago because they never got along with anyone, including each other.

Or rather, I *thought* they went extinct. The last dragon I saw was in France in the plague years, and I know that one didn't go on to lead a long and fruitful life because I killed it.

I'm basing my understanding of which animals are and are not extinct on my own witness testimony, and I appreciate that since I'm only one person this is a less-than-comprehensive survey. But unlike most of the unlikely creatures on this island and elsewhere in the world, dragons don't have the presence of mind to keep their existence hidden. Their intelligence is about on level with a wolf or a parrot, and since modern people know about wolves and parrots I would think they would also know about the non-mythological iteration of dragons, if dragons were still around.

A fully mature dragon is typically between a hippo and an

elephant in size, has an incredibly thick, scaly hide, can run on all fours at the same speed as a horse and can engage a man in combat as a biped, on hind legs and swinging powerful forearms. Its paws come with long claws, its head—oblong and lizard-like in shape—has a set of very sharp teeth, and it has a tail that can be swung like a weapon. Also, thanks to what I imagine are some serious dietary problem, dragons tend to smell like sulfur. I suspect this is where the fire-breathing aspect of their legend came from.

If encountering a dragon, it's always a good idea to have a vampire, a mercenary demon, or a very fast horse on your side. If you don't have any of those things, but you do have a decent broadsword and some skill with it, there's a puncher's chance at survival because dragons have a soft spot in their scaly armor just below the neck, but that's about all.

I had none of those things, and if the dragon wanted to eat me he could do it well before I made it up the nearest tree. And as I said, even if I did make it, for all I knew he could climb trees too.

"Hi, buddy," I said, as nicely as I could. I was adopting a defensive posture that would do me exactly no good if he pounced. "You wouldn't want to… go extinct for me now, would you?"

The dragon stood where he was: on all fours and facing me. While the light wasn't great, it didn't look as if he was treating me like a threat. There was a distinctive *whoosh-whoosh* sound, and he was swaying.

He was wagging his tail, and sniffing at the air. Then, in what I thought at first was a charge, he lumbered past me and to the spot I'd been sitting not so long ago.

He was rooting around in the leaves.

It was Bruno's sulfur. Sulfur attracted dragons. This was news to me.

This would have been a super time to climb a tree and escape, but I had gone past being afraid and had settled on curious. Something around his neck was glowing gently. Not like a throbbing neon sort of glow, more like the defensive action of a jelly-fish. It was weird, because dragons aren't battery-powered and don't glow.

I took a few cautious steps forward. The dragon noticed, and fell back until we were face-to-face again. He stood his ground, but not in a way I'd call threatening. He looked anticipatory, mostly. Like he was at least self-aware enough to recognize he was the most terrifying thing in the jungle—aside from whatever it was he'd scared off—and knew the best way to keep people at ease was to avoid any sudden motion.

I stepped closer, my hand out in front and at the same level as his head. A few more steps, and I was close enough to pet him.

Which I did. He tilted his head toward the hand like a dog, and as jarring as the entire concept was, I realized that was essentially what I had in front of me: a gigantic lizard-dog.

He licked the side of my arm and I tried not to panic.

On closer inspection, the glowing thing around his neck turned out to be a collar. It was about three inches wide and made of some kind of plastic with a built-in fluorescence. It gave off a gentle yellow-green light, which made the writing on it easy enough to read:

HELLO MY NAME IS BUSTER. I AM FRIENDLY.

"Oh," I said. "Hello, Buster."

I nearly lost my arm then, because Buster got very excited when he heard his name, and my hand was still holding onto the collar at the time. He jumped up and down and ran in a small circle, and then he growled something that sounded an awful lot like his name.

The parrot analogy wasn't entirely without merit. I did hear a dragon speak once before, but it was mostly an act of mimicry, not with any real sense of understanding language on a level we might expect from a fully cognizant being.

"Okay, Buster, okay. Calm down."

Buster was kind of adorable. Terrifying dragon, sure, but

adorable terrifying dragon. He was easily the friendliest pet monster I'd come across in centuries and his enthusiasm over having met me appeared to be something he couldn't fully contain. This put the entire landscape at risk, but so far he hadn't accidentally damaged me.

"Um, sit," I said. "Sit down."

Buster sat. Someone trained him well.

"Stay," I said.

I took a few steps around the tree and the land Buster had just been rooting around in. I found the tin of sulfur first, then Bruno.

The incubus was dead. My guess was he had been for a little while, likely passing while I was asleep and holding onto his sticky hand.

He seemed to be dissolving at an accelerated rate. I won't bother to describe what that looked like, but suffice to say the sleeping bag was no longer something anyone else would be able to use.

I decided to leave him where he was. Gordana was supposed to return in the morning; she could figure out whether or bury him or what. Whether I was there with him when she got back was an open question. I had a new mystery to solve, and waiting around until sunrise wasn't going to solve it.

I pocketed the tin and returned to Buster, who stayed put like a good boy. I figured there was more information on that collar, something that would tell me who tamed him and where he lived. An "if found, please return to…" statement of some kind.

There wasn't any such thing on the collar though, which I guess made a little sense since nobody on the island had a real mailing address anyway. There was only one other word on the collar at all, and to get to it I had to rotate it 180 degrees.

The word was PULL. It sat above a tiny tab.

I pulled, several layers of the glowing collar unspooled, and soon I had a fifteen-foot leash in my hands.

Buster's tail wagged again, and nearly took out my legs. He looked up expectantly.

"Home, Buster," I said. "Take me home."

And then we were off.

~

*I*t almost goes without saying that following the meander of someone's pet dragon through a jungle just contributed to the challenge of figuring out precisely where I was.

I knew only a couple of the estates near the top of the island on sight, and then only from certain angles. Two or three times, I caught a glimpse of the lit side of a building, and one or two of those times I thought maybe I recognized the building, but I considered that insufficient to start knocking on doors. Too many people around this part of the island reacted negatively to strangers, and after the tsunami I had plenty of reason to think a negative reaction would only be more strident.

Plus, I thought Buster was going to lead me to *his* home, which I expected to be in a house. I also expected him to get me past any gates.

I began to question this assumption around the time the angle of our ascent reached a degree of steepness that made it seem a lot more like rock-climbing than hiking.

Soon, it became impossible to pace Buster in any meaningful way, because he was a better climber and appeared to be traveling a well-known route. It was still dark out, though, and I'm not the kind of person to free-climb an unfamiliar cliff face in the dark when I have a choice. Sure, if I'm fleeing someone or something, I'll scale whatever you've got, but otherwise, I'd rather go around or wait for someone with ropes to come along.

Buster was the one who came up with a solution. When it was clear I couldn't climb with him, he simply stopped and lay down on the ground on his belly, and looked up expectantly, until I figured out he was suggesting I get on his back.

It took a really long time to figure this out, because *ride a dragon* has never been something I've considered before. It was about as likely as my someday meeting a friendly demon, basically.

I hopped on. With no saddle apparatus to speak of, I grabbed onto a couple of his scales and held on as well as I could. The surface was a just shy of sandpaper-rough, which made it easier to hang on but also put me at risk for a bad rash if I slid too much.

It wasn't far, though. About halfway up the climb became literally vertical, at which point I began eyeballing the taller trees underneath in case I had to make a quick trajectory decision during a rapid descent, but it never came to that, because then we arrived at Buster's "home".

Buster lived in a cave. This would have made a ton of sense if he were a wild dragon, but since someone went through the trouble to tame him (and, I'm assuming, breed him and perhaps also grow him in a lab or something) I was thinking whoever did that also lived in the cave.

Or at least *near* the cave, the problem being that there was no *near* to be found. The cave was on the side of a steep part of the hill. There wasn't anything man-made beneath us and as far as I could tell it was a pretty big hike to get to anything above. I saw no ladders, ropes, winches, elevators, or anything else suggesting someone visited the cave except by using the route the dragon took.

"Is this home, Buster?" I asked, just to be sure. I mean, it was possible he didn't know what the word meant, and took me to the cave out of some basic loss in translation. Maybe I was about to be eaten by a cavern full of little baby Busters.

He wagged his tail and bounced up and down a few times and then pointed with his nose toward the mouth of the cave.

I used to like caves, and lived in them quite a lot in the early days: *caveman* and all that. They were about the only place to get a proper night's sleep for a very, very long time, because the good ones had no back door so there was no chance of getting snuck up on from behind by something with bigger teeth. There were disadvantages too, like if something sufficiently vicious showed up at the door and couldn't be fought off, we had nowhere to run. Also, there were a lot of smart predators out there who figured out that humans had to eventually leave the cave if they wanted to get any food, so lying in wait near the entrance became a thing. This made the walk (or run, more frequently) from the cave mouth to the first set of trees a deeply terrifying experience.

My fondest memory of a cave involved one on the Atlantic coastline of South Africa. I don't remember when I was there or for how long, but I do remember that it was pretty easy, relaxing living. The high tide used bring in all sorts of small sea creatures —crabs, oysters, a bunch of things that may no longer exist—and strand them in pools along the shore at low tide. We would literally just run down to the beach, grab as much as we could carry, and bring it all back to the cave, which was in a hillside just above the high tide water mark. We'd spend the day cracking open shells and eating what was inside, and that was all we had to do for food. There weren't any predators to speak of, because none of the big ones cared for the ocean.

I heard it said once that it was a "brave man" who tried the first oyster. Whoever said it probably never had to worry about hunting for a protein source, though, because tide pool food was the best food. None of those creatures tried to bite me back.

We never stayed in caves for all that long, just in general, because it was hard to be nomadic while calling a cave home, and it was hard to be hunter-gatherers without being nomadic. Even the oceanfront cave didn't last too terribly long, because there was no fresh water source nearby. Eventually, we grew to reconsider caves, as something to be threatened by rather than relieved to discover. In the heyday of large land animals, it was pretty hard to find one that wasn't occupied by something violent, and harder still to evict that violent something.

It was this last part that had me standing near the mouth of this cave and wondering if I'd made a terrible mistake.

But, up and down weren't fantastic options either, so I let Buster lead me out of the moonlight and into the dark cave mouth.

It took a while for my eyes to adjust, and that wasn't by a lot, because there was hardly any light to help. I had Buster's glow-in-the-dark leash, but that was about all.

The ground was cold, smooth rock initially, then turned into dirt and pebbles my feet didn't entirely appreciate. Nothing truly jagged, though, which was nice. I could lose a whole limb to a sharp enough jutting rock in this darkness.

The sides of the cave never narrowed all that much, and soon I started to pick up the sounds of things ahead that indicated I wasn't in a cave at all; I was in a cavern.

It was rushing water I was hearing. Hopefully, an underground fresh water source, because I'd run out of water eight hours earlier.

The path opened up into a larger space. I couldn't see this happen, but I felt it, because the air cooled, and carried the occasional light mist, and the pitch of our own footsteps changed. There was a faint light high above us; my eyes started to pick out details in the room.

"What manner of being are you?" a deep voice asked. More exactly, it was a deep, booming, rumble of a thunderclap that somehow formed words. It was the voice you always hear in movies when a god is talking.

I let out a decidedly non-masculine shriek and jumped a couple of feet at the sound.

"Hello," I said, in my normal, non-godlike voice.

"What manner of being are you?" he—I was assuming the

voice belonged to a male—repeated. The question seemed to come from every direction, like I was standing inside of the questioner. I'm nearly positive sentient islands aren't a thing, but I've been wrong before.

"I'm a man. Human, I'm human."

Buster wanted to keep going into the room but I had no interest in going any further, so I let go of the leash and watched him run off. It gave me a better idea of the scale of the room, which perhaps was not as large as it seemed.

"A human? No."

"I'm… pretty sure I am, yeah."

"Are you special?"

"Special how?" I asked.

"In some way. Humans are ordinary, and we're all special here. How are you special?"

"There are so few humans on the island, would that alone not make me special?"

He grumbled.

"No, it wouldn't."

I was trying to resist the urge to speak to the ceiling as if I were actually addressing a sky god. The echo did sort of make it seem like that was the source of his voice, but I was pretty sure he was about thirty or forty feet in front of me. That was where Buster ran, before disappearing around a corner. If I was correct in assuming I spoke to the dragon's owner, it made sense Buster would head for him.

"I'm unusually old for a human, is that better?"

"Oh! You're *that* human."

"Um…"

"Leewan Sean."

That was an interesting thing to say, because although this was certainly a name I'd used in the past, it was in the very, very distant past. I'd never used it on the island or anywhere else in many centuries. It's popular with some elves, in the same way most vampires recognize me as Apollo.

"Does some one here call me that?" I asked.

"I have heard. There was another… Adam? The first man?"

"Coincident name choice."

"I am sure."

"So what kind of name do they have for you?"

"Come closer."

"I can't really see anything. How much closer are we talking?"

"Ah yes, human being, human eyes. A human nose will serve you well. Let me get the lights."

There was an echo of a click as something mechanical was flipped or pushed or triggered, and then electrical lights hidden in the walls joined the one already lit near the ceiling.

The room was a dirt-floor cavern space with water trickling down a far wall from an unknown source. The half wall on the other side of the room still hid my inquisitor, but only half-hid Buster, whose tail was out. He was lying on the floor beyond the wall.

"The room is artificial," he said. "Most of the rock on the island is volcanic, which makes proper underground caverns less likely. The natural ones are also not as nice as this. You can come forward, I won't bite."

I took a few steps and then started to pick up a somewhat familiar smell. It was body odor, of a specific type.

When I turned the corner I found what had to be the third or fourth impossible thing in the past twenty-four hours. It was a troll, wearing glasses, khakis and a polo shirt, and sitting beside an extremely large custom-job of a computer.

"I'm Grundle," he said. He stood, which was just utterly terrifying, and extended his hand, which was also terrifying. "It's a pleasure to meet you, sir. Welcome to the middle of the mountain."

~

*G*rundle was an adult male troll, which made him about 1/3 larger than Gren, who given the name might have been an ancestor. (Or, they were deeply uncreative when it came to names.) He smelled awful, but not as awful as I remember the last troll smelling, although it helped I was in a high-ceilinged room with decent air flow for a cave. Plus, there were no rotting corpses lying around.

"Can I get you some water?" he asked. "And a chair? You look like you've had quite a night. Here, some water, I have some right here."

"Uh, sure, water."

His normal speaking voice was only a little higher than the voice-of-God boom he treated me to initially, which I suspect was used specifically to ward off intruders. This was a little funny, because *being a troll* seemed like a superlative way to scare people off.

I took a seat. He had a normal human-sized chair on the other side of his little room, an indication he sometimes took in guests, and those guests weren't other trolls. He disappeared down a corridor on the other side of his desk, and returned a moment later with a bottle of water.

It was cold. He had a refrigerator somewhere.

I drank some of the water—which was wonderful—as he sat back down. A few seconds later, I realized I was staring.

"Sorry," I said. "I thought I reached my limit at non-extinct, tame dragon, but I was wrong."

He laughed. I never heard a troll laugh before. It was somewhere between Santa and Satan.

"Buster is something else, isn't he?" he said.

"Buster is impossible," I said. "I'm pretty sure you are too."

The singular defining characteristic—and weakness—that every troll before this one had, was abject stupidity.

I guess that's sort of a cruel descriptive, but "childlike simplicity" isn't really sufficient. I'd use that to describe a pixie, and pixies can be taught to read. I would have never tried teaching a troll to read, although in fairness most of the ones I knew, I became acquainted with before there was written language. Maybe, then, this is my personal bias and not truly a valid characteristic at all. The problem is, when you take away stupidity, a troll doesn't have a weakness that I can see, and that makes me uncomfortable.

"We're both quite rare, you're correct," Grundle said. "Dragons more than trolls."

"How about trolls who can form complete sentences?"

It wasn't until after I said this that it occurred to me it might be an offensive thing to say. It had been a long day.

He smiled, and took it well.

"You have encountered trolls prior to myself?"

"A few."

"I've only known a couple. I wasn't raised in a traditional manner, but suffice it to say a troll's native intellectual capacity is higher than an elderly fellow such as yourself might have learned to expect."

"Or you're a savant."

"A little of both, we'll say."

This was like finding a four year old conversant in quantum theory, or a demon working as a professional sommelier. Grundle seemed adequately self-aware to appreciate this, but I didn't want to press the issue.

"I feel like I may need to come to a new understanding for how this island came to be and what it actually is," I said. "How long have you been here?"

"Oh, some years. I'm on the committee."

"You're on the island committee."

"Sure. I vote in absentia."

"Honestly, I think I may be losing my mind."

He laughed again.

"There are a few places in the world where the special beings gather in groups, and this is one of them. It isn't all that crazy. I'm sure I am not the only intelligent troll on the planet, any more than Buster is the only living dragon. We had parents, both of us. We're only rare, not impossible."

I thought about all I'd come to understand about species propagation, and tried to figure out how that corresponded with the likelihood that there was a coordinated effort to train and keep dragons as pets without my knowing about it. Then I wondered if Grundle was telling me the truth or if he only thought he was.

This wasn't a special breed of dog we were talking about. This was a dragon.

"So who paid for this place?" I asked.

"I did," he said, pointing to his computer. "Computer coding for hire can be very lucrative if you know what you're doing, and nobody on the Internet much cares what I look or smell like. You're being very kind, by the way."

"How do you mean?"

"The smell. I know it's there. I can't really smell it myself, but I'm sure you can. I'm afraid I can't do much about it. When I host dinner parties I sit behind glass so as not to ruin everyone's palates."

"Parties?"

"I'm quite the chef."

"All the trolls I knew liked their food raw."

"Still do! Sashimi, steak tartare… I'll do some cooking. I have a stove. Oh, are you hungry? Where are my manners?"

~

"*S*o what brings you to my home?" Grundle asked, later, after I had a sandwich of rare roast beef washed down with a beer. The latter was a particularly pleasant surprise.

"Buster did," I said. The dragon was sitting on a large bed in the corner of the dining room, chewing on a bone that looked like it used to belong to a mastodon.

The dining room was quite elegant for a cave. There was a stone table in the center of the room, rough-hewn and only approximately rectangular, polished on top but rough on the bottom. The room itself was only sort-of oval, being as it was a space carved out of the middle of a mountain.

I wanted to ask how many more rooms he had, but that seemed oddly inappropriate. I was only gradually coming to appreciate that despite Grundle being a troll living in a cave on a mountain, this was the equivalent of a visit to a wealthy person's private estate.

"He likes you," Grundle said. "He usually takes to strangers only reluctantly."

"This helped, I think." I pulled the tin of sulfur powder from my pants and put it on the table. "He likes the smell. And I'm glad, because his attraction to it may have resulted in him saving my life. He chased off… well, something. I don't know what."

The troll looked very excited by this.

"Wait, was it one of the howlers?"

"I think probably, yes, if that's what you call them. Have you seen one?"

"No! No, I almost never leave the cave, but the committee is abuzz about those things. I sent Buster out to gather intel."

"Is…is Buster going to start talking now?"

"No, no."

He whistled. Never heard a troll whistle before. Didn't think their lips could do that.

Buster jumped up and walked over. Grundle reached under

one of the scales on the dragon's head and extracted a tiny metallic box.

"Camera," he said. "I can usually monitor what he's seeing from my console, but the island's wireless network has been down since yesterday."

"When the wave hit," I said. I briefly entertained the thought that he knew nothing about the tsunami, as it would have had little direct impact on him in his cave.

"Yes," he said, nodding slowly. "Awful thing. We've called in rescue, but it will be a few days. We all fear the worst. I hope they can hold out until then."

"They?"

"The survivors."

"Are you in touch with survivors?"

"Intermittently."

He shook his head sadly.

"There are so few, though," he said. "If this were an ordinary tourist destination we would have emergency ships here much sooner, but we have to balance secrecy with humanitarianism. Or, I suppose, in-humanitarianism. In honesty, when Buster brought you here, I just assumed you were one of the tourists from the lower island who managed to wash up mid-jungle."

"I couldn't imagine it would be any faster, if large portions of the world are unaware the island even exists. Convincing someone you're real isn't the best way to start a rescue operation."

"Yes. This is very true. The same could be said for most of the species sharing this island, but we—all of us—have favored the privacy of the collective over the safety of the individual for centuries. This I am sure you know better than most anyone."

"Where are the survivors? How are you reaching them?"

He smiled.

"You're looking for someone in particular."

"My girlfriend is missing. She was swept away with the wave.

I don't think she made it to the lower island, though, I think she's in the jungle."

Or, she was dead.

I was still trying to keep that thought away, but it was getting more difficult with every passing hour.

Grundle's general demeanor suggested his mind went to more or less the same place.

"If she went downhill with the wave, the odds—"

"She's very capable."

"I'm sure."

"Can we reach someone down there?"

He smiled again. I'm not really accustomed to trolls who have emotions that extend beyond anger and confusion, so interpreting the subtleties of his facial expressions was an entertaining distraction. I was nearly positive the one I was getting at this moment was a variant of pity.

"We can try," he said.

* * *

"The first floor was largely washed away, Mr. Adam. But those inside and on the second floor, we think most of the ones on the leeward side of the wave are still alive."

The person on the other end of the conversation was Paul, the hotel manager. I didn't need to recognize the voice to know the speaker, because nobody else called me Mr. Adam. Vocal identification would have been difficult, because the signal was intermittent. We were using a radio that appeared to rely upon line-of-sight communication. Our end was using an antenna array near the top. Best guess, Paul stuck his antenna out the window of his second floor office. If so, it would mean the water had receded below the second floor.

"That's good," I said. "Well, not *good*, but not as bad as it could be."

"The rooms happened to be sealed to account for heavy rains. They weren't built to withstand consistent water pressure of this kind, but many held strong. We've tried to contact as many guests as possible by phone. It seems the plumbing has held, so there is water for us, but no food aside from what was already in the rooms. What power we have is generator-based."

"Do you have a boat? Maybe you can start getting people out."

"The water is still receding. In another day we may be able to walk upon the ground again. And… there is the other thing."

"What other thing?"

"Let me go to the window."

There was a pause, as Paul carried the microphone to the nearest window.

"I will open this only in brief, so you can hear," he said.

A couple of seconds later, he opened the line.

I heard the now-familiar banshee cries, only this was considerably more terrifying. In the hills, they came intermittently, a regular call-and-response sort of thing. These were cries atop cries, coming from near and far. It didn't sound like communication in this setting, more like the persistent cawing of a flock of birds.

Then the line was closed again, as Paul let go of the transmit button and—I assume—slammed the window closed.

"The nights have been like this since the wave hit," he said. "In the day, they calm down somewhat. We don't know what they are, but they're in the water, and they appear hostile. Esteban thought so."

"Stubby? Stubby's there?"

"Not here, we spoke by radio. He was off duty when the wave hit."

Stubby had a small ranch house on the lower island not far from the town but a good distance from the hotel. It was near the base of the mountain, a short walk from the road leading up. The wave would have taken out the whole house.

"Off-duty and *where*?" I asked.

"Not sure. The radio was spotty when we spoke and I haven't

heard from him since. He had a deputy with a boat he promised to send to us, but that was some hours ago and no-one has seen this deputy, and Esteban hasn't attempted to establish new contact."

"Did he say if he was alone?"

"I didn't ask."

"I'm looking for Mirella."

There was a moment before Paul responded, which told me all I needed to know.

"I'm sorry, we haven't heard anything about her, Mr. Adam. If we regain contact we will ask."

"All right, thanks. Stay safe. When the water recedes... well, stay safe. I'm told help is coming."

"You as well."

I put down the microphone. The radio was located in the same room as Grundle's computer, which was where he was sitting.

"They're in the water," I said, thinking aloud.

"What was that?" Grundle asked.

"Something Paul said. Have you looked at the footage from Buster's camera yet?"

"I'm looking at it now. Would you like to see?"

He pulled up a still image of the banshee his pet dragon encountered. The image was blurry, but he appeared to be running some sort of program to improve the resolution.

"There are only about five seconds of footage in which the camera captures all or part of the creature," he said.

"Buster scared it off."

"A healthy reaction."

"Did you get anything on the lower half?"

"The legs?"

"I'm not sure they're legs."

"Let me see."

He went to a file of images. In the time it took me to talk to

Paul, Grundle had broken up the video into separate frames. The clean-up he was doing on an image was being performed on one of these stills, but it was one that didn't have the kind of detail I was looking for.

"There," I said, pointing to one particular panel. "Just when Buster arrives, his head was down. It looks like he caught some of the lower half."

He clicked on the shot, which was more than a little blurry. It was a glowing smear of white against a black background.

"That's not much," I said.

"Hold on."

He applied some filters. The image got a little crisper.

"Doesn't look anything like a pair of legs," he said. "I think it was moving too fast at this moment."

"I don't think it was."

There was a pair of *something* on the screen, but while they looked like they began as normal legs coming out of the lower torso, they flared out, like a pair of bell-bottom pants, only much bigger.

"You saw this with your own eyes," Grundle said. "Are you saying this image is accurate?"

"Yes, that's what I'm saying."

"It looks like two hoop skirts side-by-side. This can't be practical."

"Not on land, maybe."

Grundle nodded slowly.

"You know what it is!"

"I might," I said. "And I can't believe I'm going to say this out loud, but I think that might be a goddamn mermaid."

CHAPTER 12

"*A* mermaid," Grundle said flatly.

"Or merman, I guess."

"My skepticism remains."

"I appreciate that, but look at it. Pull up the other image."

Grundle went back to the picture the computer was still clarifying.

"If you had to design a being that was roughly humanoid but could survive in deep water, wouldn't it look about like that?"

He grunted. "Maybe. Torpedo-shaped skull, muscular but covered in fat for insulation… there are some aquatic creatures who glow like this in light."

"I was told they're more dangerous at night. Sunlight must be rough for them."

"They would burn easily with skin so fair. Who told you it was more dangerous at night?"

"That's not important right now," I said.

I'd sort of put the whole prophet-with-a-cult matter behind me. In another hour or two Gordana would be arriving at Bruno's final resting place. She might see the damage done to the jungle in that approximate spot and assume the worst. What that meant to her and her leader's understanding of the future was impossible to guess, but not really my problem.

My troll friend wasn't happy with the answer.

"I think it could be important depending on when they said it. It's been less than two days since the wave struck and before that these things were a curiosity, not a threat. I assume you left nobody behind when Buster led you here."

"Nobody alive."

"Explain."

I did. It took a while, and I had to stop and elaborate on what a prophet was, as the lexicon of known creatures he was working from didn't include them.

"And you don't know where they might be hiding?" he asked.

"She didn't give exact coordinates. I was pretty lost anyway. I'm not so sure I know where I am right *now*, to be honest, at least not in comparison to any part of the island I'm familiar with."

"Well. This is very interesting. Answers a great many questions. Not sure how to use the information."

"This is what I was saying. Not important. What is important, is *mermaid*. I need to find out if Dr. Cambridge survived. Did the hospital get hit bad?"

"I don't know. I haven't heard from anyone there, and I have no way to get a good visual. But I don't know that Cambridge was there."

"What makes you say that?"

"I monitor most of the island's public communications. In an official capacity, I mean. I speak for the committee on several matters. I happen to know Dr. Cambridge failed to show up for work for the past week."

"That's crazy. I had a drink with him... when was that? Same day Stubby showed me the hotel room vandalism, whenever that was."

"Interesting. It's possible you were the last to see him before he disappeared, then."

"Funny, yeah. And he was talking about mermaids."

"Was he."

"Yes, but not *this* kind. He was fixated on the more traditionally depicted sort. Kind of an obsession. I figure if anyone can help us with a firm identification of that thing on the screen, it's him."

"Certainly, but you would have to solve the mystery of his disappearance first."

"You said nobody saw him after I did?"

"I can't say for sure. Esteban was conducting a quiet investigation. I don't think he considered it foul play, so I suspect there was no formal attempt to establish a definite timeline. We all thought he either just left, or went on a long hike and got lost. Humans can be flighty."

"We have to find out where the cult is hiding."

He smiled. Troll smiles look a little like crevasses in rock.

"A minute ago you claimed they weren't important," he said.

"I did. But the succubus said they had a doctor with them."

"Could be a different doctor."

"Could be. But there aren't a lot of people in the world who specialize in the medical needs of impossible creatures, and this island isn't all that big."

Grundle continued to look amused, provided I was reading his body language accurately. I looked forward to a time when I might enjoy his company in less trying circumstances. Dinner, maybe, after the island was rescued and dried out and rebuilt, and all the dead were found, and Mirella was back.

It sounded more plausible in my head.

"I understand your resistance toward a cult run by a prophet," Grundle said, "but you have to enjoy the irony. If you had done as they asked you could have been getting those answers right at this moment."

"Yes, but they would have been answers to questions I didn't have yet. I still like this way better. I just don't know how to find them now."

"You could go back to the spot she left you, they may still be there."

"I don't know where that spot *is*. I was led out in the dark by an excitable dragon. Buster seems pretty smart, but if I were to ask him to lead me back I wouldn't even know what to tell him to lead me to, and I might not recognize it again. The best solution is to find a camp that nobody has been able to find. It's up here somewhere."

He arched an eyebrow, which was quite a thing. Troll foreheads are rather pronounced.

"Nobody knew to *look* for them up here," he said. "The estates mostly self-police, as you know."

"You have an idea."

"I have a thought. Let's go visit a friend."

~

isiting a friend didn't appear to involve exiting the cavern. One would think of that as a minimum requirement for going on a journey, but it turned out the internal network of passages—some combination of natural and artificial —was extensive.

We began by heading deeper into the middle of Grundle's living space until we reached the source of the flowing-water sound. This was a small pool fed from above by a steady drizzle. It looked like a low-pressure shower. I wondered if that was how it was used.

"It's replenished by rain water," the troll said, "but since it doesn't rain consistently enough to keep all of it from traveling down the mountain, we have a recycle that sends some of the water back up. Real waterfalls tend to be closer to the bottom of mountains."

"Larger mountains," I said.

"True. Our little hill is a striver. Come along."

To the side of the pool was a natural staircase of sorts, which led up and into a passageway. It was big enough for me to walk around upright, but a pretty tight fit for my host.

"It will get steep from here," he said. "Will you be all right without shoes? I'm afraid I have nothing in your size, but I can put you atop Buster. Or carry you, if you don't find that offensive."

"As long as it's lit, I should be fine."

We climbed in silence for possibly a half an hour. I couldn't be sure as I had no watch on, and the passage of time is really hard to guess in this sort of situation, but that was what it felt like. At one point, Grundle stopped and pulled hard on a thick rope dangling from the ceiling: two quick tugs, a pause, and then a third tug. My guess was, this was somebody's doorbell. I became concerned that we were perhaps about to be greeted by someone even larger than a troll.

The sound of trickling water got louder again as we neared the surface, and then the light ahead began to look more like sunlight.

It was evidently morning.

The water became a pool and the path we were on became the side of that pool, and then we came to the cavern opening and I realized I'd been here before.

We were standing on the inside of Dmitri's grotto.

The elf gangster's footman was standing at the mouth.

"Gaugin, isn't it?" I asked.

He was dressed in the same coat-and-tails I'd seen him in the last time, and he still looked completely out of place in it. On seeing me there, he shot a look at Grundle that was subtle enough to be almost impossible to read. Guests, I surmised, did not get brought to Dmitri through this particular route.

"Yes sir," he said. "You look as though you've had an unfortunate couple of days."

"Not nearly as unfortunate as most of the people on the island."

"Yes."

He looked at Grundle again. I had the sense he wanted to discuss with the troll how it came to be that I was emerging from the caverns, but his butler responsibilities weren't allowing him to speak quite that freely.

"Let me bring you inside," he said. To Grundle, he asked, "Can I bring you anything?"

"No, thanks Go-Go. I'll head back down. Give a ring if I'm needed. Adam, it was a pleasure. I hope we talk again soon."

"You aren't coming?" I asked.

"I don't leave the cave," he said.

I thought there was more to be said around that point, but the necessary explanation was perhaps too long for the time available. He probably just didn't want to be picked up by any cameras, but the idea that modern trolls might be naturally agoraphobic sprang to mind. It would certainly explain why they tended to hide under and in things, and why so few people encountered one.

Yes, I was pretty much just looking for a new weakness to replace the one Grundle contradicted. Force of habit.

Gaugin led me from the mouth of the grotto along the poolside and past the cabana where I'd last sat with his boss.

"Is she alive?" he asked, as we walked.

"I don't know. Have you heard from Esteban?"

"I've heard from nobody. I have ten family members downhill and no way to reach any of them. Each would know how to get in touch with me, and none have. What happened to her?"

"The wave reached the house. We had a hold of each other, and then we didn't."

He stopped at the door and adjusted his coat-and-tails in a way that looked like a nervous tic.

"She was spared the worst, then. If she's smart, she'll make her way here. Possibly not via the same path as you. Come."

We entered a house that was echoing with gunfire.

"Don't alarmed," he said. "Nobody is shooting anyone."

The entryway was just as I'd seen it before: modest in size but aspiring to be grandiose. The floor was marble, and there was a knock-off of a Greek statuette on a pedestal in the center of the floor. It portrayed a young Olympian preparing to throw a discus. While it wasn't an original, I was pretty sure I knew the artist being imitated. I think I might have even known the model.

We went past the statue and around the bottom of a staircase, to another door. On our way there we went by an open doorway leading to a dining area. A pretty young elf girl in a housecoat was eating breakfast quietly, alone, while looking at a handheld electronic thing. She was easily young enough to be Dmitri's daughter, but *girlfriend* was just about as likely. I decided the social awkwardness inherent in determining the answer to that question wasn't worth it, and kept quiet.

The door under the up staircase led to another staircase leading down. As soon as Gaugin opened it, the sound of gunfire got substantially louder. Having spent part of the early morning walking toward rushing water, I was now heading toward machine gun fire. I felt like I should be attempting to compose some manner of poetry around that idea, which was as sure a sign as anything that I needed some sleep and a lot of alcohol.

The basement was pretty similar to the caverns I'd just left behind, except this space appeared to be self-contained. It definitely occupied a larger footprint than the house above it, but not *that* much larger. It could have benefited from better sound-proofing, though, because as we continued to descend the sound of the gunfire, while intermittent, became loud enough to suggest it might cause damage to our hearing.

There was a table at the bottom of the stairs holding sets of ear muffs and protective glasses. Gaugin gestured to them silently as he put on a set of each himself.

Properly muffled and protected, we continued to the firing line.

Dmitri was standing on the other side of a bulletproof glass wall, at a table. The remainder of the room was mostly dead space terminating on a set of targets at the far end. He was with a young goblin I didn't recognize. The goblin was the one firing the gun. Dmitri was offering instruction.

We stood at the door that would admit us to the live gunfire side of the room and waited as the goblin fired his rounds. He appeared to be having trouble with the sensitivity of the trigger and the severity of the kickback, as the bullets were ending up high and to the left of the target.

Gaugin pressed a button next to the door, which flashed a light on the ceiling above the firing line table. Dmitri saw it, turned, nodded, and then took the gun from the young goblin, said a few words we couldn't hear, and dismissed him.

Soon, I was standing in front of a mobster who was holding a sub-machine gun, alone, in a basement.

Sometimes I really don't understand how I end up in these situations.

"Adam," he said, less gregariously than in our last encounter. "Welcome. I'm glad you're here. We will need all of the experienced hands we have at our disposal. I trust you know how to fire one of these?"

~

After about a half an hour of thoroughly unnecessary target practice, we went upstairs where a table could be found so as to facilitate a proper conversation.

I know how to fire most guns, including ones that only exist now as antiques. It isn't something I do for pleasure. It was evident, though, that I had to do it for at least a little while before Dmitri was ready to discuss why I was actually there. It was kind of a dick-measuring thing, really. Annoying, but basically impossible to avoid.

We were sitting outside, at a patio table. It was still early in the morning and cool enough that a cabana, and the shade it provided, weren't necessary. Weather-wise, it was shaping up to be a very nice day. Good weather right after a natural disaster is pretty common, for some reason.

The patio faced the downhill side of the mountain, and I was pretty sure were it not for some tall trees we'd be able to see all the way down to the town. Or, where it used to be.

"That is quite the story," Dmitri said, once I finished the explanation for how I ended up at his secret back door. "I'm glad you met Grundle. Terribly misunderstood, his kind."

"I've only known them as imbeciles," I said. "For me, it wasn't a lot different than having Buster start to talk, to be completely honest."

"I've *heard* Buster talk."

"Mimicry, though, yes?"

"Well, yes. He'll say his own name sometimes, but it's not clear he knows he's saying his own name."

"So what's with the guns?"

He laughed.

"So direct! But you should know exactly what they are for, you've met one of those things. Call them what you want: mermen, banshees, that other word, it doesn't matter. What they *are* is an invading army. This island is our home and we have to defend it, and we must act quickly."

"Why quickly?"

"Before the rescue operation commences. There are people trapped down there, *our* people, and we can't get to them. When the medical transports arrive, they won't be expecting a hostile force. We have to make sure they don't encounter one."

"Who is *we*?"

He laughed. "Oh, you, me, the boy Vincenzo you just met. Us three, down the mountain to wipe out an army."

"You forgot Go-Go."

"Yes, yes, him as well. No, Adam, I mean *us* as in the residents of the top of the island. We're working out the details, but the plan is for an assault beginning as soon as we are sure the waters have receded enough for vehicular travel on the lower island."

"You'll forgive me, I hope, Dmitri, but combat experience isn't the first thing that comes to mind when I think about most of your neighbors."

"Largely so, yes, but some are quite skilled, and there are a few you don't even know about. You didn't know we had a troll and a dragon until yesterday."

"Fair point."

I could think of at least two species that would be fantastic to have on my side in a fight like this, but neither played well with others. I'd probably try and swim to the mainland if he had one of them.

"You have doubts," he said.

"I do. You don't know the size of the enemy."

"How many of them could there be? The island is not that large."

"Yes, Dmitri. But the ocean is huge."

He sighed, and gestured something to Gaugin, which Go-Go apparently understood the meaning of. A moment later, a bottle of scotch and two glasses were on the table. Things were looking up.

"Drink with me, Leewan Sean," Dmitri said. I made a conscious effort not to respond to the name choice.

He poured us some scotch, and we drank. It was very, very smooth, and probably wildly expensive.

"I am not what you would think of as a particularly evolved man," he said. "I understand what violence is and I'm willing to respond with greater violence, and I sleep well at night despite the commission of that violence. I also understand diplomacy, and if I don't recognize when a circumstance calls for that instead of violence, I surround myself with people I trust who *do* recognize it. In life, this has gotten me far."

This was an understatement.

He continued: "I suspect the only man on this island, and possibly on the planet, with a greater appreciation of the applicability of violence than myself, is you. If I were to interpret the legends surrounding the great Leewan Sean accurately, I would also have to conclude that three of us—four if we bring Go-Go—actually *is* sufficient to eradicate this menace from our shores."

"Never believe a legend if your life depends on it," I said.

"An excellent piece of advice, thank you. They're untrue, then?"

"They're exaggerations. It would take too long to explain exactly how."

"Well, that *is* a shame."

What he was talking about had to do with a specific set of myths known to elves—and to a lesser extent, goblins—regarding me specifically. These aren't exactly like the ones you hear from time-to-time about Dionysos (most of Greece knew me by that name for about five or six hundred years) because a lot of those were originally about different gods. The Leewan Sean—or Lixian Xian depending on where you're from—myths all came from stuff I actually did.

What that stuff was, I won't get into right now.

"How about your legendary wisdom?" he asked. "Aside from the wisdom of not accepting the legend of your wisdom."

"My wisdom isn't too bad, but I'm only one drink in, so don't expect it to improve. I say an assault of any kind probably won't end well, but I don't have an alternative right now."

"You want to find these people you think are hidden in our jungle."

"Yeah."

"Because you think they have Dr. Cambridge."

"Basically."

"Why do you want the doctor?"

"There's a decent chance he knows more about mermaids than anyone else on the island."

"There are eight year olds who could claim extensive knowledge of mermaids, that doesn't make the information valuable."

"Right, but this feels more concrete. Look, attacking a non-human enemy you know nothing about is a bad idea. If you want to do this right, you have to figure out why they're here, how many to expect, and what it will take to kill them."

"Rapidly moving projectiles have proven effective, historically."

"Not always. Ever tried to shoot a demon? Or a vampire?"

"I've shot a vampire. But yes, it was less effective than tying his wounded body to a fence post and waiting until morning. I see your point."

"So can you help?"

"Let me reach out to the neighbors and see if we can figure out where these squatters are located. I can't promise we'll find them, and I can't guarantee if we do, the owner of the property they've claimed won't act badly. But we can start there. In the meantime, possibly we can get you another set of clothes, and some shoes? You're a sight, and as my guest I can no longer abide it."

～

I thought a decent shower and the rest of what was in the scotch bottle was just about all I really needed, but a change of clothes was pretty nice too. What I ended up with was a guest bedroom with an attached shower to go along with the change of clothes, plus a pair of shoes that fit. But I didn't get the scotch bottle, and while that was probably for the best I would have traded all of the above for it. It had been that kind of day.

After using the shower, I drifted off on the bed for long enough that Go-Go had trouble waking me when it was time to do so.

"Does he have something for me?" I asked, sitting up slowly. I had dressed, thankfully, before deciding the bed looked soft.

"He thinks so, yes," Gaugin said, in the midst of a particularly unpleasant stare. "Why are you here?"

"Is that what he wants to know? Because I thought he knew."

"It's what I want to know."

"You mean, why am I here instead of wandering around the jungle shouting for Mirella and banging a steel drum or something."

"Yes."

"I appear insufficiently concerned, to you?"

He didn't respond, which was an answer.

I was pretty sure whatever happened while I was sleeping included him either receiving or overhearing a description of the cult, which would have included a description of the succubus I heard about it from. He undoubtedly arrived at the most unsavory conclusion imaginable. As I said, some goblins look down on human-goblin relations, and I'm sure this information only fed into that.

"I could gnash my teeth and rend my garments," I said, "but I like my teeth the way they are and I'm only borrowing these clothes, and it won't help me find her any faster anyway. Better to work on what I can control and hope she turns up alive."

He gave a *humph* and walked out of the room, almost faster than I could follow.

The shoes in question were a new pair of running shoes, and I nearly fell just trying to re-accustom myself to the idea of them. They went well with the loaned tracksuit, though. I thought maybe all I needed to complete the whole "extra in a mafia movie" look was a gold chain or two.

I followed Go-Go down the stairs and into a study that was one of the rooms I'd not yet seen in Dmitri's little mini-mansion. He was at his desk—an expensive-looking slab of polished oak—and examining what looked like a map of the island.

"I've made some calls, and Mr. Grundle has performed a few environmental searches, and I don't think we've found them," he said.

"You brought me down to say you have no news?"

"No, Adam, I brought you down to receive the news that I believe you're mistaken, and they are not where you think they are."

"I think you're underestimating the ability of a future seer to find a part of the island where it's safe to hide."

"But where would that be?"

He gestured to the map. I'd never seen a map of the island before from this particular perspective: a bird's-eye with the top of the island in the center. The property lines were drawn out precisely along the elevation contours, with gaps indicating public pathways. Each of the buildings, swimming pools, tennis courts, treeless lawns, gazebos, artificial ponds, mini-golf courses, and so on were clearly visible and easily identifiable. It looked like there was plenty of room to spare.

"The property lines aren't marked by fences in all instances, are they?" I asked. "I mean, you have a nice big one, but most of these places don't."

"No, they don't. There are three fences: mine, Reginald's over here, and Lady Tzu on the other side, here."

He identified each with a thump of his index finger. The property lines for these sections were slightly thicker, denoting the fence.

"That leaves several without fences," he said.

"Right. Do you have proximity alarms or something?"

"Yes, after a fashion. Nothing electronic; it seems they're too easily tripped by naturally occurring jungle events, or by a certain freely-roaming pet dragon, or a few other things that would legally constitute an incursion on private land but which we're generally okay with. We want to keep out squatters, overly curious tourists, and any assassins that might drop in, but pets and wild animals are all right."

"If not electronic, then what?"

He smiled a clever sort of smile that made me think the next thing out of his mouth was something he thought of personally.

"Pixies," he said. "Trained pixies. We each have a few dozen. As a matter of course, they're sent out to survey the respective properties and to report back on what they've found. They are quite helpful in recognizing the overstepping of all manner of species."

"That *is* clever," I said, and I meant it. I'm the only person I know who's in the habit of taming and employing pixies, or I was until this moment. Clever, then, because it was actually my idea first.

"So they've seen the banshees, haven't they? The last time we talked about them…"

He was nodding.

"I know you're thinking I kept things from you that day, but I did not. We sent pixies out to identify the source of the howling, but they came back with no useful information. No intruders. An animal, they said, but the descriptions didn't make sense so we stopped asking. My point is that I've contacted each of my top island neighbors and asked them to perform a pixie sweep. All reported back that there is no evidence of squatters. And as you can see, there's hardly any other place to look."

I stared at the map for a while, trying to find a hole in his argument. It must have been because I was still groggy from the nap, or maybe I'd lived on the island long enough to ignore the obvious because everyone else did, but I didn't see it right away.

"How about here?" I asked. I pointed at the center-most part of the map.

"The summit?"

"Did you look there?"

"No of course not, it's terrible up there. No tree cover, relentless winds. Why do you think nobody put a house on the top?"

"I know all that, I've visited it."

"Well there's your answer. Tours hike up there all the time. This cult has supposedly been in hiding for weeks, and you mean to say they're living on the most visible part of the island?"

"It's only the most visible from the air, and there are ways to camouflage from an aerial survey. And I'll bet there hasn't been a tour of the summit recently."

"Maybe there hasn't," he said, still not convinced. "But how could they be so lucky as to choose to live there for a stretch of time in which there just happened to be no tours?"

"As I said, never underestimate the ability of a future seer to hide."

~

*A*s it happened, the wealthy residents of the top of the island were notified well in advance of any authorized incursion to the *actual* top of the island. The tours were planned at the hotel, with local guides walking however many people wished to go, on the long hike that didn't actually start at the bottom of the mountain. This would take too long. Instead, a carload of intrepid persons was driven to a small parking area well above the mid-point and just below the private estate property lines.

From there, the expedition followed a well-worn and clearly marked narrow uphill path that wound its way to the very top.

The trip up took most of the day, invariably exhausted everyone involved, and generally discouraged participants from ever doing it again because it just wasn't all that interesting of a hike.

Since so many people living near the top responded poorly to strangers, someone saw the wisdom of establishing a notification procedure to make sure there were no unpleasant surprises for anyone involved. It would have worked a little better if these notifications were widely shared, but at least someone was trying. The important thing was, there was a schedule, and once Dmitri reached out to Grundle—the *de facto* tech support for the top of the island—we had that schedule too, and were able to verify that from the time the wrecked hotel room was discovered to the day of the tsunami, there had been no official visits to the summit.

I was convinced I was on to something, but Dmitri wasn't swayed.

"I should continue with the preparations," he said. "Scheduling an operation like this, it has many moving parts. I can't stop and restart so easily."

"You also don't believe me."

"Not that I do or I don't, I don't see how your path can alter mine at this time. You should keep to yours, and I will help, and hopefully you'll prove me wrong before I've ended up dying for the arrogance of not having listened to your advice."

"It's solid advice," I said.

"I don't doubt this."

"Attacking an enemy without a grasp of their strengths and weaknesses is a really bad idea."

"I understand. But premature action is all we have when inaction isn't an option. So tell me, how I can help you complete your quest?"

"Some clothes more appropriate to the outdoors, maybe some hiking boots. Oh, and a guide."

"I can't spare a man, but I can get you a map."

"I wasn't thinking of a man."

~

A little while later, I was trying out a pair of boots and cargo shorts, while getting to know a pixie named Ha.

Pixies are more or less exactly what you think they are: tiny flying women with gossamer wings that look approximately like Tinkerbell from the Disney cartoons, only without the clothing. They're nearly impossible to find and catch, but if you know how to find and catch one, they're remarkably easy to tame and very loyal once they've been tamed. They're also intelligent enough to be self-aware, but not *too* smart, and they're terribly naïve.

I've known a few pixies, and a couple saved my life once or twice. The last one made a habit of it, until she was killed in a way that's going to take me a couple of generations to get beyond.

I wouldn't have asked for a pixie guide, then, if I saw any other option.

"It's nice to meet you, Ha," I said. I was walking around the lawn behind the house. We were on the other side of the yard, next to a free-standing structure that looked like a remodeled pigeon coop. Ha was one of several pixies, but the only one flying around. The others just sat and ate and ignored me.

The walking was to get used to the shoes, which were not new, but also not broken in by my feet. I didn't know who owned them, but thankfully they had the same shoe size. I would have resumed my barefoot walking, but the top was cold and rocky. I was planning to shed them as soon as I started downhill again.

"Yeah okay," she said, zipping past my head.

This would be the first time I worked with a pixie I hadn't tamed myself. I didn't really know what to expect.

"What do you do for Dmitri, usually?" I asked.

"Check the line for treppers."

"Treppers?"

"Treppers."

"Trespassers?" I guessed.

"Yes. I said that."

"So you did. My mistake."

Dmitri also provided me with a backpack, a decent amount of water and dried beef (no protein bars) and dried mushrooms for Ha.

He also had a radio for me.

"We will be on channel seven," he said. "Reception is spotty. Grundle believes our visiting friends may be causing some manner of atmospheric interference, but he can't explain how. If you need to communicate, keep trying and we will make do with what we get."

We shook hands.

"Best of luck, Dmitri," I said.

"And to you. See you downhill."

He pulled me closer. He was surprisingly strong for someone as old as he was supposed to be.

"I also promise you," he said, "if I find your woman I will keep her safe until you arrive."

"Thank you, that's really kind."

~

*I*t was past midday by the time Ha and I got going, which would put us at the top at around sundown. This was not the best timing imaginable, but it couldn't be helped.

The pixie led us off Dmitri's property and to the path, and continued to provide detailed step-by-step instruction right until she realized I knew the way from there, and then she started to get annoying.

"Okay, I go back now?" she asked.

"No, I'd like you to stick around."

"You know way, I go back."

"What I need is for someone such as yourself to range ahead and notify me of any dangers."

"Dangers," she repeated. I wasn't sure she knew what the word meant.

"Trespassers."

"Treppers? No treppers on path. Can't be."

It has been my experience that pixies don't grasp concepts like ownership and private property. It appeared Ha *only* grasped these concepts and nothing else.

"What do you look for, when you look for trespassers?"

She buzzed around for a little while without answering. When a pixie flies in tight circles like this, it means she's thinking. Kind of like pacing, in a human.

The path we were on wasn't all that challenging. I remembered being on this stretch on the one or two occasions Mirella and I hiked to the summit, but I had no idea at that time how close I was to Dmitri's land. That probably would have been useful information, or at least *interesting* information to have.

It did get steep from time to time. I tried to imagine doing it while carrying an incubus on a stretcher and decided it wouldn't have been possible without a lot more people being involved.

"Look for people," Ha said.

"People, like me?"

"Like you and Di-Di, and Go-Go and like Grund. Talking people."

"But not animals."

"Animals hard."

"But they're a lot smaller than people, and they walk on all fours."

"Four what?"

"Never mind."

"Some animals big. Big animals okay too."

"Like dragons?"

"Buster okay."

Even the island pixies knew dragons weren't extinct and I didn't.

"Dogs okay too," Ha added. "Pigs okay."

"There are pigs on the island?"

"Nobody own pigs, pigs okay."

"Wild pigs, then."

"Uh-huh."

"Fish okay."

I laughed.

"You run into fish on the island a lot, do you?" I asked.

"Walking fish, silly," she said, and I went a little cold.

"You've seen a lot of walking fish?"

"Uh-huh. Big. Smelly like water, because fish."

"Where have you seen them?"

"All over. But okay. Animals okay."

"What do you mean all over? Is there one near us right now?"

She flew away, while I stood completely still, held my breath, and did a quick inventory of all the gods I could think of. Poseidon would be a good one to pray to in this situation, I decided.

Ha came back pretty fast.

"No," she said. She was incredibly unconcerned, but it wasn't like she was at risk. I'm so used to a tame pixie worrying about my wellbeing I forget sometimes that pixies are incredibly hard to kill. It's like worrying about a laser beam getting eaten. Then again, it was that kind of thinking that might have contributed to my last pixie being murdered.

"Did you ever tell Dmitri about the walking fish?" I asked.

"No," she said, in a tone that was a little condescending. "Animals okay, fish animals, fish okay. Talking people not okay."

I wondered how often he sent pixies to find the source of the banshee howls, and how many times those pixies found a "walking fish", concluded that wasn't what they were there to report on, and came back saying everything was okay.

"I go home now?" Ha asked.

"No, Ha. I want you to fly ahead and tell me if there is anyone on or around the path. I *especially* want to know about any walking fish you find."

"Okay. Other animals too?"

"How about, anything the size of a dog or larger?"

"Okay."

~

J've probably spent more time walking through jungles than I have through just about any other natural environment, which is to be expected given my history. I have really good instincts when it comes to distinguishing between forest floor sounds that represent possible danger, potential prey, and probably nothing important.

I'm saying this because there is no good explanation for the fact that the afternoon climb to the summit was one of the most terrifying afternoons I'd had in a profoundly long time.

Not only am I really good at identifying the beasts of the jungle based on sight and sound and spoor and track, I had an obsessive/compulsive pixie checking in every few minutes to re-notify me that there was nothing up ahead, everything was okay, and can she go home *now*?

My heart was racing the whole time anyway. It was probably because of how little I knew of the banshee/mermaid/walking fish things sharing the jungle with me, and that was not at all helped by the frequency of their cries.

But, I reached the top unmolested and only bothered by a couple of mosquito bites and one annoyed pixie.

As Dmitri accurately described, the summit was an unpleasant place. The surface was a mess of jagged rocks and the wind was completely unreasonable. I couldn't see the lower island, either, and the view was supposed to be the best reason to make the climb. The hill beneath wasn't steep enough to turn this into a compelling lookout spot, though. Instead, in the direction of town there was a drop-off, then a leveling, which lasted long enough to block anything beneath that point. Trees and ocean, and that was all to see.

Also, and to my tremendous disappointment, nobody was living up there. I should have known this already, since Ha would have notified me if anything larger than a dog was ahead of us, and this would have included the summit. I didn't think of that until I got there, though.

I walked around it anyway.

"What you want here?" Ha asked.

"I was looking for people."

"Oh. No people, I go home now?"

"Not yet. How about any evidence of people?"

"Dents?"

"Evidence. Things people own."

"Like tent?"

"Yes, like a tent."

This was an incredibly specific response from her, considering all the different things people could potentially own.

"Did you see a tent?" I asked.

"Uh-huh."

She led me to the lip of the summit, and then down the gentle slope of what I would call the back of the mountain if I were looking at the top of it from the bottom.

Just below the wind was a tent the same approximate shade of dark gray as the rocky top. It was the sort of thing that might just go unnoticed in an overhead surveillance if one weren't looking for it.

I scrambled down the slope, taking note as I went of the number of tent-spike holes. There were more than I could count on quick review, but enough to indicate that at one point, recently, there had been a lot more tents.

The one remaining tent was nothing special. It was several steps up from a standard-issue army tent, but not as luxurious of some of the better ones I've seen. I've never been a big fan of them unless it happens to be raining out and I can't find shelter any other way. I don't like the idea of sleeping behind walls that aren't strong enough to protect me but *are* strong enough to keep me trapped inside and unable to see or hear something looking for dinner.

But—and I probably overstress this—I came of age when the likelihood of being eaten during the night was pretty high.

There was nobody inside. The tent offered decent shelter from whatever wind made it past the lip of the summit, and had a floor that would have kept any rain washing off the top from getting under the walls, but I had to assume whatever cot or sleeping bag used—the ground under the tent was not at all forgiving—had gone with the inhabitants when they left.

The only question was, why didn't they take this tent with them too?

The answer may have involved the one thing in the tent that wasn't me or Ha.

Sitting in the center of the vinyl floor was what looked like a small ice cooler, the kind with a handle on the top for transporting small quantities of chilled beer.

A note was taped to the cooler, but it wasn't bright enough in the tent to read it, so I carried the whole thing outside into the fading sunlight. It would be dark in under a half an hour, which meant I had about that long to decide where I was going to take shelter for the evening. The tent was an option, but I've already explained my objection to tents, which held strong in a circumstance where the woods were full of walking fish and my only companion was an obnoxious pixie.

The note read: *She is too sick we have to take her to the hospital. Doctor thinks he can save her. Meet us there. Good luck.*

I read the note twice, and then I read it aloud for Ha, who was curious and apparently couldn't read.

"Who she?" Ha asked.

"Their prophet, probably. They tend to be sickly. Can't imagine anyone else so important that they'd risk going to the hospital."

"Hospital good."

"Hospital was just under water until recently. It's probably wrecked."

"Oh. I go home now?"

"No, not yet."

I reached into my backpack and laid out some dried mushrooms for her so she's shut up for a few minutes.

I wondered what made anyone involved in this think I'd willingly follow them down the mountain. The safe play was to head back to Dmitri's and wait for the expected rescue from the mainland. Surely it would be possible to call in a whole lot of guns—if necessary—to deal with the banshee issue. If that didn't work, and Dmitri insisted I couldn't stay and had to go fight with him, I could probably hide out with the troll instead.

I had options, in other words, that didn't involve chasing a prophet down a mountain and into the teeth of undeniable danger. Granted, those options also included signing off on the possibility my girlfriend was dead or dying somewhere, but I wasn't too far away from accepting that already. I just didn't have enough alcohol to cope with it appropriately yet.

I also didn't know what putting myself in extra danger would do to change that.

But I wasn't done deciphering what was left behind. There was the cooler to attend to.

A symbol was on the side of the cooler, some kind of company logo I didn't recognize: rectangles representing bottles on a vertical line representing a table. It was an extremely old pictogram that used to refer generically to a store or shop but looked to have been borrowed for a more pharmacological reason by a modern company. I doubted they fully understood what it was when whatever marketing company responsible for corporate branding found it in an Internet search.

Anyway, modern eyes probably saw something representing medicine. I saw alcohol, but I'm probably the exception.

I pushed a button on the front, which allowed the top to swing open. For a second or two I wondered if maybe this was a bad idea, since coolers from medical facilities tend to hold bad things whenever they turn up in movies, which is my only frame of reference. But, I couldn't *not* open it after all of this, and on top of that I can't get sick anyway.

This is not to say opening it wasn't a mistake, just that those were the concerns I worked through beforehand. And it was definitely a mistake.

There was a lump of... something, inside. It was a semisolid piece of white fleshy matter. I reached in and picked it up, and it nearly oozed out of my hands.

"What the heck is this?" I asked aloud.

It felt a little like I imagined picking up a jellyfish might feel like, had I ever tried to pick one up. I was also reminded of some of the things I used to eat out of that tide pool near the cave on the African coast, way back when. Protein. Slimy, gooey protein that had to be swallowed whole, but protein.

"Fish," Ha said, buzzing past.

"Did you see a walking fish?"

"No see, smell."

"This?" I took a sniff of what was in my hands. It did have a fishy smell, but it was faint. "Smells a little like fish."

"Smell like walking fish."

"It's skin," I realized. "Something shed this. Why would they give this to me?"

"Walking fish smell," Ha repeated.

"Yes, I know it's the same smell."

I didn't fully appreciate the point she was making, which either underscores how clueless I was being about the entire situation or how much smarter pixies are than I really give them credit for. Either way, I began to notice the banshee howling—a constant throughout the afternoon—had begun to accelerate in frequency.

They also sounded like they were getting closer.

"Ha…" I began, but she had already zipped away. I threw the skin back into the cooler and closed it, which only did me a little bit of good since I also had the smell of it all over my hands. I needed a shower, but I was a long ways away from one.

Ha returned.

"Is someone here?" I asked.

"Yes."

"Walking fish?"

"Yes."

"Where?"

"All over."

They were attracted to the smell. And until I found a way to get it off my hands, they were also attracted to me.

My eyes drifted to the last line of the note taped on the cooler. *Good luck*, it said.

CHAPTER 13

My first impulse was to open throw the contents of the cooler as far away as possible and then run in the opposite direction, but while that wasn't a terrible idea, this was not the best place to try misdirection. Instead, I grabbed it by the handle and located Ha, still buzzing in nervous-tension circlets around the vicinity.

"I need a path down the mountain," I said. "Can you show me?"

"Uh-huh, you fly?"

"No, I can't fly."

"Okay, harder."

"I know. I can climb, though, if I have to and there's a tree nearby."

"Okay, but you should learn to fly."

"I agree with you completely."

"This way."

My last pixie—her name was Iza—used to provide directions by doing a gentle hover in front of my face at a pace that was easy enough to follow from anywhere between a brisk walk to an all-out sprint. Ha appeared to have never been in a situation where she led a human-sized being anywhere, because she kept zipping ahead and then doubling back, making loud huffing noises, circling five or six times as if this would speed me up, and then shooting ahead again.

The route we took had no attendant footpath, which was really okay because we were going downhill. The great thing about heading downhill rapidly was even if you made a mistake you tended to end up going in the correct direction anyway. Sure, you could land on something more durable than you are, but you were still falling the correct way.

I was carrying the cooler—not heavy, but awkwardly large— and a backpack that was more than half-full of water, so I was a little more weighted down and a little less in balance than I was used to, but I could still get down the hill at a decent clip. Not decent enough to keep the pixie happy, but better than your average two-legged prey.

Ha was less than understanding about the vagaries of the terrain, though, which became a problem when she indicated a left turn into a drop that was about ten feet steeper than I was okay with. I skidded to a stop.

"Come on!" she yelled. It was worth noting that the sun was still going down, and in a very short time I wouldn't be able to see her any more. Unlike Tinkerbell, pixies don't glow.

"I still can't fly," I said.

A howl not at all far behind us nearly convinced me to try flying anyway, but then Ha was redirecting, left and around the precipitous drop and we were away again.

Then I lost sight of her.

"Ha?" I said, my voice slightly elevated but not up at the, *everybody here I am*, level of loud. I kept running straight and hoped she expected me to do that.

She didn't. I navigated around a large tree, and on the other side of it was one of the mermen.

He looked essentially just like the one I'd seen a couple of nights earlier: torpedo head, strong arms, large belly, something approximating legs below the waist.

He opened what I guessed was probably his mouth—it was in the right place for it—and unleashed an intolerably loud bellow. The jaw appeared to have no hinges, and his cheeks billowed like sails and expanded like balloons. These features contributed to produce a low bass roar that was probably audible across the entire island. I bet under water, a cry like that carried through the entire ocean.

I was very nearly incapacitated by the sound. I didn't continue toward him, certainly, but I didn't go anywhere else either. I stopped in my tracks. To my credit, I didn't also fall over.

"This way," Ha said, in my left ear. She also smacked me on the left cheek, in case I'd lost my hearing completely, which was good thinking. I hadn't, but my ears were rung pretty bad. I wagered she was doing even worse. Pixies have pretty sensitive ears.

I headed left, and the bellowing merman moved to follow, or perhaps to cut me off.

I was still quicker. These things moved in a way I'd never seen anything move before, but there was no substitute for legs with knees when it came to jungle travel. He got only within a few yards before I was past and continuing.

"You may need to keep yelling in my ear, left or right, Ha," I said. "I can't see you any more, and I'm not sure how well I can hear you."

Ha didn't respond, which I took to be a bad sign. I couldn't hear my own voice; maybe she couldn't hear it either.

Once past the merman with the impressive set of lungs, I was okay for about ten minutes of rapid downhill transit, which got us to the other side of sunset, and the discovery that there is a certain advantage to being prey in a jungle full of glowing predators.

I didn't need a pixie's help to tell me three mermen were

waiting on the other side of the next set of trees. I could see them, or parts of them, just fine. They couldn't see me.

They could probably smell me though.

I checked behind to verify I wasn't about to be ambushed by a chaser, then knelt down and opened the cooler again.

"Not this way!" Ha said, in my right ear this time.

"Where do you want me to go?"

"You missed turn, go back."

"No going back," I said. "I have another idea."

I extracted the skin sample from the cooler. It was glowing in the moonlight too, but only faintly. I threw it downhill and to the right, as far as I could. Then I threw the cooler—still open and with that nice note taped to it—uphill in the rough direction I had come.

"Now I go forward," I said.

"No forward, only back and left."

"I'm surrounded, you're saying."

"No, back and left."

I knelt down again, and started untying my boots.

"I was thinking I'd go up," I said.

"You say can't fly."

"I can't."

"You take off shoes to fly?"

"Not exactly, no."

～

*A*n hour later, it was completely dark, with little help from the moon. I was in a tree, relaxing and enjoying a piece of dried meat and a bottle of water, while my pixie guide was trying to find a polite way to ask, again, if she could go home.

There were four mermen milling around under the tree. It wasn't necessarily the same four as the ones I spotted earlier;

they could have been rotating new ones in. There was really no way to tell, since to my eyes they all looked the same.

Their close-up language was a series of clicks, somewhere between dolphin and Khoikhoi. Their vowel sounds all came out of a hum, like a teeny tiny version of the roar that temporarily deafened me earlier. They were equipped with a different vocalization apparatus than anything on land, this much was clear. Based on the amount of gesturing I saw, much of the nuance that came with aquatic resonance was lost, absent the water.

They hadn't figured out yet that they should be looking up. The last evidence of my existence was a pair of boots on the hill not far from the tree, and whatever spoor transference occurred when I touched the trunk before climbing, but that wasn't translating into any effort to gaze skyward.

It appeared they had no necks. Maybe that was the problem.

"I go now," Ha said.

"But we're having so much fun."

The mermen did not appear to have good hearing, which was nice.

"Not fun."

"I'm joking."

"I go get help."

"That's sweet, are you worried about me?"

"I go get help," she repeated.

"Who would you get?"

"Di-Di come help."

"I think Dmitri's already heading in the other direction, but he'd probably love to come up here with a few guns."

"So? I go get help."

"I'm fine."

"You stuck."

"I'm not stuck."

"You can't climb down. You climb up? You fly?"

I laughed.

"I appreciate your concern, Ha, but I'm exactly where I want to be. Do you see that tree over there? The one whose branches are woven with this one?"

"Uh-huh, sure."

"Jungle canopies are their own highways if you know what you're doing. As long as they can't climb trees I'll be fine."

"Oh no!" she said, and then she flew off.

This was a tiny bit disconcerting. I held my breath until she returned, which was only after a minute.

"You trepping!" she said sternly.

"I am?"

"Uh-huh."

"Dmitri's land reaches this far?"

"Not Dmitri, other."

"You know all the property lines up here?"

"Uh-huh."

"That means they're trespassing too," I said. "And so are you."

"I too small, they animals."

"They aren't animals, Ha. They're like people, but people from the water."

"Walking fish."

"Swimming people."

"Hm, okay. I should go."

"Why now?"

"I tell about treppers."

"Tell who?"

"Pixies."

"You're all like a tiny little security force up here."

"Uh-huh," she said, with a teeny shrug. "I go?"

"How many pixies are we talking about?"

"Dunno."

"What are you guys supposed to do when you encounter a trespasser?"

"Tell owner."

"That's all? What if the owner isn't around?"

She shrugged.

"How about this," I said. "You go tell whoever you want about those trespassers down there, but leave me alone."

I kind of liked having her around, but I could no longer think of a use for her, and it wasn't a terrible idea to propagate the notion—among the pixies—that the creatures under my tree weren't okay.

"But you also trepper."

"Dmitri gave me permission to trespass."

This was untrue, but if she flew back to him and asked he'd back me up.

"You not trepping?"

"No. Just them."

She flew in a circle to think about this.

"Okay. I go?" she asked.

"You can go."

"Okay, bye."

Ha flew away, and that was that. Then it was just me and the mermen.

~

A little while later, one of them figured out why they kept smelling my presence around the tree, and decided the world must include a third dimension. Then they looked up. I don't know if they could actually see me, because I wasn't doing any glowing. They had large black eyes that looked to have no pupil, and I had no clue how good those eyes were at detecting things in near-total darkness. If they spent most of their time in the deep sea, though, their eyes were probably pretty good.

Unless they used their other senses more regularly when they were underwater, in which case, never mind.

This is what I mean by knowing your enemy. I had no experience with these creatures, and didn't know what was normal for them. Faeries presented a similar problem, although in theory I could probably figure out how to get back into their realm so as to gain a better understanding, and they still lived in a land-based world so it wouldn't be so bad. With these guys, forget it.

One of them put his arms and his tail around the trunk. At first I thought he was planning to squeeze the tree until it collapsed—and who knows, maybe they were strong enough to do that—but then he started to climb.

The little flagella things on the bottom of his... fin, let's call it, were somehow helping propel him up the tree. It was slow, and he looked about as surprised as anyone that it worked, but it did work.

That was my cue to go. I got to my feet as carefully as possible, secured the backpack, and felt my way down one of the extended tree limbs until I reached a spot I'd eyeballed back when Ha was still with me. I jumped.

It was the satyrs who showed me how to travel by treetop. An adult satyr has a vertical leap of something like twenty-five feet, so I could have probably found a better teacher, but some of the rules translated well. For example, only use live trees with a robust network of branches and leaves. When jumping from tree to tree, always reach for the largest limb you can find, and if you can't find one, scoop up all the small ones. If this doesn't work, don't panic, because you're bound to hit a good one on the way down.

In a real forest it's frankly not all that scary or difficult to travel this way, it's just that humans stopped spending time in trees so long ago we forgot how easy it was. I mean, aside from the occasional Tarzan movie, not that those were remotely accurate. Rope-sized vines that happened to be secure on the other end just aren't common.

Generally, the jumps aren't all that long, and sometimes they're completely unnecessary, especially in your more robust rainforests. If the trees are mature enough and close enough, they're woven together in such a way that the hard part is often just recognizing when you're relying on a part of the tree in front of you instead of the one behind you.

Parts of the island jungle were like this, especially near the top of the mountain. This was where I was starting from, so for a little while I moved at a pretty decent downhill clip. It wasn't nearly as fast as it would have been if I was on the ground and running, but it was better than nothing.

After probably an hour of downhill travel, I'd made a couple of disturbing observations. The first was that the mermen on the ground were definitely in communication with one another, and as much as it sounded like undifferentiated howling, complex ideas were being exchanged. I say this because their tactics were evolving as I moved.

They were still climbing trees, but appeared to recognize that traveling among them the way I did was a physiological impossibility. They could still get up to the low branches, though, which reduced my choices because one of the things they communicated was, where I was going and what trees to get to before I got there.

As I went downhill, in other words, I stopped seeing mermen in trees behind me and started seeing them in trees in front of me.

There were still plenty of trees from which to choose, though, so I continued around the obstacles and hoped they didn't have a large enough army to cut me off completely.

The second observation was one I'd made thousands of times before, only generally in situations that were less perilous: civilization can sometimes ruin everything.

There were, as I've said, a lot of private lands hidden in the woods. For the most part, the property owners did what they could to maintain the forest cover, because they valued secrecy almost more than they valued direct access to sunlight, but that didn't mean there was no manipulation of the natural landscape. Ground had been cleared, fences were erected, paths were put in... and trees were pruned, thinned, and eliminated.

I reached a certain point in my travels where the trees started to get not-so-close together. The jumps became more perilous, and whenever I tried to alter my course in the direction of thicker tree cover, I found the route cut off by one of the mermen.

I was being herded.

I'm intimately familiar with the concept, but this was probably the first time I'd ever been the target instead of the one coordinating the herding. The frustrating part was, even realizing what was going on I couldn't do anything about it. I wondered if this was how the mammoths felt when we forced them off cliffs or into the devastating fists of a troll.

About the only change I could make was to slow down, and so I did. Once it was obvious traveling faster wasn't going to get me to a point where there were no mermen and I was safe, I had no reason to go so quickly that I risked making a mistake. (Note: forty feet above the forest floor is always a bad place to make a mistake.)

The next hour, then, was a somewhat leisurely trip. At each tree I got to eat a little, have some water, rest my legs, and then take the next tree pre-selected by my pursuers. It was relaxing, in its own way.

I got pretty close to the road at one point. I knew this because I could see the red taillights shining through the leaves, and caught the sound of a revving engine. For about two seconds I thought maybe Ha reached Dmitri and I was getting rescued, but the sounds were faint and the SUV's were clearly heading the wrong way. Dmitri had begun his assault on the lower island.

Then I remembered he'd given me a radio. I dug it out of the bag and tuned it to the right channel. As soon as I kicked up the volume, though, the night was filled with the sound of impenetrable static. I tried anyway.

"Dmitri, this is Adam, over," I said.

Static.

"Dmitri, can you hear me? I could use a bunch of guns right about now."

More static.

I fiddled with the dial for a few minutes longer, but there was no escaping the white noise. I caught a voice here and there—I could swear one of the voices was Esteban, but that might have been my mind playing tricks—but that was all. No clear channels.

It was the mermen. Somehow, they were impacting the electrical field on the island. I know exactly enough about electricity to successfully avoid being killed by it, and that's all. But I also knew we all had clear radio communications before, and I knew there were dozens of mermen within a hundred feet of me, and I don't believe in coincidences.

～

*T*he end came when I reached a tree at the edge of a clearing. It was obvious almost immediately, and not because there were no trees left to jump to once I got there—although that was true. No, it was obvious because the clearing was occupied by a committee of impatient mermen.

All of them were staring up, waiting. I decided that as much as I had been studying their behavior over the past few hours, they'd been studying mine, so they understood that when my pace slowed it was because I became aware of their tactics. It was reasonable, on their part, to conclude that they didn't need to send anyone up this particular tree to shake me down.

I'm a tiny bit more stubborn than that when it comes to facing my own probable demise, though, so I stayed in the tree and ate some more dried meat, and drank my second-to-last bottle of water. I figured eventually one of them would give a shout along the lines of *why don't you come down from there already?*

That moment came, but not in the form of a shout. One of the mermen stepped forward, looked past my tree and gave a wordless salute to someone in a tree uphill. It was the last tree I'd been in before arriving at the clearing, actually.

I looked over my shoulder. One of the pursuing mermen had made it halfway up the trunk of the tree: a big, wide, very old specimen that looked lush and alive when I was sitting in it a little earlier.

I heard an odd hissing noise, apparently coming from the spot where the merman and the tree met. Then there was a puff of white smoke, and the tree groaned. Really, it was just the first stages of gravity pulling down the tree that made the noise, but it sounded like the plant actually cried out audibly.

The merman was either exerting a great deal of force or extruding an acid of some sort, but the outcome was the same: he brought down the tree, and in only about thirty seconds. Looks like they *could* bring them down if they wanted.

The signaling merman—evidently a leader, which was actually good information to have—looked back up at me.

"All right," I said. There was no reason to think he could understand, but I said it anyway. "I'm coming down."

My arrival in the clearing caused something that in humans would be called a *buzz*, as the assembled mermen—there were ten of them—murmured to one another. In them it was a bunch of clicks, like gossiping dolphins.

The leader raised a fist, which shut up everybody. He stepped forward, sniffed me, and stared. More clicking from the rabble, another call for silence, then he turned to them and spoke some words.

I didn't *hear* most of what he said. There was a lot of what I'd call whistling, some clicks and clacks, and something amounting to heavy breathing. I decided what was going on was that most of his vocalizing was subsonic. I was pretty sure if there were a dog nearby, he'd be going nuts.

Buster could probably hear it, I decided. There was no reason for that to be true, because dragons and dogs are about as far apart evolutionarily as mosquitos and whales, (I'm guessing) but I liked the idea. It filled me with irrational hope that a dragon was about to burst into the clearing and come to my rescue. I'd never in my life wished for such a thing before, but it had been a weird couple of days.

The merman leader turned back at me and pointed. His hands only had two fingers and an opposable thumb, so he was essentially pointing with his entire hand, but I got the concept of the gesture all right, I just didn't know what it was meant to convey.

"Hello," I said. "My name is Adam."

His response was to do his banshee-howl thing, only not at full volume and only for a couple of seconds. It had no discernible syllables to it. I mean, it could have been his name— the first name I ever had was Urr, and to be fair the noise he made wasn't all that far off from that—but it probably wasn't.

"I don't know what you're expecting from me?"

He sniffed again, and pointed.

"The smell," I said. "I don't know what you want to know. I could use a bath, sure."

The lead merman leaned down and rubbed his hand against what could generically be referred to as his thigh. It wasn't a thigh at all—the longer I spent near them the more it became obvious that everything below their mid-torso was a pair of fins —but it was where the thigh would be located.

After rubbing himself for several seconds his hand came up with a thin layer of his own skin.

He threw it on the ground at my feet, pointed at it, and then pointed at me again.

"Yes, I understand," I said. "You want to know why I smell like one of you. I think I was tricked."

He howled and chittered and did the low whistle that soon exited my range of hearing.

"Well I don't know why I was tricked, but someone put some of that in an ice chest and I picked it up."

Click click, he said.

"Yes, I think it was stupid too. In hindsight, certainly."

This would have gone better if either of us knew what the other was saying, but nobody was trying to kill me yet, so that was good.

He howled more emphatically, and for longer, and pointed at the dead skin again, and at me, and then he pointed down the hill, and at himself.

"You want me to go down the hill?" I guessed.

One of the other mermen, on the edge of the semicircle, was having a problem. I'd been noticing it for a while, but couldn't tell if what I was seeing was normal for them or not. Basically, he kept flicking his arm around quickly at the air near his head. I didn't think much of it until the one next to him started doing the same thing.

The leader didn't notice this, or in noticing, didn't care. He was a lot more interested in getting me to understand whatever it was he was trying to convey.

"I was already going down the hill," I said, "before you stopped me."

To elaborate, I gestured this out, by pointing to myself, then to him, then holding my hand up like a cop stopping traffic.

Pretty sure something was lost in the translation. He took a couple of oozy steps forward until he was standing in front of a rotten log, about halfway between us.

He shattered the log with a powerful swing of his arm, and then went back to pointing at me, pointing at himself, and pointing in the direction of the town.

He wanted me to go where I had already been going, but to do something for him when I went there, or... or something. Something involving a hunk of merman flesh in an ice chest.

We were at a pretty tough conversational impasse, and I was probably about to be in a lot of trouble. If option A was to get me to understand and do something particular and that didn't pan out, option B was to hit me until I shattered like a rotten log. It didn't get to that, though, because the two mermen having odd fits became four mermen. Also, the general swatting at the air became something like a collective seizure.

It was a pixie swarm.

I'd like to say I figured this out on my own, but Ha had to fly next to my ear to implore me to run before I realized I was being given an opportunity. It wasn't a dragon riding to the rescue, but it would do.

"Hurry hurry!" Ha shouted. It looked like the mermen were fighting nothing but the wind, and it probably felt like that to them, except the wind had teeny tiny fists that kept hitting soft patches. Their pained howling sounded like a bunch of creaking doors.

The pixie assault opened up a gap in the line, so I ran through the gap. It felt like passing through an airlock, with wind rushing past my face as the pixies got out of the way.

I started to wonder exactly how many of them there really were, and if it was enough to hold off the entire merman line. Then I wondered if maybe I should have been a touch more afraid of pixies, historically.

Once I was ten yards on the other side of them, the leader gave a tremendous, deafening shout, and five more mermen manifested at the far edge of the clearing, ready to cut off my escape route.

"Still run!" Ha shouted in my ear. I headed straight for the middle of them. They closed ranks, but then there was a rush of wind from all around and I got the sense I was now traveling in a pixie bubble of safety, which is probably the best description of what was happening.

The vanguard of that pixie bubble reached the defensive line a few seconds before I did, and committed enough damage to open up a hole. I had to do some ducking and dodging, and at one point I dove, rolled, and slid, but soon enough I was back on my feet and running through the woods, and there was nobody in front of me any more.

～

I can travel pretty fast downhill, darkness or not, because it's essentially like falling in a controlled manner. If this were daytime and I was both sufficiently motivated and unimpeded, I could probably make it back to the house well before sunrise, even though it took two days to make it all the way up the mountain in the first place.

I was absolutely sufficiently motivated, because while the mermen weren't as fast as I was, there were a lot of them. They kept popping up along the hillside to my left and my right. Only twice did one appear in front of me, and both times the halo of pixies took care of him. I almost hoped one day we would develop an ability to communicate so they could tell me what it was like to be attacked by a pixie cloud.

I don't know how long I was running, because I'm trained to run for days and once I get started I tend to zone out and lose track of time. If this were a continent, I'd probably just end up going until I hit civilization.

I couldn't run forever here. I was still on an island, surrounded by the water the things chasing me *lived* in. Long-term, there was no escape, and I would eventually have to face them again and play another game of charades until we either figured one another out or somebody clubbed me to death out of frustration.

These were not happy thoughts, so I tried not to dwell on them.

While I don't know how long I ran, I do know it was a while, because at some point the sky started to brighten. It was that creepy half-light signaling the sun would be making an appearance on the low horizon within the hour.

It was around then that I concluded something *else* was chasing me.

This something else triggered old instincts, because whatever it was, it was in the trees. My gut said it was a large cat. My head told me there were no large cats on the island, and mermen didn't travel like cats could, so it had to be a third thing. This did nothing to assuage my gut.

I kept running, until the sky brightened enough and the timing was right enough for a quick look at my pursuer. He or she was man-sized and man-shaped, and that was all I could tell for sure. I nearly stopped and called out, but then I heard another banshee wail and decided announcing my location for any reason was a bad plan, and I kept going.

"Ha," I said, for I could still hear her buzzing around my head, "how close are the walking fish?"

"Close," she said. "Look."

"I don't want to look, because then I stop watching where I'm going."

"You should fly."

"I can't fly."

"Oh."

I kept running, and things were all right for a few minutes because I no longer got the sense that I was being hunted by a predatory feline. Then it landed on me.

I was hit in the back and knocked facedown onto the ground. I was thankfully crossing a moderately flat space with few large rocks or upturned roots, or it would have been a lot more painful.

I heard a rush of wind as the pixies attacked as I rolled over to face my new foe.

It was Mirella.

"Ha, stop!" I shouted. The pixies dropped the attack, which was good because they were probably about to blind her.

Mirella was dressed exactly as she had been when I last saw her, only now she was covered in two days' worth of mud and blood, and she could really have used a comb for her hair. Her eyes were wild and she looked practically feral.

It's possible I was never happier to see someone in my entire life.

"Oh thank goodness, it's you!" I said, maybe louder than I should have.

"Follow me," she said. "Follow me *exactly*."

She grabbed my hand and pulled me into a full sprint, which is what I was doing already, so the interruption seemed sort of dumb. Also, no hug or *happy to see me*, or anything, which was surprising enough to be a tiny bit scary. I wondered if the situation we were in was drastically different than what I thought it was.

I followed her steps exactly, which got us to a low hill on the other side of which was a rocky outcrop. She pulled us down to the ground behind the rocks.

"What's going on?" I asked. The cloud of pixies settled into a buzzy morass in the air some distance behind the rock, using it for shelter more or less the same way we were. This turned out to be smart.

"Shh!" Mirella said.

We poked our heads up over the rock to have a look at what turned out to be a charging army.

The forest was two-deep in mermen. Ha was right; they were close. I had no idea how close.

"We have to keep moving," I said.

Mirella put her hand on my shoulder.

"No," she said. "Just wait."

The sunrise lit up the sky to our left, and then the earth in front of the mermen erupted in a tremendous explosion. We ducked behind the rock as debris flew past the shelter. The pixies scattered.

We huddled there in silence for several seconds, until the noise died down.

I poked my head up again.

Half the forest, it seemed, was gone. So were all of the mermen.

PART III

THE PRIESTESS

CHAPTER 14

I've never been in the middle of a modern war, so when I saw the hillside erupting in packets of flame carried by the concussive force of high explosives, I could only connect it to bomber raid scenes in Vietnam War movies. This would have made more sense if a bomber had flown by, though, and there wasn't one I could see.

"What the hell was that?" I asked.

Mirella just looked at me silently for a few seconds, and then we hugged.

"Hi," I said.

"Hi."

"I thought maybe you were dead."

"Did you really?" She seemed surprised.

"It came to mind a few times, yeah. You?"

"A moment of weakness, perhaps, but I decided this world is too stubborn to let you die."

I laughed.

"Fair enough. What did I just see?"

"Cousin made bombs," she said.

"Stubby did that?"

"I've asked you not to call me that," Esteban said, emerging from the underbrush downhill of us. "Haven't I?"

The island's sheriff didn't look all that much like a law enforcement officer any longer. He was in shorts, and had a pair of swords lashed to his back and a gun on his hip, a bandanna on his head, and nothing else. He held out his hand and helped me to my feet.

"It's good to see you among the living, Adam," he said, which was nice because I never thought he really liked me all that much. "You smell terrible."

"I know, it's a long story."

"No, I'm sure it was necessary for your role as lure."

"My what again?"

"Your friend," Mirella said. "From the top of the mountain, she told us to expect you. That was all very clever."

I looked back up the mountain, and the smoking ruins of the hillside. Esteban managed to clear out a whole lot of real estate at once. It would have taken a long time to put all of it together, and he would have had to know an army was going to be showing up in the field in the first place.

There was a lot here to unpack.

"Was it your idea?" Esteban asked. "We assumed as much."

"Stubby, not only was it not my idea, I learned about it the same time that squad of mermen you just blew up learned about it. We should talk."

They both looked surprised.

"We have a camp not far from here," he said.

"Mermen?" Mirella asked. "Is that what you said?"

~

We were joined by four of Esteban's deputies, all dressed more or less as he was. Then we climbed down to their camp, which was just below the next ridge, in a rocky recess that didn't entirely qualify as a cave. It afforded a decent view of the lower island, the first one I'd really gotten in two days.

On our way down, I learned everything Mirella had been up to since we last saw one another. Not much, as it turned out. Not *nothing*, but it was fair to say my three days had been more eventful, if a tiny bit less dangerous.

"I was carried off the side of the road by the wave," she said, "where I landed on top of a tree. The water found the lowest point while I stayed above it. It was hours before I could move from that position, and then only to another tree. The ground was underwater for more than a day. I tried to make it up to the road so as to get back to the house, but it was nightfall before I even touched land again."

"That was when I found her," Esteban said.

One of his deputies—I didn't know any of their names—got to work starting a fire. This seemed like a bad idea, and I was about to say so when Mirella caught my expression.

"It's all right," she said. "They come out in force at night, but by day it's safe in the open spaces, as long as we're on land."

"They lurk in the water on the lower island at all hours," Esteban said. "They like the water. They hate the fire and they don't care for the sun."

What followed was a tale that amounted to the small band of goblins behaving like guerillas against an invading force from the ocean. At night, dozens of the white-skinned creatures turned up all over the island, attacking anyone and everyone without explanation, so they decided their best option was to keep to the trees and pick off the enemy in coordinated assaults.

"Swords work on them," Mirella said. "Their flesh is thick so you must be careful or you will not get the sword back. It's better to confront them on dry land, if at all. Their attacks are less effective on land."

The sunrise showed a down-island landscape still covered in

water, but from my vantage point, it looked to be less than two feet deep.

"There are parts of the island that don't qualify as being *on land* any more, I take it?" I asked.

"I would say anything deeper than a puddle gives them an insuperable advantage," Esteban said. "Cousin said you called these things banshee, now you say merman. Have you seen them before now?"

"No."

"So regardless of the name we choose, we still don't know how to make them go away."

"Blowing them up seemed pretty effective," I said.

"That was a major blow, I agree," he said. "But we've killed many of them already, and always there are more. I'm afraid this is like fighting a hydra: we kill two dozen, and four dozen arrive in their place."

"What did you even use to do that?" I asked. "Do goblins know how to build munitions out of rocks and dirt, because that's a cool trick."

Esteban looked embarrassed by the question.

"Cousin has caches of weapons hidden on the island," Mirella said.

"*Really*? Why is that?"

"He's paranoid," she said. "Or so I would have said a week ago, had I known about the caches a week ago."

"I've been to war too many times not to anticipate the next war," he said. "I purchased decommissioned explosive devices on the black market before ever agreeing to terms regarding my employment. In my official capacity, I was able to identify regions of the island considered off-limits to the public, and buried stores there."

"That's alarmingly prescient," I said.

"Not so much as you would think. Although packing them in

waterproof containers was modestly insightful, if I'm to brag about anything."

Mirella smiled. "Cousin subscribes to a philosophy that the day will come when humans decide to eliminate all of us. He considered having so many of our kind concentrated in such a small place a foolish idea for this reason."

"Yet here he is, stuck on the island with the rest of us."

"I decided if the attack was to come, I would make sure everyone here was ready for it."

"With bombs buried in the hills."

"Yes. Only I expected that attack to come by boat and by plane, not in the form of gelatinous nightmares rising out of the ocean."

"We looked for you, as we hunted," Mirella said. "Until your messenger came. Then we knew you were safe and what you were planning, so we prepared accordingly."

"Yes, I'm surprised you were unaware of the weapons cache, given the instructions."

"This is what I'm trying to tell you," I said. "I didn't know about this until I got here."

"How is that possible?" Mirella said

"Well, let's start with how much I hate prophets."

~

J told them everything from the moment Bruno and Gordana found me to the part where the hill exploded. It had been their understanding that I was running toward a known trap, and all they had to do was make sure I didn't accidentally trip over a bomb on the way down. This was why Mirella had to intercept me, as it was clear I didn't know which way to go on my own.

They were disappointed when I explained that Dmitri's armed caravan wasn't part of any plan I had put together, although the caravan itself didn't come as a surprise: they were alerted to keep the roads clear, and assumed that was why.

"That is a remarkable story," Esteban said. He was disappointed, but tried not to make that too obvious. Basically, everyone thought I had some big master plan that was going to save everyone, when it turned out I was just some idiot with fish goo on his hands running for his life with a cloud of pixies.

The pixies, by the way, were nowhere to be found. I assumed they just flew back home, and hoped nobody was hurt in the blast. I called out for Ha a couple of times, but that just got me weird looks, and no pixie.

"The most interesting part, I think, is the Internet troll who as it turns out is an actual troll using the internet," Mirella said.

"He's really nice, though," I said.

"I'm sure."

"If we survive this we'll have to have dinner together. I understand he's a good cook."

"Survival is also my primary concern," Esteban said. "But I'm having issues putting together all you've told us with the timeline. You're saying you reached the summit and discovered this cult was already gone."

"I assumed they were waiting for me, but couldn't wait any longer."

"This would have given them only a day's head start at the most, and as you said they were traveling with someone who was supposedly sick. How do you imagine they made it down faster than you and evaded both the white monsters and us?"

"That does seem unlikely. Have you seen any helicopters?"

"No."

"You spent all last evening commanding the full attention of the mermen," Mirella said, "and we spent the entire day and all last evening preparing the trap. This could have given them their opening."

"That still isn't enough time to get down," Esteban said.

"Maybe," I said. "Can you describe the person who told you to expect me?"

"She wasn't a person," Mirella said. "She was an auburn-haired harlot." The tone in her voice told me more than the description.

"A succubus, then. That would be Gordana."

My assassin girlfriend raised a threatening eyebrow at me, and I was smart enough to be a little scared.

"What does this tell you?" she asked.

"It tells me I've been getting played for a lot longer than I realized. She must have gone downhill when she left me alone with Bruno, rather than up to the campsite. That's the only way she would have had enough time."

"I don't see how that resolves this," Esteban said.

"The cult had already left the top of the mountain by then. They might have a three-day head start, not one. What happened to her after she told you what to do?"

"She claimed she had to help execute the second portion of your plan," Mirella said.

"That's great. Did she happen to say what that was?"

"No. Only that it was important she get to the hotel."

This was interesting, because I was pretty sure the rest of the cult was headed for the hospital.

"I wonder what's at the hotel?"

"She declined to say," Esteban said. "But we didn't press the point because we thought she spoke for you. She went by boat, yesterday when the water line was higher and a boat was a possibility. Colin took her."

Colin was, I assumed, a deputy. Since at one time or another I'd been introduced to all of them, it was now too awkward to act like I didn't know their names, even though I didn't know their names.

"Are you in touch with him?"

"We have radios, but the interference is tremendous, so

communication is spotty."

"Right. I've encountered that too. See if you can reach him anyway."

"All right. For what reason?"

"I want to know why she went there."

~

Thanks to Gordana's liberal use of my name when manipulating Esteban and Mirella, things were now a little awkward. It had been assumed that once I got there, everything would be okay. I was there, but I had nothing to offer, aside from a weird side-quest involving the hospital and a cult that may or may not exist.

It was dispiriting.

I just didn't have anything else to offer. Everyone agreed that continuing to fight the invaders from the trees—or blowing them up—wasn't going to resolve the problem. Likewise, Dmitri's assault could well be sufficient to allow the survivors a chance to escape, but that also wouldn't be enough.

Enough meant making sure the army of mermen didn't keep attacking, which meant figuring out why they were attacking in the first place. Since my encounter with them the prior night was the closest thing to an exchange of information, any answers had to begin there. The problem was, I didn't get anything out of that summit. And I was probably the most experienced person on the island when it came to first contact with a new species.

There was still a strong need to go forward and effect change, somehow, and that's basically how we ended up walking downhill, toward town. It was ostensibly because of my stated interest in getting to the hospital and the understanding that if this was to happen, it had to happen before the sun went down. But that doesn't mean our decision to start walking was based on a concrete plan.

First, I was given a change of clothes. Esteban had a bottle of rubbing alcohol on hand, and I used most of that to try and clean the stench of merman catnip from my hands. Once that was done I couldn't smell it any more, but my goblin girlfriend with the better nose insisted it was still there. Hopefully, the walking fish didn't agree.

By the time we heard from Colin, we'd been moving for long enough for the sun to nearly make it to the top of the sky. I put it at around 11:00 AM or so. One of Esteban's men was working a radio the whole time we walked, and it was just about the only thing we heard for a lot of that time, so the morning was spent with the repeated mantra *Colin, come in*, and it was exactly as annoying as it sounds.

Colin did come in, though, and the two deputies spoke quietly for a little while, at which time the news was delivered: Colin had no clue where the succubus went.

Esteban was as unhappy with this as I was, and took the radio.

"Colin, it's me," he said. "How did you lose track of her, over?"

"The situation here is unstable," Colin said. "We... constant..."

Static was already starting to reclaim the channel.

"I didn't catch that, over," Esteban said, but the channel wasn't open because Colin was still talking.

"...fighting... and... gone but... k... everyw..."

"I think you're losing him," I said.

"Yes, thank you," Esteban said.

"...was gone...ver."

"Colin, has Dmitri reached the hotel yet? Over."

The answer was a burst of static. Stubby shook his head and threw the radio back to his man.

"Try and get him back," he said. He turned to me. "You and I will have to come to a decision soon, regarding our eventual destination."

"Why don't we see what the afternoon brings, first?" I said.

But the afternoon brought no particular clarity.

We continued on a path that led directly down the hill, rather than along the road we crossed twice, because the path was the most immediate route to the lower island. A couple of times, we took to the trees to get our bearings and to see if anything alarming was coming up, but nothing was. These were the moments when I wished I had tried harder to endear Ha's affection, because she would have been pretty useful as a scout.

The banshee howls continued. After the explosion on the hillside, the cries went silent for the first time since the tsunami, but picked up again at around midday. They seemed to be coming from where we were headed, rather than where we'd been. I didn't know what that meant, but assumed it wasn't anything good.

Still, we encountered none of them, and precious little else. It seemed whatever wildlife still lived on the island was determined to remain hidden.

We reached the high water mark late in the day. This was where the top edge of the wave hit the island, and it meant we were about parallel with our house. There was only a little damage to the land, but the lingering odor made the ocean's recent landward incursion self-evident.

"This place is going to smell of rotting fish for a long time," Mirella said.

"Gonna bring down the property values," I said. "Maybe we should move."

She smiled.

"Sell in a down market? This seems unwise. And where would you like to go next, now that we've lived in paradise?"

"Maybe we can find an old bomb shelter in a landlocked city somewhere."

"I would need a view."

"Either that or outer space."

"Space would be interesting."

"Yeah, I've never been. I hear good things."

She laughed, and took my hand.

"I'm glad you're still alive," she said. "You would be very difficult to replace."

"But not impossible?"

"No, of course not. I'm sure there are dozens of immortal men out there."

"If you two would refrain from the banal chatter," Esteban said, "and remember we are in a life-threatening situation, please."

"I bet that's the first time he's ever had to say that on a mission," I said, slightly more quietly.

"Possibly."

"And I was just about to discuss what sex in space is supposed to be like."

"Oh, were you?"

"Dear lord, please stop talking," he said.

~

J got my first real up-close appreciation of the damage done to the lower island a few minutes after a diverting conversation involving intercourse in zero gravity harnesses that Esteban likely regretted enormously. (The other four goblins in our band seemed to enjoy the subject.)

We reached a road, and it was clearly the road I took to drive down to the town. It was also, for a change, the most direct route, so we stayed to it. Shortly, we reached the point where the natural brush and trees fell away and the entire vista became apparent from our slightly elevated position.

If it seemed as if the devastation was total when the wave first hit, it looked hardly any better now. Possibly, it looked worse, because at least when the water covered all the buildings it just looked as if an ocean had replaced everything. Now that the water had receded to below knee-levels and the buildings (or what was left of them) reappeared, the scene was more manifestly horrific.

There was the structural damage, of course. That was impossible to ignore: buildings either wholly relocated or dragged off their foundations in pieces; standing A-frames with nothing beneath them; overturned cars; and wood, metal and glass fragments everywhere. A bungalow that belonged on the beach where the wave hit was sitting on top of an apartment house roof on the opposite side of the island. A sun umbrella from one of the hotel pools drifted in the shallow water down the middle of one of the streets like it was looking for a particular shop. Really, the only building that looked to have survived okay was *The First Pub*, which sat alone on a little hill just above the town. It still looked abandoned and appeared to be missing its front lookout window.

Ordinarily, my first thought would have related to the alcohol contained within the pub, and the likelihood that it still existed in sealed containers. It wasn't my first thought, though; it was my second. My first had to do with the part of the town's devastation that really drove home what had happened here: the bodies.

There were a lot of bodies: on top of buildings, caught on signposts, floating casually like an upside-down sun umbrella. They'd been lying more or less in the same spot since the wave hit, and had all that time to bake in the sun. Most of them looked unmistakably dead, although one or two appeared to just be resting. One fellow—an imp from the look of him—remained in the wicker chair he'd been resting in when the wave struck. At the right angle it would have seemed as if he was sleeping.

It was like looking at the Pompeii victims.

I recalled my first instinct, right after the wave hit, of wanting to avoid stepping on an aquatic creature recently displaced by the water. Going forward from here would mean accepting that I end up stepping on a different kind of dead.

"We're going to need a car," Mirella said.

"And a drink, maybe," I added.

I expected her to protest, as this was surely not the time, since we were still racing the sunset. Instead, she nodded.

"That sounds like a good idea."

~

*T*he problem with a lot of top shelf liquor is that bars actually keep them on the top shelf. I mean, I understand: they're the least-used bottles so they should be in the hard-to-reach spot. Plus, it's where they're most visible and showy. That's fine. But when your bar has been hit by a tsunami, it's really helpful to all the people who plan to loot your establishment in the future if the expensive alcohol is on the bottom shelf, where it's less likely to fall from a height and shatter.

I also appreciate that looters can't be choosy, and bar owners would no doubt prefer circumstances in which they are neither looted nor struck by a tremendous wave, but life isn't perfect, and so here we are.

The owners of *The First Pub* were a couple of gay Scandinavian elves named Trevor and Ivar. Nice guys, regardless of their top shelf policy. They lived in a house a tiny bit higher up the mountain than we did, and so were probably spared a direct hit. Despite that, they weren't on the premises. This made the looting easier, but I felt bad about it.

Their tavern iffrit was there, though.

Iffrits are, on average, ten inches tall, can hold their liquor as well as a 400 pound linebacker, and are generally great to have around if you like to drink a lot. They are also deeply obnoxious when anyone involved is sober, or is a woman, because iffrits are also naked and perpetually horny.

On the mainland, there's probably at most one iffrit per metropolitan area, and nobody there knows they exist. On the island, every bar has one, and everyone knows about them. They appear to be considered good luck here, a belief tragically and thoroughly disproven by recent events.

This one's name was Steven. He was incredibly depressed about the whole matter with the tsunami, but thankfully hadn't acted out in the way his kind tended to, which was to A: drink all the alcohol, and B: set fires. Regarding the second point, it's possible he just couldn't find anything dry enough to ignite. Regarding the first, he'd left us about half of the bottles.

I found a cheap rum and sat at one of the three undamaged tables, on one of the seven undamaged chairs, opened the bottle, and had a swig. Esteban, in another one of the chairs, had the decency to appear disgusted, and the grace to accept the bottle once it was passed to him. This was after Mirella had her own pull.

Stubby's men took one of the adjacent tables and dug up bottles of beer for themselves. Steven remained on the ruined bar, semi-conscious with a mostly-empty bottle of cognac, muttering quietly and for the most part ignoring us.

"Can we assume Dmitri has reached the hotel by now?" I asked, opening up what felt a lot like a war room strategy session.

"I do not know that we can," Esteban said. "The more substantive question is how much of a difference that makes."

"Have you tried them on the radio?"

"Even knowing what frequency they're using, I have no reason to think they're in active communication. With the atmospheric interference considered... if I were them I would rely upon line-of-sight as much as possible."

"It's too bad you didn't say hello when they drove by last night."

"We thought we were all working from the same master plan," Mirella said.

"Well, we sort of are," I said. "It's just that none of us know what that plan is."

"This prophet," she said. "You mean it's her plan."

"I wouldn't say *plan*. Think of it as a game of billiards. I might conceive of a strategy that would allow me to sink three successive balls. A prophet could coordinate which balls go in which pockets on the break. They adjust what can be adjusted to enable an outcome, but the path there involves chaos and randomness."

"You aren't making any sense," Esteban said. "And it doesn't matter either way, because if this woman is predicting the future, we have no special decisions to arrive at. We do what we think is best."

"So," he added, taking the bottle from my hands, "what do we think is best?"

"You have an opinion, cousin?" Mirella asked, possibly sensing something I wasn't, or referring to a conversation that took place before I got there.

"Our first priority should be to get the survivors off the island as quickly as possible. Residents and tourists alike. This place is no longer safe, and we've no idea how to guarantee that safety in the future."

With the existence of a malevolent force of mermen established, it seemed reasonable to say nobody standing in view of an ocean was safe—worldwide—but I didn't think it was worth pointing that out.

"Dmitri has the right idea," he said. "We should meet up with his group and secure a perimeter. You said rescue ships will be arriving shortly."

"That's what I was told. But those ships are coming across an ocean full of a motivated army."

"We don't know that."

"They *are* coming out of the ocean, right?"

"They are. I'm disputing the word *full*. Surely there are limits to their population."

"Well I don't know. Before a couple of days ago I'd never laid eyes on one, so maybe. But the ocean is pretty big. These aren't competing ideas. There could be millions."

Esteban made a hissing noise of dissatisfaction I'd heard before, like every third time I called him Stubby without thinking.

"We have to operate based on what we know at this time. Any further speculation and we may as well stay here and complain about our coming doom, as that creature does."

Esteban pointed to Steven, who was aware enough to recognize he was being referred to. He sighed and farted and rolled over.

"We push to the hotel, as quickly as we can, support the evacuation, and then go find this prophet you are keen on locating."

"She may be at the hotel," Mirella said. "We know your succubus friend went there."

"You think he's right?" I asked. "Do you want to go with him?"

"I go wherever you go, Adam, you know that."

"I don't think the prophet is at the hotel. They went to the hospital."

"What is it you expect to accomplish in finding her?" Esteban asked.

"I have no idea."

Esteban looked at his cousin, then at me, then back to her again.

"And you feel this is a solid decision?" he asked her.

"As I said, I go where he goes. He doesn't often know why he does what he does, but he is usually correct. He has an instinct for the serendipitous."

This, incidentally, was the best description of my life I'd ever heard.

"We're going to the hospital," she said. "You can push to the hotel. We'll be fine."

"We could use a car," I said. "And a gun or two. Do you have any spare guns?"

CHAPTER 15

*E*steban offered the use of his handgun, but it came with an explanation.

"Their fat is too thick," he said. "A head shot would do some harm, I think, but we never got one off. Those big guns I saw Dmitri with, those would likely commit damage, but this little pistol? You're better off with a sword."

Of course, a goblin would say that, because goblins will always favor a blade over a firearm, but that didn't mean he was wrong.

I searched the bar for something bigger, but it looked like Trevor and Ivar also had no firearms on the premises, probably for the same reason: elves also prefer blades.

Plus, it's a nice island. The need for an under-the-counter shotgun is somewhat lessened by the pre-arrival vetting process. If only we could have asked the mermen for references beforehand, this would have gone better.

So I didn't bother to take Esteban's handgun. I did end up with an iffrit, though. I wouldn't call this better or worse, only different. I supposed if I had to, I could throw Steven. This wouldn't hurt anyone—except for Steven, I guess—but it would be terribly confusing, and sometimes that's enough.

He decided to get off the bar and ask to tag along at around the same time Mirella and I were looking into the process involved in hot-wiring the jeep located behind the pub.

"I can tell youse where the key at," he said. "If you wanna."

"Then tell us," Mirella said.

"I'm comin'."

She looked at me, and I shrugged.

"Fine with me. Do you know how to drive?"

"Adam," Mirella said.

"He can't be worse than I am."

We already decided it would be best if I drove the jeep while Mirella stood ready to defend us with her sharp things. If we had located a big gun, this might have been a more complicated conversation, but as it was, the car was the only weapon I was going to be using on this expedition. This is not to say I'm not any good with a sword—I'm actually quite good indeed—only that Mirella is better.

Unfortunately, this meant relying upon my driving skills, which is another area in which she excels compared to me. In this arena, though, a sixteen year old with a learners' permit is also a step up.

"He can't reach the pedals," she said.

"I can be a lookout," Steven offered.

"Sure, whatever," I said. "But why? You have enough alcohol in there to last a while."

"Yeah, you think I'm safe here?" he said. "Them things come 'round every night. I gotta shatter bottles on the floor to keep 'em out, and it's breakin' my heart every time."

He tossed me the keys.

"All right, come on then," I said, sliding into the seat.

The vehicle had no roof or doors, only a roll bar. It also sat closer to the road than the boxy monstrosity I'd been piloting for the past two years. I actually felt more comfortable behind this wheel than I ever did in a comparable position in other cars. I wondered if the problem all along was the inability to rely upon my peripheral vision.

"How does breaking bottles keep them away?" Mirella asked Steven, as he climbed in behind us. It was one of those cars with a tiny back seat. It was perfectly suited for an iffrit. "Is it the glass?"

"It ain't the glass, it's the alcohol. They don't like it. 'Course it's the good stuff they hate, not so much the wine or the beer. I got lotsa wine and beer, but no, it's gotta be the vodka and whiskey and bourbon."

I started the jeep. It was the noisiest thing any of us had done since blowing up the hillside, so I held my breath for a while, to see if the sound drew any attention. It didn't, but it was still daytime. In a couple of hours, when the sun set, I could see the engine's noise attracting them. Hopefully, we'd be at the hospital before then.

"If they don't like alcohol, why do they keep returning to a pub?" Mirella asked.

"Lady, I don't know. They just do. I'm hidin' when they there. They're lookin' for something, and they know somebody's inside, but they dunno to look for someone my size so they keep comin' back like it's a big mystery. And they go around the alcohol on the floor every time."

"It could just be the glass," she repeated.

"I'm sayin', it's not the glass."

~

*W*e checked in with Esteban, and then got going. He and his team were proceeding on foot, but only for as long as it took to locate a second vehicle. This being the sheriff and his deputies, they had a decent understanding of who owned what cars and where those cars could be found pre-tsunami. This might sound unlikely, except the committee mandated a strict limit on the number of motorized vehicles allowed. The local police knew who owned most of those cars.

Anyway, they had a plan, so I wasn't going to worry about it. We had patchy radio contact with them, and that was enough.

The parking lot at the back of the pub was reachable via a narrow strip of pavement that swung around the corner of the building and descended to the lower island street-level. From there, it was probably only a mile to the front door of the hospital. If this were a remotely ordinary situation—if, for instance, I was using the jeep to transport an unwell bar patron to the emergency room—I could expect to be there in under half an hour. But the roads were still a foot deep in water and corpses and debris, so the question wasn't really so much about how long this might take, as it was about whether or not there was even a route that would get us there.

We only got a hundred feet before the most direct course became impassible.

"That looks like a roof," Mirella noted. It was one of the Bermuda roofs, common enough in the residential parts of the island, and apparently it was sturdier than the house it use to rest atop. The roof was intact, albeit upside-down, and no longer attached to the structure it used to protect.

I came to a slow, reluctant stop ten feet in front of it. Reluctant, because the water level stopped just below the front bumper, and I was worried about what might happen if I stopped too quickly and the water splashed up into the engine. I was half-convinced the engine compartment had an actual fire inside of it that made the car run. I'm still a caveman.

I put the jeep in reverse, which got water into the car itself, and headed to the left. We could only barely see the road; I had to rely on the positioning of buildings to guess where the streets were.

I ended up on a side street that opened into some more residential space, which eventually hooked up with the main road again on the other side of the roof.

"I keep expecting to hear someone cry for help," Mirella said, "but there is nothing. Did they all drown?"

"Maybe. Or maybe they were attacked. It's been two days, though, and nobody has been out here to tend to the injured. I don't expect things have gone well."

It wasn't that it was quiet, precisely. We could hear the banshee wails all around, and without trees to knock down the sound it carried pretty far. It also felt like it was coming from the water itself, which was probably pretty accurate.

The smell was ghastly. It was late afternoon, and the sun had been baking the island all day, which only made things rot faster. A low ground-fog of evaporating water gave the place a quality one tends to associate with dreams. Or rather, nightmares.

"We are wading through death," Mirella said. "Have you ever experienced anything like this before?"

"Well I mean, metaphorically, you just described my entire life. Literally? Sure. Only most battlefields aren't this wet."

I could only take the car up to about ten miles an hour, and only in short bursts. Mostly, we were going around five, which was almost slow enough to make walking seem like a tempting alternative. I would have suggested it, but there was something vaguely unsettling about the water.

Several more zigzag routes presented themselves as we got closer to the town proper and the debris became more concentrated. In an hour, we only made it about halfway.

"Do you feel that?" Steven asked. I'm conditioned to assume that when an iffrit says something like *do you feel that*, what's coming next is a dick joke and it's probably best if you ignore the question. That was likely not the case here.

"Feel what?" Mirella asked.

"In the ears," he said. "I think they coming."

She stood up, braced herself on the roll bar, and looked

around. I still couldn't hear anything unusual or feel anything unusual, but maybe what the iffrit was detecting was the same sort of thing only smaller creatures—like him, or like pixies—and animals could sense before an oncoming storm or a volcanic eruption. This would mean a squad of mermen was the equivalent of a natural disaster, and I was mostly okay with that.

"Maybe you guys are good luck after all," I said to Steven.

"Of course we're good luck. Gotta rub us though."

Now that was definitely a dick joke.

"Adam," Mirella said. She was calm, but an entirely different kind of calm. "You need to drive faster."

I looked in the mirror.

"What's back there? I don't see anything."

"There is something in the water."

"It's barely a foot deep."

"Again, there is something following us in the water, and you need to drive faster. We can discuss the physics of this phenomenon another time."

"I don't know how much faster I can go, but hold on tight."

I goosed the engine, and we lurched forward a little, but sluggishly. We were as much a poorly designed boat as a car in a few spots, and speeding up only helped the tires find more opportunities to lose contact with the surface.

"Faster, please," Mirella said.

"I can't go any faster. And we have a turn coming. No way I make it at this speed."

This speed was twenty-three miles per hour, and the turn was a hundred and ten degrees, but I was imagining the consequences of trying a turn like that in a boat and not liking those odds.

On my left, something curious was happening in the water. What had been a smooth wake produced by the front of the jeep became two wakes, as it appeared there was something traveling next to us, beneath the surface. The thing was swimming pretty fast, which was remarkable for the fact that it didn't appear to be there. I saw a white cloud under the water, but nothing I'd call substantial.

"It appears we're being chased by a men's shirt," I said.

"It looks like a jellyfish," Mirella said. "It isn't a jellyfish."

I *had* to slow down. The other option was to commit to the turn at our current speed and run a serious risk that we all learn the value of a roll bar and seatbelts, the problem being not all of us were wearing seatbelts.

When I slowed, the thing in the water shot past the front bumper. I skidded into the turn.

"That wasn't so bad," I said, as I straightened us out.

The water in front of the jeep erupted, and up sprang a merman. Just logistically speaking, this was probably the worst place he could have chosen for an attack, because I was already traveling in his direction, and saw no compelling reason to stop doing that.

We rammed him. This wasn't fun for anyone. He didn't present as an entirely immovable object, so the jeep didn't come to a full and complete stop, but we did slow down quite rapidly.

Mirella, already standing, had time to jump, which was good enough to get her over the windshield and into a somersault and an upright landing far enough ahead that when the jeep came to a stop it didn't also run her over.

Steven—somewhat less athletic and also too small for a seatbelt—ended up clinging to the wrong side of the windshield.

"That sucked," he said, before letting go and sliding down the glass to the hood.

I, fortunately, had on my seatbelt. Otherwise I'd be looking at a broken leg or two and a face full of glass. What I did end up with was a sore shoulder and ribs from the strap, but that was all.

I put the car in park and stepped out, into the tepid seawater that surrounded us, and walked around the front of the jeep. The car had a dent that made it look like it had struck a boulder that was just a bit shorter than the top of the hood. The merman was nowhere to be seen.

"I think it went under the car," Mirella said. She had two swords out and stood in a ready crouch.

"You don't think it's dead, or stunned?"

"I truthfully do not know."

"Have you killed one yet?"

"I have. They fall when they're cut. But I did this on land. In water, I'm told they are less solid."

"Yeah but you'd think blunt-force trauma would…"

Then there was a rush of water, right next to me, and a second later I was falling backwards and the merman I'd hit was right above, arms up and ready to strike. I knew it was the one I hit because his side had a jeep-shaped bump in it. If they had ribcages, I broke his. Considering his jellyfish-swimming trick, they probably didn't, but you get the point.

He didn't get a chance at a downswing. He assumed I was the biggest threat, possibly because I was the driver, although I'm willing to consider sexism even across species. It was a mistake, anyway, because Mirella only needed a couple of seconds to cut through his thick neck and remove the stubby head from it.

A spurt of algae-green blood followed, and the thing collapsed in a disarticulated heap of flesh.

Mirella waited for it to spring back to life anyway.

"I think you got it, dear," I said, climbing to my feet. I was soaked in seawater now, and not all that happy. It was going to be a long time before I stopped associating the smell of brine with the horrors of the lower island, probably.

"We can't assume their head means as much to them as ours to us," she said.

"Yeah, I think we can."

"Start the car."

I climbed back into the driver's seat and turned the key. The engine made a sound like it really wanted to start, but didn't know how to any more.

"I think the fire went out," I said.

"What?"

"It won't start. I think he broke it."

"It's flooded!" Steven said, breaking out into laughter that really didn't fit well with the quality of the joke.

Mirella looked neither amused nor calm.

"We'll have to run from here," she said. "And quickly."

"We have another hour before sundown."

"You saw how it traveled. It went faster than the car. So let's hurry, shall we?"

∿

*W*e stuffed Steven into my backpack and got moving. This was preferable to leaving him behind, but only barely. From an ethical standpoint, I didn't really have a huge problem making him stay in the jeep or finding his own way back to the *First Pub*, but that had more to do with a bias against his species than with him. He'd actually proven useful, and could be again if we ended up getting caught outside after sunset; hearing them coming before we did was a valuable asset.

I was now traveling with one of Mirella's swords. She had the other one, plus all her knives, so she led the way.

Moving rapidly through water this deep was basically impossible.

"Are you coming?" She asked, the third or fourth time she had to slow down for me. It was embarrassing, as I am probably one of the best long distance runners alive (not that I'm bragging) but these were conditions I'd never tried to marathon in before.

"I can't swim because it's too shallow and I can't run because it's too deep."

"Pick your knees up, as though clearing low hurdles. Or hop."

"Hopping is worse. And the other thing is exhausting."

"You have nothing to save your energy for, we're only going a short ways."

"I'm not saving myself for anything."

"Then you're getting old. Come on."

She was sort of right. I probably was holding back a little, but only because that's very nearly always a good idea. I didn't want to be the game that got too tired to defend himself when the predator caught up.

I high-step-ran for a little while, and this did get me going faster, but it was murder on my legs. Mirella, being in better shape, and a goblin, did better. I wasn't going to be keeping up with her no matter what I did.

"Someone's coming," Steven said in my ear. He was probably wishing he'd never tagged along; the bag he was in was bouncing around a whole lot more than the jeep did.

"We have to get out of the water," I shouted ahead. She nodded and veered to the left, to the ladder on the side of a standalone building. It was small one-family in a neighborhood of identical buildings.

We were traveling through an area of the island consisting of housing for staff. All the places had been built at the same time. On the mainland, it would have been called projects, or public housing, or a Levittown, if that's still a thing.

This unfortunately wasn't one of those projects where the houses were really close together. That would have been great, because we could have traveled from roof to roof. As it was, all we had going for us was the ladder each house had on the side, so residents could clean the roof gutter traps and maybe sunbathe up there.

Mirella scrambled up, and I followed. No sooner had my feet left the water, when I heard the rush of something traveling past.

It was like dealing with an invisible shark.

"There were two of them," Mirella said when I got to the top. "I don't think they're looking for us specifically."

"What does it feel like," I asked Steven. "Are you hearing them?"

"They're talking under the water," he said. "It's like this weird hum. Feel it in my head and my gut, more than my ears. It's like an electrical charge. Dunno if I'm turned on or if I'm gonna be sick."

"I'd appreciate if neither of those happened while you're in my bag."

"I gotcha."

"Let's go," Mirella said. "I can see the hospital."

"I think that's the library we're looking at."

"Are you sure?"

"No, but I can never keep them straight, they're built the same. Where's the general store?"

She scanned the skyline.

"Over there, I think."

"I think you're right. Let's head there first, I have an idea."

"An idea?"

"Well that and I know the way to the hospital from there. As much as I'd enjoy being trapped overnight in the library instead, maybe another time."

We scampered back down and proceeded with the hop-running in a direction we thought put us on a path to the general store. Soon, we exited the projects and reconnected with one of the main roads, one I was pretty sure I drove down routinely on my way to the store's parking area.

We nearly made it to that lot when Steven sounded out another warning, only this time we had no roof nearby.

"Quickly!" Mirella yelled, doubling her speed to get to the store. This was great for her, but I didn't have another gear to shift up into, so I was stuck going the same speed I had been.

Then something swam past my leg. I was already stopping when the merman rose up in front of me.

It was a weird thing to watch, somewhere between an umbrella closing and a person emerging from a swimming pool. Mostly, it looked like a special effect from a *Terminator* movie, which was jarring to see happen in real life.

I held the sword up.

"I don't want to fight you," I said as calmly as I knew how. I figured even if he couldn't understand me he could understand tone of voice okay.

"Please fight him," Steven said in my ear.

The merman roared, and raised his fist, so I went at him with the sword. That went pretty well.

I'm not as fancy with sharp things as a goblin, but I'm okay. Mirella already showed me the best way to do this, but I didn't have a clean angle on his head because of his raised arm, so I took off part of the arm instead, spun around as he recoiled and used the power from the spin to propel the blade through his neck, and that was that.

Then, of course, there was another one coming. I got maybe ten paces before he was in my way.

Up ahead, meanwhile, it looked like two of them were facing off with Mirella. We were going to lose a game of numbers soon.

I slashed at the merman in front of me but didn't wait around for an opening to make a kill. Instead I let him stumble aside in pain—from losing a hand, or a fin or whatever we're calling this appendage on them—before continuing toward the store.

"Just wound them and keep moving!" I shouted.

Mirella understood the reasoning all right. She made a deep, slashing cut into the torso of one of them and buried a knife in the shoulder of a second, somersaulted over both, and kept running.

We made it to the lot. I knew this as much because of the crushed seashells under my bare feet as from the building itself.

Another merman materialized in front of the door, took a throwing knife to the face, and fell aside, and a second later we were in. A few seconds after that, the rushing water that followed us (it sure felt like we were being chased by the water itself) abated. They didn't try to come into the building. Maybe they only did buildings after sundown.

I still locked the door. I wasn't sure how rational that decision was, since the water was also inside the store. After what we'd just seen it was possible mermen physiology didn't concern itself with things like doors. If that was the case we really were fighting sentient water.

There was not, however, as much water in the store. That was a little surprising. The floor was on the same level as the street outside.

Looking around, I saw why. Someone had been using a sump pump. It was sitting on the counter near the register, and looked like it had been employed recently.

"All right, we're here," Mirella said. "Now how do we get to the hospital without being overwhelmed?"

"Oh, right," I said. I was still piecing together the pump thing. "Go to the paint aisle."

"I'm confused," she said.

"It's right down there."

"No, not about the location of the paint aisle. It's clearly marked. This entire building was under water two days ago, but things are in their proper place and look relatively clean. Did the wave miss the building?"

"Someone cleaned up."

"I see. And now we're looking for paint?"

"Not paint, rubbing alcohol."

She shot me a look that indicated she thought I took this detour for a beverage. I didn't, but it was a fair assumption.

"They don't like alcohol," I said. "Steven said so."

"I did, yeah," the iffrit confirmed.

"We can load it in those insecticide sprayers."

She nodded. "That's... a clever idea."

"Thanks. Did you hear that?"

I was looking up. Someone was above us.

"No, what did you hear?"

"Do you know if the store has a second floor to it?"

"Not a public one, surely."

"I think somebody might live up there. Someone who hates water but came down here and cleaned up anyway, and doesn't know any better than to try and get rid of an island-wide flood with a sump pump."

I stepped around the front counter.

The store was owned by a talkative imp named Aloysius Carmichael Poe. The story of how Aloysius Poe ended up on the island selling goods was remarkable, probably about three quarters fictional, and much too long to tell here. Plus, I couldn't do the story justice, because nobody but an imp could, not really. It's the one thing they do really well.

Anyway, Mr. Poe wasn't around. I didn't know where he lived, but I did know that the place he lived was not atop the store. Someone else was up there.

There was a door behind the counter, only it didn't look like a door because there were things—bits of metal encased in plastic and stuck on hooks—hanging on it. I found a doorknob, though, and pulled it open. This rattled the bits of metal, but nothing fell.

A staircase was on the other side.

I was pretty sure I knew who was up there, and it was the sort of creature one made an effort to not surprise.

"Hello?" I called. "It's Adam. Come on down."

Nothing, at first, and then the entire ceiling shook. A massive figure darkened the top of the stairs.

Across the room, Mirella—a second ago loading alcohol into a canister—put a hand on the grip of her sword.

I shook my head at her.

"Hey, Leonard," I said. "How's it going?"

"Hey Adam!" the demon greeted enthusiastically. "Is the water gone yet?"

"Not yet, no."

"Okay, I'm'n'a stay up here. Hey, you want, come on up. I don't get guests much but you're all right, yeah?"

I took a look at Mirella, who shook her head violently.

"All right, sure," I said.

I took off the backpack containing Steven and put him down next to the sump pump.

"Make yourself useful and help her out," I said.

"Sure, sure," he said. I think he heard the word *alcohol* and figured helping her was going to be more fun than it really was.

The stairs were terribly creaky and the way up surprisingly narrow. It was probably never intended for a demon's use, but very few things in the world were.

The room at the top was a combination storage area and living space. In one corner was a large bedroll that looked like it was probably two or three sleeping bags zipped together. Next to the bed was a tall refrigerator attached to a portable generator. Next to that was a door leading to a toilet.

Everything else looked like extra products for downstairs, sitting in wet cardboard boxes. The windows on one side of the room were blown out, but the glass had all been cleaned up.

The whole room smelled like mildew and unwashed demon.

Lenny shook my hand and gave me a little hug, two things demons are known to be very bad at, generally.

"Great to see you!" he said. "Glad you made it!"

"Good to see you too. I... I have to admit, you're probably the last one I expected to see make it through the flood. I thought demons couldn't swim."

"Yeah we can't. I tried it once, but you know we just sink."

"Did you just hold your breath or something?"

He laughed.

"I did! Saw the wave comin' through the window there and took a real deep breath. I can hold for like an hour, maybe. Good thing the water didn't knock me out though, I would'a been done. But I saw it comin'."

"The water didn't recede in an hour."

"Naw, more like two, three hours before there was enough air at the top of the room to reach. Here, I'll show ya."

He walked me around to one corner of the room. There, tied to the wall, was a half-dozen oxygen tanks.

"They're for the cutting torches construction guys use, I think. But, like, there's air in 'em."

"That's really clever, Lenny."

"Hey, thanks! I appreciate it."

Demons weren't known to be dumb, certainly not as dumb as trolls were supposed to be. They did have a history of being governed by their emotions, though, and calmly assessing a situation in which a failure to do so would result in drowning was not the sort of even-handed behavior I expected from one of them.

Between Grundle and Leonard, I was beginning to think the problem was my preconceptions, and not their failure to line up with those preconceptions.

"So is anyone else alive?" he asked.

"Are we... am I the first person you've seen since the water came?"

"Yeah. I was thinkin' I'd go look around once the ground was dry again, but it's takin' its time huh?"

"There are a lot of us still alive. There's actually a rescue operation underway. We could use your help."

"Sure! Sure, just as soon as it's dry again."

The first time a demon tried to kill me, I escaped by jumping in the nearest large body of water and swimming away. For a long time I assumed my success was due to demons not knowing how to swim or to being otherwise unable to swim. This was true, but it's also accurate to say demons have a phobia. From that perspective, the last few days had to have been horrific for Leonard. And again, historically demons deal with complex emotions by hitting things. The fact that the store wasn't a pile of rubble by now was amazing.

"We actually have to go pretty fast. Like, in the next ten minutes. We have to get to the hospital before the sun goes down."

"Why's that?"

"Have you heard the howling? They're worse at night."

"*Yeah*! And the glowy things and stuff, yeah! What the heck is all that?"

"Well, that's why. We want to get to the hospital before they come out again."

"Yeah... I mean, sure, yeah, I'd like to help, Adam. You're a pal. But... I mean, water, right? What if it decides to come back? I gotta be near the tanks, you know? I mean, water will kill ya, and it don't matter how hard you hit it."

I laughed.

"Lenny, if you're looking for punchable water, I have good news."

~

*J*t took a few more minutes to convince him to come with us, mainly because what I was saying didn't make a ton of sense to anybody who hadn't already experienced it first-hand. And he still wasn't at all happy with the prospect of wading through any water that went past his ankles.

But he did come down. On this point, the other members of the party were less than overjoyed.

Steven, who was evidently unaware that a demon lived on the island, shrieked and ran off to hide in the plumbing aisle. This was an appropriate response, most of the time.

Mirella was on a first-name basis with Leonard, and had had

multiple conversations with him, but she looked just about as happy.

"Mirelly!" he greeted. He walked over and gave her a hug, and if I could adequately describe the expression on her face I would.

I knew she never trusted him, because we'd had that conversation a couple of times, but these were always somewhat academic conversations, because we lived in an island paradise and didn't imagine a circumstance in which we needed to concern ourselves with Lenny in a combat situation.

If she could have pulled me into a private chat to elaborate on exactly why this was a terrible idea, she would have. But we didn't have that kind of time, and no privacy.

And I mean it was sort of a terrible idea. Trusting a demon to direct his rage—and in Lenny's case, to unlock that rage in the first place—at only a certain subset of living things was always risky. When employing them in wars the best thing you could do was put them in the front of the army and make sure they continued to face away from your core troops. If they got turned around and their ardor was up, the odds were pretty decent they'd start killing the wrong people.

On the other hand, we were going to lose the sun very shortly, and we barely made it to the hardware store alone.

It was a calculated risk.

"All right, are we ready?" I asked. "Where's Steven?"

Steven made a strangled noise from somewhere inside a pipe on the other side of the store. I hunted him down and coaxed him out.

"Oh hey, looka that. Hi, little naked guy," Lenny said. Steven gulped and waved, but didn't speak. Leonard, who was accustomed to people suddenly losing the ability to form words in front of him, didn't appear to notice.

Mirella handed over a canister with a hose.

"You can have this," she said. "I prefer using a sword. Not that I distrust your instincts regarding alcohol."

A few minutes later, we exited the building, in exactly the wrong order: Mirella first; me with a sword in my hand and Steven hanging out of the backpack on my back, holding a spray canister of rubbing alcohol; and Lenny the water-phobic demon bringing up the rear. It was the wrong order for the reasons I already gave, i.e., always put the demon in front so he knows which direction to attack.

These were not normal circumstances, though.

"Geez, I dunno, Adam," Lenny said as he put his first foot into the shallow water of the parking lot. Any other time I would have told him not to worry, the water wasn't going to jump up and bite him, but since that exact thing was a genuine possibility, I didn't.

"It's not going to get any deeper," I said instead. "I promise. The ground is right under it, just where it's supposed to be."

"Feels gross," he said.

"On that we agree."

He got past his discomfort enough for us to break into a jog. Soon after that, Steven relaxed and started talking again, which was important since we needed him to let us know when we were about to be attacked. Mostly, he wanted to discuss the suddenly-important question of whether demons bathed, and if so, how.

In some measure of irony, we made it only as far as *The Fancy Mermaid* before the first attack.

"Incoming!" Steven shouted, interrupting a rambling dissertation on the theory that demons perhaps don't sweat and therefore don't smell and thus do not bathe. It would have been a very interesting subject if we were both drunk and not facing imminent death.

Mirella stopped and did a quick 360.

"Where?" she asked.

"All around," he said, which wasn't helpful.

It was correct, though. The water erupted, and for the first time in my life I heard a demon shriek like a child. He composed himself enough to declare, "what the shit, you weren't kidding, holy fuck," and then he reconnected with his inner monster and started punching mermen.

I really, really wish I could have just sat back and watched the demon vs. mermen event unfold, but I had two of them right in front of me, so there was no time. I engaged one with the sword, turning my back to the second and hoping Steven wasn't hiding in the bottom of the bag. A couple of seconds later I had my answer.

Most of the banshee screams I'd heard to this point had been a form of communication. I didn't know this up until I heard the sound they make when they're in significant pain. I didn't even hear that when I was cutting off limbs. A whole different noise, the scream of pain was a lot higher, and conveyed real anguish, and it also didn't make my eardrums want to explode, which was nice.

"The alcohol works," Steven reported, somewhat under-statedly.

"No kidding."

I turned to examine the results, but there was no merman to see.

"Oh, he ran off," the iffrit said. "Or, you know, swam."

I turned around to continue hacking away at the other one with the sword, but he was already gone.

"Adam!" Mirella shouted. She had four of them on her. Lenny had five, but he looked like he was enjoying himself, and I didn't want to interrupt. Plus I'd never heard my girlfriend call for help before, so it was probably important.

I jumped into the fray. I'd love to say my expert swordsman-ship was instrumental in clearing the scene, but the iffrit on my back, power-spraying alcohol, was probably more crucial. Still, I mean that was my idea so yay me.

It took only a few seconds for the alcohol to drive them off, and then we were clear to move.

"Lenny!" I shouted. He had nobody left to hit, and was now eagerly punching the front façade of the pub. "They're all gone!"

For maybe half a second, the look in his eyes was the kind of feral you just never want to see in one of his kind.

Just a half a second, though.

"A got a few of 'em, Adam, did you see?"

"I saw!" I gave him a thumbs-up like we were talking about a great baseball catch or something. "Gotta move!"

Lenny was unreasonably happy about being able to hit things that he was already predisposed to hate, and not get in any trouble for it. I decided what must separate him from the other demons wasn't anger management so much as it was a native moral code. I'd never met one who had one of those before.

This time, the demon was ready to lead and we were ready to let him. Thankfully, he decided the best route to the hospital was along the street and not directly through windows and doors and brick walls, because he was freight-train prepped to plow through all of that.

Twice, mermen appeared in front of him. He went at them with a frenzied glee that was genuinely disturbing. Even Mirella was taken aback.

"I'm beginning to see why you didn't want me facing one," she said, as we ran. She was referring to an event a few years back in which she—acting as my bodyguard—dispatched a demon with sharp objects and a lot of patience.

"You've never seen a demon in a war," I said. "They have a whole different level."

We were still getting assaulted, in the wake of Leonard's forward thrust, but nobody stuck around for long because we switched from swinging swords first to spraying alcohol. This did more to repel them than the threat of losing a limb or a head.

I'm tempted to reach for garlic/vampire comparison, but that's inadequate. More like salt to a slug.

Lenny got us to the hospital just as the sun was disappearing over the horizon.

The building had an ordinary-looking double door front entrance that properly deserved to be up a set of stone steps but wasn't, because everything on the island was low and squat and kind of unattractive.

The doors were wood, set in a cement frame in a brick wall, and as I said, it looked just like the library the next block over. The only way to tell the difference was the caduceus sign out in front of the hospital.

I assumed the door was locked or barred and was about to tell Lenny to kick it in, when someone opened it from the inside. A man I didn't know was holding it.

"Come in, come in!" he shouted, with a light accent that I thought was probably Haitian.

Leonard stopped just before the door and stepped aside to let us through first. I think he recognized that if he hit the entrance at full speed he might damage the door and perhaps the building. The doorway wasn't demon-sized.

Once we made it through, he stepped in carefully, and let the man close the door and bolt it.

The hospital's waiting area was on the other side of the door. It was empty, so far as I could tell in the waning light.

"You were expecting us?" I asked, although it wasn't really a question. It was obvious enough.

"Of course! I'm so glad you made it. I am Henri."

He offered his hand, which I elected not to take.

"How did you know we were coming?" Mirella asked.

"Well, she hasn't been wrong yet, has she?"

He winked at me, like I was in on some kind of joke, and I sort of wanted to punch him. That would have been a bad idea, because I was pretty sure he was a werewolf.

"Hey, Adam, that was great!" Lenny said. "But, ah, I kinda don't feel so hot."

Lenny sat down in one of the waiting room chairs.

"You all right, champ?" I asked. "You did great."

"Woo, I don't know, I'm light-headed. Never felt light-headed before."

He was sagging, so I put my hand on his shoulder to steady him.

"Just the exertion, buddy, I'm sure."

"Adam…" Mirella said.

"What, he's fine," I said. I took my hand away, and discovered his flesh was sticky. At first all I could think of was Steven's question: do demons sweat? This didn't feel like sweat, though. It felt like Bruno's skin when *he* was dying. Then I realized what Mirella was seeing, and understood. Something was drastically wrong. Lenny was shrinking before my eyes.

"I dunno," he said. "I feel real funny. I…"

He drifted off without finishing the sentence, looked over my shoulder like he was seeing something only he could see, and then with a great gasp, Leonard the demon completely disintegrated.

CHAPTER 16

There are still things in this world that I've never seen before. It doesn't happen often, but when it does it usually occasions a moment of hesitation to marvel at the very fact that this is even possible still, after all this time.

Then there are occasions such as this one, in which a creature I called friend more or less melted in front of my eyes. This was new, yes, but *horror* and *revulsion* were the words I'd reach for, way before *marvel*. There was still a pause, though.

Mirella uttered a prayer to a minor goblin god of combat before speaking.

"What happened to him?" she asked.

"I don't know."

I was sick, and expected to spend the next several years remembering the moment I convinced Lenny to leave the safety of his second-floor room.

"You," Mirella said, to the werewolf who let us in, "what is this? What's going on?"

He looked about as stunned as we were, though.

"I... I was only here to hold the door and show you upstairs."

She looked about ready to take his head off with one of the swords.

"If you can't explain it, lead us to someone who can. We wouldn't have gotten here without that demon, and I would like to find out who's responsible for what I just saw."

"I don't... we didn't have... I mean..."

"Son, maybe you'd better just do what you're here to do," I said. "It's been a long few days for everyone."

He nodded quickly.

"It's this way."

Henri led us out of the waiting room, through the empty emergency area I'd never been into before, and to a hallway and a stairwell.

Mirella continued to look about ready to murder everything that moved.

"Are you all right?" I asked, quietly.

"Leonard was a warrior and that was not a warrior's death. I'd like to correct this."

I forget sometimes what it must be like to deal with the specter of one's personal demise as a matter of course. What I mean is that even though I end up in situations where my life is at risk—this happens slightly more regularly than it should, to be honest—I don't go to bed at night understanding that one day I will actually die, if not from the sword then from old age. I never had to cope with personal mortality as a consequence of time, in other words.

Mirella had to, though. So did everyone else who wasn't me, or a vampire, or Eve, my redheaded counterpart. (Also, vampires almost don't count, because they do die from the ravages of time, it's just that the ravaging is psychological.) I thought Mirella was interpreting Lenny's death a little more personally than I was, essentially.

"This man," she said, pointing a dagger at the back of the guy leading us up the stairs. "He is no man. What is he?"

"Werewolf. You can tell by the hair and the musculature. The jawline is a pretty good indication too."

"It's not a full moon."

"No, it's not."

Werewolves don't need full moons. They're like that all the time. The whole moon-transformation thing is just a myth. So is the idea that they're half-wolf.

"But he couldn't have done that?" Mirella asked.

"To Lenny? No."

We reached the second floor, an area defined by a long corridor that appeared to have been unaffected by the tsunami.

Doctor Lew Cambridge stood in front of a door about halfway down.

"Adam!" he shouted, before practically running up to greet us.

He looked pretty rough, like he'd been living in the wilderness for two weeks. I probably looked just about as bad.

"So glad you're here, this is *so* exciting!" he said.

"Hi Doc," I said. "What's exciting?"

I could think of a lot of answers to that, but I figured he was speaking about something very different than anything on my mind.

"I can't just explain, I have to show you!"

He reached out to take my hand, but had to stop when Mirella put a blade against his neck.

"Hi... Mirella, isn't it?" he asked, in a decidedly less bubbly tone.

"*He* could have done it," Mirella said, to me. "This doctor."

There was a world of information hidden underneath the way she pronounced the word *doctor*. He was a human on an island of non-humans, doing research on those non-humans, and there were a lot of residents who thought there was something wrong with that. It struck me mostly as unnecessarily paranoid, but I knew the doctor pretty well and always saw him as coming from a place of innocent curiosity.

I didn't think Mirella was one of the people who thought poorly of doc Cambridge, but maybe before this she hadn't been.

"Done what?" he asked, in a tone consistent with a person unaccustomed to being threatened.

"Lenny," I said. "The demon. Did you know him?"

"Of course, sure."

"He just disintegrated. Downstairs. He's a puddle on the emergency room floor by now."

"You know, when demons die—"

"Yeah he was alive when it happened."

"Oh. Yes. Yes, I know what might have happened there, but I had nothing to do with it. None of us here did. There's a lot you don't understand right now."

"Then help us to understand," Mirella said.

"I will. But you really need to come with me so I can show you. I can't do that without a head."

I put my hand on Mirella's arm.

"He's probably right about that."

She lowered the sword, turned, and said under her breath—so only I could hear—"I may have to go back outside to kill more of those things."

These are the kind of mood swings you have to expect with someone like her.

"I'm sure we can find someone in the hospital for you to kill. Now let's see what the nice doctor can show us."

His general demeanor substantially tempered, doc Cambridge led us silently down the hall, while Henri the werewolf followed from a considerable distance.

The doctor paused at the door.

"Do you remember what we talked about the last we spoke?" he asked.

It seemed like an awfully long time ago, but I did. I nodded.

"Good."

He opened the door.

On the other side, was what I'd call the standard trappings of a biological laboratory space. I could make that association because I once spent several months in and out of a medical research facility, unwillingly, while a small team of scientists tried to figure out what made me immortal and disease-proof. There were a few things I recognized, I'm saying, although I couldn't necessarily speak to what all of them were called or how they were used. I knew what I was standing in, though.

It wasn't the kind of place I'd expect to find in a hospital. Maybe this was my being naïve, but I associate this sort of research with exploitation, and hospitals with healing, and those don't traditionally go together. Or, they do, and I'm wrong.

But I'm burying the lede.

At the far end of the room, in a large tub, was a mermaid.

The sides of the tub were polished steel and the water inside was churning under Jacuzzi jet power so it was hard to see all that much of her, but I'd been looking at the male version for along enough to recognize that this one was both the same species and a different gender.

At least, outwardly.

"Is that what I think it is?" Mirella asked, perhaps excited by the possibility of someone to kill soon.

"Yes, but she's sick," Cambridge said.

The mermaid had the same bullet-shaped, hairless head, but her face was a little rounder, her nose more pronounced, and she had breasts, which was really the big differentiating characteristic.

"Sick how?" I asked. "No, actually, let's back up because I need to know more of this story. You told me in the bar that you had a piece of a mermaid up here. That's a pretty big piece."

"Oh, that? No, that turned out to be nothing. They are *very* different than anything popularly depicted, as you see."

"We've seen," Mirella said.

"I was approached, not long after you and I spoke, Adam. A

very persuasive young woman who promised she had a mermaid, and promised to take me to her."

I assumed we were talking about a succubus. Gordana, possibly. There weren't a lot of persuasive techniques that could convince a man to drop everything and go live in the woods with the specious promise of a mermaid. True, there actually was a mermaid at the end of this particular promise, but that seemed like a statistical anomaly.

"So you ran off to live in the woods," I said.

"For a while, yes. And fortunate to not be here when the wave came! I wish my colleagues had been as fortunate."

"Continue, then," I said. "She's sick."

"Yes. I did what I could at the camp, but there is really no substitute for the equipment in this room. If I had any chance of making her better, it had to be here."

We stepped a little closer. Mirella, recognizing the lack of immediate threat and the changing reality of the situation, finally put her sword away, and actually started to look less bloodthirsty and more curious.

"How is she sick?" she asked.

"That's a complicated question," the doctor said.

The mermaid's arm—only slightly less muscular than the merman versions I'd been avoiding—rested on the edge of the tub. Her head was tilted back and her eyes, though open, appeared unfocused and staring at a point on the ceiling.

I touched the top of her hand. This evoked a response: she noticed for the first time that there was someone else in the room. Her hand flipped over and took mine in something almost like a handshake. Her grip was weak, but not insubstantial. There wasn't any anger in her eyes, which was more than I could say for any other member of her species.

The flesh of her hand was sticky.

"I can only assume now that she's not the only one," Cambridge said. "If what you described…"

"Lenny fought with a sick one, contracted it, and died of an accelerated version of what's happening to her," I said. "I understand now. Did you treat Bruno as well?"

"Bruno? The incubus? No, why?"

"He was sick too. He died from wounds inflicted by one of her kind, but he suffered from the same condition. Thing is, he had it before the wave. He had it as far back as the hotel room."

"I don't understand. What hotel room is this?"

"It's not important."

"Well if he *was* sick, he didn't bring it to my attention, and he could have contracted it from our friend in the tub."

I looked into her eyes again. None of the rage I saw in the rest of her tribe was there. She seemed to be aware that the doctor was trying to help.

"Either she gave it to him, he gave it to her, or they both caught it separately. I'm not sure I like any option. But I understand now."

"What is it you've come to understand?" Mirella asked.

"Just about everything, I think. Doctor, I need you to take me to her now."

"Her who?"

"You know exactly who. The prophet and I need to have a conversation."

~

*C*ambridge, and the werewolf Henri, brought us to another room on another part of the floor. This section was devoted to patient rooms, but—like most of the place, really —had more of an office building feel than anything. I don't know if I can fully explain what the distinction is. Narrowness of corridors, maybe. I thought if Lenny had survived long enough to get a room here, it'd be a problem since the doors weren't wide enough to admit a demon on a crash cart.

Although the crash carts weren't big enough to hold a demon, either.

It was obvious enough which room we were heading toward, once we rounded the corner. Ahead of us was a makeshift camp-site set up in a small open space that had a previous existence as a waiting room and nurse's station. It now had a hot plate, a microwave, a small refrigerator (I assumed the latter two were scavenged from whatever kitchen was in the building) and five people I didn't know.

In a cursory review, I counted one human man, a succubus, a male and female elf, and a male goblin. The human was the only one out of place, and it's possible I was missing something that would indicate a more exotic lineage, but I wasn't curious enough to stop and verify.

All of them looked about like what you'd expect from a band of people who had been living off the land for an extended period: hungry, dirty, tired and uncomfortable. They appeared to know who I was, though, because I commanded all of their attention as soon as I came into view. Mirella is a lot better on the eyes and she was heavily armed, but nobody treated her to as much as a glance.

We didn't pause for introductions. The door to the first ward room on the other side of the lobby was ajar, and that was where we headed.

The room was small enough to hold only one bed. It had a bathroom and a closet and a window. The blinds were drawn, but if my sense of direction could still be counted on, I was pretty sure the view from that window would be of the part of the island on which the hotel was located.

It was nighttime, but the building had electricity, and the overhead lights were on. They were dimmed, but it was still easy enough to see.

Next to the bed, in a chair, was an imp with a notepad, a pen, and a lively look in his eyes. In the bed, evidently sleeping, was a human woman: the prophet who'd been ruining my life for at least the last week, and possibly longer.

She was Asian, and perhaps as old as sixty. Her skin was loose, baggy but not all that wrinkly, so it was hard to pin down an age because she could also have easily been in her forties but dying from consumption or something. Also, most prophets don't survive into their sixties, and the weight of prophecy tends to age people prematurely.

Prophets are only lucid for short stretches. Most of them live short, miserable existences in which they are dealt with by whatever method the society of the time employs to handle the insane —and no society in history has dealt well with the insane—or they're put to the sword for witchcraft. To say a prophet who develops a following is "lucky" is stretching things, but they are marginally less unlucky for having found people to care for them.

"Hello," the imp in the chair said, ignoring Mirella to address me specifically. The doctor came in after us; Henri evidently decided to stay in the hallway, possibly because out there nobody threatened him with a sword.

Mirella took up a position at the window and, after concluding nobody in the room constituted an immediate physical threat, pulled aside the blinds and looked outside. There was no glass in the window frame—the wave blew it out—so we could hear the banshee wails and distant gunfire pretty clearly.

"Hello to you," I said to the imp.

"I am Thelonius D'Artagnan," the imp said. "And you are the eternal man."

"I go by Adam, most of the time."

"I prefer the more grandiloquent monikers," Thelonius D'Artagnan said.

"You're an imp. That's to be expected. Are you really her scribe?"

"Yes, I am!"

"That's either the most brilliant idea or the worst."

He laughed. It was an infectious sound. It made you want to join in and have a seat and swap stories.

Stories are what imps are good at, which is why attaching one to a prophet may just be an act of genius; if there's anyone who can draw a comprehensible line between two irrational statements, it's an imp. On the other hand, imps have only a casual acquaintanceship with the truth, so the resulting story could very well be purely fictional.

"I need to speak to her, not to you," I said.

"You can speak to us both! She knew you were coming, and is scheduled to awaken momentarily."

"All right. How about if I look at your notes while I'm waiting?"

"My notes?"

"Your documents. You've been her scribe for how long?"

"Oh! Two years, perhaps."

"Splendid. Then I expect there are two years' worth of note pads lying around here. I can read most languages."

"But there are no such things!" he said with a laugh. "Notes, I mean, not languages, there are *many* languages, of course. Why, one time…"

"Let me stop you. We've no time for a charming story on your discovery of a new language today. Please explain why there are no records, since you're her record-keeper and you're holding a pad of paper and a pen."

He laughed again. "Why, I keep this ready to capture her immediate impressions, but only in the moment. She often prophesises rapidly, and I need time to absorb the information. I'm ashamed to admit even needing it, but I am getting on in years, you understand. Oh! Perhaps you don't!"

Imps have unusually long lifespans, so it's hard to pin an actual age on most of them. This one looked to be a portly fifty years old, but they all look portly, vaguely paternal, and roughly fifty for something in the neighborhood of a century. I had no idea how old he actually was, and wouldn't unless he told me.

"All right, so you take notes. What happens to the notes?" I asked.

"Why, I destroy them!"

"But, again, you're her scribe. Keeping the records is what you do."

Then I understood.

"Oh Zeus, It's all in your head, isn't it?" I said.

"Why of *course*!"

This was like some extended nightmare. If I wanted to know the truth about something, an imp is the very last person I would seek out. It was an imp who was responsible for turning me into a Greek god, and trust me when I say that no matter how cool that sounds, it was *not* cool at all.

The doctor was checking the prophet's vitals.

"She's dying," Mirella said from the window, "isn't she?"

"Yes," Cambridge said.

"What's killing her?"

"In the short term, I'd say malnutrition. Holistically... sometimes the body just gives up after enough abuse."

"She has been abused?" Mirella asked, looking concerned.

"Not in the way you're thinking," I said. "Having a mind stuck in a different state than the rest of the world takes a physical toll."

"That's more or less so," the doctor said. "But she has also suffered physical abuse. There are old wounds, long healed. I don't know where they came from, and she never explained. Ah. Here she comes."

Her eyes flickered open. They took in the doctor first, since he was closest. She gave him a brief smile and squeezed his hand. Then she took note of Mirella, at the window. Then me. They stopped there.

"And now we are here," she said. "At last."

She had a strong voice for such a frail-looking woman. Her

English was sketched with a Chinese dialect I couldn't put my fingers on. She seemed lucid, focused, and lively.

"At last?" I repeated.

"The ending."

"Whose ending?"

She didn't answer. She just kept staring.

"What is your name?" I asked.

She didn't answer this, either. I looked over at her scribe.

"Her name?" I asked him.

"She never gave any of us a name. I had hoped that in this moment she might provide one to you, given your import. I've assigned her the appellation of Lorelai, and she answers to it on occasion."

"All right."

I turned back to her. It felt uncomfortably like being in the presence of an oracle. Oracles had a habit of waiting for a formal question before acknowledging the questioner's existence. It was creepy.

Instead of posing a question right away—and I did have a couple—I went in another direction.

"Lorelai, then. Let me tell you what I've put together so far. You and your band of followers arrived on this island in secret, decamped in a hotel room for a while, and then went up into the hills. At first, I didn't understand why you did this, but now I think I do: it was to capture a mermaid."

"Capture?" the doctor said. "She's sick. They found her and tried to help her."

"I agree that they found her, and that they tried to help her, but I also think had they done neither of those things she'd have returned to the ocean and died there. I don't think she stayed willingly. She wanted to leave, didn't she?"

Lorelai still had no words, because that wasn't the question she was waiting for. I looked at the scribe.

He gave a nearly imperceptible nod. It was without question

the most understated thing I'd ever seen an imp do, so I knew it represented the kind of story he didn't want to tell.

"When she couldn't leave," I said. "She called for her people. And they came looking, because for some reason or another, that mermaid is important to them. Very important, as it turns out. She's the queen bee."

For this point I got a flicker of a nod from the prophet. Her imp scribe looked bewildered, as it appeared I was coming up with a version of the story he hadn't considered.

"You knew exactly what that meant and what would happen," I said, "and you did it anyway."

"Well of *course* she knew!" Thelonius D'Artagnan said. "How else would she have helped us escape the great wave? And to send help to you! She is the keeper of the future!"

"You misunderstand. She's the keeper of *all* of the futures. This is the nature of her curse. She sees an outcome, and can act to alter it. My issue is that the outcome she manipulated the future toward was one which involved a tsunami that drowned half of the island."

Appropriately, the imp gasped, because as soon as he said it he realized I was right.

"Adam, now, come on," the doctor said. "That doesn't make any sense."

"Doc, I don't know how it's possible for those things out there to manufacture a tidal wave, but it's a more credible explanation than coincidence."

"It's preposterous," Mirella agreed. "But it fits the evidence."

"We knew the creatures were looking for something," I said, "and I was all right with the idea that whatever they were looking for washed ashore with the wave. But Doc, you examined the mermaid two weeks before the tsunami, so I know that can't be right. She isn't here because of the wave. The wave came because she was here."

"It's a magnificent story!" Thelonius said. "But let me be the first of my kind to say such a thing: it sounds impossible!"

"Maybe you just haven't lived long enough to appreciate how often the seemingly impossible happens," I said. "But we have someone in the room who can tell us what the future would have looked like without the captive mermaid. So. Am I right?"

She stared for a while. I'd say she was hesitating because she didn't want to answer, but it seemed more like she was waiting for the right moment in history in which to respond, like we hadn't reached the part yet where she was supposed to acknowledge this question, and we were all going to have to wait until it came up.

Finally, she nodded, slowly, and then went back to staring and waiting.

"But why? If you knew what would happen if you kept her, why did you keep her?"

"It was the more desirable outcome," she said.

"Because I got to live? Your succubus told me this was why you came to the island. I'm not nearly that important. Plus I was doing great before you sent a tsunami in my direction."

"You are all."

"I am all? I mean, I'm flattered, but…"

"Princes, kings and awful things, and sprites in flight all dust. The man behind the table is always in the shadows, and the shadow is death. Unstable is the world without the one who walks the path. Do you see?"

"No. I mean it kind of rhymes, which is cute, but no."

God, I hate prophets.

She looked a little exasperated, like what she just said was the clearest thing ever, and maybe for her it was.

"The beginning must be here for the ending, or the impossible will be. Do you see?"

"Again, no."

I looked over at the imp in the corner, scribbling down what she just said.

"A little help?" I asked.

"I will offer an interpretation, but I need time to meditate on it."

"Super."

"Can you give me something a little less cryptic?" I asked her. Her response was to close her eyes and resume waiting. Or something. I mean, I knew she could see the future, but a little improvisation never hurt anyone.

"The battle's escalated," Mirella said. She was back to looking out the window.

"What's going on?" I asked.

"Hard to say, it's too far. But gunfire has escalated, and I just heard something which sounded suspiciously like a rocket."

"Don't suppose you can tell who's winning?"

"No, but the field of battle is very wide." She looked me in the eye, to underline the point she was about to make. "It is undoubtedly drawing the mermen in the direction of the hotel and away from the streets."

"I understand. I'm nearly ready. First I want Lorelai to tell me why I'm so important."

"But of course you're important!" Thelonius said. I ignored him, because his prophet was busy having an event of some kind.

She opened her eyes, and I felt like I'd unlocked the next phase of this prophecy or something. Then the eyes rolled up in the back of her head, just long enough to worry me that perhaps this was the start of a seizure. Then she spoke, but what came out of her mouth wasn't in English.

When she was done, she closed her eyes and sagged back into the bed, as if she'd just accomplished something that took great effort. Maybe it did, who am I to say?

"I don't know what that was," the imp said. He was writing

anyway, though, I assume just to capture the utterances phonetically.

"What language was that?" Dr. Cambridge asked.

"It was Elamite," I said. To the prophet, I asked, "Do *you* even know what you just said?"

She didn't respond. Possibly, she went back to sleep, which was kind of rude, really.

"What *did* she say?" Mirella asked.

"It's a bit of ritual doggerel. The kind of thing you say when you want a god to show up and help."

"A prayer."

"Sure, kind of."

"Did it answer your question?"

"No, it raised new ones."

"I don't think you're going to get a chance to get your new questions answered," the doctor said. He had his fingers on her neck. Why she wasn't hooked up to a machine that beeped her heart rate out I didn't know, but then again I'd never been in a hospital that specialized in non-human patients before. Maybe heartbeat wasn't as important here.

Either way, something was wrong. He began to minister to her, slowly at first and then more frantically, while her scribe stepped between us and the door.

"She left me in charge of a final message," he said quietly.

"She's dying," I said.

"Oh yes. And she wanted you to know that if you are to accomplish what you're about to do, the time to do so is right now. The opportunity will pass otherwise. So go."

I looked over at Mirella, but she was already vacating her spot at the window and heading for the exit

"One thing," Thelonius said, grabbing my elbow. "What *are* you about to do?"

"Save the day," I said. "Or what's left of it."

CHAPTER 17

The easy part was locating an ambulance.

The island only had two, and calling them ambulances was generous because they were essentially box vans with the back seats removed.

One of the two was still in the bay at the back of the building, and the only reason it was there was because it had been stored inside and protected by garage doors. The doors didn't keep the water out, but it did prevent the vehicle from being washed away. My guess was, that was what happened to the other one.

Much harder was getting the mermaid to the ambulance. First we had to find her again, which was not a small challenge given the non-intuitive floor plan of the hospital. Once we located the ambulance bay, and after several minutes of aimless wandering, we decided to follow the directions nailed to the wall—one of those "you are here" maps that would have served me so well in the Middle Ages—to get back to the lobby, from which we retraced our steps.

On the way, we found Steven, who I actually thought was still in my bag. He was leaned up against a wall in the hallway that took us to the mermaid, drunk, and unconscious.

I checked my bag verify that the tank containing alcohol was still there. It was; he'd found another source.

"She's this way," Mirella said, urging me to step past the drunk iffrit and proceed down the hall.

"Yeah, hang on a sec."

I pushed open the door next to Steven. A storage room was on the other side.

Ten minutes later we'd found a wheelchair that wasn't doing anything else and loaded it down with as much rubbing alcohol as we could find.

The mermaid was where we left her, and in about the same state.

"We need something to move her on," I said.

"You mean like the wheelchair you've loaded with alcohol?"

"Yes, *like* that, but not that."

Mirella went off to find something that would help, while I dealt with a much more challenging problem: if the mermaid didn't want to come with us, we didn't really have a way to make her. My assumption was that for most of her stay on the island, she'd been too weak to defend herself adequately, because I didn't see anyone in the prophet's entourage strong enough to over-power her. I also wasn't strong enough, and neither was Mirella. We could kill her and drag her, certainly, but that would be somewhat self-defeating.

I sat down on the side of the tub again, as before, and put my hand on the mermaid's. Her big black pupil-less eyes blinked open and found my face. I held my hand out, palm up.

"It's time to go home," I said.

She looked around the room, and noted we were alone. A low whistle came out of her mouth that sounded like a dolphin cackle. I appreciated the lack of volume. She could probably burst one of my eardrums at this distance, as well as notifying everyone in the hospital that something was up.

She reached out and took my hand, and then I stood. The

intent was to help her to her feet, but she neither had feet nor actually required my help. When she stood, it involved gathering her fins beneath her torso in a way that would have been impossible for a being with proper legs, and pulling them together into a firm, conic shape. It was pretty cool, to be honest.

Mirella returned with a gurney a moment later, and wheeled it up next to the tub.

The mermaid examined Mirella, and the gurney, and then me.

I don't know that she understood what we were there to do, or that she would have agreed with the decision had she understood. I do know that for whatever reason, she decided we were people she could trust. I also suspect she felt as if she had nothing to lose by doing so. She was already dying alone in a tub in a strange building, surrounded by the wrong species. I had to think she saw no downside to seeing if we could improve her circumstances. Anyway, she accepted the situation for what it was, and with our help climbed up onto the gurney, lay down, and allowed us to strap her to it. I covered her with a blanket, although I couldn't tell you why. It just seemed appropriate.

"All right," I said. "Let's go."

～

The building had exactly one elevator, and like everything else there it was in a location that wasn't immediately obvious. And, since it was not intended for public use—it was ostensibly a freight elevator—none of the maps were helpful.

We did find it, though, and it was actually working, which I appreciated. I wasn't looking forward to taking the mermaid down a flight of stairs, as this would unquestionably force her to re-examine the decision to trust me in the first place.

The elevator dropped us off right at the ambulance bay, and that made some sense. A few minutes and lot of struggling later, she was loaded in the back. That was when doctor Cambridge showed up.

"What are you doing?" he shouted. He was alone, and didn't have a gun in his hands, so I had no reason to pay any attention to him.

"I'm bringing her back to her people," I said.

"But she's still sick!"

I slammed the back of the ambulance closed while Mirella climbed into the driver's seat.

"I know she's sick. Did you manage to make her better?"

"I don't know. I was trying something... I had an idea, and I wanted to... Adam, I'm still studying the condition, but I need more time! I am *so* close!"

Her species was tearing the island down around us and he thought he had time to run some more tests. I wondered if Lew Cambridge was always this clueless and I just never noticed before.

"You're out of time," I said.

"This is irresponsible, you're killing her!"

"She's not the only one that's sick. Lenny caught whatever they have and it killed him in about ten seconds. It killed Bruno, too, and he was an incubus, so whatever this is, it jumps species. You realize you may have started an epidemic, right? But either way, you're going to have more subjects to study soon enough. And how do you know her people don't have a cure already?"

"I don't know how advanced they are."

"Let me help: they're advanced enough to create a tsunami. Look, go ask your prophet, I'm pretty sure she'll tell you this is the only way."

"She's dead."

"Then ask her scribe. Oh, and don't let him disappear, he and I have a lot to discuss."

"Adam, we have to go," Mirella said.

"I'll be back," I said to the doctor. "Assuming I live through this."

Mirella pushed a button inside the ambulance that was of the standard garage-door variety, and worked in exactly that manner. A second later, she was revving the engine, I'd jumped into the passenger seat, and we were staring at more foot-deep water covering an open road.

"What's the plan?" she asked. "Can't we just find a merman and hand her over?"

"Let's go to the largest concentration of them we can find."

"That would be the hotel."

"Then let's go to the hotel. And turn on the flashing lights."

"The dome lights."

"Yes, those."

~

*W*e ran into no interference for the first few blocks. It seemed Mirella's assessment of the scene outside was accurate: the mermen were being drawn toward the hotel by the concentrated resistance there. If they began with the assumption their queen's disappearance was an act of malice, it made sense that she would be held in the most fortified place. At the same time, the efforts of the leader I met in the jungle made me think they were willing to consider a negotiated settlement.

At least, that was what I was counting on.

I was in the passenger seat with plastic bottles of alcohol and one of Mirella's knives, intending to puncture one and toss it out the window at the first sign of resistance, but after a couple of blocks I put down the knife and dug the radio out of my bag.

I opened a channel and got a lot of static, then something that sounded almost like Esteban, the sound of gunfire, and more static.

"Esteban, is that you?"

Static.

"Adam, I..."

Static.

This was going to be more frustrating than it was worth.

"Mirella, does your cousin know Morse code?"

"How would I know?"

"I dunno, maybe it came up at reunions."

"It didn't. But he might. I don't."

"It's not something goblins are taught as children or something?"

She just glared at me, so I dropped it, and started sending a message using the radio static. I figured if Esteban was listening to the channel and nobody else was trying to use it, *and* he could understand Morse, it would get through.

Basically, I couldn't control the fact that there was static on his end every time I hit the transmit button on my radio, but I could control the length of time I hit that button. So I sent a bunch of dashes and dots in a repeating message.

"That's modestly clever," Mirella said. "What are you telling him?"

"We're in the ambulance, don't shoot us."

"I would hope they already know not to shoot at ambulances."

"Wait."

Esteban replied.

Surrounded. Bring atomic bomb if you have one.

"What did he say?" Mirella asked.

"That things could be going better."

We turned the last corner before the avenue leading to the hotel's front parking area.

The contrast in how this scene looked, between the last time I was there and this time, was pretty drastic. Dmitri and his collection of ex-mafia, retired celebrities, former CEO's, accountants and attorneys had formed a makeshift defensive wall against enemy incursions with their Humvees and minivans and SUV's and jeeps. Now they were standing on top of those vehicles and firing down at the mermen. It was a good idea, tactically, with the one problem being that they didn't have a way to block off the water, so it was just a matter of time before the approaching army figured out they could swim under the cars, and pop up on the other side.

Esteban, it seemed, was anticipating exactly this, because as we drew closer I spotted him and two of his deputies, swords out, in front of the hotel doors.

The army of mermen was hard to recognize at first because they didn't pop out of the water often, and were tough to spot below the surface. Dmitri had lights trained on the surface, and his people were firing at all the moving water they could identify, which out of context looked kind of ridiculous.

Twice, I saw an attacker surface far enough to get cut to pieces by a hail of bullets. This seemed like an irrational approach. I had a suspicion their bodies were more jellyfish-like when they were submerged than when they were out of the water, and I didn't think bullets would do lethal damage to a jellyfish. Or perhaps it could, but not easily. But, they weren't my bullets.

"Much closer and the creatures will target us instead of the convoy," Mirella said.

"I know, that's the idea."

I flipped on the siren.

We were just at the edge of the parking lot, past the gates. As anticipated, the siren had a much more dramatic effect than the dome lights did, because these were beings who relied a good deal more on sound than on sight. It worked, in other words, which was why we didn't get a whole lot further than the edge of the parking lot before the first attack.

Two popped up in front of us. Mirella jerked to the left to avoid them, only to discover three more. She turned again, and clipped one of them, which rocked the whole vehicle sideways and onto two wheels for a half second. We settled back down, and Mirella floored the gas.

We were on a beeline for the convoy, and traveling thirty-five miles an hour. I was pretty sure even a head-on with a merman wouldn't stop us at that speed.

It didn't take a merman: just a curb. The parking lot wasn't uniformly flat. There were raised curbs here and there to help define the regions within which one could park a car versus where one might drive one's vehicle to and from the parking area. We couldn't *see* any of the curbs because it was dark out and there was over a foot of water hiding everything. Speaking for myself, I forgot they were there at all.

So we hit a curb, on my side of the vehicle. This lifted us up onto two wheels again, for about ten feet. Had we remained unmolested, we would have righted ourselves, but then a couple of mermen surfaced and effectively finished the job of dropping us on our side.

We skidded to a stop on Mirella's side of the van, with me on top of her on account of my not having on a seatbelt.

We lay there quietly for a few seconds. The siren perished in a strangled warble, so all we had was the sound of gunfire outside.

"Are you okay?" I asked.

"Yes."

The whole ambulance rocked. Something was hitting it hard from the outside.

"I'm looking forward to the rest of your plan," she said. "Maybe you can set us on fire next."

"You're almost right. Can you get to the back and make sure she's okay?"

"Once you get off of me, yes."

I climbed off of her.

The inside wasn't really meant to be moved around in when the whole thing was sideways, so the going was awkward, but I was able to get my hands on one of the bottles of alcohol. Then I climbed, until I made it to the passenger door, pushed it up and climbed onto the side/top of the van.

We were completely surrounded by mermen, and I was being spot-lit by someone from the convoy. You know, just in case any mermen a half-mile away couldn't see me.

"Adam, don't move!" It was Dmitri, using a megaphone, from the end of the convoy. "We will come get you."

"Stay there!" I shouted. I didn't think he could hear me, though, so I shook my head and held my hands up and hoped he understood the universal symbols for *don't fucking do that*.

The mermen surged, and one punched the side of the ambulance. It rocked and I nearly fell off.

"Okay, okay, hang on!" I said, this time to the surrounding army. I raised the jug of alcohol with a theatrical flourish, popped the top off. I flung some of the contents at the one who punched the ambulance.

He recoiled with a shriek.

"You all know what's in this bottle now, right?" I said.

I knew they couldn't understand me, but whatever. I swung the bottle around to get everyone to take a step back, and then I poured the contents over my head.

It took sixty thousand years, but I finally found a problem where a bath of alcohol was the answer.

I walked to the back of the ambulance and jumped down. The mermen at that end gave me plenty of room. I locked eyes with one of them. He looked a lot like the one I'd conversed with on the mountain, and it would have been nice to say it *was* him, and here we were again, settling things, but in truth they all looked basically alike to me.

"Hello," I said. I held my hands out, palms up, arms open. For most tribes of human and non-human, this indicated I had no weapons, and could be trusted. Hopefully it meant the same thing to them, but considering they probably had to deal with octopi, who knows?

I knocked on the doors.

"Mirella, are you ready?"

A voice muffled by the layer of car between us answered.

"What am I ready for? What are you doing out there?"

"Is she free of the gurney?"

"Yes."

"Then open the door."

She pushed from the inside and the lower door opened, and fell. I reached under and pulled the other door open, so it looked like I was helping—and perhaps directing—what happened next.

What happened next was, the mermaid came out. It was slow, and she was clearly not doing spectacularly well, which may have had as much to do with being strapped to a gurney in an ambulance that was currently sideways, as it did with whatever disease she was fighting.

Still, she climbed out, using Mirella's hand for support. I would have helped too, but I was covered in alcohol, and I was pretty sure she didn't want any part of that.

She perked up as soon as her fins hit the water.

Then she let out an ear-splitting shriek. I reacted by nearly letting go of the door, which would have been really bad because she was still under it.

Her cry was met by something akin to a cheer from the mermen that was, collectively, even louder than what she'd done, but a lot more diffuse, and not issuing from a single source right near my head, so it wasn't as intolerable.

She walked forward, then dove into the water, and disappeared.

I didn't know, yet, if that was a good thing or a bad thing.

"Now what happens?" Mirella asked, fingering the hilt of one the swords on her back.

"I don't know."

"Perhaps we will all just wear alcohol all the time from now on."

"I could think of worse."

The lead merman—the one I locked eyes with a minute earlier —took a step forward and looked me up and down. I lowered the door, and resumed the posture: arms open, hands open, palms out.

He responded by howling, which could have been bad. But it was possible I'd begun to understand them a little bit, because I could tell by the tone that this wasn't a threatening cry.

He mirrored my posture, and we stood there like that for a few seconds. Then he raised one arm with a closed fist, held it, and then opened his hand.

Around us, the mermen dispersed, which was kind of stunning. Since they sank into the water as miraculously as they appeared to rise from the water, it looked like all of them melted collectively.

After maybe thirty seconds of this, it was just me and Mirella and the last merman. Then he did something that was nearly a bow, tapped his chest with his fist, turned and performed his own vanishing act.

We stood there in silence, alone, for a time. Mirella was ready to draw at the first sign of an attack, but it looked like we were in the clear.

"Well," Mirella said, "I find it hard to believe that worked."

"Me too."

"Next time, can we try it without the car accident?"

"Hey, you were the driver."

"I mean, why not just release the mermaid right away?"

"You have no respect for pageantry," I said. "Besides, she couldn't be seen as escaping. We had to hand-deliver her. Otherwise, they'd probably still want to kill everyone."

~

*D*mitri took a while to convince.

Absent a mode of transport, Mirella and I walked across the parking lot to the edge of the convoy, under the judgmental gaze of the spotlight. It was a little unnerving because while I was pretty sure nobody was going to be shooting at us intentionally, this was a trigger-happy bunch, they were sleep deprived, and they'd been firing at ripples in water for the past few hours. Every whorl and perturbation could be misinterpreted, and I didn't want to be in the middle of an unnecessary hail of bullets. Or really, any kind of hail of bullets.

I tried to explain via shouting and gesticulation that all was well and they could stand down and things were cool, but again, I was dealing with people who'd been shooting at malevolent shallow water. Trust was going to come slowly. So we walked carefully, trying not to trigger an overreaction, until we got within earshot.

"What did you do, my friend?" Dmitri asked. The voice came from one side of his spotlight, but I couldn't see him because of said spotlight.

"I gave them who they were looking for," I said.

"Did you now? And who was that?"

"It's a really long story. Can you shine that light somewhere else before my girlfriend takes it out with a knife?"

"Was that a suggestion?" she muttered.

"Absolutely."

"Adam, are we truly to believe they just took their... whatever... and went home? That we should not anticipate a renewal of hostilities?"

I looked around. The island behind us was silent, almost tranquil, in the way cemeteries were tranquil. I held my arms out and spun around a little, as if to invite a renewed attack.

"You can anticipate whatever you want," I said, "but they're gone. And personally, I don't feel like going through the rest of my life waiting for an attack from a pool of water. There's too much water to worry about."

Dmitri cut the light, and after my eyes adjusted it became clear Mirella and I were standing in front of an actual firing line. It was peopled by some of the wealthiest beings in the world, which just made the whole thing that much weirder. The 1% stood ready to gun us down.

"How can we be sure?" Dmitri asked.

"You can't," I said. "We speak different languages, so I couldn't exactly get a guarantee from them. But they were heading for the ocean last I checked, so if you want to row out there and see how you do on their home turf, have at it. Thing is, I understand there's an evacuation that needs managing, so if I were you, I'd focus on that while I could. I would personally love nothing more than a drink and a hot shower, so can we all go inside now please?"

～

I declined the opportunity to get directly involved in the rescue operation, because I had other things that needed attending to, including the securing of a stiff drink.

But before that happened, I had to acknowledge some of the basic pleasantries that come along after everyone has decided a siege is finally over and everyone's safe.

Esteban made it through. I got a chance to say shake his hand and express sentiments along the lines of *I'm glad you too are still alive*, which was nice. Dmitri offered me the use of any illegal thing I wanted at any time in the future, which was also nice. Paul took a minute to thank me for whatever blah-blah thing I might have done (he had no idea, he only heard I fixed things somehow) and then he was off, a list of guests in his hand and an expression that suggested what came next was definitely going to suck more than what had already happened. And there were others, whose names I mostly didn't know, and mostly we were all happy to have survived.

Then the hard part began.

Someone was able to get a hold of Grundle, which I guess was easier without all the electrical interference. He was the lifeline to the mainland, so any coordination of the rescue teams would go through him. He was already in touch with the necessary parties.

Paul, Esteban and Dmitri, meanwhile, had to go through that guest list and start counting the living, as a way to tally the dead, at least so far as the hotel itself was concerned. (The dead resident count was going to have to wait.) This task meant going from room to room.

Mirella volunteered to help. I declined, and nobody gave me a hard time about it. I had something else to do that was probably more important, but I didn't want to tell anyone about it, including my girlfriend.

So it was that a couple of hours after ridding the island of a banshee infestation, I sat in the dark at one end the bar in the hotel's night club, enjoying the best bottle of bourbon I could find.

I wasn't alone.

"Y'understand, if you pour it in a proper glass it breathes nice and taste better," Calvin the vampire said.

I was drinking straight from the bottle.

"Tastes fine like this."

"Yeh sure, it tastes *fine,* just that it could taste *better.*"

As a guest, Calvin wasn't asked to help with the door-to-door canvassing currently underway, but even if he had been he likely would have turned it down inasmuch as this would probably take all night and half the day, and he had a certain aversion to daylight.

"You want some?" I asked. I was standing on the bartender side, because that was where the alcohol was located. It didn't exactly feel unfamiliar; as you can imagine, tending bar is one of my favorite jobs.

"Alright sure."

I dug up two rocks glasses and filled both with bourbon. I could have maybe offered him blood, but I didn't know where that might be stored behind the bar—I never tended one that catered to vampires—and he couldn't have any of mine.

"Now you swish it round," Calvin said, rolling the liquid in his glass, as one does.

"I promise, I have more experience drinking alcohol than you do," I said. "I'm not interested in savoring this, I'm interested in drinking the hell out of it. Cheers."

We clicked our glasses together.

"So what did this prophet say to you?" he asked.

I'd been recounting how I spent the past few days, which was way more interesting than how he spent them. He woke up underwater, but not much had happened since. He didn't even take part in the battle outside, which is a shame since he probably would have been an excellent ally, if he knew how to fight at all. He may not have. I've met my share of pacifist vampires.

"I already told you," I said. "A bunch of crazy."

"Sure, but what *kind* of crazy?"

I wasn't sure how to answer. In the time since I'd been in Lorelai's company, I hadn't had much opportunity to dwell on the particulars. There was the middle part—the official prophecy I was going to need her scribe's help in unraveling—but the beginning and end were pretty clear, in my head.

"I think she actively enabled the events which lead to this entire disaster," I said, "and I think she did it specifically so I would still be here at the end of it all, and I don't know why. And that's kind of messing with my head."

"Oh. Well."

Calvin gulped his drink, perhaps coming around to my way of thinking. This was not a time for sipping.

"Well that sounds like bollocks," he added.

"Maybe. I don't think it is. But I'm really tired of people dying because someone thought I was worth saving."

"I can see that, yeah." He refilled his glass and thought about what he might say next. I was half-expecting one of those pithy *you can't blame yourself* speeches that always tend to surface around conversations like this. I'd both received and delivered a version of that exact speech on dozens of occasions, and they never really worked in comforting the afflicted. Maybe Calvin was old enough to appreciate this. Or, maybe he thought it was appropriate to blame myself. Either one.

"So is that why we're drinkin' now?" he asked. "You feelin' bad about yourself?"

Honestly, this might be half the reason I drink, just in general.

"No, actually. Although that'd be a pretty solid reason. I'm drinking because I'm not ready yet for what comes next."

"Yeah, not following you."

I refilled my glass, emptied it, and then refilled it again. It was easier when I was drinking straight from the bottle.

"The prophet had three messages for me. The first was that she killed an entire island because I was more important than anyone here. The second was *why* I was more important, although it was gibberish. The third was to notify me that someone else was coming."

"Right." He gulped his drink and I wondered if being around me caused people to drink more. This would hold up, historically. "Still not following."

"Elamite," I said. "The prophet spoke Elamite. You understand prophets see the future and not the past, yes?"

"Sure. So she looked into the future, and in that future, someone spoke the language. So what? She could'a seen you. You speak it, yeah?"

"You're right, and you're wrong. She was quoting the future. But she wasn't quoting me."

CHAPTER 18

I arrived at room four twenty-two a couple of hours later, less sober but not drunk, which was more or less my default state for most of history.

The door was unlocked, which wasn't a real surprise. *All* the rooms at the hotel were unlocked. It was a security feature that existed for exactly this situation, i.e., when going door-to-door looking for people who can't open doors for themselves. Although honestly, Paul may have been saying that to hide the fact that all it took to gain access to any room was a large-scale power interruption.

It didn't look like the interior had been hit by the water. This was perhaps one of the reasons the prophet chose it. The room looked more or less precisely as it had when I was there last. All except for one detail: Gordana was sitting in the chair next to the window.

She looked as if she'd been waiting for me the entire time, as she may well have been.

"There you are," she said, smiling. "The shrieking stopped, and I hear people in the hallway, so I know it's over. Yet you leave me waiting."

She was dressed exactly as she was when we parted, but looked a little better for having had access to a shower, and the opportunity to at least rinse her clothing. I imagine I looked considerably worse than when she saw me last, because I hadn't gotten *my* shower yet.

"I didn't see any reason to hurry," I said.

Perhaps the only good thing about prophecy is that since it's unavoidable, whatever time I showed up in the room was the right time for me to show up in the room.

"I was worried someone else would get here first and I would end up evicted."

"They're searching occupied rooms," I said. "This one is notoriously unoccupied."

The message was still on the wall. I took a minute to try reading it again, this time with the words the prophet spoke laid over it.

The sounds lined up. That is to say, repetitive consonants from the words belonging to the ancient ritual landed on the same characters in the phrase on the wall. Hard 'G' was the same squiggle in three places, for instance. Not that I had any doubts; it was just good to see that for myself.

If I read the passage aloud, I could have created the circumstance by which the prophet looked into the future and heard me speaking the words. But I didn't know how to read the message until I heard her recite it in the hospital room. Her getting it from *me* getting it from *her* would just create a paradox that honestly made my head hurt.

As much as I wasn't looking forward to what was about to happen, I also didn't want to deal with any kind of paradox. It just seemed like a bad idea.

That said, just because Lorelai heard someone read it didn't mean she knew how to *write* it. At some point I would need to account for her receipt of the Elamite text.

But not right now.

"She told us it was a summoning," Gordana said.

"I guess it is, sure. Or a prayer. Or a chant. They're all pretty close to the same thing."

"I think a summoning is different, no? There's an expectation of an arrival. Is it to summon a god?"

"No. Well, yes but also no. A human considered a god."

"To summon you, then."

I smiled.

"At a different point in history, maybe. Not in Elam, though, and not with this phrase. The last line on the wall there... in the ritual, it's only spoken once, while the rest of it is repeated as long as it has to be to realize the coda. Translated, it means *the priestess comes.*"

"Priestess. A woman."

"Yes. I've been many things, but never a woman."

I sat down on the edge of the nearest bed, and added this to the list of situations it was weird to be in with a succubus without sex being involved.

"I should have figured it out earlier," I said. "I'm not the only immortal in the world. Did I tell you that? There's another: just like me, but older. She would have been just as drawn to a city-state like Elam as I was. Only, not as a laborer. That wasn't her style."

Gordana jumped in the chair, startled by something that had just happened behind me. I knew without turning what that something was.

The priestess came: Eve was in the room.

That she had appeared out of nowhere, silently, without the use of the door, was one of the few things that separated us. It wasn't magic, but it was about the closest thing to it in the world. I sort of know how she does it, but I can't do it myself. Maybe one day.

Eve began by reciting the incantation on the wall, closing

Lorelai's temporal circle without creating any paradoxes, which was nice.

She always spoke with a curiously melodic cadence that echoed languages even older than I was. I think to modern ears it sounded southern European, but I heard ancient African tongues.

I turned, and waited for her to finish the stanza. She looked as amazing as ever: bright red hair and pale skin, with stunning blue eyes. I chased her for ten thousand years, in part because she was the only other immortal I knew of, and in part because she was the most beautiful thing I'd ever laid eyes on.

"Hello, Urr," she said quietly, noting the presence of other people in the room for the first time.

I still found it difficult to find my breath and my voice when sharing the same space with her. This was true even after our last encounter, when Eve made it clear she more or less hated me, and for some really good reasons. The sting from that conversation was still there, and I had no reason to expect anything different this time around. Maybe she was here to harangue me for letting everyone on the island die, like I wasn't beating myself up enough for that already.

"Hi," I said. Eve could kill me any time she wanted, the same way she was capable of appearing in a room without using the door. I sometimes have trouble sleeping, knowing this.

She looked at Gordana.

"The message, is it yours?" Eve asked.

Gordana shook her head mutely.

"Well. My thanks to whomever put it there, as I would not have found you otherwise, Urr. Or should I call you Adam now? I have been looking for some time."

"That's… a little terrifying, actually. I don't suppose you have *good* news."

Or maybe she changed her mind after the last time and decided she did want me dead after all.

She took a step in my direction and stumbled a little, as if she was having trouble with her shoes... except she was barefoot. I reached out to steady her, but she caught herself in time, on the edge of the bed.

"Are you hurt?" I asked, surprised.

She was in a simple white sundress; if she were bleeding from somewhere, it would be obvious.

"I... I need your help, Adam. Something awful is..."

Then she collapsed into my arms.

Gordana, stunned and frozen to this point, leapt to her feet.

"She's ill!" the succubus said.

"No, no, she can't get sick. This is something else. We have to check for wounds."

With Gordana's help, I got Eve onto the bed, forming a tableau: her unconscious body beneath the Elamite phrase. If I saw the future, and witnessed this moment, it would probably stick out for me too.

There weren't any obvious wounds or bruises on Eve that I could see. Gordana, searching under the dress, came up empty too.

"A blow to the head, maybe," I said. "Or an internal wound. We should get doctor Cambridge here."

"Are you *sure* she isn't sick?" Gordana asked. "She's burning up."

Of course I was sure. It was the one thing I could count on in my own ridiculously long life, and one on which Eve's even longer life also depended: we simply didn't get sick.

And yet...I put my hand on Eve's forehead. Gordana was right, even though she couldn't be.

"She has a fever," I said, mystified.

"This is what I'm saying. For a being who cannot be ill, she is surely displaying the symptoms of illness."

When I took my hand away from Eve's forehead, I realized the skin on her body was sticky.

"It can't be," I said, although clearly it was. "It's... impossible."

ABOUT THE AUTHOR

Gene Doucette is a hybrid author, albeit in a somewhat round-about way. From 2010 through 2014, Gene published four full-length novels (*Immortal, Hellenic Immortal, Fixer,* and *Immortal at the Edge of the World*) with a small indie publisher. Then, in 2014, Gene started self-publishing novellas that were set in the same universe as the *Immortal* series, at which point he was a hybrid.

When the novellas proved more lucrative than the novels, Gene tried self-publishing a full novel, *The Spaceship Next Door,* in 2015. This went well. So well, that in 2016, Gene reacquired the rights to the earlier four novels from the publisher, and re-released them, at which point he wasn't a hybrid any longer.

Additional self-published novels followed: *Immortal and the Island of Impossible Things* (2016); *Unfiction* (2017); and *The Frequency of Aliens* (2017).

In 2018, John Joseph Adams Books (an imprint of Houghton Mifflin Harcourt) acquired the rights to *The Spaceship Next Door.* The reprint was published in September of that year, at which point Gene was once again a hybrid author.

Since then, a number of things have happened. Gene published three more novels—*Immortal From Hell* (2018), *Fixer Redux* (2019), and *Immortal: Last Call* (2020)—and wrote a new novel called *The Apocalypse Seven* that he did not self-publish; it was acquired by JJA/HMH in September of 2019. Publication date is May 25, 2021.

Gene lives in Cambridge, MA.

For the latest on Gene Doucette, follow him online

genedoucette.me
genedoucette@me.com

SCI-FI

The Spaceship Next Door

The world changed on a Tuesday.

When a spaceship landed in an open field in the quiet mill town of
Sorrow Falls, Massachusetts, everyone realized humankind was not
alone in the universe. With that realization, everyone freaked out for a
little while.

Or, almost everyone. The residents of Sorrow Falls took the news pretty
well. This could have been due to a certain local quality of unflappability,
or it could have been that in three years, the ship did exactly nothing
other than sit quietly in that field, and nobody understood the full extent
of this nothing the ship was doing better than the people who lived right
next door.

Sixteen-year old Annie Collins is one of the ship's closest neighbors.
Once upon a time she took every last theory about the ship seriously,
whether it was advanced by an adult ,or by a peer. Surely one of the
theories would be proven true eventually—if not several of them—the
very minute the ship decided to do something. Annie is starting to think
this will never happen.

One late August morning, a little over three years since the ship landed,
Edgar Somerville arrived in town. Ed's a government operative posing as
a journalist, which is obvious to Annie—and pretty much everyone else
he meets—almost immediately. He has a lot of questions that need
answers, because he thinks everyone is wrong: the ship is doing
something, and he needs Annie's help to figure out what that is.

Annie is a good choice for tour guide. She already knows everyone in
town and when Ed's theory is proven correct—something is
apocalyptically wrong in Sorrow Falls—she's a pretty good person to
have around.

As a matter of fact, Annie Collins might be the most important person on the planet. She just doesn't know it.

~'

The Frequency of Aliens

Annie Collins is back!

Becoming an overnight celebrity at age sixteen should have been a lot more fun. Yes, there were times when it was extremely cool, but when the newness of it all wore off, Annie Collins was left with a permanent security detail and the kind of constant scrutiny that makes the college experience especially awkward.

Not helping matters: she's the only kid in school with her own pet spaceship.

She would love it if things found some kind of normal, but as long as she has control of the most lethal—and only—interstellar vehicle in existence, that isn't going to happen. Worse, things appear to be going in the other direction. Instead of everyone getting used to the idea of the ship, the complaints are getting louder. Public opinion is turning, and the demands that Annie turn over the ship are becoming more frequent. It doesn't help that everyone seems to think Annie is giving them nightmares.

Nightmares aren't the only weird things going on lately. A government telescope in California has been abandoned, and nobody seems to know why.

The man called on to investigate—Edgar Somerville—has become the go-to guy whenever there's something odd going on, which has been pretty common lately. So far, nothing has panned out: no aliens or zombies or anything else that might be deemed legitimately peculiar… but now may be different, and not just because Ed can't find an easy explanation. This isn't the only telescope where people have gone missing, and the clues left behind lead back to Annie.

It all adds up to a new threat that the world may just need saving from, requiring the help of all the Sorrow Falls survivors. The question is: are they saving the world with Annie Collins, or are they saving it from her?

The Frequency of Aliens is the exciting sequel to *The Spaceship Next Door*.

Unfiction

When Oliver Naughton joins the Tenth Avenue Writers Underground, headed by literary wunderkind Wilson Knight, Oliver figures he'll finally get some of the wild imaginings out of his head and onto paper.

But when Wilson takes an intense interest in Oliver's writing and his genre stories of dragons, aliens, and spies, things get weird. Oliver's stories don't just need to be finished: they insist on it.

With the help of Minerva, Wilson's girlfriend, Oliver has to find the connection between reality, fiction, the mythical Cydonian Kingdom, and the non-mythical nightclub called M Pallas. That is, if he can survive the alien invasion, the ghosts, and the fact that he thinks he might be in love with Minerva.

Unfiction is a wild ride through the collision of science fiction, fantasy, thriller, horror and romance. It's what happens when one writer's fiction interferes with everyone's reality.

Fixer

What would you do if you could see into the future?

As a child, he dreamed of being a superhero. Most people never get to realize their childhood dreams, but Corrigan Bain has come close. He is a fixer. His job is to prevent accidents—to see the future and "fix" things before people get hurt. But the ability to see into the future, however limited, isn't always so simple. Sometimes not everyone can be saved.

"Don't let them know you can see them."

Graduate students from a local university are dying, and former lover and FBI agent Maggie Trent is the only person who believes their deaths aren't as accidental as they appear. But the truth can only be found in something from Corrigan Bain's past, and he's not interested in sharing that past, not even with Maggie.

To stop the deaths, Corrigan will have to face up to some old horrors, confront the possibility that he may be going mad, and find a way to stop a killer no one can see.

Corrigan Bain is going insane ... or is he?

Because there's something in the future that doesn't want to be seen. It isn't human. It's got a taste for mayhem. And it is very, very angry.

Fixer Redux

Someone's altering the future, and it isn't Corrigan Bain

Corrigan Bain was retired.

It wasn't something he ever thought he'd be able to do. The problem was that the *job* he wanted to retire from wasn't actually a job at all: nobody paid him to do it, and nobody else did it. With very few exceptions, nobody even knew he was doing it.

Corrigan called himself a fixer, because he fixed accidents that were about to happen. It was complicated and unrewarding, and even though doing it right meant saving someone, he didn't enjoy it. He couldn't stop —he thought—because there would always be accidents, and he would never find someone to take over as fixer. Anyone trying would have to be capable of seeing the future, like he did, and that kind of person was hard to find.

Still, he did it. He's never been happier.

His girlfriend, Maggie Trent of the FBI, has not retired. Her task force just shut down the most dangerous domestic terrorist cell in the country, and she's up for an award, and a big promotion.

Everything's going their way now, and the future looks even brighter.

Unfortunately, that future is about to blow up in their faces…literally. And somehow, Corrigan Bain, fixer, the man who can see the future, is taken completely by surprise.

Fixer Redux is the long-awaited sequel to *Fixer*. Catch up with Corrigan, as he tries to understand a future that no longer makes sense.

FANTASY

The Immortal Novel Series

Immortal

"I don't know how old I am. My earliest memory is something along the lines of fire good, ice bad, so I think I predate written history, but I don't know by how much. I like to brag that I've been there from the beginning, and while this may very well be true, I generally just say it to pick up girls."

Surviving sixty thousand years takes cunning and more than a little luck. But in the twenty-first century, Adam confronts new dangers—someone has found out what he is, a demon is after him, and he has run out of places to hide. Worst of all, he has had entirely too much to drink.

Immortal is a first person confessional penned by a man who is immortal, but not invincible. In an artful blending of sci-fi, adventure, fantasy, and humor, IMMORTAL introduces us to a world with vampires, demons and other "magical" creatures, yet a world without actual magic.

At the center of the book is Adam.

Adam is a sixty thousand year old man. (Approximately.) He doesn't age or get sick, but is otherwise entirely capable of being killed. His survival has hinged on an innate ability to adapt, his wits, and a fairly large dollop of luck. He makes for an excellent guide through history ... when he's sober.

Immortal is a contemporary fantasy for non-fantasy readers and fantasy enthusiasts alike.

Hellenic Immortal

"Very occasionally, I will pop up in the historical record. Most of the time I'm not at all easy to spot, because most of the time I'm just a guy who does a thing and then disappears again into the background behind someone-or-other who's busy doing something much more important. But there are a couple of rare occasions when I get a starring role."

An oracle has predicted the sojourner's end, which is a problem for Adam insofar as he has never encountered an oracular prediction that didn't come true ... and he is the sojourner. To survive, he's going to have to figure out what a beautiful ex-government analyst, an eco-terrorist, a rogue FBI agent, and the world's oldest religious cult all want with him, and fast.

And all he wanted when he came to Vegas was to forget about a girl. And maybe have a drink or two.

The second book in the Immortal series, Hellenic Immortal follows the continuing adventures of Adam, a sixty-thousand-year-old man with a wry sense of humor, a flair for storytelling, and a knack for staying alive. Hellenic Immortal is a clever blend of history, mythology, sci-fi, fantasy, adventure, mystery and romance. A little something, in other words, for every reader.

~

Immortal at the Edge of the World

"What I was currently doing with my time and money ... didn't really deserve anyone else's attention. If I was feeling romantic about it, I'd call it a quest, but all I was really doing was trying to answer a question I'd been ignoring for a thousand years."

In his very long life, Adam had encountered only one person who appeared to share his longevity: the mysterious red-haired woman. She appeared throughout history, usually from a distance, nearly always vanishing before he could speak to her.

In his last encounter, she actually did vanish—into thin air, right in front of him. The question was how did she do it? To answer, Adam will have to complete a quest he gave up on a thousand years earlier, for an object that may no longer exist.

If he can find it, he might be able to do what the red-haired woman did, and if he can do that, maybe he can find her again and ask her who she is ... and why she seems to hate him.

But Adam isn't the only one who wants the red-haired woman. There are other forces at work, and after a warning from one of the few men he trusts, Adam realizes how much danger everyone is in. To save his friends and finish his quest he may be forced to bankrupt himself, call in every favor he can, and ultimately trade the one thing he'd never been able to give up before: his life.

Immortal and the island of Impossible Things

"I thought I'd miss the world."

Adam is on vacation in an island paradise, with nothing to do and plenty of time to do nothing.

It's exactly what he needed: beautiful weather, beautiful girlfriend, plenty of books to read, and alcohol to drink. Most importantly, either nobody on the island knows who he is, or, nobody cares.

"This probably sounds boring, and maybe it is. It's possible I have no compass to help determine boring, or maybe I have a different threshold than most people. From my perspective, though, the vast majority of human history has been boring, by which I mean nothing happened, and sure, that can be dull. On the other hand, nothing happening includes nobody trying to kill anybody, and specifically, nobody trying to kill me. That's the kind of boring a guy can get behind."

Nothing last forever, though, and that includes the opportunity to *do* nothing. One day, unwelcome visitors arrive in secret, with impossible knowledge of impossible events, and then the impossible things arrive: a new species.

It's *all* impossible, especially to the immortal man who thought he'd seen all there was to see in the world. Now, Adam is going to have to figure out what's happening and make things right before he and everyone he loves ends up dead in the hot sun of this island paradise.

Immortal From Hell

Not all of Adam's stories have happy endings

"Paris is romantic and quests are cool. But the threat of a global pandemic kind of sours the whole thing. The good news was, if all life on Earth were felled by a plague, it looked like this one could take me out too. It'd be pretty lonely otherwise."

--Adam the immortal

When Adam decides to leave the safety of the island, it's for a good reason: Eve, the only other immortal on the planet, appears to be dying, and nobody seems to understand why. But when Adam—with his extremely capable girlfriend Mirella—tries to retrace Eve's steps, he discovers a world that's a whole lot deadlier than he remembered.

Adam is supposed to be dead. He went through a lot of trouble to fake that death, but now that he's back it's clear someone remains unconvinced. That wouldn't be so terrible, except that whoever it is, they have a great deal of influence, and an abiding interest in ensuring that his death sticks this time around.

Adam and Mirella will have to figure out how to travel halfway across the world in secret, with almost no resources or friends. The good news is, Adam solved the travel problem a thousand years earlier. The bad news is, one of his oldest assumptions will turn out to be untrue.

Immortal From Hell is the darkest entry in the Immortal series.

Immortal: Last Call

"I'm something like sixty-thousand years old, and I've probably thought more

about my own death than any living being has thought about any subject, ever. I used to be unduly preoccupied with what might constitute a "good death", although interestingly, this has always been an after-the-fact analysis. What I mean is, following a near-death experience, I'll generally perform a quiet review of the circumstances and judge whether that death would have been objectively good, by whatever metric one uses for that kind of thing. I'm not nearly that self-reflective while in the midst of said near-death experience. Facing death, the predominant thought is always not like this."

A disease threatening the lives of everyone—human and non-human—has been loosed upon the world, by an arch-enemy Adam didn't even know he had.

That's just the first of his problems. Adam's also in jail, facing multiple counts of murder, at least a few of which are accurate. He may never see the inside of a courtroom, because there remains a bounty on his head—put there by the aforementioned arch-enemy—that someone is bound to try to collect while he's stuck behind bars.

Meanwhile, Adam's sitting on some tantalizing evidence that there might be a cure, but to find it, he's going to have to get out of jail, get out of the country, and track down the man responsible. He can't do any of that alone, but he also can't rely on any of his non-human friends for help, not when they're all getting sick.

What he needs is a particularly gifted human, who can do things no other human is capable of. He knows one such person. He calls himself a fixer, and he's Adam's—and possibly the world's—last hope. That's provided he believes any of it.

Immortal: Last Call is the sixth book in the *Immortal Novel Series*, and also the end of a long journey for one immortal man.

∾

Immortal Stories

∾

Eve

"...if your next question is, what could that possibly make me, if I'm not an angel or a god? The answer is the same as what I said before: many have considered me a god, and probably a few have thought of me as an angel. I'm neither, if those positions are defined by any kind of supernormal magical power. True magic of that kind doesn't exist, but I can do things that may appear magic to someone slightly more tethered to their mortality. I'm a woman, and that's all. What may make me different from the next woman is that it's possible I'm the very first one..."

For most of humankind, the woman calling herself Eve has been nothing more than a shock of red hair glimpsed out of the corner of the eye, in a crowd, or from a great distance. She's been worshipped, feared, and hunted, but perhaps never understood. Now, she's trying to reconnect with the world, and finding that more challenging than anticipated.

Can the oldest human on Earth rediscover her own humanity? Or will she decide the world isn't worth it?

~

The Immortal Chronicles

~

Immortal at Sea (volume 1)

Adam's adventures on the high seas have taken him from the Mediterranean to the Barbary Coast, and if there's one thing he learned, it's that maybe the sea is trying to tell him to stay on dry land.

~

Hard-Boiled Immortal (volume 2)

The year was 1942, there was a war on, and Adam was having a lot of trouble avoiding the attention of some important people. The kind of people with guns, and ways to make a fella disappear. He was caught somewhere between the mob and the government, and the only way out involved a red-haired dame he was pretty sure he couldn't trust.

Immortal and the Madman (volume 3)

On a nice quiet trip to the English countryside to cope with the likelihood that he has gone a little insane, Adam meets a man who definitely has. The madman's name is John Corrigan, and he is convinced he's going to die soon.

He could be right. Because there's trouble coming, and unless Adam can get his own head together in time, they may die together.

Yuletide Immortal (volume 4)

When he's in a funk, Adam the immortal man mostly just wants a place to drink and the occasional drinking buddy. When that buddy turns out to be Santa Claus, Adam is forced to face one of the biggest challenges of extremely long life: Christmas cheer. Will Santa break him out of his bad mood? Or will he be responsible for depressing the most positive man on the planet?

Regency Immortal (volume 5)

Adam has accidentally stumbled upon an important period in history: Vienna in 1814. Mostly, he'd just like to continue to enjoy the local pubs, but that becomes impossible when he meets Anna, an intriguing woman with an unreasonable number of secrets and sharp objects.

Anna is hunting down a man who isn't exactly a man, and if Adam doesn't help her, all of Europe will suffer. If Adam *does* help, the cost may be his own life. It's not a fantastic set of options. Also, he's probably fallen in love with her, which just complicates everything.